PRAISE FOR
A LONG TIME GONE

"In the dark, icy heart of a Minnesota winter, Deputy Packard, a smart and courageous gay cop, embarks on a mission to uncover the truth about his brother's disappearance. *A Long Time Gone* is an atmospheric, gripping, and emotional mystery about the intersections of family, memory, grief, and healing. Joshua Moehling's novel dives headfirst into the raw pain of the past, the dangers of today, and the ghosts who haunt us from within."

—Margot Douaihy, bestselling author of
Scorched Grace and *Blessed Water*

"A big thriller with an even bigger heart! Moehling deftly weaves together a riveting present-day crime with closely held family secrets and sins of decades past, proving once again that the most compelling thrillers are written about the ones we love but fear we will never truly know."

—Lisa Gardner, *New York Times* bestselling
author of *Still See You Everywhere*

"On top of being everything you could want in a mystery—riveting, layered, unfolding in surprising yet inevitable ways—*A Long Time Gone* is a gorgeous story of loss and redemption that broke my heart, then put it back together. It's been a long time since I've loved a character like I love Ben Packard, with his deadpan humor and warm heart. Moehling is a literary star with a gift for observing and conveying humanity, and he's written a mystery of the highest order."

—Ashley Winstead, author of
Midnight Is the Darkest Hour

"With *A Long Time Gone*, Joshua Moehling returns with the highly anticipated, hard-hitting third installment of his beloved Deputy Ben Packard series. Moehling has once again penned a thoroughly engrossing police procedural with all the trimmings: intrigue, suspense, memorable characters, shining prose, and an ending that is equal parts heart-stopping and heart-tugging. *A Long Time Gone* firmly secures Moehling's place as the newest tour de force in the thriller genre."

—Heather Gudenkauf, *New York Times* bestselling author of *The Overnight Guest* and *Everyone Is Watching*

"With a page-turning plot, vividly drawn characters, and a compelling, gay protagonist with a dry, deadpan wit, *A Long Time Gone* is the kind of book you don't just read but devour. Set in a *Fargo*-esque town, Ben Packard investigates a brutal crime while also unravelling the mystery of his brother's disappearance decades earlier. Sharp, complex, and emotionally powerful, I love everything about this series."

—Christina McDonald, *USA Today* and Amazon Charts bestselling author of *What Lies in Darkness*

"*A Long Time Gone*—unflinching as a Minnesota winter—is equal parts compelling mystery and riveting family drama, and I'd follow its hero, Deputy Ben Packard, anywhere. His relentless pursuit of the truth will keep you hooked from start to finish."

—Jess Lourey, Edgar Award–nominated author of *The Taken Ones*

"Ben Packard is one of the best new mystery series on the market, and each book just gets better and better. In the third installment, two cold cases intertwine to reveal a suspicious death and the devastating truth about Packard's past. At turns harrowing and laugh-out-loud funny, action-packed and deeply personal, *A Long Time Gone* hits on every level. If you're not reading Joshua Moehling yet, clear your schedule and start today!"

—Mindy Mejia, *USA Today* bestselling author of *To Catch a Storm* and *Everything You Want Me to Be*

"Joshua Moehling is a star! This book is the proof of his singular talents: a superb and gripping story with an immersive setting and unforgettable characters, all gorgeously structured and beautifully written. Only Moehling can craft such an entertaining page-turner of a mystery, an outsider's tale, with life-changing themes and surprising solutions. *A Long Time Gone* is ultimately and uniquely heartbreaking, redemptive, and rewarding. Standing ovation."

—Hank Phillippi Ryan, *USA Today* bestselling
author of *One Wrong Word*

"In his third Ben Packard novel, Joshua Moehling takes us into this protagonist's tragic past, adroitly peeling back the layers of his brother's disappearance thirty years ago. With great skill, he evokes the snow-encrusted terrain and characters in his fictional Minnesota town, Sandy Lake, balancing humor with intense detective work. Above all, Packard, a gay man and member of law enforcement, defies stereotypes of police and gay men; he is a new sort of law enforcement hero, rich with complexity and fresh in his perspective; it's a thrill to follow his journey through this series!"

—John Copenhaver, award-winning
author of *Hall of Mirrors*

PRAISE FOR
WHERE THE DEAD SLEEP

"When a diabolically wealthy family pits themselves against each other, it's hard to know who to believe, unless you're Deputy Benjamin Packard. Josh Moehling lays out a deliciously complex plot and turns sleepy Sandy Lake into anything but."

—John McMahon, author of *The Good Detective*

"With *Where the Dead Sleep*, Joshua Moehling solidifies his place as one of the best new voices in the mystery genre. Moehling nails the spirit of small-town life in Minnesota's unique North Country. His understanding of the darkness that can haunt the human spirit twists his story in wonderfully unpredictable ways. Fans of Walt Longmire or Joe Pickett or my own Cork O'Connor have reason to celebrate and look forward to a long life for Moehling's series and its fresh, vibrant protagonist Ben Packard."

—William Kent Krueger, *New York Times* bestselling author of the Cork O'Connor series

"Small-town secrets have never been so deadly in this compelling thriller featuring my new favorite deputy, Ben Packard. The plot will grab you; the characters keep you coming back for more."

—Lisa Gardner, *New York Times* bestselling author of *One Step Too Far*

"In *Where the Dead Sleep*, Joshua Moehling continues the compelling journey of tough as nails and conflicted Deputy Ben Packard as he patrols his old stomping grounds of Sandy Lake, Minnesota. Exploding with secrets, this novel has everything you want in a riveting mystery: a brutal crime, fast-paced action, expertly drawn characters that thrust the story from the page, and a jaw-dropping ending that you won't see coming. Looking for a new favorite hero to root for? You've found him in Moehling's Ben Packard."

—Heather Gudenkauf, *New York Times* bestselling author of *The Overnight Guest*

"A well-paced whodunit that doubles as an evocation of Minnesota small-town life in all of its messy, dysfunctional glory... The real suspense emerges as Packard figures himself out, defying expectations in quiet, sometimes devastating ways."

—*New York Times*

"Evocative and charming with a deadpan wit, Joshua Moehling's *Where the Dead Sleep* is a richly satisfying mystery with fully-drawn characters—especially the winning and deeply human protagonist, Sheriff Ben Packard. Joshua Moehling's skill as a writer and storyteller is evident on every page. I can't wait to read the next installment in this excellent series!"

—Nick Petrie, bestselling author of *The Runaway*

"This title has all the elements of a good mystery: a puzzling crime, dark secrets, fast-paced writing, and deadpan humor… Riveting and a real page-turner; fans of C. J. Box's Joe Pickett novels or Craig Johnson's Longmire series will feel at home."

—*Library Journal*

"Observant and authentic (and funny, too), *Where the Dead Sleep* is a perfect mystery, the literary descendant of *Fargo* and *Mare of Easttown* and an exploration of all the nooks and shadows that make Sandy Lake, Minnesota, an ideal place to spend a summer and a chilling place to pass a winter. I'd highly recommended it to every fan of crime fiction but especially those reading in a lake house just after sunset."

—Adam White, bestselling
author of *The Midcoast*

"*Where the Dead Sleep* sticks the landing… And if you think you've got the mystery solved in the first few chapters, you're dead wrong. Moehling has some tricks up his sleeve."

—*Associated Press*

"Joshua Moehling has quickly become one of my favorite must-read authors, and *Where the Dead Sleep* shows exactly why. The characters are rich, and the small-town setting, where everyone has a secret and everyone is a potential suspect or victim, is brought vividly to life. This is a suspenseful, gut-wrenching page-turner of the highest order. Not to be missed!"

—David Bell, *New York Times* bestselling author
of *Try Not to Breathe* and *She's Gone*

"*Where the Dead Sleep* is a beautifully written mystery that had me on the edge of my seat. Joshua Moehling has created unforgettable characters in a story that kept me guessing the whole way through. *Where the Dead Sleep* is not to be missed."

—R. J. Jacobs, author of *This Is How We End Things*

PRAISE FOR
AND THERE HE KEPT HER

"A dark and complex mystery that will consume you, starring a protagonist who is equal parts quirky Milhone and steady Gamache."

—Julie Clark, *New York Times* bestselling author of *The Last Flight*

"Joshua Moehling is a fresh, powerful new voice in crime fiction. His debut novel is a twisted ride with a detective you won't soon forget. This book isn't just unputdownable, it's the definition of the word."

—Samantha Downing, international bestselling author of *For Your Own Good*

"When Deputy Sheriff Ben Packard investigates the disappearance of two teenagers in Sandy Lake, Minnesota, he exposes the seamy underbelly of a small American town. *And There He Kept Her* is a sharp, intense thriller combining a dark plot with a relentless pace. An absorbing, impressive debut."

—A. J. Banner, #1 Amazon, *USA Today*, and *Publishers Weekly* bestselling author

"*And There He Kept Her* plays out like something on TV, resembling *Yellowstone* in its small-town setting and larger-than-life drama set against captivatingly detailed scenery... *And There He Kept Her* is a great opportunity to get into a new detective series at the ground level. Especially if you like the idea of the hard-boiled detective novel but prefer your stories set in modern times with light touches of current social issues. Moehling's is a strong debut."

—*Associated Press*

"There's a terrific new voice in crime fiction, and it belongs to Joshua Moehling. *And There He Kept Her* is a taut, beautifully written thriller reminiscent of Karin Slaughter. A novel with heart, its protagonist, acting Sheriff Ben Packard, is the kind of hero we need today, a man wrestling with his sexual identity as he searches for missing teens in a small Minnesota town guarding secrets of its own."

—Jonathan Santlofer, author
of *The Last Mona Lisa*

ALSO BY JOSHUA MOEHLING

And There He Kept Her
Where the Dead Sleep

A
LONG
TIME
GONE

JOSHUA MOEHLING

Poisoned Pen
PRESS

Sourcebooks, Poisoned Pen Press, and the colophon are registered trademarks of Sourcebooks.

Published by Poisoned Pen Press, an imprint of Sourcebooks
P.O. Box 4410, Naperville, Illinois 60567-4410
(630) 961-3900
sourcebooks.com

Library of Congress Cataloging-in-Publication Data

Names: Moehling, Joshua, author.
Title: A long time gone / Joshua Moehling.
Description: Naperville, Illinois : Poisoned Pen Press, 2025. | Series: Ben
  Packard ; book 3
Identifiers: LCCN 2024019352 (print) | LCCN 2024019353 (ebook) | (hardcover) | (epub)
Subjects: LCGFT: Detective and mystery fiction. | Novels.
Classification: LCC PS3613.O3344 L66 2025 (print) | LCC PS3613.O3344
  (ebook) | DDC 813/.6--dc23/eng/20240429
LC record available at https://lccn.loc.gov/2024019352
LC ebook record available at https://lccn.loc.gov/2024019353

Printed and bound in the United States of America.
LSC 10 9 8 7 6 5 4 3 2 1

For Lisa

CHAPTER ONE

THE CASE BEING HEARD that afternoon on the third floor of the Sandy Lake Government Center involved a property dispute brought by Jim Wolf—real estate agent and developer—against Robert Clark. Wolf had acquired the lot adjacent to Clark's knowing that his septic and well were on Clark's land due to a long misunderstanding of the actual property lines. As the new owner, Wolf was claiming adverse possession gave him legal right to an additional thirty feet of Clark's land that included a flower garden where Clark had scattered his wife's ashes.

The judge had warned everyone not to be late but not forcefully enough to make anyone early, leading to a crush of trial participants, jurors, and interested spectators trying to make their way through security at the last minute.

"Place bags on the conveyor. Empty your pockets of all items—keys, wallet, cell phone—and put them in the basket before stepping through."

Deputy Ben Packard watched the overhead lights as a woman passed under the metal detector, then reminded her not to forget her things. Another deputy watched a video monitor as bags went through the scanner.

Packard said hello to the people he recognized, smiled at the others, repeating again and again the line he heard in his head when trying to fall asleep at night. *Place bags on the conveyor. Empty your pockets of all items—keys, wallet, cell phone—and put them in the basket before stepping through.*

Jim Wolf stepped out of the elevator with a man in a suit by his side. They both got in line and Wolf watched Packard with a satisfied smirk on his face.

"Oh, how the mighty have fallen," Wolf said as he got to the front. "From acting sheriff to purse patrol. Your career's headed in the wrong direction, Packard."

Wolf was in his late fifties, gray beard, bald on top. He was the chair of the county board of commissioners and had led Howard Shepard's campaign team in last fall's election for sheriff. After reluctantly agreeing to run, Packard lost to Shepard in a three-way race by a wide enough margin that he couldn't console himself by calling it close.

"Empty your pockets and come through," Packard said to Wolf.

"It's fine work you're doing, looking in ladies' handbags and counting their tampons," Wolf said. He put his hands behind his head like he was getting scanned at the airport as he stepped through the metal detector. "You're a real asset to our community, Deputy."

Packard put his hand on Wolf's back, pushing him along, saying nothing. Wolf's lawyer looked at Packard apologetically as he followed behind his client.

Once everyone got through security, Deputy Blanchard moved inside the courtroom to serve as bailiff, leaving Packard alone on the floor. He paced back and forth between the bag scanner and a high window that looked down on the parking lot where the winter's snow had been plowed into temporary monuments that would endure through May. He was tall with dark hair kept short and a trimmed beard. He had broad shoulders and a wide back from swimming and pull-ups. Standing all day in full uniform with forty pounds of gear on his back and around his waist also helped keep him lean.

Packard took out his phone and checked the time. The jury for Wolf's case had been selected that morning and was finally being seated now that lunch was over. Packard had four hours until his shift ended. Four hours to stand there, rock on his heels, and wait for court to adjourn for the day. He'd be the last one off the floor until the custodial staff came in later that night to clean.

Wolf wasn't wrong.

Being demoted to chief bag-checker and light-turner-offer was definitely a low point in his career.

It was late February. Howard Shepard, winner of the election in November, had officially been sheriff of Sandy Lake County for a month and a half. Packard and Shepard had had a contentious relationship long before they swapped roles. Packard had been ready to fire Shepard for violating department policy and jeopardizing his last investigation, but the optics of doing so during the election gave him pause, so he decided to let voters decide whether Shepard stayed employed by the sheriff's office.

And now Shepard was his boss.

After being sworn in, Shepard hired a new chief deputy, then reorged the entire department, taking Packard off investigations and putting him in charge of court security. His new responsibilities included maintaining order and decorum in courtrooms, transporting inmates from the jail, screening entrants, and maintaining a high level of safety and security for those conducting court business.

The job was as far down the hierarchy of responsibility from acting sheriff and lead investigator as Packard could get. Packard knew it. Shepard did too. He called it cross-training. Everyone else saw it for what it was: a power play.

Deputy Jill Thielen, Packard's closest confidant and ally in the department, still had her job as a lead investigator—Shepard couldn't very well replace both of them at the same time—which meant she was doing her job, Packard's job, and training Deputy Reynolds, the department's newest hire.

Kelly Phelps, head of administration, was within spitting distance of retirement but hadn't pulled the plug. Packard had let her run things how she wanted, recognizing that Kelly was the cog that kept everything turning. She hadn't suffered Shepard's foolishness when he was a deputy, and she'd shown no more appetite for it now that he was her boss. If Shepard had a plan to put her in her place, he hadn't executed it yet. He mostly looked terrified of her, as he should have.

What could any of them do? They could have resigned or retired, like two deputies and a dispatch operator had done before Shepard took the reins. But retired and done what? Resigned and paid the mortgage how? Packard supposed he could have looked for a job in a neighboring county and added a lengthy commute to the beginning and end of his days. He also could have gone to barber school and cut hair on the side. That wasn't going to happen either.

For now, he was stuck. Shepard had won the election fair and square. Packard truly wanted Shepard to be an effective sheriff and was willing to help if asked. He hoped they would find common ground eventually.

Thielen and Kelly weren't as optimistic. Thielen was exhausted and ready to fucking kill somebody. Kelly hoped Shepard would get pulled into a piece of farm machinery.

The judge hearing Jim Wolf's case called a thirty-minute break at 2:00 p.m. There were restrooms and vending machines and plenty of places to sit inside the secured area. A few people put on their coats and took the elevators down to smoke or get fresh air.

Deputy Blanchard was short and stout and walked with his chin pulled into his neck. He gave Packard an update on how the case was going. "Not looking good for Clark," he whispered with his back to the room. "I'm no expert, but it sounds like the law is on Wolf's side."

Packard hated to hear it. The last thing Jim Wolf needed was to make more money at someone else's expense.

"Will it go to the jury this afternoon?"

"Probably tomorrow. Clark's lawyer still has to present his case," Blanchard said, hitching up his pants. "I'm gonna hit the head before things start up again."

The jurors stood by themselves, awkwardly pacing or checking their phones, trying not to make eye contact. Packard had testified in enough trials to know jurors had been instructed not to discuss the case with one another and not to interact with either party during the break. Wolf stood near the window with his lawyer, smiling.

A woman wearing two cardigans over a turtleneck sweater came up to Packard. He had recognized her face when she went through security earlier but couldn't recall who she was. He'd met a lot of people while campaigning last year.

"Do you remember me?" she asked him.

He smiled and gave her a sideways look. "Tell me your name again."

"Phyllis Egan," she said.

Now he remembered. "Egan's Five and Dime," he said, shaking her hand. Packard and his siblings had frequented the store as kids. It had closed decades ago. Packard met Phyllis last fall while looking for a murder suspect who had rented a dark, depressing room in her basement. "We talked last year about your renter."

"I'm glad you remember," she said smiling.

The elevator bells chimed, and Packard looked over Phyllis's head to see Robert Clark get out. Packard didn't know him as anyone other than the guy sitting opposite Jim Wolf in the courtroom. Clark's attorney was still in there looking over his notes. Clark was heavyset and jowly. He was wearing suspenders over a black and green flannel shirt messily tucked into a pair of old jeans. He had his coat draped over his right arm.

"Do you remember that I said I might vote for you?" Phyllis said.

"I do remember you saying that."

"Well, I did vote for you. Just wanted you to know."

"Thank you. I appreciate it, Phyllis."

Clark was standing on the other side of the secured area, which was separated from the unsecured areas only by a trio of metal stanchions with retractable ribbons that directed people through the metal detector. The illusion of security depended on the vigilance of the deputies on duty. Clark had a pack of cigarettes and a lighter in his left hand that he was trying to tuck into the front pocket of his flannel shirt. Packard didn't like how he couldn't see what was in Clark's right hand because of the way his coat was draped over his arm.

"Excuse me for a minute, Phyllis," he said. He took his position next to the metal detector. "You ready to come through, sir?"

Clark got his cigarettes put away and smiled. He moved his coat from one arm to the other. There was nothing in his hand. Packard relaxed a hair.

"Not yet. I need to make a call," Clark said. He reached in his front pocket and took out his phone.

"I still can't believe I rented to a murderer," Phyllis said behind Packard. "How was I supposed to know? He had a lot of tattoos. Maybe that should have been my first clue."

Deputy Blanchard was out of the bathroom. He stood in the doorway to the courtroom and loudly announced the break was almost up. "We will be in session again in five minutes. I need everyone in their seats in four minutes."

Packard felt his attention pulled in multiple directions. On Clark, on Phyllis, on Blanchard, on the people already moving toward the courtroom, and on the elevator doors dinging. He watched Clark reach behind himself with his right hand. *He's pulling up his saggy jeans,* Packard thought.

The elevator doors opened, and a woman in a puffy green coat that went to her knees got off the elevator behind Clark. She could see what Packard couldn't, and by the time he registered the look on her face, Clark's hand had come around with a black pistol in it. The sight of the gun made Packard feel like the tiniest details were blown up to the size of a movie screen. He knew Clark's gun was a Glock by the shape of the trigger guard. It looked small in his hand. Six-round magazine. It would fire as quickly as Clark could pull the trigger.

The woman in the green coat quickly stepped backward into the elevator before the doors closed.

Packard tapped the body cam on his chest. "Everybody get down! Drop the gun, Robert!" he shouted as he slid back the restraint and pulled his own weapon in one smooth movement.

Clark was a step ahead of him, gun raised, aimed at Jim Wolf.

Packard heard screams and then the flat crack of Clark's gun. He heard Blanchard yell for everyone to get down. Packard had to step through the metal detector to get a clear shot. It beeped in protest.

Clark got off two rounds. He turned and looked at Packard as he fired a third time.

They made eye contact.

Packard shot Robert Clark in the chest.

CHAPTER TWO

A COURTHOUSE SHOOTING IN northern Minnesota was a big enough story to make the morning news in the Twin Cities. Packard watched a clip on WCCO of Sheriff Howard Shepard giving his first-ever news conference. "Yesterday, a man who was a party in a court case being heard at the Sandy Lake Government Center opened fire from outside the secured area, killing one man. Two Sandy Lake sheriff's deputies were on the scene providing court security at the time of the shooting. One of the deputies returned fire and killed the gunman. That deputy has been put on administrative leave pending the outcome of an independent investigation. Names of those involved are not being released until family notifications are complete."

It was the first crisis of Shepard's administration, and he had no more idea what to do than a toddler with a textbook.

Yesterday, after emergency responders had arrived and taken over assisting the dead and the wounded, Packard had called Shepard from the scene.

"Goddamnit, Packard. You think I need you shooting someone when I'm one month into this job? What am I supposed to do?"

"We have an internal procedure that tells you exactly what to do in the event of an officer-involved shooting," Packard said. "Ask Kelly where to find it and then read it. Deputy Baker was the first uninvolved officer on the scene. He's already collected my firearm. I'm going to come downstairs, change out of my uniform, and allow it and my equipment to be collected as physical evidence. I'm going to submit blood and urine samples. Then I'm going to go home and wait to be called back to give a statement. I'm officially on administrative leave until we both agree I should come back to work. You need to call the BCA and get an investigator out here to conduct a criminal investigation of the matter and start preparing a statement for the media. It's all in the procedure."

Packard turned off the morning news and took his breakfast dishes to the kitchen. He had barely slept at all. In the dark of night, he couldn't stop seeing the look of tired acceptance he'd seen on Robert Clark's face right before shooting him. Packard didn't know anything about Clark, but in that moment, guns drawn, it wasn't his own life that flashed before Packard's eyes; it was Clark's. He imagined a local boy who had grown up, married, worked hard, and who now, as an old man, was alone and weary from the long winter and did not understand how the law might take away something that so clearly belonged to him. Packard imagined Clark looking out a window where his wife's garden and ashes were buried under the snow and deciding he had nothing left to lose.

Mark Quinto, a juror who was walking toward the courtroom after Deputy Blanchard called five minutes, ended up taking a bullet in the back of the neck meant for Jim Wolf. He died before anyone could help him.

Packard knew his actions were justified by the circumstances. He'd done his job according to procedure the whole time. He was at his post and already on alert based on Clark's actions after getting off the elevator. There were cameras all over the government building, including outside the courtrooms, that would have captured Clark in the parking lot, in the elevator, and pulling his gun from outside the security station. Packard had given a verbal warning before either one of them fired a single shot. His body cam recorded everything else. It was all on a hard drive somewhere.

There were those who would wonder why he couldn't have shot Robert Clark in the arm or the leg. Those people didn't understand that once your weapon is drawn, your goal is to keep yourself or others from being killed. You may only get one shot and you don't want to miss. The human body presents the largest target through the torso, so that's where you aim.

Packard's name hadn't been mentioned in the morning news report but it might be by the evening news or the next day's. He took out this phone and sent a message to his family group text that included his mother, father, brother, and sister.

> Was involved in a shooting at the court-house yesterday. I'm fine but two others were killed. I'm on leave for the time being.

He had an OMG and prayer hands from his sister before he could finish typing the next part of the message.

> We need to have a family Zoom call tonight. There's other news I need to tell everyone. It's about Nick.

CHAPTER THREE

THIRTY YEARS AGO, NICK Packard snuck out of his grandparents' house two nights after Christmas and never came home. Ben Packard was twelve at the time and the last family member to see his brother alive. He'd come downstairs to go to the bathroom and caught Nick putting on his coat and boots near the back door after everyone else was asleep.

"I want to go with you," Ben said. "I'm bored and not tired at all."

"Forget it," Nick said, using his helmet to push Ben back into the kitchen. "I'm meeting a friend. We don't need you hanging around."

Ben threatened to wake up their mom and dad. Nick called him a tattletale baby. They wrestled at the back door. Ben was a boy, Nick almost a grown man. He yanked his little brother outside and shoved him in the snow in his pajamas so he'd be too cold and too wet to do anything but go inside.

Nick took off on a snowmobile. Divers found the sled three days later in open water after a searcher spotted a frozen glove near the edge of the ice. It looked like someone had struggled to climb out.

Divers searched underwater for days, and again in the spring. Boats labeled SANDY LAKE SHERIFF patrolled the shoreline. The lake was over ten thousand acres and more than one hundred feet deep in spots. Nick's body was never found.

Last spring Packard had gone in search of Nick's file and found that it was missing from the cold-case storage room. It wasn't until the previous sheriff, Stan Shaw, died and his widow gave Packard the box that he realized his boss had connected him to the boy who disappeared all those years ago. Packard hadn't tried to keep it a secret. Like so much else in his life, he let it go unsaid.

After the election was over, Packard finally opened the box only to find everything was missing, replaced by stacks of blank pages and a handwritten letter from Stan.

Ben,

It took longer than it should have to connect you to this case. In my defense, it was a long time ago and the drugs I'm on make things awful hazy. I wasn't on the drugs when we first met so that's no excuse. I don't blame you for not bringing it up. There are things a man has the right to keep to himself.

I remember this case. It was two years old when I joined the department as a deputy. The lead investigator felt like they'd had all the answers they were going to get. They found the glove and the sled. No body but Lake Redwing is wide and deep and there are some things the water won't let go.

Bullshit.

I circled back on this every year or so for a few years until it was shelved for good for a lack of new leads. I would check in with your parents and grandparents. Check in with the people who had been interviewed before to see if they had remembered anything new. Paw through the paperwork to see if anything had been missed. You know how it is with cold cases.

There was one guy who would never return my calls. Every year I'd have to hunt him down in person and every year I got the sense he was bracing himself for my return, that he knew he might spend the rest of his life answering questions about the missing Packard boy. His answers never changed. He didn't know anything. Didn't see anything. His kids' answers were the same as their dad's.

You know as well as I do that there are things you know and then there are things you can prove. I had nothing but a gut feeling about this guy. He had no record, no previous encounters with police. We had no evidence to make a case against him.

All of this came back as I read through the file again. I ran a search and found him still alive and still living in MN. I called him, reminded him who I was, and we had a long chat spread out over several phone calls. We talked about getting old and being sick. We're both in bad shape, him possibly worse than me, if you can believe that. We talked about the things that keep us awake at night. We both agreed, looking back, that there were times when we vastly overestimated our ability to imagine a worst-case scenario. There were times when we had no idea how much worse things could get.

We talked about his family and about another family who still didn't know what happened to their boy. I didn't get all the answers but we made a deal. He'd give me a location to search in exchange for protection for his family. Otherwise, he was taking what he knew about your brother to his grave.

You'll be angry at me for this and I don't blame you. I had limited time and limited options, but I thought you would want this above all else.

I'm sorry for what I've done, Sheriff.

Stan

There was a hand-drawn map with Stan's letter. Packard's first instinct was to head there immediately and start digging. He had called Deputy Thielen while stepping into his boots.

"I need your help," he said when she picked up. "We need dogs, deputies. The snow is going to be deep in spots so we'll need a plow. And lights."

"Hey, slow down," Thielen said. "What are you talking about?"

"There's a body," Packard said. "It's Nick. It's my brother."

That was back in January. Thielen had convinced him not to round up the cavalry until they had time to inspect the location for themselves. They'd waited until morning and then followed the crude map Stan had drawn on the back of his letter. A two-lane road took them to a gravel turnoff that they followed until they were bordering state forest land. The directions said to climb a small ridge and search the low area on the other side. If there had ever been a trail, they couldn't find it under all the snow. Not even a snowmobile or an ATV had been out this way recently.

They parked, put on snowshoes, and made their way up the rise in the land. There was nothing to see but dense trees and deep snow in all directions, nothing to indicate if they were even close. The winter forest was starved and skeletal. Dead trees leaned precariously against the living, their limbs tangled in a fraught embrace.

"The ground here could be frozen three feet deep," Thielen said. Her nose was red and putting out steam.

"Makes me wonder how they buried my brother when he disappeared at Christmastime. It would have been just as cold and frozen."

"We don't know if he was buried or dumped," Thielen said. She had read Stan's letter on the drive out. "If it was the latter, there might not be much left to find after all this time."

Packard sighed. "And if it was the former, we have no idea where to start digging with all this snow." They needed a more precise location before they could talk about snow removal and ground warmers. They couldn't attack things with shovels or a grader for fear of damaging the remains and any evidence they might hold.

Thielen sniffled. "A cadaver dog could find a body under all this snow. Our K-9 isn't trained for that," she said, telling Packard something he already knew.

"It'll be a special request to get one up here," he said.

"You really need to wait until this snow is gone and that's going to be April." Three months away.

"Fuck," Packard said.

———————

He'd waited a few weeks after visiting the site with Thielen before approaching Shepard with the idea of searching for Nick's remains. He showed him Stan's letter. Shepard only glanced at it before setting it aside.

"You know the budget better than I do," Shepard said. He smelled of cigarettes and had gained weight since Election Day. Packard imagined a lot of celebratory dinners and a week in Mexico drinking piña coladas while sitting in warm pool water.

"Do we have the money to pay for all the equipment and overtime to find this brother of yours?"

"Probably not without making cuts elsewhere," Packard conceded.

"We can't very well blow our wad on a private investigation into your family matters, now can we?"

"I'm not sure I'd call it a private investigation or a family matter. It's a cold case involving what might be a homicide within the borders of our county."

"*Might be*," Shepard said, making air quotes with his fingers. "I think we need more to go on before we start digging up the forest. I'll put Reynolds on it. It'll be good experience for him."

"You're going to put Reynolds on a cold case that's older than he is? A case with no file and no leads to follow up on? Where would you suggest he start?" Packard asked.

Shepard shrugged. "I dunno. I'm not a detective. That's not my job. Thielen can help him."

"I'll help him."

"Not during working hours. You're court security now. And no overtime for this."

A month had gone by since then and Packard still hadn't told his family about what he did and didn't know about Nick. How was he supposed to tell them that his former boss had traded away all the information in the case file and that his new boss had no interest in the matter at all?

Two days after shooting Robert Clark, Packard had his family gathered on a Zoom call. He told them briefly about what happened at the courthouse and answered their questions about how he was feeling (fine) and how long he thought he might be on leave (he didn't know). As soon as he could, he switched the subject. "There's been a new development in Nick's case," he said.

His sister, Anne, was sitting on the couch, drinking red wine in a hooded sweatshirt and connecting via the iPad in her lap. His brother, Joe, a cop in a Saint Paul suburb, was practicing putts in his basement and only half paying attention to the phone propped on his fireplace mantel. Joe was two years older than Packard, Anne three years younger, the baby of the family.

"What do you mean, a development?" Joe asked, pausing his putting and coming closer to the phone.

"It's a long story," Packard said. What he told them next was part truth, part lie, and a whole lot of omission. "Stan Shaw, the former sheriff, was working the case from his sickbed after he connected me to Nick."

"You never told him?" his mom, Pam, asked. The sun was high and bright in Arizona. She was sitting outside and holding the phone at arm's length. She had a wide hat pressed down on long hair that had gone gray-white. She was wearing a blue chambray shirt and a big turquoise necklace. Packard could see her desert-scaped backyard reflected in the window behind her.

"I didn't tell him, and now that's he gone, I can't even think of why I thought it was better not to. But he figured it out, started cold-calling names from the case file, and he got a lead on where we might find Nick's body."

"What do you mean find the body? In the lake?" his mom said.

"No," Packard said. "Nick didn't drown in the lake. Stan's notes are incomplete and he died before he could tell me any of this, but from what I can decipher, Nick died somewhere—I don't know where—and someone moved the body to the woods. How he died and who was involved is still unknown."

"Are you fucking kidding me? Are you telling us that Nick was murdered?" Anne asked.

"Maybe," Packard said. "I don't know." He reminded them that the case had never been completely closed, just shelved for a lack of new information. Some believed the body was in the lake and hadn't been found. Others, including Stan Shaw, who spent years following up, thought the sled in the water and the glove nearby were too convenient in the absence of a body. Over time everyone got to make up their own mind about what they believed.

His family all talked at once. Packard's dad, Terry, who had audio but no video because he couldn't figure out how to use the app, was the only one who was silent.

"Dad, you're on mute if you're talking," Packard said. "Touch the microphone button to come off mute."

"I haven't been saying anything," his father said. "I'm...I don't know what. In shock maybe." Terry was calling from Florida, where he lived with his second wife and their two labradoodles. They drove a golf cart everywhere they went and only left the borders of their senior retirement community to flee hurricanes.

Packard told them what he knew about the location had come from scant notes that Stan had left behind. He lied and said he still needed to go through the rest of the file to figure out who Stan had been talking to. He didn't tell them he didn't actually have the file or that Stan had destroyed it in exchange for the location information.

Packard's cell phone rang with a call from Suresh, the department's digital forensics expert. He muted the call and turned his phone facedown.

"Listen, this is going to be slow going. There's too much snow to do any kind of thorough investigation of the area. And it doesn't help that I'm off the investigation desk and on administrative leave because of the courthouse shooting."

"Get your partner to look into it," his mom said. "The lady who runs all the triathlons and things."

"Thielen's going to help but she has a full caseload of her own. I'm telling you this now because I need you to be patient and I want you to be prepared in case word gets out. If I have anything to say about it, the official word from the sheriff's department will be no comment until we have further details. Don't believe anything you read or hear unless it's from me."

Packard recognized the hypocrisy of his statement considering he had just lied to them. He didn't plan on making a habit of it.

"I can't believe this," Anne said. She had her stemless wineglass pressed to the side of her face like an ice pack. "I always thought of Nick as being the spirit of the lake…like a shadow back in the trees or part of the morning fog. Now you're telling me he was never in the lake. And that he might have been murdered? It's…devastating." She looked like she was on the verge of tears.

His mom was clutching the chunk of turquoise near her throat. "I'm going to do a crystal grid tonight and let him know we're coming and that we love him," she said.

"For god's sake, Mom. Enough with the crystals," Joe said. To Packard, "Do I need to come up there and help you figure this shit out? I can take the time." He was leaning on the mantel with his elbow and had his whole face in the phone.

"No. No one needs to come here," Packard said. "There's nothing to see, there's nothing to do. I need time to figure out the next steps and we need spring to come. By then I should know a lot more."

"Well, I'm coming up there and I don't care what you say," his mom said.

"Mom, don't do it."

She shook her head. "I need to see the place, and you need family energy around you right now. It's traumatizing to learn this information about your brother after all these years. And now the shooting on top of it. We hold trauma all knotted up in our fascia, you know. I can show you some exercises to help release it. I'll rent a car at the airport and get a hotel so you don't have to do anything. I'm hanging up now. I'll send my flight info when I have it."

Her window closed and she was gone.

Packard and his siblings just looked at each other. Their dad's window was a phone number in a black box. "I'm proud of you, son," his disembodied voice said. "I know the election was hard news, but you're doing great things up there. You saved your cousin Jenny from that maniac. The shooting at the courthouse could have been so much worse if you hadn't been there. Now you're going to find your brother after all these years. I'm sorry I don't have more guidance. I need to talk to Janet and process all this. It's a lot to take in suddenly."

They wrapped up the call with Packard promising regular updates even if the news was there was no news.

Packard closed his laptop and called Suresh back. "What's the word?" he asked.

"I have two words for you: 'double tap,'" Suresh said in his thick Indian accent.

"What do you mean?"

"To activate sound and video recording on your body cam, you have to double tap it."

The body cam Packard wore while on duty was always buffering thirty seconds of video with no audio. When double tapped, the camera would save the previous thirty seconds prior to the tap and start recording the incident in real time as it happened. "I did double tap it."

"No, you did not. There's nothing to download from your body cam from the courthouse. Did you hear it make two beeps when you tapped it? Did you see the light turn from green to red?"

Packard took a breath to calm himself. "Suresh, I didn't stop to listen for two beeps or wait for the light to change colors. I double tapped it while I was drawing my weapon. I was yelling at a man to drop his gun and trying to prevent a mass shooting."

"Yes, of course. I am just telling you there is nothing to download. The camera was never activated."

"What about Deputy Blanchard's camera?"

"His recording starts after the first shot is fired. He was in the courtroom and by the time he gets out to where you are, all the shots have been fired. He has audio but not eyes on you during the shooting."

"And the cameras on the third floor?"

"There is only one security camera. It has no audio, and it was angled too high to capture the area where you and Clark were standing. No good."

"Thanks, Suresh."

Packard hung up and put his head in his hands. The policy said they were to activate their camera anytime a situation became adversarial, which he had tried to do. Whenever there was supposed to be body-cam footage and there wasn't, the public assumed the officer or the department was trying to hide something. A recording of the incident from his point of view—even from Blanchard's—would have made this an open-and-shut case. Without it, his fate would be determined by external investigators and largely based on what other people remembered.

Packard wiped his hands down his face and back against the grain of his beard. The news from Suresh was the last thing he needed.

The second-to-last thing he needed was his mom to come to town.

CHAPTER FOUR

FOLLOWING AN OFFICER USE-OF-FORCE incident, the Minnesota Bureau of Criminal Apprehension is in charge of an independent criminal investigation to establish the facts for review under Minnesota statutes. BCA agents interview witnesses, collect evidence, and write a report that is presented to the prosecuting attorney, usually within sixty days of the incident, for charging decisions.

The bodies of Robert Clark and the juror he shot were sent to Saint Paul for autopsy. Packard gave his statement to a BCA agent during questioning at the sheriff's office and again on the third floor where the shooting occurred. When asked why he didn't activate his body camera, he said the same thing he told Suresh. He thought he had.

"Didn't you listen for the double beeps?" the agent asked.

Packard said nothing.

The list of witnesses had twenty-two names on it. Packard was less than assured by the number. Twenty-two witnesses would likely provide twenty-two different versions of events, giving the county attorney more opportunity to interpret things in the absence of video evidence. That the county attorney was a close friend of Jim Wolf's only made Packard more nervous.

An article about the shooting in the *Sandy Lake Gazette* said Robert Clark had worked as a butcher and meatcutter before retiring a decade ago. His wife had died three years earlier. Their two grown children both lived in California. The people who knew him were shocked and saddened by what he'd done.

After giving his statements, Packard had been instructed to remain available but no one called him. He was supposed to get a psych eval but didn't feel like talking about what happened. Mostly he stayed home. He went grocery shopping late so he wouldn't run into people. He walked his dog—a three-legged rescue corgi named Frank—and worked out and listened to music. He struggled to sleep. He struggled with the endless empty hours without work. He thought a lot about Robert Clark.

———

When Packard's mom arrived ten days after the shooting, it was like a whole circus coming to town. She was bright-eyed and jewel-toned and her cold-weather clothing consisted of enormous knit hats and flappy mittens and a lot of tasseled blankets and serapes that went over her head or around her shoulders and smelled like essential oils. She reminded Packard of a desert mule loaded and ready to descend into a canyon.

She got in late the first day. There was just time to get her situated at the hotel and take her grocery shopping to stock the small fridge in her room. On the second day she came to his house and they took Frank for a long walk and played Scrabble. His mom cooked potato soup, a thin milky recipe from Packard's childhood that he remembered sieving in search of the ground sausage she used to add to it. Now she was a vegetarian and the sausage had been replaced by kale.

On the third night, after another whole day together, Packard decided he wanted to see people and he wanted to see life, so he took his mom to a brewery for a late dinner. The Hopfenstopfen had officially opened the week before Christmas and was gaining popularity with the locals and the out-of-town snowmobilers. Packard had held his election night party there. Wasn't much of a party.

Kyle Hill, one of the co-owners, poured a sample of their piney IPA for Packard's mom. She sipped it, then tried not to make an unpleasant face in front of the guy who brewed it. "Well, that's interesting. But not for me," she said, smiling.

Kyle took her glass and asked Packard if he wanted to sample anything. Packard had a list of things he wanted to sample on Kyle—a handful of his dark hair, the scratch of his five-o'clock shadow, the texture of the scar on his upper lip. He'd thought maybe they'd had a moment at his party but there hadn't been time to investigate since then on account of how badly he lost that night.

Then it was the holidays.

Then he'd read a letter that contained a map to the location where his missing brother's body was buried.

Then he shot and killed a man.

It had been a busy winter.

He'd taken his mom to the place on Stan's map before they went to the brewery. Snow had filled in the tracks he and Thielen had left the last time he was here. He wanted his mom to see what they were dealing with—the deep snow and all the trees and not a landmark or depression in the ground or anything to go by—so she could back him up with the family about why the only option right now was to wait for spring.

"I feel something here," she said, closing her eyes and moving her head like she was drawing a picture with the tip of her nose. "There's an energy that doesn't belong."

They walked around a bit and then Packard waited patiently while his mom took a bit of fabric out her coat pocket, unwrapped a pink crystal the size of a tennis ball, and held it out in the four directions while she whispered a prayer or a spell or whatever it was she believed in currently. Her spirituality was an ever-evolving casserole of new age, Wiccan, Native, Buddhist, feminist, sex-positive beliefs that only made sense to her.

Packard's feet were freezing and his mom was crying by the time she finished her ceremony. Their whole family was on the verge of having to let go of everything about Nick they had convinced themselves might be true. After all these years they were close to finding some answers. It was a raw feeling, sore but welcome. He hugged his mom and they walked down the hill while a flock of red-winged blackbirds spiraled overhead.

They finished a large cheese pizza at the brewery. Packard ate most of it. Kyle found plenty of time to chat and wipe the bar on either side of them, even though no one was sitting close by. He was wearing a flannel shirt over a white thermal, the sleeves of both pushed back. A gray beanie drooped off the back of his head.

"When's the last time you went by Grandpa's house?" his mom asked.

Packard shook his head. "Haven't been there once the whole time I've been here."

"Not even to drive by?"

"Nope."

"Maybe we could go there tomorrow," she suggested. "It'll be nice to see Louise after all these years."

Packard shrugged. He was running out of things to do to keep his mom busy. If they were idle for too long, she'd ask him to lie down so she could do Reiki on him or massage his fascia.

"Let's do it. I've never felt like going there alone. It'll be nice to go together," he said.

Kyle dropped off the tab after they asked for it. Packard's mom grabbed the folder and moved her reading glasses down from the top of her head. "He didn't charge us for the beers," she whispered.

"That's nice of him. Leave a big tip."

"He sure was attentive. Do you know if he likes older women?"

"Mom, I don't know if he likes older women, or younger women, or wet pool noodles. Just put your card in there."

She moved her glasses to the end of her nose and watched Kyle set down two foaming pilsner glasses at the far end of the bar. She turned back toward Packard. "You two haven't—you know." She stuck her pointer fingers out and tapped the tips together—international sign for bumping dicks.

Packard grabbed her fingers in one of his large hands and pushed them down to the top of the bar. "No, we haven't...done that. I don't even know him. What's wrong with you?"

"For god's sake, Benjamin. I know how things work with you boys. My hairdresser calls himself an ethical slut. You should—"

"Nope," Packard insisted.

"But you—"

"Uh uh."

His mom looked disappointed in his response. She signed the bill with a flourish. "Don't be so uptight," she said. She leaned away from him, moved her hand in a circle in front of him. "Your energy's all blocked. You need to relax. You need to unclench your butt and let your root chakra breathe."

"And you need to find another ride back to your hotel."

CHAPTER FIVE

THE NEXT MORNING, PADDED and protected from a cold that felt interstellar, he picked up his mom and they drove twenty minutes out to Lake Redwing where Packard's grandfather had purchased a lake home in the 1950s. The house was built in 1912, two-and-a-half stories with a cement-block foundation. A bump-out on the front that was originally a porch had been finished and turned into living space. On the back, a sagging set of concrete steps rose up to the door on a small addition that had been added to make room for another bathroom. The house was painted dark green—something between John Deere and L.L. Bean.

Even before they stopped the truck, Packard noticed something. "No one is doing snow removal. There's no lights on. Looks like the house might be empty."

"I'm sure Louise still lives here. I get a Christmas card from her every year."

"Did you get one this year?"

His mom had to think. "I don't know for sure."

They parked on the side of the road and trudged through knee-deep snow, past the two-car garage, making their way toward the house. Packard reached back and held his mom's hand as they wobbled forward. The snow squeaked like Styrofoam under their boots.

Nothing about the place had changed since he was a kid. He knew that in the summer there would be two dirt tracks under their feet and a weedy lawn that never got very tall, and that at the bottom of the back steps was a patio of paired bricks set in an alternating pattern. The house seemed smaller but the angles and the color and the old trees were the same. At any moment he expected the back door to fly open and younger versions of himself and his siblings to come flying down the stairs, an avalanche of mittens and hats and plastic sleds. He suddenly remembered the mulled cider his grandmother always kept warming in a Crock-Pot set to low and how it was the first thing you smelled coming back into the house after playing in the snow.

He cleared a path up the back steps with the side of his boot and opened the storm door. Taped in the corner where the door met the framing was a bright-orange sign declaring the premises had been sealed by the Sandy Lake Sheriff's Department. Entry was forbidden without permission.

"This doesn't look good," Packard said.

"What does it mean?"

"Something happened here and the house has been sealed. No one's living here for sure."

"You didn't know about it?"

"I didn't."

He took out his phone and called dispatch and asked about calls to the property. Packard said, "Uh-huh… When was that…and who responded?" He watched his mom standing at the bottom of the steps, shivering. Too many years in Arizona had melted the Minnesotan in her. She was a desert lizard in the wrong habitat.

"I see… Got it. Thanks, Mac. 'Preciate it."

"And?"

"Louise died last summer. She fell down the basement stairs. It was days before anyone found her."

"Oh my god," his mom said, horrified. She pressed her hands together in front of her face, closed her eyes, and said a prayer. "Poor Louise," she said when she was done. "She was such a sweet woman. She and her husband used to live next door. They bought the house from your grandparents. They wanted extra space and didn't want to renovate their house, which was not that thing."

She pointed to a brick McMansion with arched windows and porticos and a gabled roof. It was a high-end home at the time it was built. Now it looked every bit a relic from the 1990s.

Packard had been so busy time traveling through his memories that he hadn't taken note of all the things that had changed. Primarily the houses on either side of them. He remembered two girls who lived in an eggplant-colored American foursquare next door. It was also gone, replaced by an A-frame bowed like the prow of a ship with towering glass windows looking over the lake. Grandpa's house looked like a stubborn holdout against changing trends in architecture and sky-high home values.

"Now what do we do?" his mom asked.

"Don't you want to go inside?"

"It says to stay out."

"It says to stay out without permission from the sheriff's department. I'm with the sheriff's department. Maybe you've heard of my career in law enforcement."

"Hush, you. It's okay even if you're on leave?"

He assured her it was. He was on leave from his current role as court security. He was still a sworn deputy with all the rights, responsibilities, and access intact.

"How are we going to get in?"

"Remember where Grandpa always kept a spare key?"

His mom had to think for a minute. "The dryer vent?"

"Bingo."

Packard went down the stairs to the triangle-shaped vent on the back of the house. He stuck his hand inside and came out with a magnetic case. "This is the same key holder Grandpa had."

"I bet Louise never changed the locks," his mom said. "Why would she?"

Packard used the key inside the case to cut through the sheriff department's seal on the back door, then tried it in the lock. It worked.

They stomped their boots on the linoleum inside. There were pantry shelves and coat hooks on their left. To their right was a half bath with a washer and dryer in it, and straight ahead another doorway into the kitchen. Here in this cramped addition was the last place Packard saw his brother Nick.

"Nick and I argued right here," he said. "He was putting on his boots when I came to use the bathroom. 'I want to go, too,' I said. 'Take me with.' He told me to go to bed."

His mom put a hand on Packard's arm. "You really looked up to him as a boy. You and Anne and Joe fought all the time because you were so close in age. The age gap between you and Nick made you want to do what he did. Nick was becoming a man. His interests didn't always include hanging out with his little brother."

"I can't blame him. Especially when I told him I was going to tell on him for sneaking out. He said, 'You want to come with, then let's go.' He picked me up and carried me outside. I didn't have shoes or socks or a coat on. He dumped me in the snow at the bottom of the stairs. I was so mad at him."

Packard's mom had heard this story before. He'd told it many times, the same words, the same details. It would have been interesting to read the case file and find out if the story he told as a kid was the same one he was telling today.

"That didn't stop you, though, did it? You tried to go after him on the other sled."

Packard looked at her and shook his head. "What are you talking about?"

"You came in and got your winter stuff on and tried to follow him on the other sled. You don't remember that?"

"I don't remember that at all."

"You got maybe a mile down the road and rolled it in the ditch. You had to walk home. You didn't tell us about it until we couldn't find Nick and both sleds were gone."

"How can I not remember that?" Packard said.

He felt like he'd been hit in the face with a snowball. It was shocking to him that there were details of his brother's disappearance that were new or unknown to him. Even without the case file, he considered himself the authority on what happened that night. He was the last one to see Nick. No one else could claim that right. He remembered being cold and wet and watching from the back door when Nick rode away on the snowmobile. Or did he? Were his memories of that night actual memories, or had they been replaced by the stories he'd been telling himself for years?

His mom suggested they take off their wet boots before tracking through Louise's house. It was nearly as cold inside as it was outside. The kitchen was unchanged from Packard's childhood; purple laminate countertops, dark oak cabinets, and a wallpaper border of vines and plums around the ceiling. "Grandma and Grandpa certainly made some bold design choices," Packard said.

"This was high style in the early eighties," his mom said, sniffing the air. She made a face. "Is that smell what I think it is?" she asked.

Packard nodded grimly. It was the smell of a dead body left alone for too long. It got stronger the further they went into the kitchen.

There was a small saucepan on the butter-yellow stove and next to it a coffee mug with a tea-bag string draped over the rim. The refrigerator was unplugged and the door left open. A look inside the cupboards showed them still stocked with dry and canned goods and mismatched dishes.

On the other side of the kitchen wall was a set of narrow wooden stairs up to the second floor and, on the other side of that, the dining room. The living room was on the front of the house. Louise had a set of matching furniture covered in a maroon fabric and lots of small tables and lamps scattered around.

"I want to look upstairs," his mom said. The wooden steps creaked as she climbed.

A folded quilt lay over the back of the couch and a large-print John Sandford book from the library rested on the arm. Packard opened the book to a business card used as a bookmark and held it in his hand like a preacher. Dispatch said a deputy was sent to the address the weekend after Memorial Day to check on Louise. At some point she had been reading on the couch, then got up to make herself a cup of tea and fell down the basement stairs. The notes dispatch read to him said a broken bottle of bourbon was found beside the body. Maybe it wasn't her first drink of the night. Maybe she'd been nipping at the bottle all day. Seemed unlikely. Packard didn't know a lot of drunks who were also dedicated readers.

The deputy who made the welfare check was Howard Shepard.

Last summer Packard was acting sheriff and buried under the landslide of paperwork and media requests and family inquiries that followed the discovery of the bodies of the missing women found buried on Emmett Burr's property. An accidental death like Louise's would have required an autopsy but not an in-depth investigation by the sheriff's department. Maybe it had made Thielen's radar, maybe not. With Shepard first on scene, it got the least amount of atten-tion possible.

Packard could see his breath and feel the cold at the tip of his nose. He heard his mom walking around upstairs. The old house had dried out over the years. Every footfall landed with a thud or a creak. Images of Louise's final night in this house rode a tide of a million memories spent growing up here—running out the front door in bare feet, across the dirt road that passed in front of the house, to the beach and the dock on the other side. Long summer days when the sun never seemed to fully set and cool nights that smelled like bonfires and the lake. A closet under the stairs filled with board games and his grandparents' winter clothes and the smell of mothballs, eating hot dogs on the back steps, bike rides, boat rides, waterskiing, snowball fights, sledding and snowshoeing, a Christmas tree at home and another one here at the cabin. Anne cutting off all her hair when she was six, Nick driving them to town when he got his license.

Also, that night with Nick on the back steps, the calls to the police, sitting upstairs by the bathroom vent listening to the adults talk downstairs, a sher-iff's deputy saying, "We found a snowmobile in the water." The bad months and years that followed when no amount of sunshine or Christmas lights could bring the cheer back to this house or fill the space where Nick should have been.

It felt like being barraged with punches. It felt like a time machine phasing him in and out of the present. He was in his grandparents' home, in Louise's home, his brother was missing, Louise was falling down the stairs, the memories of a child, the thoughts of an adult.

His mother came clomping down the stairs. "Your father got me pregnant with Anne in that room up there."

And...firmly back in the present.

Back in the kitchen, standing at the purple peninsula, his mom set her purse down and took out a stack of photographs. They came from the case file, the only things that Stan hadn't destroyed. There were less than a dozen, including a nine-by-six of Nick's junior-year school photo circa 1990. His hair was longer, parted off-center, and pushed back in arcs that curved around again near his temples. There were photos from that summer at the cabin of a young Ben with Nick and Joe and Anne wearing wet swimsuits, eating ice cream sandwiches on the front porch, holding sparklers at the end of the driveway.

In one photo, people were lined up three deep in the backyard, adults and kids from infants to the elderly. Packard could only name about a third of them. Another photo was of Nick and a girl in the lake, up to their necks in the water. She was behind him with her chin on his shoulder and an arm around the front of him. A boy was sitting on the edge of the dock, only half turned to the camera. The girl and the boy might have been brother and sister based on their similar features. It was late afternoon by the way the faces were in shadows and the sun on the water washed out the photo.

"Do you know these two?" he asked.

"I don't remember them. Does the file have their names?"

"It might. I'll check next time I'm in the office," Packard lied. "The clothes and the hair and the low-resolution photos make this feel like a century ago," he said.

"It was the nineties, dear. Not that long ago."

"I was a child and there was no internet."

"It does sound like forever when you put it like that," his mom said.

Packard studied the photo of his brother in the lake but felt his attention drawn to the basement door. It wasn't the smell. Something about the door opening outward and Louise falling down the stairs didn't sit right with him. He could understand if it opened inward and she leaned against it or pushed it open and missed the first step. Also, why would an eighty-year-old woman keep her whiskey in the basement or head down the stairs with a full bottle in her hand?

A loud knock at the back door caused both Packard and his mom to start.

"Who's in here?" a woman's voice asked.

"It's Deputy Packard with the sheriff's department."

A woman came up the back steps wearing a gold three-quarter-length parka. She had a white knit hat pulled down over a mass of curly blondish-brown hair. She looked to be in her early forties. Snow on her pants up to her knees. A neighbor.

"I'm Andrea," she said. Packard shook her gloved hand. She had something heavy in her coat pocket making it hang crooked on her. A gun, he thought. Or a big can of soup to brain an intruder.

"This is my mom, Pam. She was a friend of Louise's."

"You heard about what happened, I assume," Andrea said.

"We heard," Packard said.

"So what are you doing in her house? Are the police looking into it again?"

The truth was they had no business being there. Having lived here once and knowing where to find the spare key gave them no rights. Letting themselves into the house was about nostalgia, not department business.

Packard dodged the question. "Were you close to Louise?"

"Fairly close," Andrea said. "We had dinner sometimes with Max and Linda on the other side."

"Was Louise a drinker?"

"She said a shot of bourbon at night helped her sleep and kept her young. Who knows if it was more than a shot?"

Packard nodded in agreement. "Any word about what's going to happen to the house?"

"It's tied up in probate from what I've heard. She doesn't have any family. Lot of interest in the place." Andrea looked around at the kitchen like she had her own ideas.

"Interest from who?" Packard asked.

"From anybody with money."

They were interrupted by another knock at the back door. Someone said, "Sheriff's department."

Packard groaned quietly. Their quick visit to the family home was now police business. He called out to Deputy Baker—black hair, early forties, graying goatee—and invited him inside. Packard introduced his mom and Andrea.

"A neighbor called. Said there wasn't supposed to be anybody in the house," Baker said.

Packard glanced at Andrea but she shook her head. "Wasn't me. I came over to handle it myself."

Packard looked at the weight in her coat pocket and wondered what she meant by *handle it*.

"Dispatch told me you were on-site," Deputy Baker said to Packard. "I still thought I should check it out."

"Why are you on-site?" Andrea asked. "What are you doing here?"

"This used to be our family's house. When we saw it was empty, our curiosity got the better of us. But we're done now," Packard said. "We can go."

His mom swept up the photos and the three of them followed Baker out of the house. Packard locked the door and pocketed the key, deciding in the moment to hold on to it rather than put it back where he found it. Neither Baker nor Andrea thought to ask where he got it.

As he came down the stairs, Packard watched Andrea try to navigate her tracks in the deep snow back to her house next door. When he looked to the McMansion on the other side of Louise's, he saw a man watching from a floor-to-ceiling window with a pair of binoculars clutched in both hands in front of his chest. Packard gave him a friendly wave. The man didn't move.

CHAPTER SIX

HIS MOM WANTED TIME to meditate and do yoga before dinner so Packard dropped her off at the hotel. They made plans that she would drive her rental car out to his place in the evening for dinner.

When he got home, he let Frank out and they went for a walk. Off the leash, the Pembroke corgi ignored the shoveled sidewalk and headed for the deepest snow in the yard. He rolled on his back, pounced like he was hunting something, and ran around as best he could on three legs. His tongue flapped like a scarf caught by the wind.

Back inside, Packard toweled Frank off and stoked the fire in the wood-burning stove before the two of them got comfortable on the couch. Packard sat with his laptop open as he made notes in the new digital case file he was creating for Nick's disappearance. So far, it contained Stan's letter, the map he'd left with directions to the supposed location of Nick's remains, notes and photos from the visit to the site with Thielen, as well his conversations with Shepard about what to do and not do in the near term. He had digital copies of the photos his mom was carrying. He had started a list of people he recognized in the large group photo and left question marks for those he didn't. He had question marks for the young man and the woman in the water with Nick.

Finding out that he had taken the other snowmobile in pursuit of his brother was new and interesting, but he wasn't sure it was useful. Packard leaned back and closed his eyes and tried to find his lost memories. After a couple of minutes, he wasn't sure if the things he was recalling—the sound of the machine, the snow in the headlights, a trail that climbed steeply and the feeling of the sled starting to tip—were memories or imagination. Where had he gone? What was he feeling before the sled tipped? What was he thinking when he decided not to tell anyone what he had done? He couldn't answer any of those questions.

He noted the information anyway and that the source was his mother. He recorded the date and time of their visit to Louise's house, the appearance of Deputy Baker, then accessed the department's files via remote log-in. The original incident report regarding Louise's death had been completed by Shepard and included information about the request for a welfare check to the address and what he found on entry. The report was dated June 5. The next day's report was written by another deputy and documented his conversation with the neighbors and his inability to identify any family.

Packard recognized the name of the person who had made the initial call for a welfare check. Raymond Wiley was a lawyer with a small firm in town. His daughter was Lisa Washington, a public defender Packard had most recently consulted with on the Bill Sandersen murder. That case still hadn't gone to trial.

Packard didn't have a personal number for Raymond but he had one for Lisa. "I wanted to ask you about a friend of your dad's. He made a 911 call last summer to ask someone to check in on her."

"You're talking about Louise Larsen," Lisa said.

Packard heard the rattle of a cookie sheet going in or coming out of the oven. "That's her," he said.

"So sad. Dad and Louise were bridge partners. We were out of town the week before, on a vacation to Colorado. When we got back, she didn't return Dad's calls or pick him up for bridge, so he called you guys. I heard she was at the bottom of those stairs for days."

Packard had been imagining the smell of chocolate chip cookies in Lisa's kitchen. Now he recalled the smell coming up from the basement at Louise's house. "I saw in the report that your dad said Louise didn't have any immediate family."

"Yeah, it's true. Dad was probably her closest friend. Also her attorney. Our firm is handling probate for her estate. We can't find a single living blood relative anywhere."

"Were your dad and Louise romantically involved?"

"My dad is seventy-six, Sheriff."

"Deputy," he corrected her.

"Sorry, sorry. My brain refuses to believe you didn't win that election. Sorry."

"Don't worry about it." He got up and threw another log in the stove, then came back to the couch. Frank nuzzled in close again.

"As I was saying, my dad is seventy-six. He's blind in one eye. He was friends with Louise and her husband long before her husband died, which was probably fifteen years ago now. I'm not sure they did anything more than play bridge. On the other hand, who knows? I've heard assisted-living centers and nursing homes are full of horny seniors and rife with STDs. You could ask him yourself if you wanted to be certain."

"What's in the will if there's no one to inherit?" Packard asked.

"I've only glanced at it. My dad is handling the estate. She had a couple of charities listed, including the Sandy Lake Public Library. That place has already been the benefactor of the Henkels' wealth. They're about to get a nice check from Louise as well, once the estate settles." Jim Henkel was a local author who had made millions over a long career of writing bestselling science-fiction novels.

"How big is the estate?"

"Surprisingly large. She and her husband did a good job investing their money. She's got that house on Lake Redwing. That'll be worth a bundle regardless of the condition."

"I was there today with my mom."

"Really. What for?"

Packard decided to tell her everything since he had technically trespassed in her client's home. He told her that his grandfather used to own the house, how he'd spent summers and winter breaks there as a child, about Nick's disappearance, and the letter from Stan Shaw.

"Holy shit, Ben." They'd been talking so long, he heard a timer go off and the next batch of cookies come out of the oven. "I know that you know there's plenty of gossip about you in this town, but I never heard any of that. Oh my god."

"Some folks remember the boy who disappeared all those years ago, but I'd say most don't remember his name. I purposely didn't make it known during the election and no one brought it up."

"Well, if you want to talk to my dad about Louise, let me know. I should go with you. He's not exactly your biggest supporter," Lisa said. Packard could hear the ratchet of a cookie dough scooper.

"What did I do?"

"He's very conservative, first of all."

Hates gays, Packard interpreted.

"And there's our family connection to Howard Shepard."

"I don't know about the connection," Packard said.

"You didn't know my sister, Robin, is Howard's wife?"

Packard tried not to laugh but failed. "Are you kidding me? I had no idea. I don't know that I've ever had the chance to say more than two words to her. I never would have guessed you were related."

"We're nothing alike. Her husband is a moron and she…has no problem being married to a moron."

Packard could hear Lisa's eyes rolling over the phone.

"Anyway. My dad is thrilled that his son-in-law is now sheriff of Sandy Lake County. It's been a bit of good news in a hard year for him. He misses Louise."

"He lives on Lake Redwing, correct?"

"He does. On the upper lake."

"Has he lived there long?"

"My whole life. He's still in the house I grew up in."

Packard was thinking of all the unidentified people in the photos he had from the case file. Someone like Ray, who'd lived on the lake forever, might be able to put names to faces. "I think I will take you up on that offer to meet with your dad. Could we do it tomorrow?"

"I can't go tomorrow. I'll be in St. Cloud with my daughter."

"Find out if he's free. I'll take my mom to protect me from your mean old dad."

Lisa laughed, her mouth full of cookie. "I'll find out and text you later. I know he's got bridge sometime tomorrow. He and his new partner, Ralph, are still trying to get to know each other's styles."

"It must be hard to start over with a new partner after so many years."

"He once told me trying out a new bridge partner is like getting to know a new lover. And now I don't know what's worse, the idea of him and Ralph as lovers or him and Louise. Ugh."

"I'll leave you to work that out," Packard said. "Thanks for the help."

The woodstove was raging, the dry heat like a weighted blanket. He made a few more notes on the computer but his eyes didn't want to stay open. In a minute, he and Frank were both asleep.

He woke from his nap to a text from Lisa with her dad's address and an invitation to stop by anytime after noon the next day. He took Frank for another walk and started prepping risotto and char-roasted vegetables for dinner. A beer from Kyle's brewery fizzed in a glass while he grated a weightless pile of Parmesan cheese. A Yo La Tengo album spun in slow circles, releasing music like a fragrance.

The kitchen and the dining area were the only parts of the house he'd yet to remodel. Both were raised up a step from the rest of the living area, allowing him to leave the original floors, which were terrible. The cupboards were without doors, and the linoleum countertops had been pulled up and thrown away back when he had a construction dumpster. In their place he had put down plywood and brown paper from a giant roll that he burned in the fireplace when it got dirty.

His mom showed up with a bottle of wine and snow in her hair. He poured her a glass while she shed her layers. "That stove looks forty years old," she said, taking the glass from him and peeking inside at the vegetables.

"It is. It probably cost less than $200 at the time and it still works great. Makes it hard to find the motivation to start the remodel."

"It's not the kitchen that makes the chef. I don't know where you learned how to cook. Certainly wasn't from me," she said, tipping back the rosé.

His mom had been a fine if unimaginative cook. What home cook was imaginative in the kitchen in the eighties? She had cooked hearty meals meant to fill up and shut up a family of six: sloppy joes, chili, tuna hot dish, potato soup.

"I watch a little YouTube, a little Food Network. I learned a lot from Marcus," Packard said, ladling another cup of vegetable stock into the risotto.

He and Marcus had met during the police academy. After years of stolen looks and uncomfortable silences, they ended up in bed one night after too many drinks. Afterward, they had to hide their relationship to keep it from affecting their careers. Marcus was willing to be more open about it, but Packard struggled with the idea of being known as a gay cop. He pushed back at the idea of being out at work. Their relationship suffered because of it.

Marcus was killed responding to a domestic disturbance. Finding out Marcus had made him the executor of his will and left him all his death benefits had shaken Packard to his core. It made him realize all the things Marcus had wanted that Packard wasn't ready to accept. He still beat himself up for what it cost them both.

After dinner, after Frank licked their plates, and after the dishes were done, Packard made himself an old-fashioned and his mom poured another glass of wine. He stoked up the woodburning stove and put on a Linda Ronstadt album his mom liked when he was a kid. They sat kitty-corner from each other on the L-shaped couch with a Scrabble board on the coffee table in front of them.

"How are you feeling about the shooting? How is your mind?"

Packard groaned. For as much as he hadn't wanted his mom to come to town, he was glad now she had. Running around with her had helped distract him from Robert Clark. There was no forgetting. It still found him at night like something staring out from the darkest part of the closet. "Not great," he admitted. "Just when I thought things couldn't get any worse at work, Robert Clark had to pull a gun in court."

"You know you didn't do anything wrong," his mom said.

"It's not about right or wrong. At the end of the day, a man is dead by my hand. I killed him. I can't stop thinking about every decision in his life and mine that led us to intersect in that moment, and what tiny change might have produced a different outcome. It's a maddening game of what-if."

His mom nodded sympathetically and rearranged the tiles in her tray. Of course, she understood the what-if game. She had spent thirty years playing it with Nick's disappearance. "Please tell me you're going to get your psych eval. You need to talk to someone."

"I'll do the eval eventually."

"Meditation would do wonders for you, too," his mom said with a knowing look.

"Let's talk about something else."

He told her about his conversation with Lisa Washington and the plan to visit her father and ask for his help identifying the people in the photos.

"Maybe you should buy Grandpa's house when it hits the market," his mom said.

"I can't afford Grandpa's house. Our whole family could pool its money and we still wouldn't be able to afford Grandpa's house."

"Could you make a side deal with Lisa before it hits the market?"

"I'm pretty sure she's obligated to get the best price for her client."

"Her client is dead," his mom said.

"I don't think that matters."

Packard played FLOUT. His mom played INLET off his T. Packard used all seven letters and played ASTEROID off her I. "You jerk," she said, writing down his score.

She got up and brought the bottle of wine to where they were sitting and poured another glass. As she studied her tiles and the board, Packard asked the question he'd been wondering about for a while. "Mom, why did we stop talking about Nick?"

When she looked at him, her eyes took a second to find his face, a sign of intoxication he recognized from years on patrol. "What do you mean?" she asked.

"Never mind," he said. "Now isn't the time."

"No, you asked the question. Tell me what you're thinking."

Packard sat forward with his elbows on his knees. "Speaking of the what-if game. I wonder what would have happened if I hadn't moved back here. Would we ever have gotten any answers? Was anyone still asking for them? We hardly talk about Nick at all anymore."

His mom sighed. She took off her glasses and rubbed her face. Packard felt the same way. Exhausted by his own questions.

"Do you remember the days and months and years when we talked about nothing but Nick?" she asked him.

Packard sat back. He remembered the chaos right after Nick disappeared. They stayed in Sandy Lake for days after the holiday break ended, unable to leave the house, until his parents finally sent him and his siblings home to go back to school. For what felt like a long time after, one or the other or both of their parents were up in Sandy Lake. Then, for a time, they didn't go back at all.

The fact that Nick's disappearance didn't involve an abduction and that they found the sled in the lake meant the story wasn't big news much beyond the immediate area. Kids at school still found out about it. Packard remembered looks in the hallways and whispers behind his back. He was the kid with the dead brother. He had another classmate, a girl named Stephanie, whose mom had died the year before. Stephanie had seemed radioactive after that, pulsing like a neon sign that said Dead Mom. Kids avoided her as if she gave off the thing that had killed her mother and might kill them too if they got too close.

Packard hung on to most of his friends. They didn't know what to say about Nick and neither did Packard, so they didn't talk about it. He and his siblings all saw counselors, which felt new and interesting for a while, but then started to feel like a chore. When his brother Joe got angry about it, Packard adopted the same attitude until his parents finally relented and the sessions ended.

"For me, your brother was a door I couldn't stop walking through," his mom said. "I couldn't close it or put it behind me. It was a threshold I crossed every time I woke in the morning, every time my thoughts came back to him from something else. On the other side of it was...." She closed her eyes and shook her head.

"Nick was all any of us thought about or talked about. Then it became something else. Like a secret," Packard said.

What he couldn't say, even though they were supposedly speaking the truth, was that what he eventually felt was shame. He was embarrassed that this was the story of his family, he was ashamed of his parents, and these feelings were tangled up with the trauma of puberty and the physical attractions he couldn't verbalize. He was terrified of being found out. He was terrified that something bad would happen to him. His parents couldn't protect him. Look what happened to Nick. Look how they had failed him.

"You kids had to have a childhood that wasn't all about Nick. You had to have experiences not tainted with tragedy. What happened to Nick was a bomb that wounded all of us. It ended my marriage to your father. It scarred all of your childhoods. We did our best to make things as normal as possible for you kids. I don't know that we were very successful."

"Stan Shaw's letter said he called annually for a few years before the case finally went cold. He didn't believe the body was in the lake. Do you remember those calls?"

His mom nodded and drank her wine. "He talked to your father more than me. The news was always the same. Nothing to report."

"So after we stopped talking about it and after the police stopped calling, what happened? Did you make peace with not knowing?"

A look of anger flapped across his mother's face like a bird hitting a window. "I haven't known peace since the day your brother disappeared. Not a day." She picked up her wineglass, then put it back down without drinking. "You're not a parent, but I know you know how to empathize. It's what makes you a good police officer. You should be able to imagine what it's like in my mind, knowing every day that the first child I gave birth to just…disappeared. He was by my side his whole life, on the verge of not needing me anymore, and then gone. Not on his own. Missing. Presumed dead. Which one? Both? I didn't know what to do with that kind of uncertainty. I decided to have hope and protect it as best I could."

"Did you think there was a chance he was still alive all this time?"

His mom ran her hands through her white hair, pulled it back and twisted it, then let it fall loose again. "For some years, yes. Then no. The hope turned into something else over time, or got so small as to be meaningless. I know you kids like to make fun of my rituals, but have you ever stopped to consider that these talismans and protections are what I need in order to live every day in this body, in this mind, in this world without my son?"

He hadn't. Or he had and he still made fun. When your mom told you to unclench your butt and let your chakras breathe, it was hard to know where the line was.

"How do you feel now, knowing what we know?" he asked.

His mom stared at the Scrabble board. She rearranged the tiles in her tray. "Mostly sad. And hopeful again."

"Hopeful for what?"

"For the truth. If we get the answers, if we find his body, it brings Nick back from the theoretical." She put her hands up beside her head and moved her fingers. "He exists in a realm of infinite possibilities right now. The truth will bring him back to us, not alive, but back among us in a way that he hasn't been for thirty years."

Packard stared at the fire. A knot in the wood popped and flashed brightly inside the stove. Frank had fallen asleep between them. "Are you ever going to take your turn?" he asked.

"I thought it was your turn."

"I played JUMP," he said, pointing at the board. "And don't think you're driving back to the hotel tonight after drinking most of that bottle of wine. The guest bed is made up. I'll give you something to sleep in."

"In that case, I might as well finish it." His mom emptied the bottle into her glass with a rushing pour. She picked up her glass. "Cheers, son. I love you."

"I love you too, Mom."

CHAPTER SEVEN

IN THE MORNING, THE smell of coffee roused his mom from the guest room. She was wearing a black T-shirt he had given her, tucked into a pair of track pants that she had rolled down several times at the waist and cuffed at the legs to keep from dragging on the ground.

"Why did you let me drink so much last night?" she asked. Her face was drawn and puffy at the same time.

"You're a grown woman. You don't need me to tell you anything." He poured a bowl of scrambled eggs into a pan that already had onions and peppers and broccoli in it. His mom found a coffee mug and poured herself a cup. "My head…" she said.

"Is there a crystal you can rub on your forehead or put under your tongue to make it better?"

She gave him a dirty look through one eye over the rim of her coffee cup. "No, but some ibuprofen would be nice. Smart-ass."

"Hall closet," he directed her.

They ate. After breakfast, his mom disappeared with a large glass of water into the infrared sauna in his bathroom. She emerged an hour later, showered and dressed in her clothes from the previous day, looking revived.

———————

The day was bright blue and eye-wateringly cold. They scooped up Frank and poured him into the extended cab of Packard's truck. As he drove, Packard told his mom about the Emmett Burr case. His family knew the details as they pertained to Jenny Wheeler, the daughter of Packard's cousin, Susan. After Jenny was rescued, investigators uncovered the remains of three other women on Emmett's property. One had yet to be identified.

"Emmett Burr abducted his first victim about five years after Nick went missing. I spent more than a few nights lying awake wondering if Emmett might have had anything to do with Nick's case."

"Is he mentioned in the case file at all?"

Packard had no idea so he dodged the question. "Not that I remember. I feel pretty comfortable ruling him out. Emmett abducted women, kept them in a room in his basement, and buried them on his property. It was only women."

"He killed Jenny's boyfriend."

"Yes, for breaking into his house. He also killed a friend of his and dumped the body and a tow truck into a flooded quarry. He killed when he needed to. I can't draw any lines connecting him and Nick."

They kept driving and made their way around the lower part of Lake Redwing, taking the long way to Ray Wiley's house. His mom had the group photo with the unidentified people in it and kept looking from it to the houses passing by. "Your grandparents could have told you who lived in every single house on this lake. Your father and I spent a lot of time up here but I never really paid attention to who was who or where they lived."

The address from Lisa took them to a house that looked like two sides of an isosceles triangle with four garage stalls and a living area down one leg, a large kitchen in the center, and bedrooms down the other leg. It wasn't small but it was modest for the neighborhood, where a house on the nearby point had sold for $12 million recently.

They left Frank in the truck and rang the doorbell. Ray invited them into a house that smelled like dusty books and an old man's cologne. He was large with an age-spotted face and thick glasses and white hair combed straight back, heavy with pomade. He still had half a pot of coffee from that morning, and everyone said yes to a cup. An Irish setter named Daisy followed Ray around the kitchen, then lay down beside his chair.

"Well, that election certainly didn't go your way," Ray said by way of an opening.

Packard sat beside his mom on the couch. He laughed. "No, it did not."

"Not sure what made you think you had a chance in hell, given your proclivities. Marilyn Shaw should have known she was wasting her time trying to get you elected. The homosexual agenda doesn't play well this far from the Cities."

Packard could feel his mom stiffen next to him. He smiled, shook his head, leaned forward to put his coffee mug on the table in front of them. "There was no homosexual agenda. I ran on my experience and my record. I thought that might be enough."

Ray scoffed. Coffee ran down his chin and dripped onto the front of his shirt. He wiped himself with the back of his hand. "You obviously don't know how politics work. I'm happy to see Howard in the job. It was long past time for Stan to go. He had a blind spot for people he liked and carried a grudge against those he didn't."

"I never witnessed that about him," Packard said. "He seemed incredibly fair to me."

"You were in his blind spot," Ray said.

Packard opened his mouth to respond but his mom interjected. "Ray, I wanted to know if you remember my father," she said. "Franklin Harris. He had a house on the lower lake. His grandson went missing over the winter break almost thirty years ago."

"I remember Franklin," Ray said. He sat with his hands folded across his wide belly. "I remember that boy going missing."

"That was my son," Packard's mom said.

Ray looked at Packard. One of his eyes was gray and fixed like a sink drain. It didn't move with the other one. "Your brother?"

"Yeah, he is. Was. My older brother," Packard said.

"I'll be damned," Ray said. "I forgot the boy's name but never forgot the story. Franklin lived in the green house. Louise and Charles bought it from him."

Packard reached across the coffee table and handed Ray the two photos they'd been carrying. "These photos came from my brother's case file. There's been some new developments and we're trying to ID some of the people who were around that summer and winter. Lisa said you've been living here a long time."

Ray grunted as he leaned toward the lamp next to his chair. He turned on the light and picked up a magnifying glass the size of a dessert plate. Packard had to wonder how Ray saw the cards at bridge if his eyes were so bad.

Ray looked at the photo with the three rows of people for a good while. Pam went around behind his chair and used her phone to film the photo as Ray pointed and gave them four more names they didn't know. "Of course, they're all dead now," Ray said.

"Dead recently or a long time now?" Packard asked. He was thinking of Stan's letter and the fact that the man he'd been talking to was in bad health. If he had died since then, it was only recently.

"A long while," Ray said.

The other photo of the girl and the boy with Nick by the water gave Ray pause. "I don't remember the names of these two but I remember the family," Ray said. "They had a house…" He closed his eyes to think, then pointed. "Three down to the east. He was a doctor or dentist of some kind. Middle Eastern. Muslim." He said the last word like it was regrettable. "Single dad. Had these two kids."

Ray told a story about coming home from a fishing trip with his neighbor, Chuck. Ray had dropped his tackle box on the last day, busting the lid off it. When it came time to pack up, he dumped everything in his laundry bag with a plan to sort it out when he got home.

"Chuck and I were still unloading the car when I heard my wife, Cheryl, scream. I came into the bedroom and her hand looked like a decorated Christmas tree. She had jammed it blindly into the laundry bag and had every kind of lure dangling from it, hooks deep in her palm and fingers. I thought we should go to town but Chuck said there was a doctor closer so we knocked on his door and he came over with his bag and some numbing ointment and a scalpel. Got Cheryl fixed up in no time."

Ray closed his eyes again, trying to remember a name. Nothing would come to him. "I do remember I settled the score. Might have even been later that summer. His kids got into some trouble for something, the daughter got mouthy with the police. I don't remember. Underage possession or something like that. He asked me for help and I got things smoothed out."

"Did Nick ever get into any trouble like that up here?" Packard asked his mom.

She nodded. "He was in a car with kids who were drinking. I'm sure the only reason he wasn't drinking was he was waiting until they got to where they were going. He was driving with a headlight out and got pulled over. It was a mess for a while. We kept it from you younger kids."

It was weird to think of his older brother as another troublemaking kid he might have pulled over as a patrol cop. Dying young had turned Nick into a saint in Packard's mind.

"What happened to the family?" he asked Ray.

"They weren't around long from what I remember. Sold the place and that was it."

"You said the house was three to the east from here. Are you sure about that?" If Packard had an address, he could go to the county property records and find the history of who owned the house.

Ray said he was sure. Packard didn't have any more questions about the photos so he switched the subject. "I wanted to ask you about Louise," he said.

"What about her?"

"We went by the house yesterday. Mom was hoping to say hi to Louise."

Ray took off his glasses and wiped under his milky eye with the back side of his hand. "Ah god. I miss that woman. We won the Gopher Regional bridge tournament more times than I can count. Came in eighth one year at NABC. Not bad for a couple of old farts from up north."

"We were shocked to hear what happened," Packard said. "Was there anything surprising to you about it?"

"Are you asking me was I surprised when I asked my son-in-law to check on Louise and he told me she was dead at the bottom of the stairs? Yes, I was pretty goddamned surprised." He seemed annoyed by the question.

"What I meant was did she have a history of falls or accidents? Drinking-related or otherwise?"

"No."

"And the broken bottle of bourbon mentioned in Shepard's report?"

"Louise was no teetotaler. She liked a nip now and then. She wasn't what I would call a drinker."

"So getting intoxicated and falling down would be out of character for her."

"Yes. I'm sure I told Howard the same thing."

"Was she sick or on any kind of medications that might have affected her balance or blood pressure?"

"How would I know?" Ray complained. "Where are you going with this?"

"I'm not sure I'm going anywhere. I get curious when a woman who's lived in a house for years and years by herself suddenly falls down the stairs when no one is around."

"Accidents happen, Deputy."

"So do other things," Packard said. "What can you tell me about her estate?"

"I can't tell you anything. It's none of your business."

"Does she have any heirs?"

"No," Ray said, seeming satisfied. "The whole estate is to be dispersed among her favorite charities."

"Does the estate pay you for handling the probate?" Packard knew he was poking a bear with the question. He didn't care.

"None of your goddamn business," Ray sputtered. He struggled out of his recliner. "I've had enough of your questions. Louise died in a tragic accident and I don't even want to think of how she might have suffered. I won't have you turn things into a circus. You're not sheriff anymore. You aren't even a detective. I would think being a killer cop under investigation by the BCA would give you enough to worry about. I'd leave Louise alone if I were you."

Packard wasn't sure if Ray Wiley meant his words to be a threat or just hurtful. He longed for the days when his biggest worry was being thought of as the gay cop. Being called a killer cop felt like being kicked while he was down.

He and his mom stood, put on their coats, and tried to thank Ray for his help. Ray put his hands on them and turned them around and pushed the door shut on them.

Back in the cold truck, Packard turned on the seat warmers and the windshield defrost. Frank crawled from the extended cab over the console and into Packard's mom's lap.

"That was something else," Packard said.

"What an unpleasant man. Did you have to put up with that kind of behavior during your campaign?"

"Most people weren't that bad. Most people were actually perfectly nice," Packard said, looking behind him as he drove in reverse. "Though, did I ever tell you about the Fudge Packard yard signs?"

CHAPTER EIGHT

PACKARD HAD A TEXT from Shepard the next morning. **Get your ass in the office.** No time. No subject, though he could guess.

Shepard wasn't in when Packard arrived just before 9:00 a.m. He sat at an empty computer and pulled up the Sandy Lake County Assessor website. Ray had said the doctor lived three houses to the east. Packard had his mom write down the house number as they drove by. The sales history for that address on the website showed the house was sold in 1989, 1993, 2007, and 2019. Packard clicked on the arrow for 1993 and saw the seller's name was Rassin and the buyer's name was Green. Rassin bought the house two years before Nick disappeared and sold it two years later.

The assessor's site only provided last names, so Packard picked up the phone and called the recorder's office, gave the plot number and address, and got a full name: Dr. Abbas Rassin. Packard put the name into the driver's license database and got an address in Duluth. CIBRS and criminal history came back clean. When he called the phone number for Dr. Rassin, it came back as no longer in service.

He was telling Thielen what he'd found when Shepard came down the hall.

"Packard, my office. Right now."

"What did you do now?" Thielen asked.

Packard gave her an unconvincing shrug. "Lunch today? Noon?" he asked as he backtracked out of her office.

"Yeah. I'll make time," she said.

"Bring the kid," he said, referring to Deputy Reynolds, her trainee.

Packard followed Shepard down the hall to his office.

"Close the door," Shepard said. He had a thermos in one hand and a newspaper under his arm. He took off his coat and hat and sat behind his desk.

Packard noticed Stan Shaw's citations and awards were still up on the walls. Several flattened boxes that needed to be folded and taped were leaning against a bookcase. Kelly probably felt she had done her part getting him the boxes. It was up to Shepard to finish the job.

"My father-in-law said you showed up uninvited at his house yesterday with a woman and badgered him," Shepard said as he poured coffee out of the thermos into its lid.

Packard made an exaggerated face. "The woman was my mom, and we were definitely invited. I had his daughter call and ask if he would meet with us and he said yes. There was no badgering. We showed him some photos from Nick's case file and asked for his help identifying the people in the pictures."

"He said you badgered him about Louise."

"I asked him a few questions about the circumstances of her death."

"And why would you do that?"

"Curiosity."

"It's not your job to be curious, Deputy. You're not on the detective desk. You're court security and you're not even that right now."

If their roles were reversed, Packard would have corrected Shepard. A deputy's job was always to be curious, to be on the lookout, to notice patterns and watch for things that deviated from the pattern. Didn't matter if you were a patrol deputy, a detective, worked in the jail, or stood over a bag scanner on the third floor.

"Let me ask you a question," Packard said. "You only wrote up the first incident report on Louise. Why was it assigned to another deputy to follow up?"

"I was on vacation. Took the family camping. When I got back, it didn't need follow-up. The ME determined she died from a broken skull. She was drunk and fell down the stairs. Case closed."

"Hmmm," Packard said.

Shepard sat up straight and shook his head. "Don't *hmmm* me, Deputy. I know what it means when you say *hmmm*. It means you think someone is full of shit. I heard it enough out of you the last several years. I'm not going to hear it as your sheriff."

Packard nodded. "Understood."

"I also got complaints from Louise's neighbors. Said you cut through the seal on the door and let yourself in."

"I did do that," Packard said.

"How far up my ass would you be if I'd done something similar last year when you were in this seat?" Shepard asked.

"Pretty far," Packard admitted. "I made an emotional decision because of the personal nature of Nick's case."

"Which is why you're not supposed to be looking into it. Anything you know, Reynolds should know so he can do the job."

Shepard downed the last of his coffee and stood with the newspaper under his arm. "This coffee is kicking my ass. I'm gonna go destroy the bathroom. Go home, Deputy. If I get any more calls about you, we're gonna have real problems."

At lunchtime, Thielen and Reynolds were already sitting across from each other in a booth by the time Packard got to El Toro Loco, Sandy Lake's idea of a Mexican restaurant. The house margarita tasted like green Jell-O and too much of the menu came smothered in a cheese sauce that hardened into stucco as soon as it reached room temperature. There were gems if you knew where to look.

Packard slid in beside Reynolds, ordered the street tacos with carnitas and a water to drink.

"If their margaritas didn't suck, I'd order a pitcher and straw," Thielen said. She looked sullen.

"A little early in the week for that, isn't it?"

Thielen gave him a dirty look. She was five four in shoes with short blond hair and the body of a dedicated triathlete. "You want to compare the weeks we're having when you're on leave from scanner duty?"

"Hey, that's low. I didn't ask for this. You think I was enjoying looking through purses? Do you know what women keep in their purses?"

"I have an idea," Thielen said.

"I saw a vibrator the other day."

Thielen tilted her head and stuck out her bottom lip. "Aww, that must have been horrible for you. Tell him what we saw this morning," she said to Reynolds.

Reynolds was leaning forward, sucking on the straw in his giant glass of Mountain Dew. He was a pink-faced local kid just out of college with a criminal science degree and two kids already. He barely looked old enough to babysit, let alone be someone's dad. Or a deputy. "Old guy with ALS. Lost his in-home aide. The neighbor said she was doing what she could to help out but it wasn't enough. The old guy rolled his wheelchair into the bathroom, got himself in the tub with the shower curtain pulled. Put a .38 under his chin," Reynolds said. He made a sound in the corner of his mouth of a trigger being pulled.

"All right, you win," Packard conceded.

Their food came. Reynolds had ordered a chimichanga the size of a football. Thielen had a taco salad. They ate.

"Is your mom still here?" Thielen asked.

"One more night. She's flying out of Duluth tomorrow."

He told Thielen and Reynolds about the visit to the family home, about Louise Larsen falling down the stairs, about meeting with Ray Wiley. "I've got a lead from Ray on a person of interest from Nick's case. It's a doctor whose two kids were friends with Nick. I have a photo of all three of them together and I have an address for the doctor in Duluth. I'm not one hundred percent certain but I have a feeling this might be the guy Stan referenced in his letter."

He stared at Thielen. He was going somewhere with this. He wanted her to get there at the same time.

"What?" she asked.

"Shepard wants Reynolds on this case. I could take him with me to Duluth tomorrow if you'll cut him loose."

Thielen stabbed at her salad aggressively. "Come on," she said. "We're not busy enough? Now you want to pull him away for a day? Not gonna happen."

"Okay. I'll go on my own. When it suits him, Shepard acts like this case is a personal matter that we can't devote resources to, then in the next breath tells me I'm too close to it and should let Reynolds run lead. Fuck it. If Shepard asks, I'm going to say Reynolds wasn't available."

They finished their food. While they waited for the check, Packard reluctantly made another request. "I want someone to take a second look at Louise's death."

Thielen's mouth was as small and tight as it could be.

"Why?"

"I don't think it got the attention it deserved. Ray Wiley called Shepard, his son-in-law, to check on Louise. His report is short on details. There's not even a description of the scene beyond the back door being unlocked and the body at the bottom of the basement stairs and the smell of alcohol from a broken bottle. It never came across either of our desks for a closer look."

"It came across mine," Thielen said.

"I didn't see you in the file."

"You were busy with the Emmett Burr circus. I read what Shepard wrote, I read the follow-up. I read the ME report. I told him to close it."

"Did you go to the scene?"

"No."

"I did," Packard said. "Something about the story isn't right."

"Who do you think is going to look into this again? Me? Reynolds? In our free time? It's been almost a year since she died. No one has raised any questions or concerns."

"I'm raising them now."

Thielen looked annoyed. "Why? Because she lived in your family's house? Because it's where your brother disappeared from? Are you sure you're not chasing one because you can't dig for the other?"

"That's got nothing to do with it. Something about it isn't right. It has to do with the direction the door opens. It has to do with the idea of an old woman going down the basement stairs with a whole bottle of bourbon in her hand. It's absurd on the surface."

Thielen sat back and folded her arms. "Accidents are absurd. Death is absurd. The state refusing to pay home health aides more than $19 an hour, leaving an old man no choice but to commit suicide in the tub, is fucking absurd," Thielen said. "I know you've been miserable standing next to that X-ray machine getting your balls irradiated, and being on leave must suck for you since your whole life is your job, but you don't get to make things difficult for the rest of us because of it. You don't get to make work for us because you think something is absurd."

Packard was used to being in step with Thielen. They approached work the same. They had each other's back. They were friends outside of work. But they hadn't been in sync since Shepard was sworn in. Thielen was tired and miserable and always seemed to be spoiling for a fight.

"First of all, I'm not trying to make your life difficult. You're doing a good job of that on your own with your shit attitude." Packard reached for his wallet, took out a twenty and tossed it in the middle of the table. He kept his voice low and controlled. "When someone who isn't a known drinker nose-dives down a flight of stairs with a bottle in her hand, I got questions. I got way more questions than anyone bothered to ask the first time around. Maybe I am making this personal. She died in what used to be my family's home. Our worst deputy responded while I was still sheriff and distracted with other things. I'd look into it myself if I wasn't on leave for killing a man whose only wish was not to lose the land where he scattered his wife's ashes. I'd look into it myself if I hadn't lost the election and my job as an investigator in the process."

Reynolds looked like he was watching Mommy and Daddy have a fight in public and wanted it to stop. Packard slid out of the booth and grabbed his coat from the hook on the side. "We see the worst shit imaginable on this job and give thanks every day that it isn't our family member in that tub with their brains blown out or dead at the bottom of the stairs. We still treat them as if they were. I shouldn't have to explain this to you of all people."

Packard waited for Thielen to reply while he zipped his coat, and when she didn't, when she stared at him like she was daring him to say one more word to her, he looked away and then looked around the restaurant as if trying to locate who he was really mad at.

Why are we taking this out on each other?

He left without an answer to the question.

CHAPTER NINE

EARLY THE NEXT MORNING, Packard met his mother at her hotel. Only the brightest stars still shone as the sun came up white at the horizon, pushing back the night in shades of blue. He started her rental car and let it warm up while she finished packing.

They caravanned along two-lane roads, eventually picking up Highway 200 east to Route 2, finally merging onto Interstate 35. The road climbed as they approached Duluth so that the view was all asphalt and treetops before it opened and showed them the St. Louis River, fringed with ice, and the large buildings and heavy machinery of industry. Long rectangular docks piled high with sand and coal, a scrap-metal dealer, paper and energy plants, the sanitation center. Chimney stacks put out hot air shredded by the cold wind.

They off-loaded his mom's rental car at the Duluth airport before coming back to town. The address Packard had led them away from the lake, uphill again past large brick homes and stately Craftsmans that sat on small, steep lawns.

After his fight with Thielen yesterday, he'd channeled his anger into a workout, thinking about Ray telling him how he helped Dr. Rassin's daughter with an underage drinking ticket. His mom said Nick got in similar trouble.

Packard didn't know for sure it was the same incident, but common sense said it was. If Nick and the girl in the photo had gotten in trouble together earlier that summer, a late-night meetup over Christmas break might have been the only way they could see each other.

After a quick shower, he'd sat with a towel around his neck and looked on Google Maps at the upper and lower sections of Lake Redwing. He dropped a pin on his grandfather's house and one on Dr. Rassin's house. It wouldn't have been far at all on a snowmobile. Nick could have taken a trail around the lake or driven on roads plowed across the ice that led to fish houses and temporary hockey rinks.

He'd also read Stan's letter again, this time thinking about Dr. Rassin and the two kids in the photo with Nick.

There was one guy who would never return my calls. Every year I'd have to hunt him down in person and every year I got the sense he was bracing himself for my return, that he knew he might spend the rest of his life answering questions about the missing Packard boy. His answers never changed. He didn't know anything. Didn't see anything. His kids' answers were the same as their dad's.

The truck's nav system told Packard to turn onto a slippery road hedged with tall trees that blocked the sun and then told him he'd arrived at his destination.

"This is Dr. Rassin's house, according to the driver's license database," Packard said as he turned again into a driveway that ran to a tuck-under garage on the side of the house. Off the back he could see a main-level balcony over a shaded brick patio bordered by more tall trees. To the right, a curved set of concrete steps climbed around to the front of the house.

"I'm coming with you."

"No, you're not," he said to his mom. "Let me introduce myself and get a sense for him. I'll text you if you should come up. If I come stumbling down the stairs bleeding, call 911."

"Are you kidding? Why would that—"

He put a hand on her knee. "I am kidding. Stay here."

The snowy steps had been tamped down to ice, probably by the mailman. The front of the house was brick with a teal door. Packard rang the bell and waited.

The woman who answered was in her early forties. She was wearing a beige cardigan over black yoga pants and had a blanket draped over her shoulders. She had wireless headphones in her ears and a phone in her hand. She held up a finger at Packard. "Hang on, there's someone at the door. I need to go on mute. I'll be right back."

Packard was dressed in regular clothes. He showed her his badge. "I'm with the sheriff's department in Sandy Lake County. I'm looking for Dr. Rassin."

The woman leaned in to look at his badge more closely. She unscrewed one of the buds from her ear. "Dr. Rassin doesn't live here anymore," she said. "We bought the house from him a couple of years ago when he moved to assisted living."

"Do you happen to know the name or the address of the facility?"

She wrapped the blanket tighter around her shoulders and started scrolling on her phone. "I put it in my contacts because we still get mail for him that I need to forward." She turned the screen around and showed it to him. Packard wrote the address in his notebook.

"Is he in some kind of trouble?" the woman asked.

"Not that I know of. I want to talk to him regarding an old case I'm following up on."

"It's just that you're the second person from a sheriff's office to contact us about Dr. Rassin."

Packard felt the hair on his neck stand up. "Tell me about the other one," he said.

"It was a phone call maybe a year ago. Same thing—someone saying they were from a sheriff's office. Might have been the same one as you. Sounded like an older man. Said he was looking for the doctor. I gave him the same information."

"I know who that was," Packard said. "I'm doing another follow-up. Sorry to trouble you again."

Back in the truck, his mom asked, "Well?"

Packard shook his head. "Rassin's not here but I know where to find him. I also know we're following in Stan's footprints, which means we're on the right trail."

———————

Traffic crawled as they followed the north shore of Lake Superior where it probed the space between Minnesota and Wisconsin like a finger. The assisted-living place was called the Harbor. The streets and the parking lot and all the infrastructure looked brand new. Four snowcapped condo buildings, styled like Swiss chalets, faced the enormous frozen lake. Behind them was a larger, shorter building shaped like an X that looked administrative.

Packard had to wonder as they crossed the parking lot why so many of his cases brought him to assisted-living facilities. He'd been to places like this in Sandy Lake and in Iowa and now Duluth. Old cases, old victims, old suspects.

The building they entered held the common areas. Behind the reception desk was a staircase with a grandfather clock at the top of the landing where the stairs split off in two directions and went up to the second floor. Underneath the grand stairway he saw a game room and a library with shelves of books and large leather reading chairs. Everything was wood-paneled and the carpets were dark and rich.

The young woman behind the desk smiled and welcomed them to the Harbor.

"We're here to visit Dr. Rassin," Packard said.

The woman nodded. She asked if it was their first visit to the Harbor. They said yes. She clicked her mouse, looked at something on her screen, typed. "It'll be just a moment," she said.

A minute later, a door opened down the hallway to the right and a middle-aged woman with gray hair, dressed head to toe in matching purple, came up and introduced herself as Ann, the Harbor's director. She led them over to the library, asking over her shoulder if they were friends or family of Dr. Rassin.

"Friends," his mom said before Packard could respond.

Ann closed the French doors and her expression turned solemn. "I'm afraid I have some bad news," she said. "Dr. Rassin passed five months ago."

Packard's mom looked genuinely stricken. She put her hand on Ann's forearm and they looked at each other like they both shared in this loss and felt it deeply. Packard was busy remembering another phrase from Stan's letter. *We're both in bad shape, him possibly worse than me, if you can believe that.*

Five months ago was October. Stan had died on Labor Day weekend so Dr. Rassin had made it a month longer than he did. Last October Packard was up to his neck in campaign activities. It would be another two months before he opened the box Marilyn Shaw had given him and found Stan's letter.

Dr. Rassin was the source of information from Stan's letter. And now they were too late to talk to him.

"Did he have a lot of visitors while he was here?" his mom asked.

Ann gave a sad smile and shook her head. "A few people from his dental practice. He was an oral surgeon for a long time, as I'm sure you know."

"We did know," his mom said even though Packard never told her that. "What about his son and daughter? Are they in the area?"

"His son lives in Duluth," Ann said.

"His kids were still kids the last time we saw them," Packard's mom said. "Dr. Rassin and his family had a cabin on a lake near ours. We'd love to get in contact with his son if you have a number or an address for him."

Packard had to keep from smiling. His plan was to show his badge and see how far that got them. Now he had the feeling a badge would have made Ann's eyes pop. She would have told them to make an appointment with whoever was higher up the chain of command than the director. His mom's way was working far better.

Ann led them out of the library and held hands with his mom as they walked back to the front desk. "Obviously, I can't give out information about the residents or their families. The son's last name is Rassin and he's a tattoo artist here in Duluth. I think with a little googling you should have no trouble locating him."

Ann hugged his mom and then moved in for a hug with Packard, who hadn't said a word the whole time and wasn't really ready for a hug. She was much shorter than him. He caught himself before he patted her on the top of the head.

The wind was whipping off the lake as they hurried back across the parking lot. Slabs of ice lifting and grinding together sounded like timbers cracking.

"Nice job, Detective Packard," he said when they were back in the truck.

"What? I just asked for the info."

"That's my job. You didn't give me a chance to show her my gun and tell her we can do this the easy way or the hard way."

"You're not carrying a gun. You know what I've found in the healing work I've been doing? Human touch calms people and makes them want to open up. You should try it sometime."

"You wouldn't want to hug a lot of the people I have to question."

"It's not about what you want. It's about what they need, Detective," she said sincerely.

———————

His mom googled *Rassin* and *tattoo* and *Duluth* and came up with an address for Harbor Town Tattoos way back on the other end of town from where they were now.

"We don't have time to get down there, talk to him, and get back this way again to get to the airport. It's been nice working with you, partner," Packard said.

His mom made him promise to call her that night with what he found out. She told him what time her plane was landing and how long it would take to get home from the airport. She reminded him she was an hour earlier than he was, in case he'd forgotten how time zones worked.

At the airport, he stopped beside two idling cars in the drop-off section and went around the front of the truck to pull her bags from the extended cab. They hugged goodbye with salt crunching under their feet and clouds of car exhaust billowing around them.

"When you get home, you need to call Wally the Beer Man," she said.

He didn't know who she was talking about at first. "Do you mean Kyle? From the brewery?"

"Yes, whatever his name is," his mom said. "Tall, dark, and handsome. He likes you. I can tell. And by likes you, I mean...."

She made an open fist with her hand and moved it back and forth toward her mouth while sticking her tongue into her cheek, a crude and easily recognizable gesture that no one ever wanted to see their mother make.

Packard closed his eyes at the horror. "For god's sake, Mom. Get on the plane."

From the airport, he took Grand Avenue and Highway 23 out to the edge of Duluth. A decade ago, a summer storm had dropped ten inches of rain on the city. All the rivers and creeks overflowed their banks and the steep terrain funneled all the water this way, washing out roads and flooding homes. At the zoo, some of the animals drowned in their habitats. Others floated out and were caught later roaming the streets, including two seals and a polar bear.

Harbor Town Tattoo was in an oddly shaped blue building built to fill an oddly shaped corner lot where two streets came together at a thirty-degree angle. The building was two stories, in need of paint, and looked about a hundred years old. Across the four-lane road was an auto body shop and an ugly fence surrounding a lot of shitty cars.

Packard parked by the curb and spent some time looking at the shop's website. There were links to the artists' portfolios and only two names: Alex and Hamid. Hamid did a lot of detailed black and gray work—snakes and insects and a Darth Vader head and fine-line graphics. There were no photos of Hamid himself.

The entrance to the shop was on the corner of the building. Inside was nicer than the outside. Vinyl plank floors, a pair of leather couches, and a bookshelf filled with binders and art books. There was a workstation on either side of the room, one closer to the door than the other. A light table and a giant mirror and a bathroom were on the far wall. It smelled clean, like rubbing alcohol and soap.

In the closest station a shirtless, beefy guy with a long ZZ Top beard was lying on his side on a padded table, getting a tattoo on his ribs. Two bright lights on arms lit him up. The tattoo artist was standing over him with a buzzing needle that sounded like an angry wasp.

"I'm looking for Hamid," Packard said.

"He's not working today," the tattooer said.

"Are you Alex?"

"I am."

The big guy on the table struggled to sit up. "I need a break," he said. Packard could see the stencil on his skin for a Don't Tread on Me snake tattoo.

Alex turned off his machine and took off his black gloves while the guy got up, put on his coat over his bare chest, and went outside to smoke.

"Did you want to make an appointment with Hamid?" Alex asked. He looked to be in his midforties with salt-and-pepper hair and a three-day beard. "I can look up his schedule and tell you when he's available."

Packard introduced himself and showed his badge. "I'm not here for a tattoo. I wanted to talk to him about his dad."

Alex made a face. "His dad died recently."

"He did," Packard confirmed. "How long have you guys had this shop?"

"It's my shop," Alex said. "I own the building. Hamid started working here about three years ago. He rents the apartment upstairs."

"Is he around?"

"His car is here so I'm pretty sure he's up there. Go outside to the left and ring the bell if the bottom door is locked. If it's open, go up the stairs and bang on the door. He was at Bent Paddle with some friends last night. He might be in rough shape this morning."

Packard thanked Alex for the info, went outside, and held the door for the
DON'T TREAD ON ME guy, who had finished his cigarette.

The sidewalk followed the triangle shape of the building. Packard looked
up and saw a satellite TV dish and a window air conditioner poking out from
a second-story window. The side entrance had a storm door and a steel door
behind that, both unlocked. Packard pressed the doorbell a couple of times and
started up the stairs. There was a single bare bulb at the top landing outside the
apartment door.

Packard got to the top of the stairs and knocked. Waited. Knocked again
louder. He heard movement inside and saw a shadow pass in front of the peephole. The door opened.

"Who are you?" the sleepy-looking man asked. He was wearing flannel
pajama bottoms and a zippered navy hoodie. He was dark-complected with
a patchy beard and curly hair that corkscrewed straight up from the top of his
head. A mandala tattoo covered his entire throat.

"You're Hamid Rassin?"

"Yeah. Who are you?"

"Abbas Rassin is your father?"

"Yeah. Was. He died. What do you want?"

Hamid was twenty-five years old, maybe thirty. The boy from the photo
with Nick would have been almost fifty by now.

"Damn," Packard said.

CHAPTER TEN

PACKARD ASKED IF HE could come in and talk to Hamid about his father. Hamid asked him to wait on the landing. Packard heard cans being gathered and Hamid moving from one side of the apartment to the other. A few minutes later he opened the door dressed in jeans and with a waffle-knit thermal under his hoodie. He was wearing round, black-rimmed glasses and had put on a stocking cap. His socks were wool with a spot for each toe.

The apartment smelled like weed and takeout and stale beer. Sheets of plastic were taped to the wall around each window to keep the cold air out. They didn't help much. It was freezing. Packard kept his coat on and turned down the offer of something to drink. Hamid plugged in an electric kettle and made himself a cup of tea in the apartment's tiny corner kitchen.

"Alex said you've been tattooing here for a few years now. What were you doing before that?"

"Freelance graphic design while I apprenticed at another shop. Alex was working there and decided to leave and open his own place. I followed him."

Packard sat on the edge of a craigslist couch. Hamid sat across from him in a metal outdoor chair that had a blanket thrown over it. Packard explained to

Hamid that he was from Sandy Lake and then showed Hamid the photo of Nick in the water with the girl and the boy watching from the dock.

"This photo was taken in 1990. The guy in the water is my older brother, Nick. Do you know the other two people in the photo?"

Hamid held up the photo and studied it while he sipped his tea. "I don't know them at all."

"I was told they were Abbas Rassin's son and daughter. Your dad owned a lake home for a while near Sandy Lake. My brother was friends with these two."

Hamid kept looking at the photo. "My dad had two children from his first marriage. This guy looks like my dad, for sure. I've never met them."

"How is that possible?" Packard asked.

"My father would not talk about the past at all," Hamid said. "He was an impossible man in many ways."

Abbas Rassin was a Sunni Muslim from Iraq who immigrated first to Europe where he met his wife, then to the United States. They had two children. "My mom said all she knew about my dad's first wife was that she was French and decided she wanted to go back to France. She knew my dad would never let her move away with their children so she left them behind. I think they were pretty young when that happened."

Hamid's mom was an American. She worked in the dental office and married Abbas in 1995. Hamid was born a year later. Hamid's mom didn't know what happened to the other two children because Abbas wouldn't talk to her about them. "She got the impression they were sent to live with family in Iraq. When and why I don't know. I don't think she ever did either."

"Do you know their names?"

Hamid had to think for a minute. "I don't remember."

Packard felt the bottom drop out from under his hopes for this case. Abbas Rassin—the only one who knew for sure what happened the night Nick was killed—was dead. His kids might have been involved or known something, but how was Packard supposed to find two people who may have immigrated to Iraq thirty years ago? He didn't even know their names.

Hamid said his mom died of breast cancer when he was fifteen. "My father and I on our own was a terrible combination. Part of the problem was he was old enough to be my grandfather. He was fifty-nine years old when I was born. He had old-man tendencies, an old man's energy, and an old man's view on life. He wanted me to embrace his culture and language and religion. I wanted nothing to do with any of it. I was an American kid. He wanted me to be a doctor. I wanted to be an artist. When I was in college, he threatened to not pay the tuition every time it was due."

Hamid mocked his dad's accent. "*You are a bad son. You don't deserve this money. You are very disrespectful.* When I was out from under the tyranny of his checkbook, our relationship really fell apart. He was retired. His health was poor. He was angry about everything. I didn't want to be around it. When I got into tattooing, he pretty much disowned me."

Hamid went back to the kitchen and made another cup of tea. "Why am I telling you all this? You told me where you're from. You told me you're a cop. Why so interested in my dad?"

Packard told him everything. About Nick's disappearance and the fact that his body was never found. About moving back to Sandy Lake to be a deputy and deciding to look into the old case file. About the empty binder and Stan's letter and the deal he made in return for the map to Nick's remains. He told Hamid all the details he'd gathered that made him sure it was Abbas Rassin who had given Stan the information.

Hamid was stunned. "Fuck, dude. That's fucking intense. Sorry that happened to your brother. I'm trying to imagine my dad killing somebody. Could he have done it? I don't know. I only knew my dad as an obstacle, not as a man."

They talked more about Abbas's final days. He died of congestive heart failure in his apartment at the Harbor. "We made minor amends toward the end. Now that you tell me he was talking to the sheriff about what happened all those years ago, I'm wondering if that had something to do with him calling me. I went to see him and he apologized for being a bad father. *I failed all my kids. I should have let you live your lives and been proud. You think there is nothing worse than your children disappointing you but there are much worse things in life. You don't know how bad things can get."*

The hair on Packard's neck stood up. Hamid imitating his father echoed something Stan had written in his letter.

There were times when we vastly overestimated our ability to imagine a worst-case scenario. There were times when we had no idea how much worse things could get.

"I don't know what else to tell you, man. I wish I could be—Oh, here's something. You could talk to my aunt Eleanor. She's my mom's sister. My mom was a nurse in my dad's practice and her sister Eleanor was the office manager for like a hundred years. She ran that office and probably the personal lives of a lot of the doctors who worked there. She might remember those kids. She was there even before my mom and dad got married."

Hamid called her and confirmed she was home and would meet with Packard. He got her number and address and thanked Hamid for his help. At the door, a last question came to him.

"Your dad sold his house a few years ago. Is there a storage locker or anything with all his personal possessions?"

"No. He sold the house furnished. Anything they didn't want was sold or donated or thrown away. When he died, I got a box of his clothes from the Harbor and two smaller boxes of personal items. That's all that's left."

"Could I see what's in the boxes?"

Hamid walked him around to the back of the couch where three U-Haul boxes were stacked. "It's been sitting there for months. I don't know what to do with it."

The biggest box was full of clothes. Another box had some framed photos of Abbas and his second wife and Hamid. There were DVDs and CDs and a jar of change. The last box had books and a pile of file folders and old mail. Under some catalogs and magazines, Packard spotted a large manila envelope with a

Sandy Lake return address. He opened it and took out a stack of paper that was hole-punched and two inches thick.

Nick's original case file. The whole thing.

Packard couldn't remember the last time he was this close to tears. He let out a sharp, barking laugh to mask the tremor in his throat. Moments ago he thought he was at a dead end. Now he had the file. Now he knew what the original investigators knew.

Packard told Hamid what it was. "I'm going to need to take this with me," he said.

Hamid's mouth was an O. He told Packard he could have it, no problem. "Do me a favor. If you find my brother and sister, tell them about me and where they can find me. I'd like to know them."

"I'll do that."

———————

It was dark by the time Packard left Duluth for the long drive home. It had warmed ten degrees over the day to just above freezing. He was still an hour away when it started to snow and he had to slow down. The new National album streamed from his phone through the truck's stereo.

His meeting with Hamid's aunt had been productive. She lived in a small house on a steep street with a view of the river. He burned out his calves walking up the hill to her house. Her Christmas tree was still up and filled the front window with lights.

Eleanor told him she was the office manager at Abbas's dental practice for twenty-five years, until she had a minor stroke that made it hard for her to keep up with the fast pace and all the moving parts. She'd been retired for fifteen years. She walked with a cane but seemed to be fine otherwise.

She told Packard the first wife was already gone by the time she went to work for Abbas but she remembered the kids well. They went to a private school in Duluth. She remembered the girl as a source of a lot of trouble and the boy as quiet and studious. "The girl got detention all the time. She'd miss the bus so I was constantly calling for a cab or a neighbor to pick her up at the school and drive her home. I remember she was boy crazy. Her father wanted her to be quiet and demure and she was neither."

She told him the kids' names: Faizah and Faisal.

"Faisal was the well-behaved one. He was very into religion. He wasn't orthodox. I know that's not the right word." She put her head down and rubbed her fingers together in her lap. "It's hard to think of words sometimes. I'm trying to say he wasn't a strict Muslim. He was curious. He wanted to attend a mosque but there wasn't one here back then. They had to go to the Cities. All this made his father nervous. It wasn't a good time to bring attention to yourself for being an Iraqi or a Muslim back then. And this was a decade before 9/11."

"What happened to the kids? Where did they go?"

"That's a story that I don't know all the parts of," Eleanor said. "I remember there was a scramble to get them passports, fill out the paperwork, get the photos taken, mail it all in. I'm sure you remember how everything was a lot more work back then. Before the internet."

"Where were they going that they needed passports?" Packard asked.

"I had a travel agent book them on a flight to Istanbul. Dr. Rassin said they were going to stay with his brother who lived there. I remember there was a long layover in Amsterdam and Dr. Rassin was not happy about it but there wasn't anything to be done. Remember when only travel agents knew when flights took off and landed? Seems like forever ago, doesn't it?"

Eleanor said the tickets were one-way and she never saw the kids again. "Sometime after that, I made the mistake of asking him in passing how the kids were doing. He got so mad. I can still see the look on his face. 'My children are not your concern. You do the office work. Do not ask after them again.' I can tell you I went to the ladies' room and cried my eyes out."

Packard rubbed his face and lowered his truck window to let some cold air in to help wake him up. His phone rang and a photo of his mom filled the screen.

"I've been home for an hour and you haven't called," she said.

"That's because I'm not home. I'm still driving," he said.

"You were there all day? Wait, let me pour myself a glass of wine. What did you find out?"

"Plenty," he said.

CHAPTER ELEVEN

THE DAYS PASSED FURTHER into March. A month after shooting Robert Clark, Packard knew he wasn't doing well. He didn't know how to describe how he was feeling. It was more than a mood or a funk, more adjacent to the darkness that had swarmed him after Marcus's death. He was spending too much time alone. He worked out twice a day to the point of exhaustion. Behind his house, he chopped a hole in the ice and submerged himself in the freezing water for minutes at a time. It helped produce a deep sleep, which was the only time he didn't feel something gnawing his insides.

He hadn't spoken to Thielen since their argument at lunch, both of them too stubborn to make the first move. He stayed away from the office, not that there was anything for him to do there. The sixty-day clock for the BCA to finish its report still had plenty of time on it. Their need to conduct an impartial investigation meant he had no inside access to their progress or findings. An email to Shepard asking if there was any news got a one-word response. *No.*

Packard tried to keep busy by poring over every detail of his brother's case from the file he'd recovered from Abbas Rassin's possessions. It read like an impersonal diary of the worst time in his family's collective life.

This officer responded to the Franklin Harris residence at 688 Redwing Drive on a report of a missing child. Upon arriving at the residence at approximately 1145 I spoke to Terrance Packard, son-in-law of Franklin Harris, and his wife, Pamela Packard. Terrance and Pamela reported not being able to locate their son, Nicholas Packard, age 17 (DOB 2/21/1974). The Packards' second youngest child, Benjamin Packard, age 12, reported seeing his brother leave home on a snowmobile just before midnight. (See supplement for snowmobile description and licensing information.) Terrance Packard reported both of the family's snowmobiles were missing. Nick told Benjamin he was meeting a friend.

#

A call to the Sandy Lake Sheriff's Department reported an overturned snowmobile abandoned on the Redwing Trail. This officer visited the scene and verified it matches the description of the Packard family's second sled. Additional questioning of Benjamin Packard by this officer revealed the boy tried to follow his brother Nick on the second sled. Benjamin lost control of the sled and walked home.

Here was the proof of his mom's story about him taking the other snowmobile. It felt more real to him now. Not that he didn't believe her. This printed relic from the nineties helped make it a fact and not just another story taking the place of memory.

He found the first interview with Dr. Rassin and his children, which didn't stand out from any of the other personal interviews that were conducted in the early days of the investigation. Anyone Nick considered a friend and their parents were interviewed. Nearly everyone around the lake was interviewed.

Investigators followed up on calls from the public about late-night gunshots and strange cars and lone men walking on the side of the road in the freezing cold.

Someone uncovered the report from Nick's traffic stop with two underaged drinkers in the car, and it was added to the file. The Rassins were interviewed again. Nothing about their story changed. Faizah and Faisal had last seen Nick at the Spot Café several nights before he went missing. When an investigator asked Faizah if Nick was her boyfriend or a romantic interest, Faizah said she wasn't allowed to have boyfriends.

Another discrepancy between the record and his memory was the time it took to find Nick's glove. Packard always said three days. According to the notes in the file, a storm wrapped the area in blizzard conditions and hampered the search for several days, and it was exactly a week later when a guy walking his dog on the ice found the glove. Once the sled was pulled out of the lake, the investigation switched from a missing person's case to an accident. Any and all leads originally being pursued were dropped. There were reports dated over the spring and summer from the rec deputy who organized groups of volunteers to walk the entire perimeter of both the upper and lower lakes to look for a body in the weeds. The dive team used everything they knew about the lake's depth, inflows and outflows, and wind direction to plan their dives. They logged maps and weather reports and water temperatures.

Hundreds of typed pages. All of it added up to nothing.

Even in the absence of a body, it was obvious what had happened. Kid went joyriding on a sled after dark. Ran into open water or thin ice. Struggled to get out but couldn't. The motivation and the resources to treat Nick's case as anything but an accident didn't exist.

It reminded him of a case involving an old lady who fell down the stairs with a whiskey bottle in her hand.

The last page in the file held a final surprise. It was the typed notes from the last follow-up done in 1999. At the bottom of the page, in handwriting Packard recognized were two words: *Hello, Ben.*

It was a message from Stan Shaw. He'd held up his end of the deal with Abbas Rassin, got critical information in exchange for the case file, but left enough clues for Packard to find his way here. Packard remembered how angry he felt when he first opened the box and found the file replaced by stacks of blank paper. Knowing Stan's intentions helped diminish those feelings. It was a risky move. Maybe even a careless one. But it had succeeded. One last lesson from his old friend.

What frustrated Packard the most was that even with Nick's file back in his possession, he didn't know any more than what he'd been able to figure out on his own. Abbas Rassin and possibly his children were involved in the death of Nicholas Packard. At the very least, they had conspired to cover it up. Unless he could locate Faizah and Faisal, he was at a dead end.

A Google search of their names produced a long list of hits, most of which he was able to dismiss because of the age or background of the person. A search of both of their names together got him a message that there didn't appear to be many great matches. Entering their names and dates of birth into the databases he had access to through work turned up nothing. No driver's license info, no criminal history. Nothing in the federal databases either.

It was like they had both vanished.

Another frightening possibility: they were both dead.

———————

A repeating weather pattern brought snow squalls that dropped an inch of snow every day like clockwork. The calendar said they were closer to going into the woods to look for Nick's remains. The deepening snow said otherwise.

Packard was glassy-eyed on the couch in front of the television with Frank under his wrist when he got a call from Lisa Washington.

"My dad hired an estate sale company to clean out Louise Larsen's house. If you want to see it once more for old time's sake, this might be your last chance."

"I do want to see it again," Packard said, sitting up. He'd hadn't forgotten about his interest in Louise's death. He just didn't know what to do about it. With him on leave, and without Thielen's support, there was no one to take up the cause.

He met Lisa the next day at the house after she got off work. It was dark and snowing lightly. Changing the clocks a couple of weeks earlier had pushed sunset later, but the long days of summer still felt far in the future.

Lisa drove a blue Subaru Outback with a cargo box on the roof. She pulled up next to his truck and put down her window. "I was about to call you. I got all the way out here and realized I forgot the keys," she said.

"I have a key," Packard said.

He explained to her about the spare key in the dryer vent as they tramped through the snow up the back steps.

"I'm gonna need that from you when we're done," she said.

Packard unlocked the door and handed her the key over his shoulder. "Take it."

They stepped out of their boots. The floor was cold through Packard's socks. It still smelled like a closed-up house that had had a dead body in it for a week.

"This is my first time inside," Lisa said, taking it all in. "I like the purple countertops."

"Don't be ridiculous," Packard said.

The lights were working now. Lisa said they had the electricity turned on again in advance of the work to be done. He gave her a quick tour through the lower-level rooms and described the way he remembered things. Something about the light fixtures and the shadows they cast—the same ones from when he was a kid—made him feel like he was walking on a stage decorated to resemble his childhood.

On the second floor, he showed her a room with a sloped ceiling where there used to be two sets of bunk beds when he was a kid. He showed her the upstairs bathroom with the penny-tile floor and the claw-foot tub and the large heat register that let him and his siblings listen in on conversations the grown-ups were having with the police in other parts of the house after Nick went missing.

They went downstairs again. Packard noticed the book Louise had been reading on the couch and picked it up. "I'm guessing the library would like this back. I can drop it off next time I'm in town."

Back in the kitchen, he asked Lisa about the timetable for the house.

"I think it'll take a few weeks to get it cleared out."

"Is there an agent involved on your side?"

"Dad's put Jim Wolf in charge of things."

Packard groaned. He hadn't heard a word from Wolf since saving his life by shooting Robert Clark.

"I know," Lisa said. "He wouldn't have been my first choice either. But he knows how to move properties like this."

Looking around the kitchen, Packard had the same feeling as last time when he was here with his mom. Something about Louise's accident didn't make sense. It nagged him like a chirping smoke detector. He stared at the open basement door. To the left was a tall cupboard that Packard remembered being full of baking supplies when he was a kid. He used to raid it for marshmallows or chocolate chips when he couldn't find any other sweets in the house.

"There's something I'd forgotten about," he said, pointing to the inside of the basement door. "Our growth marks from when we were kids."

The door was pushed against the wall behind it. On the middle panel were pen and pencil marks noting the height of the four Packard kids and their cousin, Susan, over the years.

Lisa bent over for a closer look. Packard stood behind her. "Can you believe you were ever this short?" She pointed to a mark a little more than four feet off the ground that said *Ben 8 1987*. "I could talk to my dad and make arrangements to take this door out if it's something you think you want. Be a shame to lose this record of your family history."

Packard wasn't listening. He was looking at the last mark for *Nick 16 1990* almost six feet up. It read like the inscription on a tombstone.

He grabbed the door by the edge to pull it shut. A two-piece eye and hook screwed into the frame and the door helped keep it closed. When Packard tried to fit the hook in the eye, he noticed it was crooked. No, not crooked. Deformed and discolored.

"This is weird," Packard said. He took out his phone and turned on the flash.

"What are you looking at?"

"It's been bothering me since my last visit just how Louise fell down the stairs," he said as he examined the eyelet more closely. "First of all, it was the middle of summer. No ice or heavy, wet boots. There's nothing she needs downstairs—the laundry is up here; the pantry is up here. See how the door is shrunk to the point that the latch no longer keeps it shut? That's what the hook is for. Also note how the door opens out instead of pushes in. Grandpa hung it that way on purpose. He didn't like the idea of his wife or kids pushing that door open and potentially falling down those steep stairs. They weren't to code back then and definitely aren't now."

"Okay, I'm following you," Lisa said.

Packard shined the light all around the eyelet. "I need the kit from my car, but I'm almost certain this is blood. I also see hair." He looked at the hook that was screwed into the door. "There's blood here, too. Blood on both means this door was closed and latched when something hit it hard enough to bend the eyelet and leave blood and hair behind."

"Could Louise have stumbled or tripped, then been disoriented or confused? There was evidence of alcohol consumption."

"There was a broken bottle of alcohol," he corrected her. "She lay at the bottom of those stairs for too long to get a reliable blood alcohol. The blood in a body starts to ferment hours after death, throwing off the reading. She was down there for almost a week."

Packard shined the flash from the phone on the doorframe. "There's a tiny drop of blood here," he said, pointing at a spot halfway to the floor. "It's hard to see because of the color of the wood. It would have dried and blended in by the time she was found."

Lisa came close to see what he was pointing at. The snow on the shoulders of her coat had melted into drops of water. "Could the blood be unrelated to the accident?"

"It could be. I need to see the medical examiner's report again. I think I remember something about a spiderweb fracture to the parietal bone. It might have been assumed she suffered the damage by hitting her head on the stairs or the concrete below. I need to know if hitting her head here could cause similar damage before she went down the stairs."

Packard stood again and pocketed his phone. "Let's say her blood pressure dropped suddenly and she blacked out and hit her head. Did she then undo the hook, step back and pull the door open, and then fall down the stairs? All while holding a bottle of whiskey?"

Lisa took a deep breath and ran a hand through her long hair. "How was all this missed?"

"There was a dead body in this house for a week in the summertime. Imagine trying to haul a leaky, hundred-pound bag of rotten pudding up these stairs. Imagine the smell. Shepard was the first on scene. I'm guessing he got a big whiff, then waited outside for the ME to come. We expect deputies to do their jobs, make informed conclusions, and write detailed reports. Shepard made assumptions that nicely aligned with the effort he was willing to expend."

"If you're suggesting what I think you are, this is not good," Lisa said.

"It's not good at all," Packard agreed.

"So what happens now?"

Packard held out his hand. "I'm going to need that key back. This is a crime scene until I decide otherwise."

CHAPTER TWELVE

PACKARD CALLED DISPATCH AND requested a patrol deputy to the scene. He called Thielen while he waited.

"Are you still pissed at me?" he asked.

"No," she said, sighing. "Are you pissed at me?"

"Of course not. But you might not be happy with why I'm calling." He told her he was at Louise's house with Lisa Washington. He told her about the blood and the hairs and the bent eyelet and why he couldn't accept the theory that Louise accidentally fell down the stairs.

"Shit," Thielen said. "I can't come out tonight. I called in sick today. I still don't feel great."

"What's wrong with you?"

"Nothing. Stomach bug. I'll be fine by tomorrow."

He told her he'd document everything at the scene and have his notes in her email by morning. "This is a case now. It needs a detective assigned to it."

"I hear you," Thielen said. "No argument from me."

The deputy arrived and Lisa got ready to leave. "You'll have to cancel the estate planner and probably push back the sale," Packard said as she stepped into her boots. "I'm not releasing this place until I'm satisfied that there's been a thorough investigation."

"My dad will be furious," Lisa warned him.

Packard shrugged. "He can add it to the list of reasons he hates me."

The deputy was there to take photos and notes. He photographed the kitchen and the doorway to the basement in detail. Packard tested the spot on the doorframe and confirmed it was blood. Using a pair of tweezers, he removed the hairs on the eyelet and put them in an envelope. He used a pair of needle-nosed pliers to remove both the hook and the eyelet and put them into an evidence bag. He had to keep from whistling while he worked. It felt good to be doing his old job again.

A tall kitchen window beside where they were working looked straight into the house next door. A man stood in his own window, watching them with a glass of wine in one hand and his phone in the other. He looked to be about Packard's age with a dark mustache. Andrea, the woman with the curly hair he'd met last time he was here, lived in that house. This was likely her husband. Packard gave the man a nod, then went back to work.

The basement stairs were uncomfortably shallow and steep. Each step had a black rubber friction mat stuck to it that was worn in the center from decades of foot traffic. Packard found another drop of blood on the top step—more evidence that Louise was bleeding before she fell down the stairs.

The last thing he and the deputy did was to remove the door handle from both sides of the basement door and put them in brown paper bags to take back to the station for fingerprinting.

Packard thanked the deputy and sent him back out. He gave the kitchen one last look before turning off the lights. It no longer felt familiar. He saw it with the cold, impartial eye of an investigator. There was a story here that had nothing to do with his family or Nick's disappearance. An old woman had been assaulted in this room and pushed down the basement stairs. He was going to find out who did it.

———

He drove to the station and logged the items collected at Louise's house and locked them in the evidence room. Back at home, he worked on his laptop with Frank by his side as he documented his last two visits to Louise's house for Thielen. Cutting through the door seal and letting his mom; the neighbor, Andrea; then later, Lisa Washington traipse through the site was not how he'd typically treat a crime scene. But had he not, he wouldn't be doing the work or asking the questions he was now.

Who would want to kill Louise Larsen? It didn't appear that the home had been burgled. She wasn't sexually assaulted. She had a sizable estate but no one to inherit it. He thought of all the people who would be interested in that house on that lot on that lake, including Jim Wolf, and imagined them like buzzards perched in the large oak with their sharp beaks and hunched wings. Killing an old woman was a great way to tie up her assets for years in probate court while an investigation ground on. But if it convincingly appeared like an accident and no one bothered to take a closer look…

Packard read through Shepard's original report again.

On Wednesday June 5 at approximately 1900 hours I responded to a call for a welfare check at 688 Redwing Drive. Upon my arrival, no one responded to knocking at either the front or back door.

Packard noticed right away a missing detail. He knew from talking to Ray Wiley that he had personally called Shepard to check on Louise. Shepard's report made no indication that the call had come from his father-in-law and hadn't gone through dispatch. It was a meaningful detail that should have been in the report.

Packard had to think back to what was going on last June. The Emmett Burr case was a month old. The news cycle had nearly moved on, but behind the scenes the investigative work into the identities of the other bodies and the mountain of paperwork consumed a lot of the department's resources. Packard was involved as a family member, as an investigator, and as acting sheriff responsible for keeping the community updated. It didn't surprise him in retrospect that Louise's incident fell through the cracks. Didn't make it right either.

```
The back door was unlocked. There was a strong odor of
decay and alcohol upon entering the kitchen. There was no
response to any of my calls. I found the home's resident,
Louise Larsen, on her back at the bottom of the basement
stairs. She had blood beneath her head. Nearby her body was
a broken bottle of Evan Williams whiskey. I radioed dispatch
for assistance. Deputy Baker and medics arrived on scene
at approximately 1930. Medics pronounced Ms. Larsen dead
at the scene. After an examination by the ME, the body was
transported to Methodist for examination.
```

If you wanted to make sure an incident only received cursory attention, you couldn't have done better than getting Shepard assigned to the case. Before winning the election in November, Shepard was doing a half-assed job as a patrol deputy. Shepard's MO was to accept things at face value and not ask a lot of questions. More questions meant more work and less time to sit around and smoke cigarettes.

The follow-up reports were written by Deputy Baker, who was an order of magnitude higher up the competency scale. Still, he seemed to have started with the assumption that Shepard had documented everything there was to know. Baker talked to the neighbors on either side of Louise to determine the last time anyone had seen her. Max and Linda Scarpetta said they had had a large family gathering on the Sunday of Memorial Day weekend and invited Louise for dinner. They ate grilled burgers and baked beans and watermelon. The neighbor on the other side—the one who had watched them process the scene from his window next door—was Brian Hopkins. He claimed not to have known Louise at all and suggested Baker talk to his wife. Baker talked on the phone with Andrea who said she couldn't remember for sure but thought she saw Louise in passing either on Saturday or Sunday of Memorial Day weekend.

Baker had talked to Ray Wiley and noted his relationship to Louise as being "friend and bridge partner and lawyer." Ray told Baker that Louise had no next of kin to contact. Baker noted in his report that Ray was handling funeral arrangements and had asked that any questions about the case or Louise's estate come to him.

Ray Wiley had raised the alarm about Louise, called his son-in-law to investigate, then directed all inquiries to be routed to himself. Something about it smelled fishy to Packard. Continuing to work with Lisa Washington—Ray's daughter—was going to be difficult if he couldn't articulate his unease without her shutting him down.

Packard switched to the autopsy details. Diagram outlines of a human from the front and the back showed Louise's injuries. She'd broken her shoulder, four ribs on her back, and her pinkie finger. She had extensive bruising on both hips. Causes of death were skull fracture and intercranial injuries.

The signature on the report was from Dr. Simon Hersh. Packard had Hersh's cell number in his phone so he called despite it being after 10:00 p.m.

"Hello, Detective Packard."

"You still up, Doc?"

"I am. The wife and I are in California this week with our kids and grand-kids. It's two hours earlier here. I'll warn you, I had enough wine this afternoon to make it illegal for me to perform medical procedures or operate a motor vehicle."

"No worries. I just have a few questions. Do you remember examining the body of Louise Larsen?"

"More details, please."

"Elderly woman. Fell down the stairs and wasn't found for several days."

"Oh god. Yes. Terrible."

"I'm looking at your diagram of her injuries. It looks like you drew two shapes to indicate blows to her head."

"Are you looking at the file? Can you email it to me so I can see it on my phone?"

Packard sent him the file and waited for Hersh to pull it up and read it. "It appeared that she hit her head two times on the way down the stairs," he said. "The stairs were steep, open on both sides with no handrail. I determined she likely hit her head on the corner of a step and then slammed the back of her skull on the concrete floor. There was a depression at the back of her head and the bone was loose in that spot."

Packard told him about the bloody eyelet and the hair. "While the door was latched with the hook, I think someone smashed Louise's head on the frame hard enough to bend the eyelet, then opened the door and pushed her down the stairs. Do you see anything about her injuries that might not align with that scenario?"

Dr. Hersh was quiet as he read through his notes again. "I don't," he said regretfully. "What I thought was the corner stair strike could have been caused by the eyelet. There was a strong smell of alcohol due to the broken whiskey bottle. I saw a cup of tea being prepared, the pantry nearby, and the open basement door. The story, supported by what I saw, was that she lost her balance after getting the bottle from the pantry and tumbled down the stairwell."

"You tested her blood alcohol."

"Yes, it was .10. Some of that could have been due to fermentation of the blood. The results are not always black and white when a body has been sitting that long."

"Your notes say you think she had been dead six days based on the contents of the stomach and condition of the body."

"Right. Her stomach contained the last meal she had. Hamburger, beans. Wine."

"That was Sunday night with the neighbors. So she died within hours of that meal," Packard said.

"Yes. The food was only partially digested, still mostly in her stomach." The doctor sighed. "I'm embarrassed to have gotten this one so wrong. I missed the eyelet when I was on the scene. After I thoroughly examined the body at the hospital, I looked at the photos and read the deputy's report again. It mentioned no signs of a struggle, nothing stolen, nothing about the blood you found on the doorframe and the eyelet. Everything pointed to an accidental fall down the stairs, which is not uncommon or unusual at all. The cause of death was definitely the trauma to the brain."

"Was there any follow-up or questions from anyone in the sheriff's department or close to Louise?"

"Now that you mention it, I got a call from Ray Wiley. He called and wanted to know what I found. I specifically remember him asking if she had suffered. He was pretty upset."

"What did you tell him?"

"I told him the truth."

"Which was?"

"That I didn't know."

CHAPTER THIRTEEN

THE NEXT MORNING, PACKARD'S plan was to get into the office early, talk to Thielen about what he found at Louise's, and get out. Running into Shepard, who was not known to be an early riser, but for some reason was hovering in the doorway to his office like he was waiting for a blind date to pull up, was not part of the plan.

"The fuck are you doing here, Packard?"

"Meeting with Thielen. You're in early."

"Yeah, thanks to you I've got a meeting with Jim Wolf, who wants to discuss the Packard problem. Sit down."

"Jim's coming here? Now?" Packard loved the idea of catching Wolf off guard. He had a lot of questions about the plans for Louise's house.

Packard had a seat while Shepard continued to look at his phone and wait in the doorway. Kelly wasn't in yet, so someone would have to let Wolf through the secure door.

"I'm guessing Wolf isn't happy about what happened at Louise Larsen's house yesterday."

"You don't know the half of it, Packard. I wouldn't be looking so smug if I were you. People are calling for your head or your badge, whichever will come off easier."

"What people? Jim Wolf and your father-in-law?"

Shepard ignored the question. Packard texted Thielen while Shepard walked down the hall. A minute later he was back with Wolf on his heels.

Packard turned in his chair and looked up at Wolf but didn't bother to stand or stick out his hand. He could tell by the expression on Wolf's face that Shepard had failed to mention that the Packard problem was waiting in his office. Wolf looked like he didn't know whether to sit or sprint for the door.

Shepard sat behind his desk, oblivious. Wolf took the seat next to Packard after pulling it away a few inches.

"Let's start with what the hell happened at the Larsen house last night," Shepard said.

Packard recounted how Lisa Washington had invited him to see his family home one last time before it was emptied and readied for sale. He explained his discomfort with the idea that Louise accidentally fell down the stairs, how it seemed unlikely that she would be going up or down the stairs with a bottle of whiskey, and about the blood and hair evidence he spotted while examining the scene.

"In other words, you're saying I did a shitty job," Shepard said.

Packard ignored the statement. "I talked to Dr. Hersh, the ME, last night. He didn't notice the things I noticed either. He did the autopsy. He thought she hit her head twice going down the stairs. He said my theory of events—that someone smashed Louise's head against the doorframe hard enough crack her skull, then shoved her down the stairs—would also fit the findings in his report." He looked at Wolf for no other reason than to make him wonder why he was being looked at.

"So this is my fault," Shepard said.

"I'm not sure you're listening," Packard said. "I'm explaining that I think a woman was murdered in her home. I don't understand how you're hearing an attack on you when I've said no such thing."

"I was the first on the scene. I found her. I wrote the report. It was an open-and-shut case. Elderly woman, accidental fall, likely intoxicated. Very sad. The end. Now you come along and say I got everything wrong."

Packard sighed. "Sheriff, this is not a comment on your work. The blood evidence was not easy to see. The door needing to be constantly latched would not be obvious unless you were familiar with the house. I'm sure when you got on the scene, the state of a week-old body and the strong smell from the broken whiskey bottle lent themselves to obvious conclusions. I didn't go in there with a magnifying glass hoping to find evidence of you not doing a thorough job. This second look wouldn't have even happened if I didn't have a connection to the house. I went there with my mom, I went there with Lisa, and between those two times I found things that led me to a different conclusion."

Wolf spoke up for the first time. "You said you've been through there multiple times with people not connected to the sheriff's department. You could have contaminated the scene or left it vulnerable to contamination."

"To what end?"

"So you can be the hero. Again," Wolf said. His tone made it sound like he was stating the obvious. "First there was Emmett Burr. Then Bill Sandersen. You thought you could ride those two cases to a full-time sheriff's job but it didn't work out for you. Now you need another excuse for all eyes to be on you."

Packard had been called plenty of names in his time. Fascist. Pig. Faggot. A very angry and strung-out prostitute he arrested in Minneapolis had called him a fucking fuckface tittybaby microdick. Names rolled right off him. An asshole like Wolf accusing him of doing this job for the attention put up the hair on his neck. "You don't know the first thing about me, Jim. I didn't join law enforcement to be a hero. This is a job of service. It's dangerous, it's thankless, the pay isn't great, and no heroes I know spend as much time filling out paperwork as I do."

Wolf messed with his tie and tried to sit taller in his chair. "I have contractors and subs and invoices for a warehouse of supplies lined up for that job. You're gonna cost me a fortune."

"I couldn't care less what this is going to cost you," Packard admitted.

"Can he even do this?" Wolf asked Shepard. "He's supposed to be on leave."

Shepard was the last person who would know what the conditions of an officer's leave entailed. Shepard only learned by doing, and no one had trained him to retrieve this particular stick. Packard answered for him. "I'm on leave from my current duties as court security. I'm still a sworn officer of this department and retain all the rights and responsibilities that come with that." It was mostly the truth. "If I say the Larsen house is a crime scene, it's a crime scene."

"And as lead investigator in this office, I'll back him up if necessary." Packard and Wolf turned in their chairs to see Thielen standing in the doorway. She had a shaker bottle of the green smoothie she liked to drink every morning. They turned back to Shepard. He looked exhausted.

Thielen said, "I also wasn't as diligent about this case the first time around. I read the report Packard filed, looked at the photos, and rereviewed the previous reports. I agree that there's enough to warrant an investigation."

Wolf was red-faced. "I have a contract to tear that house down a week from tomorrow. Packard could have planted that evidence for all we know. He shouldn't be able to interfere with my business because he's suddenly come up with some half-baked theory about a woman who's been dead and buried since last summer."

Packard said, "If I wanted to interfere with your business, letting Robert Clark get off another couple of shots outside that courtroom would have been a lot easier than planting evidence."

Wolf looked at Shepard like he couldn't believe he was letting Packard speak to him like that.

"It's a miracle I had time to tear myself away from all the tampons that needed counting to save your life. Your description of my job, if I remember correctly."

"Fuck you, Packard. What do you want? An apology for hurting your feelings?"

"I'm not the one you need to apologize to. You should apologize to Robert Clark for trying to steal his land. You should apologize to Mark Quinto who took a bullet with your name on it. Two men are dead because of you."

Wolf stood up, looking furious. "I'm tearing that house down in a week. You can take me to court if you want to stop me."

"I don't need a court. I can arrest you and anyone else attempting to disturb a crime scene," Packard said as Wolf pushed past Thielen and disappeared down the hall.

"Nice job," Shepard said after he was gone. "Any business the sheriff's department has in front of the county commissioners is going to go over like a fart in church thanks to you two."

"You know we're doing the right thing," Thielen said, sitting in Wolf's chair.

"What the fuck is in that cup, Deputy?"

Thielen swirled the remaining contents in her bottle. "Spinach, pineapple, banana, ginger, Greek yogurt."

"God, I'm getting gas just thinking about it," Shepard said.

Packard's mind was still on something Wolf had said. "What does he mean, he's tearing the house down? I heard from Lisa Washington that he was handling the sale."

Shepard shook his head. "Ray said that Wolf approached him with a business opportunity. Wolf thinks no one will buy a house where a woman lay dead for a week. Wolf wants to redevelop the lot, build a new house. That way everyone makes more money than selling it as is."

Packard was no lawyer, but the idea of Wolf using a woman's tragic death to enrich himself with her attorney's permission didn't seem entirely ethical. He wondered if Lisa knew about the plan and whether she failed to mention it accidentally or on purpose.

"Sheriff, let me take the lead on this case. I'm getting paid to do nothing while I wait for the BCA report. Why don't you pay me to look into this instead? Thielen doesn't need more on her plate right now. I can work on this quietly and it won't have any impact on the BCA's investigation. I'm going crazy sitting at home."

Crazy didn't begin to cover the state of his mental health lately. It was wholly inadequate in describing the dark thoughts he'd been trying to drown out with exhausting workouts and ice baths.

"Why do you care so much about this particular case?" Shepard asked. "Did you know Louise?"

"No."

"Does your family know her?"

"She knew my grandparents. They're both dead."

"Do you have any insight into why she might have been killed? Assuming she was killed."

"I don't."

"So why you?"

Because he needed something to do besides see Robert Clark's face in the dark and worry about what the county attorney was going to decide. Because everything about Louise Larsen felt personal. How he found it. Where it happened. The house connected Louise's case to his brother's. One dead at the bottom of the stairs, the other disappeared out the back door, both being investigated again because of his need for answers.

"Sheriff, you want what's best for your team. Your two main investigators are swamped. I'm available to help. Let me have this one, and when I close it, you get to stand up and take credit as captain of the ship," Packard said.

"I know how this works," Shepard said, sounding resigned and picking up his cell phone. "I'm going to say, 'No, leave it to Thielen.' And Thielen is going to say she doesn't have the bandwidth. And you're going to do what you want anyway because you're on leave."

Packard and Thielen looked at each other, then back at Shepard. They both nodded. Shepard was looking at his phone, already disinterested.

"Speaking of the BCA. Any word?" Packard asked.

"No," Shepard said.

"Has Wolf said anything to you about his interview with the agents?"

"It hasn't come up. I can call him back if you want. I'm sure he'd be happy to put in a good word about you to them."

"I don't need him to put in a good word with the BCA. I need him not to try to influence Phil Ayers." Ayers was the county attorney who'd be deciding whether charges were warranted. He was also the first person to defend Jim Wolf whenever anyone questioned whether Wolf's role as chair of the county commissioners created a conflict of interest with some of his business dealings.

Shepard shrugged like it wasn't his problem. "There's nothing you can do about it until the report is complete. In the meantime, you should be thinking about what you want to do when the investigation is over. Come back and follow my orders or claim PTSD and comp out while you can."

"I already told you I want to come back to work. As a detective. Not court security."

"And I already told you—that's not up to you."

Shepard didn't exactly say yes to Packard's request to investigate Louise's death, but he hadn't said no either. Packard printed all the paperwork they had on Louise and sat in his truck looking for a name. The deputy who had followed up on Shepard's original report had talked to Louise's neighbors on both sides. Packard had already met Andrea and seen her husband, Brian, through the window. The people on the other side were the Scarpettas. Max and Linda.

On the drive out of town, Packard thought about his grandparents' house being torn down. He hadn't so much as driven by the place until his mom came to town. It could have been torn down or burned down years ago and he'd have been none the wiser. Being back inside had made everything feel close again. The house was part time capsule, part portal to an alternate future. It made him feel close to Nick in a way that he hadn't felt or allowed himself to feel in a long time. He knew he had no claim on the house, no right to feel wronged. But why did Jim Wolf have to be the one behind the controls of the bulldozer? That part felt personal.

Next door to Louise's house—which was how he needed to think of it, not as his grandparents' house—was the Scarpetta house. It was all light brick and arched architectural features and irregular rooflines. It looked like a suburban Minneapolis McMansion, not a lake home. The driveway had blue reflectors on either side for the snow removal company. One of the three garage stalls was completely blocked by piled snow.

Max Scarpetta answered the door. He was in his early sixties with thick dark hair parted on one side and dressed in a Ralph Lauren sweater and fuzzy house shoes. He invited Packard in and said his wife, Linda, was at the community center walking laps with her girlfriend.

Packard had a seat at a two-tiered island shaped like a wide C. The kitchen design was faux Tuscan with stone tiles hand-painted with ivy and grapes. It smelled like coffee and soap from the dishwasher humming in the island.

"I've noticed some traffic next door recently," Max said as he poured them each a cup of coffee. "To be honest, I'm the one who called the sheriff's office the first time I saw you there. The place has sat untouched since last summer. I wanted to make sure everything was on the up-and-up."

"I don't blame you one bit," Packard said, taking his mug. "Were you and your wife close to Louise?"

"Pretty close, yeah," Max said. He came back from the fridge with something called Italian sweet cream vanilla coffee creamer. He poured a glug into his mug and offered some to Packard. "Makes it taste like melted ice cream."

Packard held up a hand. "I like it to taste like coffee," he said. "When you say you and your wife were 'pretty close' to Louise, what does that mean?"

"We would have her over for dinner once a week and send her home with leftovers. A woman that old living alone probably isn't doing a lot of cooking for herself. My wife wanted to make sure she was eating and had a home-cooked meal a couple of times a week. The two of them were the closest. They both like to read. They both like Masterpiece Theater on PBS. Sundays were when we would have Louise over. Linda cooked, I opened the wine, the two of them watched whatever was on TV, and I cleaned up. It was a fairly regular thing."

"Tell me about Memorial Day weekend."

Max drank his coffee. "We had nineteen people in our house, almost a dozen cars parked outside, people coming and going all hours, kids screaming like you wouldn't believe. Louise came over for dinner. We grilled hamburgers. There was a ton of food. I didn't spend much time with her because of all the chaos. We ate early. It was probably six thirty when I walked her home."

There was no mention in Shepard or Baker's report that nineteen people had been at the house next door the night Louise had dinner there. Another omission in the details. Packard would have gathered names, addresses, and phone numbers of all nineteen people if it had been his case. Also, the report mentioned Louise left the Scarpetta's house sometime between 6:00 and 7:00 p.m. It did not mention that Max Scarpetta walked her home, making him the last person to see her alive.

Max said he poured Louise a glass of wine when she arrived. He didn't know if she had more. He said she rarely drank more than one glass on their normal Sunday night dinners.

Packard said, "We haven't been able to locate any family for Louise. Not even distant blood relatives. Did she ever mention any family to you?"

"You should ask Linda about that." Max made jabbering puppet hands and held them up on either side of his head. "Those two did way more talking than I did listening."

"Did she have anyone who came around to check on her?"

"She had a gal who helped her manage her properties and did odd jobs." He had to think for a minute. "Tess…something. Other than her, no one else really. That was part of the problem, in my opinion. I kept trying to convince her to sell that house and move into the assisted-living facility in town. I don't know how she afforded the heating bills and taxes on that huge place. To be honest, I kept trying to get her to sell it to me so she could cash out and move someplace where she'd have more amenities."

The more Max said *to be honest* the less Packard believed the words coming out of his mouth. People who said *to be honest* used it like a sweetener to give what they were actually saying a candy coating that you were supposed to swallow without questioning.

"From what I heard, she had plenty of money. The bills weren't a problem," Packard said.

Max raised an eyebrow. "Like how much, if I can ask?"

"The estate is worth several million."

"No wonder she never took me seriously," Max said. He looked disappointed. "I worked with a local real estate agent and offered her a fair price. Even offered to rent it back to her for $1 a year if staying was what she really wanted to do."

"What was your interest in the place? Besides helping Louise, of course."

"To be honest, I'd love to tear down that house and this house, build one new, smaller house for Linda and me, and then build two cabins that we could run as rental properties."

"Sounds expensive."

"We bought this house in 2009 during the housing crisis. It was a foreclosure. Got it for a steal. Great location but I've hated this house since day one. It's too big for the two of us. This kitchen looks like a fucking Olive Garden."

"A kitchen remodel would be cheaper than acquiring another property, tearing down two houses, and building three more."

"The idea is for income from the rental properties to eventually pay for it all. Everyone wants to spend time at the lake, but no one wants the hassle of year-round ownership. You can charge a fortune on a per-night basis. Way more than enough to cover the expenses."

"Who helped you with the offer on the house?"

"Jim Wolf. He said he'd represent both of us and handle all the paperwork for only half his usual fee if Louise agreed."

"Hmmm," Packard said. "What a guy."

"I'm still waiting for news about what the plan is with the property. I know Ray Wiley was her friend and lawyer. I've left a few messages with him asking if I could buy the property before it lists."

"I think you've lost your chance. It's not going to hit the market as is."

"What do you mean?"

"Jim Wolf is working with Ray to redevelop the property and then sell it. They're going to tear down the house and probably build something worth several million dollars."

"That motherfucker," Max said. He slammed his coffee cup down hard enough that the handle snapped off with his fingers still through it. He put the mug and the broken handle in the sink. "Jim knew I wanted that house. He stole it right out from under me."

"Sounds like it," Packard agreed as he finished his coffee. "I gotta run. You should call Jim."

Packard backed out of Max's driveway, turned the wheel to the right, drove a hundred yards, and turned left into Andrea and Brian Hopkins's driveway on the other side of Louise's house.

The man watching from the window the night before came out of the house with two long guns in padded cases under his arms as Packard got out of the truck. Another man came out behind him carrying a long gun of his own. There wasn't much to hunt this late in the winter. They were heading to the gun range or shooting on someone's private land.

"Deputy. What can I do for you?" Brian Hopkins asked. He opened the back door of a black Ford Explorer with tinted windows and put the guns in the back seat. He was wearing mirrored sunglasses. The smile he wore when he turned toward Packard felt insincere.

"I wanted to ask you a few questions about your neighbor," Packard said.

Brian's sunglasses did nothing to hide the impatience that flashed across his face. "Can it wait?"

"It won't take long," Packard said.

The other man had put his gun into a white Hummer. "Go ahead. I'll lock up and meet you there," Brian said.

Water leaked across the driveway and sidewalk where the sun hit. In the blue shade of the house, the deep snow was unyielding. Packard followed Brian through a side door that opened to a long hallway running behind the garage stalls. Packard saw a laundry room and a door to a bathroom. The closest door was made of metal and opened to a gun room that was ten feet by ten feet in size. Long guns were mounted on the wall and slotted into floor racks. There was a workbench with equipment to load shotgun shells and green ammo boxes underneath. A small couch faced a large TV on the far wall.

"Impressive," Packard said.

"I like shooting," Brian said. "I was on the rifle team in college. We won the NCAA championship two years in a row."

"Doubly impressive. I met your wife the other day. Is she home?"

"She's not. She's very busy with the legislature in session."

"What does she do?"

Brian took off his sunglasses and gave Packard an incredulous look. "You don't know who my wife is?"

Packard tried to look apologetic as he shrugged.

"She's Andrea Hopkins. The state representative for this district."

Of course Packard knew who that was. Politically, she appealed to the red-meat voters in the area with her military background and speeches against crime and government overreach. She was also an endorser of Shepard for sheriff.

"She had a big winter coat on and introduced herself as Andrea when I met her," Packard said. "I didn't recognize her. When I saw her name in the report, it still didn't click. I didn't know she was that Andrea Hopkins."

Brian looked unimpressed with Packard's detecting abilities. "So what do you want to know about Louise? I watched you and the other deputy working over there the other night. I've heard you're trying to make a case that she was murdered."

"Who'd you hear that from?"

Brian shook his head like he wasn't stupid enough to answer that question. "A friend."

Since they were both being withholding, Packard said he had no hard evidence, just questions about the series of events that led to Louise being found at the bottom of the basement stairs. "Were you and your wife close to Louise?"

"Close in proximity, yes. Close as friends, no. Wave across the yard, say hi in town."

"It's curious how close your houses are. When I saw you in the window the other night, I felt like I could reach across and shake your hand."

"The original house on this lot was smaller, obviously. The people who built this place had to consider septic placement and soil stability. The new house ended up a lot closer to the property line. If money were no option, I'd buy Louise's place for the lot and knock down the house."

Another man with a plan for what to do with Louise's house. How many people had scanned the obits looking for her name? How many people were ready to snatch that house from under her at a moment's notice?

"You better talk to Jim Wolf. He and Ray already have plans for the lot. I'm not sure improving your view is a priority."

Packard could tell by the expression on his face that this was news to Brian. Wolf was getting his way with the property, but the list of people who wanted his head was getting longer. Maybe that was the secret to getting rich. Not caring who you pissed off along the way. Might not be so bad if you could live with yourself and had someone to step in front of the occasional bullet.

"Is this you and your wife's primary residence?" Packard asked.

Brian looked thrown by the question. "More or less," he said.

"What does that mean?"

"We have this house and a condo in downtown Saint Paul for when Andrea is spending a lot of time at the capitol."

"Were you here Memorial Day weekend?"

Brian looked impatient. He ushered Packard out of his gun room and locked the door. "I don't remember. I travel a lot for work. I might have been out of town."

"Do you remember the next weekend, when they hauled a dead body from the house next door? There were probably a lot of cars, an ambulance…lots of flashing lights?"

"I was here. I do remember that."

"What about Andrea? Where was she for those two weekends?"

"You'll have to ask her. We're not in the same room very often anymore. If we're done, I need to get to the range."

Brian walked down the hall and Packard followed. On the steps outside, Packard asked, "What's a good number if I want to get hold of Andrea?"

"Her office phone. You can find it online but you're wasting your time. She didn't know Louise that well. Louise wasn't even on our radar most of the time."

"Hmmm," Packard said. He took his time looking through his notes. "Do you know the last name of someone named Tess who did odd jobs for Louise?"

"Never heard of her."

"One more question. What do you do for a living?"

"A lot of different things."

"Like…?"

"I work in energy and commodities. I also do investing. Entrepreneurial stuff."

A lot of vague words that meant nothing. Packard thanked Brian for his time and left a card with his number on it.

As he drove away, Packard couldn't help but be curious about the fact that Andrea had come through Louise's back door—possibly carrying a gun—the day he and his mom were in the house, like she was personally responsible for the security of the place. Andrea said she occasionally had dinner with Louise and the neighbors. Yet her husband claimed Louise was practically a stranger. They either had very different perceptions of things or someone was lying.

CHAPTER FOURTEEN

PACKARD WORKED FROM HOME the rest of the day. He wrote up his notes from his conversations with Max Scarpetta and Brian Hopkins. A Google search of Brian Hopkins and Sandy Lake took him to a Facebook page for the Sandy Lake Rifle & Revolver Club. There was a photo of Hopkins wearing shooting glasses and holding a trophy for the range's thousand-yard record. Running Hopkins through the databases turned up a DUI that was eight years old. On the secretary of state website, Packard found three LLCs that listed Brian Hopkins as the sole member. One was called Lake Country Crypto. Another was Hopkins Enterprises. The third was Hopkins Investments. When Packard googled the three businesses, he got no hits. Whatever Brian's work involved, it hadn't left a trace online so far.

He looked up Andrea Hopkins, Brian's wife, who was into her second term as a Minnesota legislator. She was serving on committees related to families and children and veterans' affairs. In Afghanistan, she had served on an all-female civilian engagement team that went into the field alongside special operations teams, trying to counter insurgents by reaching out to Afghan women and children. The CETs allowed women to serve in combat arms positions for the first time, operating side by side with some of the most elite forces in the American military.

In 2012 a member of Hopkins's unit was killed by a roadside IED and Hopkins was wounded. Her tour ended in 2013. In 2015 she married Brian and they bought the home on Lake Redwing. News articles about her first campaign seemed to imply she targeted the district to launch her career in politics because the current representative, who was seventy-six years old, was close to retirement. The representative's son mounted a campaign to take over his father's seat, and even though he held the same values, he had the misfortune of not being blond or pretty or young or a military veteran. Andrea handily overcame his name recognition and took the seat. In those same articles her husband was described as working in finance.

Max Scarpetta also had a finance background. He was a vice president at Wells Fargo who quietly retired from the customer accounts department as news was breaking about fraud and racially biased lending activities carried out by the bank.

The influence of outside money in Sandy Lake was an old story. If you could afford it, a lakefront home was a solid investment at almost every price point. The problem was that sky-high real estate prices did little to stimulate the local economy. The money didn't spread wide or far. A lot of it passed from wealthy buyer to wealthy seller, most of whom didn't live full-time in the area.

But was a hundred-year-old house on prime lakefront property worth killing Louise over? Ray Wiley, Jim Wolf, Max Scarpetta, and Brian Hopkins all had money, and all had a vested interest in not getting charged with murder. Wolf probably only stood to make a few hundred grand on his plan after he paid the estate the fair value of the property. If Ray Wiley's fee was a percentage of Louise's overall estate, this deal wasn't going to move the needle meaningfully for him either. Brian Hopkins and Max Scarpetta would be out of pocket a ton of money to get their houses and property situated to their liking. Any profits for them were far down a long road.

Packard closed his laptop and started questioning his own assumptions. Did a couple of drops of blood mean a murder had taken place? The blood he found and the fall could have been separate incidents, as Lisa suggested. He didn't know anything about Louise's emotional state, sobriety, or mental acuity. A moment's distraction or confusion about where she was or what door she was opening could have easily led to a fall down the stairs.

But the bent eyelet. And the fact that both the hook and the eyelet had blood and hair on them. The door was latched shut when her head struck the simple lock. He couldn't imagine an accident that resulted in her hitting her head there, unlocking the door, opening the door, spinning around, and falling down the basement stairs with a bottle of whiskey in her hand. It was too Rube Goldbergian.

Assuming there was a murder and taking possession of her house wasn't the motive, what else could it be? Did Louise know something? Did she see something? Maybe there was something else of value in the estate. Ray Wiley would have been responsible for doing an accounting of all the estate's assets. The odds of him turning that over willingly when Packard's investigation was jeopardizing his business deal with Jim Wolf were slim to none.

Lisa, on the other hand…

The office of Wiley, Washington & Prentis Attorneys at Law was off Main Street. An electronic bell dinged as Packard stepped inside. There were two desks up front and a bevy of closed doors behind them. A man in dad jeans and a button-down shirt was talking to a woman wearing a headset, sitting at one of the desks. Packard had his badge on his belt and opened his coat to show it as he introduced himself.

"Of course I know who you are," the man said. He was Mark Prentis, one of the firm's partners. "This is Marsha Weber, our senior assistant." Marsha gave him a pinched smile. She was in her sixties with a heavily powdered face and drawn-on eyebrows.

"I'm looking into the death of Louise Larsen," Packard said. "I'm trying to find out more about her, including her estate. I'm wondering if I can get a copy of her probate report."

"That's Ray's client," Mark said. He exhaled with his hands on his hips and pushed his gut out. "Did you ask Ray for it?"

"I haven't," Packard said. "We're not exactly on the best of terms."

"Because of the election," Mark suggested.

"Among other things. I was hoping to run into Lisa and that she might be open to the idea."

"Lisa's in court today. I can't turn it over to you," Mark said. "But I can call Ray. If he says yes, I can have Marsha print it out for you."

"Try him," Packard said. "Maybe he's in a generous mood."

Mark was wearing his cell phone in a clip on his belt. He unholstered it and called Ray. He didn't have to put it on speakerphone for Packard to hear Ray's response.

"NO, THAT SONOFABITCH CAN'T HAVE ONE SHRED OF ANY-THING ABOUT NOTHING. FUCK HIM. TELL HIM TO GET A GODDAMN SEARCH WARRANT. AND TELL HIM NO MORE GOING INTO LOUISE'S HOUSE WITHOUT A WARRANT. FUCK HIM. GODDAMNIT."

Marsha gave Packard a disapproving look. She moved a stack of folders from the top of her desk to a drawer out of sight, as if he might snatch whatever he could get his hands on and run out the door with it.

"Sorry, mate," Mark said, clipping his phone back to his belt. "Get that warrant and we'll have to turn it over."

"Who else can I ask about Louise? I've heard she didn't have any family. I know Ray was her bridge partner. I've talked to her neighbors. Any ideas about who else she might have known?"

"I didn't know her myself," Mark said. "I'm guessing she was like a lot of old ladies—they outlive their husbands, their peers die off, their world gets smaller and smaller. It's sad."

Packard looked at Marsha, who had turned all her attention to her computer. She looked like she couldn't wait for the two idiots crowding her desk to find somewhere else to go.

"All right. I'll keep looking. Don't be surprised if I come back with that warrant."

"I'll let Ray know to expect it," Mark said.

It was after dinner when headlights washed across the front of Packard's house as someone pulled into his driveway. Packard got off the couch and went to the peephole in the garage. On the other side of the wall, the lens was hidden behind a Welcome sign to the right of the front door. It allowed him to see who was on his step without putting himself in front of the door. He wasn't being paranoid. A few months ago, someone had tried to shoot him through the door of the house he was approaching.

He couldn't have been more surprised to see who was standing on his front step.

The doorbell rang. Frank barked but sat when commanded. Packard opened the door. "Marsha," he said. "This is unexpected."

The admin from Ray's law office was wearing a long purple coat to her ankles and a matching set of pink earmuffs, scarf, and gloves. "Can I come in for a minute?" she asked.

"Of course. Let me take your coat. Have a seat."

She held up a hand and stayed where she was. "I'm not staying long. I have something to show you and then I'm leaving." She reached into the pocket of her coat and took out her cell phone. She twiddled the screen, then turned to show it to him.

"This photo and the next are the list of Louise's assets."

Packard looked at the phone, looked at her. "Should you be showing this to me?" It was a dumb question they both knew the answer to.

"Of course not. But I want to help Louise if I can."

"Come in. At least sit down. Don't worry about your boots," Packard said.

They moved inside and Marsha sat at the dining room table. She took off her earmuffs and unbuttoned her coat far enough to unwind her scarf. Frank tried to climb the front of her legs until Packard snapped his fingers and said "Bed," which sent the dog scurrying for his cushion by the woodburning stove.

"You're a friend of Louise's, I take it."

"I don't know if I would call us friends. More than acquaintances. Despite what Mr. Prentis said earlier today, there was nothing sad about Louise or her life." Marsha looked equal parts exhausted and irritated. A condition of employment working for Wiley and company, he guessed.

"How did you know her?"

"Card club. Louise loved playing cards. Not just bridge. She would murder you at hearts, spades, gin rummy, euchre, you name it. There's a group of us that get together twice a month in the meeting room at the VFW. A few of us also play at the senior center now and then. They need folks who can help keep the game moving along, as you can imagine."

Packard smiled and stole another look at the photo on Marsha's phone. "I'm happy to hear she wasn't sitting at home watching the second hand sweep around. I found a library book on her couch. It seems like she had plenty of hobbies."

"Old women are not to be pitied. A widow is not a sad creature. There are too many idiotic men running things around here, some of whom may be well-intentioned, but still say the dumbest things." She closed her eyes and put a hand on her chest. "I voted for you for sheriff for that very reason. Howard Shepard is a disgrace, and Ray should be ashamed for putting his own interests ahead of the public good by championing his son-in-law for a job he knows he's not qualified to do."

"What are Ray's interests?" Packard asked, intrigued.

"I don't know. But I've heard him refer to his son-in-law as...poop-for-brains enough times to know neither one of us thought he would make a good sheriff."

"I guess if it was a choice between a family member and a degenerate, Ray didn't have much of a choice."

Marsha blushed and didn't know where to look. She folded her hands in her lap. "You should have won that election and that's all I have to say about that."

"Thank you," Packard said. He swiped to the other photo. "Can you text these to me?"

"No. I don't want any evidence that you got this from me. I couldn't bring you a copy because every use of the printer or the photocopier gets billed to a client. You can look at them while I'm here. I don't know if this does any good but if something unthinkable happened to Louise, I want to help."

"Was she a drinker?"

"Not that I ever saw. There's a lot of drinking during card club at the VFW. Too much if you ask me. I never saw Louise drink anything besides ice water."

The first photo was a list of banking and investment accounts and their balances. Besides the current year's income and property taxes, the estate was entirely debt free. On the second page was a list of Louise's property, including the house on the lake, her car, a storage unit, and three other addresses in Sandy Lake and nearby towns.

"Do you know anything about these other addresses here? Are they rental properties?"

Marsha leaned forward and Packard handed her back the phone. "This one in Sandy Lake is downtown. It's been a few different restaurants. I remember her saying at card club something about her latest business owners not being able to make a go of it. I don't know anything about the other two."

Packard took the phone back and quickly wrote down the addresses. "No one will know I got this from you," he said. "I could have found this info in the county property records and business licenses. I have to ask—why are you showing this to me?"

"I have worked for Ray for many years. He's not the man he used to be," Marsha said. "He's gotten old and mean. There used to be a kindness to him that no longer exists. I don't know if it's age or early dementia or too much cable news. I see and hear everything that goes on in that office. I know what he and Jim Wolf are planning. I heard Lisa tell him about what you found at Louise's house and that he needed to be patient. He's furious for no reason. He's no longer thinking of Louise and that bothers me. Especially if you have evidence implying foul play."

Packard didn't tell her he'd spent the morning doubting his own conclusions. Things would be so much easier if he was wrong. He didn't think he was.

"I hope the risk I'm taking is worth it," Marsha said. "Promise me you won't let Ray or Howard Shepard or Jim Wolf or anyone else stop you from getting to the truth."

Packard reached across and took one of her hands and gave her his most reassuring look. "I can promise you that will not happen."

Marsha took her phone and he walked her to the door. He put on his coat and boots and got Frank on a leash and walked outside with her. She was driving a gold Buick that looked like it was from the '90s. Not a bit of rust on the body.

Packard opened the driver's door and stood behind it as she got inside. "Did Louise see anyone new or tell you about anything happening to her that was out of the ordinary?"

Marsha looked up at him and shook her head. "As I said, we weren't that close. Occasionally we'd sit at the same card table and exchange small talk. I don't have a recollection of anything like that. Sorry."

Packard thanked her for coming and shut the door. A huge moon made all the snow glow as he and Frank watched Marsha back out of the driveway. Packard let Frank lead them down the road in the opposite direction, and while his three-legged dog scampered, nose to the ground, Packard raised his chin to the winter sky and the frozen starlight that told a story millions of years old.

CHAPTER FIFTEEN

AS MUCH AS PACKARD appreciated the risk Marsha took by giving him a peek at Louise's estate holdings, by the next morning he'd decided he wanted to see everything. After his workout, a cold plunge, and a walk with Frank, he spent the morning filling out the paperwork for a search warrant requiring Ray Wiley to produce all his records pertaining to the estate of Louise Larsen. He explained the evidence found at her house leading him to reexamine her case. In the photos from Marsha, he'd seen Sandy Lake Wells Fargo listed on several of Louise's accounts, so he wrote a separate warrant for the bank, requesting statements as far back as they had them, as well as any information on power of attorney and the names of anyone else with access to the accounts. He sent the paperwork without comment to the judge who was sitting on the *Jim Wolf v. Robert Clark* case the day of the courthouse shooting. He hoped name recognition and his actions that day would get him the favor he was seeking without specifically asking.

By noon he had the signature he needed.

He drove into town, stopped at the court office to pick up his paperwork, then drove it over to Ray Wiley's office. Marsha was at her desk. He heard Ray's voice coming from one of the back offices.

He was careful not to display any familiarity to Marsha since their meeting the night before. "I'm back," he said. "This is a search warrant for all the records pertaining to Louise Larsen's estate. I'd like them before the end of the day."

Marsha took his papers without a word and walked back to Ray's office. A minute later, he heard Ray say, "IS THAT SON OF A BITCH HERE? RIGHT NOW?"

Marsha must have known better than to get in the way of a rolling boulder like Ray Wiley. He came tumbling out of his office wearing a heavy wool sweater and brown pants tucked into a pair of snow boots. His white hair was loose in the dry air. There was enough static in his sweater to jump-start a truck battery.

"What are you trying to do, Packard?"

"You told me to get a warrant. I got a warrant. I thought you'd be happy to see me following your orders."

Lisa Washington and Mark Prentis and Marsha Weber stood in the three doorways behind Ray. They all looked ready to slam doors and dive out of the way if Ray went off like a grenade.

"Fuck you following orders, Packard. I want to know what this is really about."

"You can read it for yourself in the warrant. I think something happened to Louise in that house, and I will get as many warrants and ask as many questions and take as much time as necessary to prove that I'm either right or wrong."

"You don't give a shit about Louise," Ray accused. "You didn't even know her name two weeks ago. This is about losing the election. My son-in-law beat you fair and square. Now you're trying to make him and anyone connected to him look bad."

"You couldn't be more wrong," Packard said. "I'm investigating the death of a woman under suspicious circumstances. That's my job. You're the one making this personal. I'll be back in an hour for those records."

He turned for the door. Behind him, Ray sputtered like a boiling pot with a lid. "YOU SONOFABITCH. YOU'LL BE LUCKY TO HAVE A JOB WHEN THIS IS OVER. FUCK YOU. FUCK YOUR WARRANT. FUCK YOU AGAIN."

———————

Packard's next stop was the bank, where he dropped off the other warrant with the branch manager and got a lot fewer fuck-yous in return.

Back in his truck, he called Thielen. "What are you and the kid doing?"

"What kid? Why are you asking me about a kid?"

"I'm talking about Reynolds. What are you talking about?"

"Nothing. I was confused," she said. "We hardly talk anymore. I'm forgetting what you mean when you say things. What are you doing? Having a spa day?"

He had to admit, taking his time that morning to work out and take care of business from home without the pressure of being on duty felt like a luxury. It felt like being his own boss. "I'll have you know I've already had two warrants signed today. I delivered one of them to Ray Wiley, then had to listen to him tell me to go fuck myself about a hundred times. That took up a good part of the day."

"All this for Larsen?"

"Yep. I was wondering if you wanted me to take Reynolds off your hands this afternoon. I can use and abuse him for a few hours."

"We're in the office now, doing evidence intake and reports. I suppose I can spare him. But don't break him. He's just starting to be slightly better than worthless."

Packard knew Reynolds was standing right there and heard everything. "I'm having lunch at the Spot. Have him meet me there in an hour."

———————

The Spot Café didn't try to be vintage. It was vintage. Trapped in amber. The stools were covered in red vinyl and the water cups were textured green plastic and behind the counter was a tiny pass-through window where tickets hung from a spinning wheel. The electric clock on the wall flipped ads written in neon ink for local businesses every few minutes.

Packard sat at the horseshoe-shaped counter and ordered the open-faced turkey sandwich for lunch. While he waited, he thought about Ray's accusations. It was true; he didn't know Louise's name two weeks ago. Now he felt like he knew plenty about her. She played bridge, she was a reader, she drank tea and liked bourbon and took care of herself and her big house. He could see her move through its rooms—the same ones he knew as a child—like a member of the family. The only photos he'd seen of Louise were the gruesome ones from the crime scene. He preferred to imagine her holding the railing, going down the front steps, and shuffling to the bench near the lakeshore, where she would watch the summer boats and sunsets with a book in her lap.

The house made the case personal on the surface. The case wasn't about the house. Even Jim Wolf's plans to tear it down only interested him in relation to the death of the woman who owned it. And no matter what Ray Wiley thought, taking up the cause to find out what really happened to Louise had nothing to do with shaming Shepard. Packard had been more than willing to help smooth Shepard's transition into his new role as sheriff—had told him so in those exact words—but Shepard didn't want help until things became an emergency.

His food came, a pale plate of sliced turkey on white bread, mashed potatoes and gravy, and enough salt to de-ice a mile of road. He dug in.

What he wanted more than anything was to get back to his old job as an investigator. If he could get back on the detective desk, that would take away the impression that he was looking into Louise Larsen's death for personal reasons. He'd have the authority to decide what needed a closer look and who would look at it. He was digging himself a big hole by investigating Louise's case without the job title or the sheriff's explicit support. If he misread the evidence and had Ray Wiley and Jim Wolf whispering in Shepard's ear, he could be fired.

Or worse—stuck on court security forever.

Reynolds showed up half an hour later and took a seat at the counter beside Packard. He had blond hair swept back from his forehead. His baby-faced complexion was normally pink, but the cold made him look like an elf in a Christmas cartoon.

"What are you guys working on?" Packard asked.

"Fentanyl bust. Pills, guns, cash. A big dog…some kind of Rottweiler," Reynolds said. "We went in there to arrest the husband and the wife. He knew there was nowhere to go and gave up pretty easily. The wife thought she could delay matters by locking herself in the bathroom, taking off all her clothes, and getting in the shower."

"Did you drag her out?"

"Didn't have to. Just turned off the hot water. You should have heard her scream."

Packard laughed. "What happened to the dog?" he asked.

"Animal Control took it in."

Reynolds had already eaten so Packard paid the bill and they stepped out into a bitterly cold wind. Any warmer and they might have walked to their first stop. Packard decided it was worth the drive. "Let's take your vehicle," he said.

They drove three blocks and pulled up in front of an empty storefront on Main Street, where all the buildings were pushed together like books on a shelf. "What are we doing here?" Reynolds asked.

"Know this place?"

"It's been a number of different restaurants. Last one was Asian or Chinese."

"Did you eat there?"

"I didn't. I'm a real Minnesotan. If it's spicier than ketchup, I'm out."

Packard had eaten there a few times. It was called the Tea Palace. It seemed like the chef had wanted to offer authentic Chinese dishes. Packard remembered a spicy hot pot, a whole fried fish, Szechuan dumplings, and dishes with tripe or pork stomach. There were also things you had to have on an Asian menu in Minnesota or you would go out of business—orange chicken, sweet and sour pork. Seemed like even that wasn't enough to save them. Packard thought the place lasted less than a year.

"Louise Larsen owns the building. The owners of the restaurant would have paid her rent to use the space. It's one of three commercial properties she owns."

They got out of the car. The building was narrow and brick and had large windows on either side of the door. A sign in one of the windows said FOR RENT.

Packard cupped his hands around his eyes and tried not to fog the cold glass with his breath. The building was empty. Not a table or a chair in sight. He saw a counter and a narrow hallway at the back.

"Let's go check out the other two," he said.

They drove to Cedar Creek, a township north and east of Sandy Lake with a much smaller downtown, and found another building fitted for a restaurant. The letters on the front door had been scraped away but still clearly said JANET'S CAFÉ. Janet's looked like it had been closed even longer than the Tea Palace. Through a film of dust on the inside windows, Packard could see an illuminated EXIT sign over the back door. He tried the front door, then had Reynolds drive them around to the alley that ran between the buildings and a pair of garage stalls sagging under the weight of the snow on top of them. The alley had been plowed but behind the café had not.

"This is a fire hazard," Packard said, looking at the deep snow that had drifted against the building and buried a dumpster like an Ice Age mammoth. "I'm guessing someone hasn't paid the snow-removal guy so he quit doing it."

"Who would pay the snow-removal guy if the old woman died last summer?"

"She had someone helping her manage the properties," Packard said. "Let's keep going. Next one is on Hollow Lake."

They headed further north. Packard asked Reynolds what he thought of working investigations. "It's all right," Reynolds said. "I think I like patrol better."

"Why is that?"

"Patrol is different every day. Investigations...tomorrow we'll be back at the fentanyl house, maybe the next day. We'll be interviewing them in jail. Trying to follow that thread as far as it will go. Patrol can be boring and I know we're supposed to be grateful for boring but I like the randomness of it."

"Have you told Shepard that?"

"I'm not sure the sheriff gives a shit what the noob thinks. It's my job to do what I'm told."

The kid was right. Most law enforcement departments were run like the military with layers of command—deputies under sergeants under captains under the chief deputy, all the way up to the sheriff, who decided the department's mission and allowed those under him to give the orders. They had a flatter command structure in Sandy Lake because of their size and budget.

"Thielen really needs your help right now. I'm glad she's got you. Do what she says. But you're allowed to make it known that investigations is not the direction where your career path lies. Nothing wrong with that."

They kept driving. The wind buffeted them from the west and sent powdery snow across the road. The chatter between dispatch and responding deputies and other agencies filled the silence as they headed further north.

"What the hell is all the way out here?" Packard asked.

"I have a feeling I know," Reynolds said.

The nav system took them down an icy dirt road to a boat landing and a ramshackle building that looked like an old house on the shore of Hollow Lake. A sign over the porch said Bell Bait & Tackle. Another sign said Closed. There were tracks from trucks and trailers and snowmobiles. The wind had blown snow into drifts against any motionless thing, including the front of the bait shop.

"Closed for the season or closed permanently?" Packard asked.

"I've been fishing up here quite a bit. It's been closed for years," Reynolds said.

"The Larsens were not great at picking commercial properties as investments. These buildings will bleed you dry on maintenance expenses and taxes if no one is paying rent."

Packard couldn't see any motive for murdering Louise based on her real estate holdings. There was no hidden treasure here. There would have to be a literal gold mine under the floor to make them worth any money at all.

They headed back to town. On the way, Reynolds said, "Thielen told me about your brother. Sorry that happened."

"It was a long time ago. Feels like we might finally get some answers after all these years."

"Why did it take so long?"

Good question. Part of it was like Stan said in his letter—there are things you know and things you can prove. They wouldn't be on the verge of proving anything if Stan hadn't reached out to Rassin again in time to take advantage of the regrets of a dying man.

"That's the thing about investigations," said Packard. "They take time. It's not like on TV or in books where everything gets wrapped up neatly in sixty minutes or three hundred pages. You've seen that evidence room—there's stuff in there relating to cases that have been open for years."

Reynolds nodded. "Another reason why I like patrol. There's an incident, you respond, you write your report, you move on."

On the radio, dispatch sent responders to a man with chest pains and shortness of breath.

Packard said, "Back to Louise. To recap, we have a dead woman in her eighties. We have evidence that suggests she may have been killed. She has an estate worth roughly three million dollars, including a huge home on Lake Redwing and the three properties we looked at, and no heirs to inherit. All of it's going to charities and foundations per her will. I've talked to her neighbors and her lawyer. I've talked to the medical examiner. Where do we look next?"

Reynolds had to think for a while. "You said she's got a property manager."

"Yes. Tess something. I haven't found a last name yet."

"Have you looked at Louise's bank statements? There's probably a check made out to Tess for managing the properties."

"I like your thinking. It just so happens that I dropped off a search warrant at the bank this morning. I didn't think of a paycheck. I was thinking the property manager would be able to make deposits and write checks from Louise's business accounts. Tess's name should be on the account."

"We going to the bank now?"

"You got somewhere else to be?" Packard asked.

"Nope."

"Good."

They stopped at the bank and Packard went inside and picked up a stack of printouts an inch thick. They stopped at the offices of Wiley, Washington & Prentis Attorneys at Law and Packard picked up a pile of paper twice as thick from Marsha. Ray Wiley had left for the day. His daughter, Lisa, was still there. "Please keep me in the loop if you can," she said to Packard. "I'll run interference with my dad. He's taking this personally for a whole number of reasons. I can't help you if I don't know what's going on."

"Did you know about the agreement your dad made with Jim Wolf to tear down Louise's house and build a new one before selling it?"

Lisa cocked her head. "I did...not," she said, sounding unsure of either the question or her answer. "Not until after I was at Louise's house with you."

"I'll be in touch," Packard said.

Reynolds drove him to his truck and they went back to the sheriff's office. Shepard was gone. Thielen was out. Kelly was at the front desk. "The hell are you two doing together?" she asked, barely looking away from her computer.

"Fighting crime, catching bad guys," Packard said.

"I don't like it," Kelly said. She pointed a long manicured nail at both of them. "He's supposed to be with Thielen. You're supposed to be on leave. I guess we all do whatever we want now."

"You're the boss. What would you like us to do?"

"One of you could rake the snow off my roof. The other could get in the kitchen and get dinner started."

"Maybe after we go through this paperwork," Packard suggested.

"Forget it. You'll just disappoint me like every other man in this world."

"We should go," Packard said to Reynolds, "before she starts listing them all."

"It all started with my first husband. No, wait. My father...." Kelly yelled after them as they disappeared down the hall. They grabbed water and settled in a conference room. Packard took the bank statements and Reynolds looked through the paperwork from Ray Wiley's office.

"I think I have a lot of the same documents you do. This is a bunch of bank statements," Reynolds said.

"I figured as much. I got two warrants so I could get her banking info from the source in case Ray felt the need to hold anything back. There should be a master list of all her accounts in your papers. See if there's anything that looks like a business account related to the rental properties."

Packard spent a few mind-numbing minutes reviewing pages and pages of account numbers and balances and automatic withdrawals. Reynolds did the same.

"Here's something," Reynolds said finally. "There's an account called Larsen Properties LLC. It's at the bank. Can you find it?"

Packard kept flipping pages until he found what he was looking for. "Here it is. There's a secondary signer here named Tess Reid." Packard looked at the records for the account and noticed something right away. "Look at this," he said to Reynolds. "This account had a standing balance of about $50,000 for a long time. In November someone withdrew it all."

"Probably wasn't Louise if she died in June."

"Very astute of you, Reynolds. You might make a good detective, after all."

Reynolds went to his desk and came back with his laptop. He looked up Tess Reid in the driver's license database and found a local address. "She's right here in town," he said.

Packard checked the time on his phone. It wasn't yet five. "Let's drop by and ask Tess what she spent $50,000 on."

"I'm hoping to get home to have dinner with my kids by six."

"What are you having?"

"Pot roast," Reynolds said. Then added, "You could join us. My wife always buys the biggest roast so we have plenty of leftovers."

"Have you ever had Thielen over?"

"No."

"Are you inviting me to make sure we get done at a reasonable time?"

"Kind of," Reynolds said.

Packard shrugged. "I'm fine with that. Text your wife, tell her I'm coming. Let's go see Tess."

———————

They took Reynolds's car again. The dashboard said it was twenty-seven degrees out as they left the station. Three minutes later, when they pulled up in front of the address, the temperature was twenty-three. A pot roast dinner cooked by someone else was sounding better and better.

Tess's house was a small yellow cube with a steep roof. The sidewalk and steps were shoveled and the porch light on. Packard talked to dispatch on the way over and found there was no record of any calls to the address in recent history.

They went up the sidewalk and rang the bell. No answer. It looked like there were no lights on inside. While Reynolds kept ringing, Packard followed the sidewalk to the back of the house and across the yard to a stand-alone single-car garage. Packard looked through the window. No car inside.

Reynolds had gone from ringing the doorbell to knocking hard on the metal storm door.

"You guys looking for Tess?"

A bearded, middle-aged man leaning on a cane stood in the doorway next door.

"We are," said Packard. "Any idea where we can find her?"

"She's gone."

"Gone where?" Reynolds asked.

"No idea. She disappeared. Left all her stuff behind. Haven't seen her in months."

Packard said, "Can we come in and ask you a few questions?"

"Yeah," said the man. "I've been waiting for this."

———————

His name was Mike Turner. He owned Tess's house, which made him her landlord. "I grew up in this house," Mike said. "When I was ready to move out on my own, my mom suggested I buy the house next door and she would move there and I could have the bigger house for my family. So that's what we did. My mom died about ten years ago. I've been renting out the place ever since."

They were sitting in the living room. Mike had a large swiveling recliner pulled up close to an even larger television. Behind it was a couch pushed against the wall and a chair turned sideways. It didn't look like the setup of a man with a family. It looked like a place where a man lived alone and watched a lot of television. The smell was of an apple cinnamon plug-in air freshener losing the battle against two cats and their litter box. Packard was very allergic to cats.

"How long did Tess live there?"

"About five years. I think she came up from the Cities. She was in a relationship or getting out of one. She's like you," Mike said, sticking out his hand and shaking it side to side.

"Like me?" Packard questioned. "She's a sheriff's deputy?"

"No. She's... You know."

"Tall? Really fit?"

"No. She likes women. Sexually."

"That's not like me at all," Packard said.

Reynolds dropped his head and put a hand over his mouth to hide his laughter.

"You know what I mean," Mike said.

"I know what you mean."

Mike described her as being short, curly brown hair shaved on the sides. She had tattoos and wore sleeveless T-shirts and shorts almost year-round. "She's not fat but she must be eighty percent whale blubber to walk around dressed like that all the time."

"What did she do for work?"

"She worked part-time as a property manager and also on the ground crew for a tree company."

"Did you know her well?"

"Pretty well. She came over and drank a beer now and then. It was nice having her as a renter because she could fix anything. Took the pressure off me. I don't get around like I used to." He bounced the end of his cane on the toe of his shoe.

"What happened?"

"I used to work road construction. Got hit by a car going too fast through a construction zone. Been collecting disability for a while now. The wife and I got a Medicaid divorce to keep me on the plan after she got a better-paying job. Eventually it turned into a real divorce. We were in each other's face too much with me not working."

"Sorry to hear that," Packard said.

Mike shrugged. "It is what it is. I gotta admit I miss Tess more than the wife. She mowed both our lawns, ran the snowblower. She was funny and always up for a good time. I went out a couple of times with her and her lady friends. Lesbians know how to party."

Packard nodded as if he knew this to be true himself. "So what happened to her? You said she disappeared."

"It wasn't like a magic trick. She came by one day and said she needed to get out of town for a while. She wrote me a check to cover rent through January and said she'd be in touch when she could."

"When was this?" Packard asked.

"November."

"She wrote you a check for three months' rent all at once." Packard looked at Reynolds. Easy to write a check for that much money when you've cleaned out $50K from your employer's account.

"She did," Mike said.

"Did she say why she had to take off?"

"No. But she seemed upset about something. I thought it might be lady troubles."

"She ever have anyone over regularly?"

"Used to be a blue Golf that would be parked out front some nights. Brenda something. She was at BB's every time we went there."

BB's was a bar outside of town. Short for the Big Beaver. That the place attracted all the area lesbians like iron filings shocked no one. How could it not?

"She paid you through the end of January. It's March now. Have you heard from her since?"

"Not a peep. Her cell phone is out of service. No response to emails I've sent. I'm praying she comes back. I don't want to throw all her stuff away but I'm gonna need to clean the place out and find a new renter soon."

Reynolds asked, "Has anyone come looking for her in all this time?"

"No one besides the two of you. No wait—that's not true. A few months ago, a lawyer came by looking for her."

"Older man? Heavyset?" Packard said, describing Ray Wiley.

"No. It was woman. Lisa something."

"Hmmm," Packard said. Lisa had asked him to keep her in the loop but had somehow failed to mention the missing property manager who helped herself to fifty grand. He was starting to get the feeling she was only telling him what she wanted him to know.

An orange cat jumped from the floor and walked along the back of the couch where Packard was sitting. His eyes were starting to itch. He imagined everything in the room giving off cat dander like a beaten rug. He twirled his pen to keep from rubbing his eyes.

"I assume you have keys to the place. We'd like to take a look around if you'll let us," Packard said.

Reynolds cleared his throat and looked at his watch.

"Tomorrow would be better, actually," Packard said.

Mike said yeah, sure, no problem. He leaned on his cane and pushed himself out of the chair. He gave them keys to Tess's house and said they could keep them as long as necessary. He had another set. Packard asked him to write down the phone number and email address he had for Tess.

"I'd love it if you could track her down," Mike said. "If for no other reason than to let me know she's okay. I'm worried something has happened to her."

"We'll do our best," Packard promised.

And then he sneezed loud enough to make everyone jump.

CHAPTER SIXTEEN

DURING DINNER WITH REYNOLDS and his family, Packard was put into service giving the baby his bottle while Reynolds changed out of his uniform and his wife, Melissa, finished feeding their toddler. The adults finally sat down to a steaming platter of roast beef and potatoes and carrots, everything roasted to a caramel sweetness.

Reynolds wanted to know if he was nervous about the BCA investigation.

"Not nervous," Packard said. "There's no point in being nervous. The report isn't going to tell me anything I don't know. I was there. I pulled the trigger. The report is for the county attorney to make a decision, it's for the public. I'd like it to be over with so we can all move on."

He realized as he said it that the report wasn't going to give him permission to move on. It wasn't a magic pill that could change how he felt about shooting Robert Clark. He would have to grapple with that, on his own, for as long as it stayed front of mind.

After they ate, Melissa put both kids to bed while Packard and Reynolds washed dishes. The antihistamine they gave him for his cat allergies and the two beers he drank had him and Frank in bed by nine thirty.

Packard dreamed he was outside the courtroom, yelling for Robert

Clark to drop the gun. Packard shot Clark, ran over to him, but Clark didn't have a gun. Packard stood up and shot Ray Wiley, he shot his mom, he shot Reynolds. He had endless rounds in his gun. He shot random people and watched them drop like tin plates in a carnival game. The elevator dinged and dinged and the doors opened and closed on a body half in and half out of the car.

Packard heard the sound of his own yell pulling him back from wherever the mind goes during sleep. Frank yipped and nudged him with his snout.

Packard sat up and leaned over to pet his whimpering dog. "Sorry, buddy. It was just a dream."

Frank got up from his spot at the foot of the bed and lay down next to his human. Packard let Frank's warmth and steady breathing ease him back to sleep.

———————————

Packard assumed there was no way Thielen was going to let him have Reynolds two days in a row, so he was surprised to get a call from the deputy the next morning asking what time they were going to Tess's house.

Packard had been up for hours. He'd spent the time before the sun came up working out, then writing search warrants for Tess's bank and phone records.

"What's wrong with Thielen?"

"She says she's got the crud that's going around. She's going to try to be in this afternoon if she's feeling better."

"I'll meet you at the office in an hour. We'll take your vehicle again," Packard said.

"Melissa wants to know if you want me to bring you a roast beef sandwich."

"You never have to ask if I want a roast beef sandwich. The answer is always yes. Tell Melissa I said thanks again for dinner last night."

———————————

Driving into town, Packard called Lisa Washington.

"You asked me to keep you in the loop about Louise Larsen," he said. "Why aren't you doing the same for me?"

"In regard to what?" Lisa asked.

"Why didn't you tell me about Tess Reid?"

"What about her?"

"That she exists. That she had access to Louise's business account. That she withdrew $50,000 and disappeared. That you've been looking for her, too."

"Wait, wait, what? She did what?"

"You didn't know?"

"That she stole money? That she disappeared? No, I didn't know that."

"Why were you looking for her?"

"My dad initially told her to keep doing whatever it was she did for Louise. I think it was around the holidays he decided it was time to cut her loose from the estate. My father does not have the most tact or consideration for people's feelings, as you are aware. I told him I'd give Tess the news. I called her a few times. I went by her house. I couldn't get hold of her. Then I got busy and told my dad he'd have to take care of it. I forgot about her after that."

"He hasn't said anything to you about her or the missing money?"

"First of all, are you certain she took it?"

"There are only two names on the account, and one of them was dead when the money was withdrawn."

"I'll ask my dad about it."

"Is it possible he wouldn't know if Tess withdrew $50,000?"

"You picked up copies of our records yesterday. Check the statements. They might be out of date if he hasn't pulled them again recently. Even if they are recent, it's possible he hasn't looked at them closely."

"Here's something else I want him to confirm. I want to know if Jim has bought Louise's house outright or if Ray's giving him permission to tear it down and rebuild without a purchase agreement."

"I'll ask," Lisa said. "Let me know if you find Tess."

Reynolds showed up in uniform again, even though detectives usually dressed more casually. "I don't have a lot of business casual clothes," Reynolds said when Packard asked him about it. "I have uniforms. The uniform means I don't have to think about what I'm going to wear to work."

Tess's rental was tiny—one bedroom, one bath, and an unfinished basement with a washer and dryer.

In the bedroom, most but not all of the clothes had been packed. The bathroom had been cleaned out of its toiletries. Packard got the sense that there was a hurriedness to the decision-making of what to take and what to leave behind. *Empty the dresser but leave most of the hanging clothes. Take the toothbrush and toothpaste but leave the large bottle of shampoo and conditioner in the shower and the dried-up washcloth hanging in the loop of the handheld showerhead.*

The dining room table had a printer on it and cables that connected to a docking station that was missing the laptop that fit there. Stacked on the table and on one of the chairs beside it was something Packard hadn't seen in a long time: phone books. Half a dozen books from Spokane, Washington; Toledo, Ohio; and Louisville, Kentucky, among other places, some of them dating to the eighties and nineties.

"Are you old enough to know what these are?" Packard asked Reynolds, who was a generation younger than him. He'd recently seen a video online of a kid trying to dial a phone number on a rotary phone. It was like watching a chicken try to use a paintbrush.

"I know what a phone book is," Reynolds said. "When I was a kid, my mom would rip the pages out of ours to keep weeds down in the garden."

Packard nodded. He opened a narrow cupboard in the kitchen and pulled out a couple of drawers. "She had a dog," he said.

"How do you know that?"

"She has a vacuum cleaner made for pet stains and a lint brush with most of the paper peeled off. I'm not sneezing my face off so it had to be a dog, not a cat."

"Is knowing she had a dog useful to us?"

"I might know someone we can call."

Their next stop was the Big Beaver. Earlier in the winter, Packard had gotten into a fight in the parking lot at this fine establishment with a murder suspect who had thrown a shovel at his head.

BB's was open but quiet. An older woman, who Packard recognized as the owner, was working behind the bar. Her husband was sitting on a stool with a cup of coffee and a shot glass of whiskey in front of him. Kelly Clarkson was on the television. There was something incongruous about daytime television in a bar. Same with whiskey before noon.

"Hello, boys," the woman said. She was blond and wearing heavy eyeliner but not much other makeup. Packard couldn't remember her name.

"Hi, Steph," Reynolds said. "Cliff," he said to the man sitting nearby.

"Looking for some food?"

"Looking for somebody," Packard said. "A woman by the name of Brenda. She's part of a group of gals that hang out here." *What was the proper term for a bunch of lesbians? A gaggle? A brood? A band?*

"I know Brenda," Steph said.

"Do you know her last name?"

Steph had to think. She pulled her phone out from under the bar and opened the contacts. "I don't. I have her in here as BRENDA!!!! If you know her, it makes sense. She's loud and crazy."

Packard took down the number. "Is she local?"

"She lives in St. Cloud. She owns a cabin and is up here with all those gals more weekends than not."

"Even in the winter?"

"Oh yeah."

Packard had to think for a minute what day of the week it was. Friday. "Think they'd be up this weekend?"

Steph shrugged. "Like I said, it's most weekends."

"What about Tess Reid?"

"I know Tess, too," Steph said. "Same group. I feel like I haven't seen her in a while."

"The two of them were dating, as I understand," Packard said.

Steph shrugged. "I think they were. I don't know for sure. I love all those gals. They come in here, they spend a lot of money, don't cause trouble. I know some of them are together, some used to be together but are now just friends. I don't pay attention to who's doing who." She made a V with the first two fingers on both hands, then slotted them together.

Reynolds was already blushing even before the crude hand gesture. He tucked his thumbs into the armpits of his vest like chicken wings and stared at his feet.

"You got any photos of Tess or Brenda?"

Steph had a lot of photos of both of them, together and separate, mostly taken there at the bar. Tess was as she had been described by Mike. Brenda had super-short hair, big red cheeks, and freckles. Steph selected the photos Packard wanted and sent them to his phone.

She couldn't tell them the address of Brenda's cabin but was able to give them driving directions. "I've spent many a night around the firepit with those gals," Steph said. "They know how to cook and eat and party. They are a hell of a lot of fun."

———————

They drove away from BB's and pulled into a parking lot for a campsite and ate their roast beef sandwiches. Wheat bread, mustard, thinly sliced red onions, wrapped in parchment. A small bag of chips for each of them.

"You eat lunch like this every day?" Packard asked.

"A lot of days. We're saving for a house," Reynolds said. "We're renting the place we're in now. Any extra income goes toward our down payment. Leftovers are cheaper than eating out and healthier than vending machines."

Another patrol car driven by Deputy Baker pulled alongside and they all shot the shit for a while about the weather and spring break. When dispatch asked for responders to a car/deer accident, Baker took off. They cleaned up the garbage and crumbs from lunch, and Packard took out his phone and made a call.

"Gary, it's Packard."

"Honey, I know who this is. It says Frank's Big Bad Daddy on my phone when you call."

Now it was Packard's turn to blush. Gary Bushwright was a retired truck driver who ran a dog rescue and boarding kennel on his property outside Sandy Lake. Packard had adopted Frank from Gary. More than forty years ago, Gary had been a male hustler and a gay porn star who survived the AIDS epidemic and eventually came home to take care of his sick mother.

"Hey, Gary, I have you on speakerphone with Deputy Reynolds. I'm wondering if you know a gal named Tess Reid. I'm pretty sure she has a dog. Lesbian. Short hair, shaved on the sides—"

"Honey, are you describing Tess or the dog?"

"Tess. Tattoos, wears shorts and short sleeves all the time."

"So you just assume I know every lesbian with a dog in this county?"

"Do you know her?"

"Well, yes," Gary admitted. "I know Tess."

Packard looked at Reynolds and rolled his eyes. "What do you know about her?"

"She got her dog from me. She did some tree trimming and brush clearing a year or so ago in exchange for kennel time. I haven't seen or talked to her in a while."

"What kind of dog does she have?"

"A brown-and-white cocker spaniel. Kind of looks like Lady from *Lady and the Tramp*. Hence the name Lady Gaga Pinot Grigio MargaretAnn String Cheese Reid."

"Wait…what now?"

"Lady Gaga Pinot Grigio MargaretAnn String Cheese Reid."

"That's the name of one dog?"

"Yes. Honey, it's no weirder than calling a dog Frank."

"I don't know about that," Packard said. "How long ago did she adopt the dog?"

"Three or four years ago, I'd say. I can look up my records if you want to know for sure."

"I'll let you know if I do. Thanks, Gary."

"All right then. Give our boy a hug from me. Come by and see me sometime," Gary said.

Packard hung up and wrote in his notebook. "Let's go talk to Brenda and find out what she can tell us about Tess."

Reynolds put the car into Drive. "Roger that, Big Bad Daddy."

Packard reached across and grabbed the steering wheel. "I will fire you if you repeat that to anyone at work. Especially Thielen."

"You can't fire me. You're not the sheriff anymore."

Packard let go of the wheel. "Damn it."

Brenda's cabin was set back fifty yards from the road, surrounded by trees and small outbuildings. Bare branches and a cloudy sky shaded the windshield as they crept down a long driveway cleared of snow and came up to a gray house with white trim that sat high above the frozen lake below.

Two women smoking cigarettes stood next to a firepit surrounded by tree stumps and chairs. A trio of dogs came running at the patrol car and then away toward a woodpile and a small tractor with a plow blade on the front.

Brenda came out of the house carrying a brown grocery sack. She looked about fifty, had an almost shaved head and walked with a limp. She threw the grocery bag into the fire and lit a cigarette.

Packard radioed their location to dispatch and got the property owner's full name: Brenda Short. He and Reynolds got out of the car. The smell of cigarettes hung heavy in the damp air. No one seemed surprised to see them, meaning Steph from the Big Beaver had probably tipped off Brenda that the cops were looking for her.

"Afternoon, ladies. I'm looking for Brenda Short," Packard said.

If Packard hadn't known who Brenda was, he would have after the other two women looked at the one standing between them. They both took one last puff of their cigarettes and threw them into the fire and headed for the house. Packard spotted two more women standing by the picture window inside.

"I'm Brenda. What can I do for you?"

Packard introduced himself and Deputy Reynolds and said they were trying to find Tess Reid.

"I don't keep up with her anymore," Brenda said, staring into the fire. "We dated for a while and then we broke up."

"How long ago was that?"

"This fall some time."

"What caused the breakup?" Packard asked.

Brenda gave him a look that asked what business it was of his. She had a flannel coat over a hooded sweatshirt and kept her non-cigarette hand in the front pouch to keep it warm. "Irreconcilable differences," she said.

"Must have been a bad breakup if you're not speaking anymore. Steph showed me a lot of photos of you guys having a great time at the Big..." He couldn't bring himself to say *big beaver* in front of a lesbian. It felt wrong for any number of reasons. "At BB's. At the bar."

Brenda looked at him. "I didn't hear a question in there," she said.

"What do you know about her job as a property manager?"

"I know that's one of the jobs she had. She collected rent, made sure bills were paid. That's all I know about it."

"How long did she work at that job?"

Brenda shrugged. "Years. I don't know for sure."

"Was Tess having money problems? Or any other kind of problems?"

"We're all having money problems, aren't we? Wages are stagnant, inflation is sky-high. It cost me $85 to fill up my gas tank the other day."

"I hear ya," Packard agreed. "I'm talking about debts or big bills. Anyone after her for anything that had her worried or scared?"

The word *scared* made Brenda blink and her eyes go far away for a second. She tried to play it off by waving her cigarette in front of her face. "I don't know about anything like that. We were friends, we dated for a while. We didn't mix our finances or move in together on the second date, like lesbians are supposed to do."

One of the dogs came over and sniffed around Reynolds. It looked like a setter of some kind with a long tail. Reynolds squatted down to pet it and got licked in the face.

"Was it the breakup that made her leave town suddenly?"

"You'd have to ask her. I told you I don't know. We don't talk."

"And you haven't heard from her since…the breakup? Since the fall?"

"Right."

"Any idea where she might have gone?"

Brenda shook her head.

"Do the other women here know where to find her or get ahold of her?"

"No," Brenda insisted. "She cut off contact with all of us."

"All of you?" Packard asked incredulously.

"These are my friends. Tess knew them through me. So after we broke up…"

"How long did you two date?"

"Less than a year."

"Interesting."

"Why is that interesting?"

Packard opened his notebook and pointed to the cocker spaniel lifting its leg over by the woodpile. "I'm guessing that's Lady Gaga Pinot Grigio MargaretAnn String Cheese Reid," he said.

If the word *scared* made Brenda blink, the dog's name made her look like she'd been slapped across the face. She was a woman standing on thin ice and she knew it.

"So you broke up, she left town, you don't speak to her, but somehow you have her dog that she had long before you two started dating."

Brenda took a long drag on her cigarette, looked up, and slowly exhaled, taking time to think. "Not me," she said. "The dog is with one of the other gals. Tess told her she couldn't have a dog where she was going."

"If I send Reynolds in the house and he asks who is Lady Gaga's owner, who's going to raise her hand?"

"Amy," Brenda said.

Packard tilted his head toward the house and Reynolds headed that way. The dogs followed him and he stooped to pet each one.

Packard said, "Listen to me, Brenda. I don't give a shit about who's taking care of the damn dog. I want to talk to Tess about the work she did for Louise. There's money missing. I also want to know if she saw Louise the day she died. Right now, I'm pulling Tess's bank and phone records. If I can't track her down through those means, then I'm going to start treating her like a missing person, maybe even a criminal suspect. I'm going to open an active investigation into her whereabouts, and that's when the consequences for lying to me get serious."

He paused and he and Brenda stared at each other. Reynolds was almost to the cabin's front door. "Reynolds, come back. Never mind about the dog."

Packard took a business card out of his wallet and handed it to Brenda. "If you hear from Tess, tell her I just want to ask her some questions."

Brenda flicked her cigarette butt into the fire and tucked Packard's card into the top pocket of her coat. "I'm not going to hear from her."

There was no place to turn their vehicle around. Reynolds put the car in reverse and backed down the long driveway. Packard watched Brenda limp toward the house, Lady Gaga Pinot Grigio MargaretAnn String Cheese Reid at her heels.

Reynolds asked. "Was she lying?"

"You couldn't tell?"

"I was playing with the dogs. Sorry."

"You're a terrible detective."

They went back to the office. Kelly had taken the day off and her desk was dark. Thielen was in, looking a bit green and sweaty.

Packard and Reynolds stood in the doorway to her office. "What is wrong with you?" Packard asked. "Are you sure you're not making everyone else sick by being here?"

"I'm not contagious," Thielen said, drinking from a giant water bottle. "I've been having stomach issues lately. I'm taking different things out of my diet to see if I can figure out what it is."

"Maybe you're pregnant," Packard suggested.

"Maybe you're an asshole who should get out of my office if you're not here to do any actual work," Thielen said.

"I brought your Padawan back," Packard said.

"Don't make *Star Wars* references," Thielen said. "I hate *Star Wars.*"

"Well, you'll love this. While we were questioning a suspect, he forgot to pay attention because he was too busy playing with their dogs."

Reynolds looked hurt. "She wasn't a suspect. She was a friend of a person of interest in the Louise Larsen case. What are you talking about, suspect?"

"I suspect she lied to me the whole time so now she's a suspect," Packard said.

"Yeah, well…Gary Bushwright's nickname for Packard is Big Bad Daddy. That's how he has him in his phone."

The color came back to Thielen's face, maybe for the first time in days. "Oh, that's very good to know," she said. "I will file that away for future reference. Now if you two dipshits will get out of my office, I'm behind on everything. Reynolds, I made you a to-do list. It's in your email. Don't let me see your baby face until it's done."

"I'm going to have you arrested," Packard said to Reynolds as they walked away.

"A night in jail might be preferable to whatever is on that list," Reynolds said. "I'll let you know."

Shepard's voice boomed from the back office just then.

"Is that Packard I hear?"

Packard walked down the hall and stuck his head in the door. Shepard was sitting behind his desk with a piece of pie on a paper plate in front of him and a cup of steaming coffee. "Got a call from the BCA. They finished their report. They want to meet on Monday."

"That was fast. Maybe that's a good sign."

"I wouldn't draw any conclusions until you see the report. Is your psych eval done?"

"Not yet."

Thielen's office was close enough that she could hear everything. "Tim can do it this weekend," she yelled from behind her desk. Tim was her husband, a licensed psychologist who worked with the department when employees needed counseling or debrief sessions after a particularly traumatic event.

"Get it done," Shepard said.

Packard nodded.

CHAPTER SEVENTEEN

WALKING FRANK WAS A balm, even on the coldest days of winter, which this was not. The snowpack around them had started to settle, letting go of the air it held like it was exhaling in acceptance of its fate. Spring still felt far off, but the light it brought was growing brighter, the days already noticeably longer. In a few weeks, the trees would start to bud and the first green things would appear on the sloped ground where the sun shone the longest.

Packard was relieved to know the BCA report was ready. Monday he'd be able to see all the evidence collected as part of its investigation. He'd know everything except the county attorney's decision.

He cooked dinner. The oven gave off the hot, starchy scent of a baked potato. In a ripping-hot black skillet he put a piece of salmon skin-side down and watched it flex like muscle before brushing the top with hoisin. He finished it with a squeeze of lime right before taking it out of the pan.

Frank took his post beside his chair and waited for bites of food while Packard scrolled his phone and ate. The house was quiet. Packard remembered a photograph of an old man praying over a loaf of bread that had hung in his grandparents' dining room when he was a kid. How closely would he resemble it if someone looked into his window right then? A man alone at a table, thankful for what he had. A phone instead of a Bible. Otherwise, not far off.

His phone rang then. He put it on speaker. "Hi, Mom."

"What are you doing?"

"Eating dinner," he said. Then, because he knew what the next question would be, "Salmon with a baked potato and broccoli."

"You're such a good eater," she said, sounding like she was talking to a five-year-old who had cleaned his plate. "I'm a vegetarian and ate cheese and crackers for dinner. I should be ashamed of myself. Is there anyone there with you?"

"Just Frank, begging as usual."

"It's not begging when you feed him scraps. It's called waiting for what he's been trained to expect."

"Is there a reason for your call, ma'am?"

"Have you called the brewery guy?"

"I have not."

"Why not?"

"I've been busy. I have a case."

"Is your leave over?"

"Not yet. Almost."

He told her about the blood he found at Louise's house on his second visit and how it had him asking a lot of unpopular questions of everyone who knew her.

"Be careful, sweetheart. And poor Louise. We should have done a ceremony while I was there, in case her soul hasn't found its way into the light."

"If I found out someone killed her, you can come back and do one then."

"Any more news on the dentist or his children?"

He said no new news since their trip to Duluth. She wanted to know when he thought they would start searching the area from Stan Shaw's map for Nick's remains and he said he really didn't know. May? June? That long, she said. Maybe, he said. I was hoping sooner, she said.

Before they hung up, she told him again to call the guy from the brewery.

"His name is Kyle."

"I'll learn his name if you decide to get married. Just call him. You should be getting fantastically laid at your age, darling. Don't waste it."

Packard sighed. "Yes, Mother."

He spent five minutes thinking about calling Kyle until he remembered he didn't have Kyle's number. He could have called the brewery. And said what? Going down there would have meant getting cleaned up and trying to think of a reason why he was there drinking by himself. Maybe he wouldn't have to make up a reason. Maybe it would be obvious and they could take things from there.

It was too much work, he decided.

Better to do actual work, he decided.

He poured himself a splash of bourbon on the rocks and wrote his notes from the visit to Tess's house, the Big Beaver, and the lesbian cabin full of lesbians. There was no doubt in his mind that Brenda was lying about her knowledge of Tess's whereabouts. Her *we broke up, we don't talk* story was bullshit. The fact that no one was worried that Tess might actually be missing or dead meant someone, somewhere, knew she was okay.

He wrote about his phone call with Lisa Washington and her claim of looking for Tess while not knowing about the money that had been withdrawn from Louise's business account. He put the laptop aside and spread out the papers he picked up from the bank and from Ray's law office. He found the statement for Louise's business account in the reports from the bank and compared it to the statement in Ray's files. The paperwork backed up Lisa's story. Their statement was dated in July, four months before someone withdrew the $50K.

Tess had worked for Louise for years, according to Brenda. What made her suddenly clear out the account and leave town? It wasn't Louise dying—that had happened almost five months prior. Maybe it took her time to work up the courage and come up with a plan. But upend your whole life and walk away from everyone and everything you know for $50,000? It was definitely enough to start over somewhere but it wasn't going to last her long.

Packard kept looking through the bank statements. It didn't take a forensic accountant to make sense of what was happening. Louise had income coming in every month from social security and what he assumed were required minimum distributions from her investment accounts. She spent very little... utilities, groceries, regular monthly gifts to things like the library and public television. She paid a lot in property and income taxes.

Her business account had no consistent money coming in. From all the statements he had, it didn't look like anyone was paying rent on any of the three buildings she owned. Louise had made a couple of large deposits from an external account to cover bills and taxes and a regular paycheck for Tess of $500 a week. There was a fairly large monthly electricity bill, which struck him as odd as it seemed none of the buildings had any activity occurring in them. Heat was more likely to have been gas or propane, and no one in their right mind would pay to heat an old, empty building through the winter.

Packard's eyes were heavy as he made a note to follow up on the electric bill. He finished his watered-down bourbon. He'd had two good days of work. Two days of running around with Reynolds, following leads and asking questions. It was the professional equivalent of a workout. Using his talents. Using his mind. He would sleep well.

CHAPTER EIGHTEEN

THIELEN'S HUSBAND, TIM, WAS in his fifties, more than a decade older than his wife. He was long and lanky with a dark beard and gray hair that curled out over his ears and behind his neck.

"Okay, last chance, Ben. It can be hard to have an open and honest conversation with a therapist when that person is also a friend. I can refer you to a colleague if that would be easier."

"I'm fine," Packard said. "You're not my therapist. You're doing a psych eval to see if I'm fit to return to work."

They'd already talked for a while about the things the two of them usually talked about—work and the weather. Tim had taken up oil painting a few years ago and had shown Packard a large canvas he was working on of a barn surrounded by tall yellow grass and slanting afternoon shadows.

Tim got up, closed his office door, and sat again. His impossibly long legs extended from the chair toward Packard in a way that seemed to distort the perspective between them. Packard had been to Thielen's home dozens of times, but never in this room—Tim's office—and never alone with Tim with the door closed. Thielen wasn't home.

"Of course, you can expect one hundred percent confidentiality. Nothing we talk about will be shared with Jill."

It was weird to hear Thielen referred to by her first name. Another thing that made this feel like anything but a normal visit.

"I trust you," Packard said. He didn't understand what Tim was expecting him to reveal in this session. They were going to talk about the shooting and his feelings about it. He didn't plan to wander far from that topic.

"Let's start with the incident outside the courtroom," Tim said. He had a yellow notepad in his lap, the same kind Packard used when he was making notes and trying to diagram all the variables in a case.

"The shooting, you mean," Packard said. Might as well call it what it was.

"That was the end result, right?"

"The end result was a man died. I killed him."

Tim nodded but said nothing.

"Aren't you supposed to ask me how that makes me feel?"

"There are no rules or expectations here. We're just talking," Tim said.

Packard studied his hands. He'd come into this thinking it would be a casual conversation, but the familiarity he usually felt with Tim wasn't in the room. They were sitting across from each other in deep matching chairs with high upholstered arms. There was a desk with a computer and a ring light behind Tim. He saw a lot of patients online, according to Thielen. Outside the window Packard could see the snow-covered yard and the creek that ran behind their property.

"I realized the other day that I've fired my gun more times since I've been in Sandy Lake than I did the whole time I was a cop in Minneapolis." Packard was a skilled interviewer, but put in a chair and told to talk about his feelings, he'd blurted out the first thing that came to mind. As soon as he said it, he regretted it.

"Tell me more about that," Tim said.

"I was a beat cop for a long time. Pulled my gun when necessary but almost never fired it. By the time you show up as an investigator, the bullets have already flown. You're there to examine the scene and talk to witnesses. Why am I telling you this? You're married to Thielen. You know it's not like on television."

"I know you both fired your weapons at Emmett Burr."

"We did," Packard confirmed. Emmett had burst out of the brush driving a Bobcat and firing his gun. Packard and Thielen returned fire after which Emmett lost control of the Bobcat and rolled it into the lake.

"Did you talk to anyone after that?" Tim asked.

Packard shook his head. "I was acting sheriff then. I excused myself from the psych eval. Did you talk to Thielen about it?"

"I did."

"What did she say?"

"You'll have to ask her," Tim said, smiling.

"Of course." Packard scratched his beard and looked out the window. "I guess Emmett was different. He came out shooting at us. And after I saw his basement and we found the other bodies on his property...I didn't feel so bad."

"Do you feel bad now?"

"I don't feel great that two men have died by my hand in the last two years. That's not what I do. That's not what law enforcement is supposed to be about. I'm embodying the worst behavior that people use to justify their hatred for cops."

"Do you really believe that?"

Packard sighed. "I don't know."

"So Emmett was one set of circumstances and variables. It sounds like you feel different about what happened at the courthouse."

"The courthouse feels different," Packard said.

"How so? You had an active shooter situation. Another man with a gun. You saved lives by ending it as quickly as you did."

"Logically, I know that. When I meet with the BCA on Monday I'm hoping they're going to say the same thing. But in my head...it's different."

"Because?"

"Because it shouldn't have had to come to that."

"What part of it?"

"All of it," Packard said, frustrated. "Robert Clark shouldn't have been in court fighting to keep his property. He was an old widower. He'd worked hard, played by the rules all his life, and now the system was changing the game on him."

"How does any of that change what he did?" Tim asked.

"Are you saying he deserved it like Emmett did?"

"I'm not saying anyone deserved anything," Tim said, sitting up and crossing and recrossing his legs. "It's not about who Emmett and Robert were as people. In the moment, it's about their actions and your responsibility. Who Robert was outside the courtroom, what kind of life he lived doesn't change the fact that he brought a gun into a county building and started pulling the trigger. His being a good man prior to then doesn't change the decision you had to make in that moment. His being a good man shouldn't add to your psychic burden more than Emmett. They both did terrible, regrettable things. Robert Clark's intention was to kill innocent people."

"His intention was to kill Jim Wolf. I have a hard time labeling Jim as innocent in all this. There would have been no court case, no angry Robert Clark, no gun in a courtroom, no juror walking in front of a bullet if it wasn't for that asshole trying to enrich himself at someone else's expense."

The look on Tim's face said now they were getting somewhere. "Is your frustration with the fact that Jim Wolf didn't get the comeuppance you feel like he deserved?"

"Are you asking me if I feel like he's the one who should have been shot and killed? No. I don't feel that way. What I feel is that it's all his fault that two people died that day. I feel like he forced my hand almost more than Robert did."

"Jim didn't open fire in a courtroom full of people."

"But Jim's the one who gathered everyone there. It's almost like he's the one who loaded the gun and gave it to Robert. Robert just pulled the trigger."

Tim suggested they take a break for a few minutes. He got Packard a bottle of water from a small fridge hidden in the wall of cabinets behind his desk. Packard stood at the window and watched a gray squirrel chase a white albino squirrel away from the trampled, dirty snow beneath the bird feeders in the backyard.

"Is Thielen feeling better today?" he asked Tim.

"She is. She's at her happy place this morning."

"The gym," Packard said.

They sat and continued. Packard briefly told Tim about the dreams he'd been having where he kept shooting the wrong person, where there were calls over his radio about an active shooter and he was the shooter. He admitted his emotions were out of whack from what they usually were.

"I'm angry at Jim Wolf. I'm sad and sorry for Robert Clark. I feel self-pity and disgust for myself. You know at the Labor Day carnival when people win those giant life-sized teddy bears? I feel like I'm hauling one of those around. I can't set it down, there's no room for it in the house. Every time I turn around, I'm tripping over it."

"You've had a traumatic experience. Multiple traumatic experiences. Trauma can rewire your thinking."

"Now you're sounding like my mom," Packard said.

Tim shrugged unapologetically. "I know you're used to working through things on your own. That's who you are. You distract yourself with work until you're convinced you've left things in the past. But what if you haven't? What if there's a cumulative effect from Robert, from Emmett, from the election." He paused. "From Marcus even."

Packard felt like he'd been sucker punched. They were supposed to be talking about the courthouse shooting and now Tim was bringing up Marcus. He'd told Tim and Thielen about Marcus, about their relationship, about Marcus being killed in the line of duty. It wasn't a secret. He just wasn't prepared for Marcus to come up as a topic of conversation in this room.

"I know you can't bring up things we talk about here when we're hanging out as friends. Feels like the reverse should be true as well," Packard said.

"We don't have to talk about Marcus. I apologize for springing his name on you. All I want you to do is think about whether there's a connection to all of this. I want you to ask yourself, have you dealt with these experiences or is the teddy bear getting bigger and heavier and harder to lug around?"

Packard was tired of sitting. He got up and stood by the window. "What's making all of this worse is being on leave."

Behind him, Tim said, "Is it making it worse or is it creating an opportunity for you to sit alone with the bear?"

"I wish I'd never mentioned the goddamn bear," Packard said.

"Forget the bear," Tim said. "Tell me what you've been doing while you've been on leave."

Packard stood behind his chair and leaned on the back. "My mom visited for a few days. We followed up on some leads related to my brother's case and the letter I got from Stan. Things petered out there. We're waiting on warmer weather to start searching for Nick's remains."

"Jill said you're looking into the death of a woman who lived in your family home."

"Yeah."

"So even while on leave from your job, you're finding a way to fill your time with work."

Packard shrugged. "What else am I supposed to do?"

Tim raised his eyebrows.

Packard dropped his head like he'd been given a terrible diagnosis. "You're saying I need to get a life."

"I'm saying—again—it's all connected. The constant work, the trauma, the unresolved issues. They go hand in hand. Listen, I've already heard enough to know you can go back to work. Your mental state does not make you a threat to the public. I'm worried about the cost to you. What are you denying yourself by staying in a constant state of motion, by always moving forward, not slowing down, not looking back?"

Packard didn't know if his resistance was fading or if he was ready to say whatever needed to be said to get out of there. He sat again with his elbows on the chair arms, his hands open. "What do you suggest?"

"Slow down. Take some time off. Put yourself out there and try to meet new people."

"Last time I put myself out there, I lost by 1,200 votes," Packard grumbled.

"Put yourself out there in a way that has nothing to do with work. Get a hobby. Go on a date."

"Now you're really starting to sound like my mom," Packard said.

"Your mom sounds like she knows what she's talking about."

"My mom also mimed giving a blow job in front of me and said I should be getting fantastically laid at my age."

"She's not wrong," Tim said.

CHAPTER NINETEEN

PACKARD'S HEAD WAS BUZZING by the time he left his appointment with Tim. He didn't necessarily disagree with anything his friend had said; he just didn't know what to do about it. Intellectually, he knew he had no choice in shooting Robert Clark. But in his heart? His gut? His spleen? He felt like he was full of sand. Heavy and unsteady.

Tim had warned him that news or the lack of news about his brother could compound the stress he was already under. "Have you thought about what it will mean to find out the truth of what happened to Nick? All this time the story has been that he drowned in the lake. What if the truth is much worse than that? Or what if this wall you've hit with the investigation refuses to topple? Are you ready for some answers but not all? Are you ready to possibly never know what really happened?"

A lot of questions, a lot of potential outcomes. It was impossible to prepare for every eventuality. He said as much to Tim.

"You need other coping mechanisms for things like this. Other outlets besides work," Tim said. He offered to continue meeting and helping Packard develop healthy habits and reactions to the stress in his life. "Your benefits will pay for all of this. You should take advantage of them."

Packard agreed to meet again in a month, and then, because he didn't know what else to do, he went back to work.

He found himself at Tess's little yellow house again. The first time through with Reynolds he was trying to get a sense of who she was by the things she left behind. This time he was looking for clues about where she'd gone and what sent her packing.

It felt colder in the house than it did outside. The kitchen faucet sputtered air, and pipes rattled under the sink when he tried opening the tap. The lights still worked but there was no heat, no water. He took out his phone and took a photo of all the things Tess had stuck to the refrigerator with round black magnets. Christmas cards and Polaroids and coupons and store receipts. There were business cards in a magnetic clip that he laid out in two columns on the countertop to photograph, each one a potential lead if they needed to start calling anyone and everyone who'd ever been in contact with Tess. He found a photo of Tess and Brenda together in winter hats and another one of them looking red-faced in tank tops on a pontoon. Curious that the photos were still up if the breakup was as bad as Brenda made it out to be.

Before entering the dining room, he spotted a key caddy hanging on the wall above a jack where a landline would have plugged in. Dangling on tiny hooks were sets of keys, all clearly labeled. He found the three sets to Louise's properties and put them in his pocket.

He was more intrigued by the pile of phone books in the dining room. What need would someone have for thirty-year-old white pages from cities far from Minnesota? He opened a phone book from St. Louis that was sitting near where the laptop would have been. He fanned the pages and was surprised to find dozens, maybe hundreds of names highlighted in pink throughout the entire book. He looked in another phone book and found the same thing. There were too many highlighted names for there to be a connection among them. If the numbers weren't thirty years old, he would have thought he was looking at a cold-call sales list.

What would Tess do with all these names?

There was a laser printer next to the empty docking station. Packard found the switch and powered it on. The draw on the house's electrical system made the lights dim for a second. The printer had a small LED window and buttons that helped him navigate through a limited menu of options. Packard found an option for "Reprint Last Job" and pressed Select. The lights dimmed again as the printer sucked paper from its tray and the internal parts groaned from the effort. The pages, three of them, came out facedown and then the printer went silent.

The first page only had ink on the bottom half of the page. Probably a limitation of what the printer could store in its memory. It was a table with four columns. The first had names, the second a street address, the third a five-digit number that looked like a zip code, and finally a column with numbers in the low single or double digits. The next two pages had more of the same. Roughly forty names to a page. The columns had no headers on any of the pages. At the bottom was a footer that identified the page numbers in an X of Y pages format. These were pages 18, 19, and 20 of 20 pages.

Packard opened the phone book again and looked up the names appearing on the printed pages and found every one he checked. The addresses in the phone book didn't match those in the table and the zip codes were for the surrounding area, not St. Louis.

He tried to think of how these names matched with unrelated addresses had anything to do with her job for Louise. It might have had something to do with her job with the landscaping company. But Mike said she worked outside on a crew, not in billing or sales. It could be this was something else, completely unrelated to either job. Might not have anything to do with why she left town. *What if all Tess needed was a fresh start, and a dead woman's bank account was too hard to ignore? What if he was chasing shadows and none of this was connected?*

He didn't believe that. Couldn't believe it. His session with Tim might have had him questioning things about himself, but this he knew to be true. There was a trail here. He sensed it as sure as a bloodhound could follow a scent. A wealthy woman. A death under mysterious circumstances. An empty bank account. A missing employee.

These were not coincidences.

He needed to find Tess.

Behind the printer and the phone books was a tray piled with opened mail. Utility bills, an invoice from a plumber, a statement of estimated property taxes. Packard remembered the large monthly electric bill and pulled out the statement from the electric co-op. All three of Louise's commercial properties were on the same bill. Each one had account fees and special taxes. Two of the addresses showed 000 for the monthly kilowatt usage. The storefront in Cedar Creek township had used 2,200 kilowatts for the month.

What was using all that electricity when the building was empty?

He did a cursory search of the rest of the house, looking in drawers and cupboards. He checked closet floors and back walls for hidden compartments. Nothing else grabbed his interest. He was looking at the home and possessions of a woman who lived alone, worked hard for what she had, and kept a tidy house. There was nothing to suggest that she might disappear with someone else's money or where she might have gone.

When he was done, Packard locked up and followed the shoveled sidewalks over to Mike Turner's house next door. Mike hollered for him to come in when he rang the bell.

"Saw you coming up the sidewalk," Mike said from his seat in the recliner in front of the television. The cat in his lap jumped down and disappeared. "Where's your buddy?"

"It's Saturday so Reynolds isn't working. Normal people like days off now and then for some reason."

"I've been on permanent vacation for five years now. It's not all it's cracked up to be. Spending your days and nights in front of the TV can make you feel like the last man on earth."

Packard had the sudden realization that Mike's life could be his own. He'd been alone watching TV with an animal in his lap, same as Mike, before Lisa Washington invited him over to Louise's house one last time. If the county attorney got the BCA report and decided to charge him, he could be on leave indefinitely. Then what?

"What's your mobility like?"

"I get around okay. I can't drive because I sometimes have seizures. Mostly it's hard to find the motivation in winter. Lost a lot of work friends after the accident. My ex took the rest."

"I know a good psychologist if you need someone to talk to. He told me I need to put myself out there. Meet people and do something besides work."

"What do you like to do outside work?"

"Work out, swim, listen to music, walk my dog. Solitary stuff. That's part of my problem. I fished a lot with my grandpa when I was a kid. Been meaning to get back into that since moving back here."

"I got a boat. We could go fishing sometime."

Packard was inclined to say sure and not mean it. What if he said yes with sincerity? Maybe this was how you made new friends as an adult. Randomly and awkwardly by taking a chance on someone. It was possible they could help themselves by helping each other. "Let's do it. It'll be fishing opener before long. I'll call and remind you."

"Cool," Mike said. "To be clear. I'm not gay. In case you were wondering."

"Hadn't even crossed my mind."

"Okay then. We're just two guys who enjoy fishing."

Packard took out his notebook and pretended to write. "Mike…just fishing. No gay stuff," he said.

"You're a smart-ass, too. I think we'll get along fine."

Packard gave Mike the keys to Tess's house and then showed him the pages from her printer. "This mean anything to you?" he asked.

Mike put on a pair of reading glasses and sat on the edge of his chair. His lips moved as he read through some of the names. "Not a thing," he said, shaking his head and handing back the pages. "I don't know any of those people."

"She's got a stack of phone books over there from different cities. Some of them thirty years old. That's where the names come from."

"That doesn't make any sense."

"Not yet it doesn't. I noticed you still have the utilities on over there. Any reason for not shutting them off?" Packard asked.

"I got everything unplugged, the pipes drained, the heat off. The electric company charges to completely disconnect service. They charge you again to reconnect it. It's easier to leave it be."

"Something in one of the empty commercial buildings that Tess managed for Louise is using a lot of electricity."

"Security system? Sump pump?" Mike suggested.

"No, it's drawing more power than that."

Mike took off his glasses and put them on top of his head. "You know where my mind goes when I hear unusually high electric usage? Fans, air filters, grow lights, watering system...."

"A weed house," Packard said.

Mike shrugged. "Maybe."

"How do you know about weed houses?"

"Let's say I used to know a guy."

Packard smiled. "Seems unlikely to have something like that, even in a downtown as small and dried up as Cedar Creek's. Every grow house I've been in stunk bad."

The cat jumped back in Mike's lap. He scratched it under its chin. "Maybe someone with the sheriff's department should go there and check it out."

"That's a good idea. You want a job?"

"Shit no. I've seen enough episodes of *The First 48* and *Forensic Files* to know I don't want nothing to do with criminals and murderers. You take care of 'em. Call me when you want to go fishing."

"Deal."

It started snowing as Packard made the drive to Cedar Creek, fat wet splats that couldn't decide if they were rain or snowflakes. The wiper blades moved slush to the bottom of the windshield. He cranked the defrost and wondered if Mike was right about the weed grow. A lot of those old buildings downtown had unfinished basements dug out where the operation could be kept out of sight. Tess worked for a landscaping company, and growing pot was definitely a job where horticultural skills would come to bear. An industrial air scrubber could deal with the smell. Still seemed unlikely. Growing weed illegally on a commercial scale didn't make sense when a dealer could make ten times the money moving tiny little grains of fentanyl or oxycodone pills.

One day the whole world would be as quiet and abandoned as the tiny township of Cedar Creek. Packard's vehicle was the only one in sight. He parked in front of Janet's Café and grabbed a flashlight from his glove compartment. The building next door was Nancy's Hair Hut and on the other side was retail space with a large For Sale sign in the window. Louise was lucky she didn't own the whole empty block.

Packard used Tess's keys to unlock the door to the café. Every small town in Minnesota and Wisconsin has a place like Janet's Café. Old wood paneling halfway up yellowing white walls. A drop ceiling with acoustic tiles laced in spiderwebs and dust. A long bar with vinyl padding along the edge. Drink coolers and a cash register. Interior design was courtesy of the Anheuser-Busch company in the form of calendars and posters and decorated mirrors and neon signs all advertising Bud Light. If the place had any charm at all when it was open, it must have come from Janet or her food.

The electricity definitely wasn't being used to heat the building. It was ice cold inside. Packard peeked behind the bar and then pushed through a swinging door into a tight, cramped kitchen. The appliances and surfaces were stainless steel and greasy and old. The vent hood over the grill was black inside. Against the back wall was the source of the electricity usage—a walk-in freezer with a struggling compressor. Packard reached for the long handle, then stopped when his eye caught a telltale spray pattern on the wall. It was the same color as old grease but this wasn't grease.

Blood.

Now that he'd seen it, he saw it everywhere. Spots on the ceiling. More on the wall next to an irregular-shaped hole in the drywall that might have been made by a tumbling bullet. More blood on the floor that had been hastily swiped at. There was a paper towel holder on the wall with a miserly amount of towels still left on the roll. Mindful of fingerprints, Packard grabbed a towel and pulled the freezer's handle. The latch clunked as it released and the door, thick as a bank vault, swung open.

It was pitch-dark in the six-by-six interior. Packard had to duck to step inside. The shelves were empty but it still smelled like frozen meat and stale air. He thumbed on his flashlight already knowing what he was about to find.

The dead woman was sitting upright in the far corner. There was a hole where most of her face had been. She was slumped to the side, her one remaining eye open and hard as a marble.

CHAPTER TWENTY

WHEN PACKARD FIRST PULLED into Cedar Creek, it was as empty as an abandoned mining town. Hours later, it was swarmed with sheriff's vehicles and an ambulance parked on Main Street and people who had driven into town and parked on the side of the road and stood in small groups in their winter coats, watching and wondering what was going on.

After calling dispatch, Packard had called Thielen and told her what he found. "You want in on this or you want me to call Reynolds?"

"Reynolds, please," she said. She sounded tired.

"I'm worried about you, Thielen. What's going on? You don't sound good."

"I'm fine. I did legs at the gym. Tim made us lunch. It's cold out and I'm under a blanket. I want to look at a dead body inside a walk-in freezer like I want to be punched in the throat."

Packard kept everyone out of the restaurant's kitchen until the crime-scene team arrived and took over. He'd reluctantly shut the freezer door again, closing the dead woman in the dark while quietly wishing he had a blanket for her, some kind of comfort.

Reynolds's first question after arriving was, "Is it the lesbian?"

Packard gave him a look. "I don't know if she's a lesbian or just bi-curious. I forgot to ask."

"I meant is she what's-her-name. Tess."

It wasn't Tess. This woman was older with long, dark hair. She had on a short-sleeved blouse stained with blood. Shoes with no socks. No coat. She hadn't come here and gotten shot in the wintertime dressed like that. There was a rime of ice built up along her hairline and around the edges of the hole in her face. She'd been in the freezer for a long time. Months.

Packard sent a deputy to find out the contact info for whoever had been running Janet's Café and the Hair Hut next door. He put another deputy on finding out who the township supervisors were, to ask them about the state of Cedar Creek's commercial district. He also wanted to know if there had been any abandoned cars towed from downtown or anywhere else nearby recently.

With the okay from the crime-scene techs, Packard put on shoe covers and gloves and entered the freezer. The compressor was still running. He could see his breath inside the tiny room.

"I don't suppose you found a driver's license or a phone in her pockets."

"Nope. No personal effects. We've photographed everything in here. We still need to see if we can get a slug out of the hole in the wall," said one of the techs. "We'll turn off the freezer while we do that. Right now she's frozen to the wall behind her. Her right hand also has blood on it and is stuck to the floor."

Packard looked at her other hand, clenched in her lap.

"We're not going to get fingerprints today, are we?"

"No. We'll ship her to Saint Paul for the autopsy. They'll thaw her out and get you a clean set. Give 'em a couple days."

Afterward, Reynolds was pacing the restaurant while Packard stood with his elbows leaning on the bar. There were no tables or chairs, no place to sit. Packard felt a dark mood settling over him. Under different circumstances, he would have loved a place like this where you could get a beer and a fried wall-eye basket and trade stories with the old woman behind the bar. There was no ideal place to get shot in the back of the head, but a greasy kitchen in a failed restaurant in an abandoned town seemed a particularly hopeless place to meet that fate. He imagined the team lifting her out of there and onto a gurney, frozen in that bent, slumped position. Would she thaw on the drive to the coroner's office? Would she finally be able to relax and lie flat?

Shepard had been notified but hadn't felt it necessary to make the trip to the crime scene. It was for the best. Packard would have wanted to grab him by the shirt collar and force his head down as he pushed him in the freezer for a closer look. *Do you still think Louise Larsen's death was an accident? There's something going on here. This is all connected.*

"If that's not Tess, do we like Tess for pulling the trigger?" Reynolds asked.

Packard dropped his head and thought of the woman who lived in the house he had searched. The landlord who missed her. The rescue dog she adopted. All the mugging with friends in the photos he'd seen of her. She didn't seem like the type to shoot another woman in the head and drag her into a freezer. Emptying Louise's bank account was a far different crime than murder. Maybe the space between them wasn't as far apart as he thought.

"Hard to say," Packard said.

Reynolds looked like he was doing math in his head. "Here's what I think. Louise confronted Tess about something. Maybe she'd been taking advantage of her access to Louise's account all this time. Louise was going to fire her, so Tess killed her in June. And this woman, whoever she is, found out about it or witnessed it, maybe tried to blackmail Tess so Tess had to kill her, too. Tess knew she was eventually going to get caught so she emptied the bank account while she still had access. Then she took off with all of Louise's money and is living under a new identity somewhere. Mexico probably."

"Now you're just making shit up," Packard said.

CHAPTER TWENTY-ONE

PACKARD FORCED HIMSELF TO take the next day off. It was Sunday and probably his last chance for a break, and it gave the coroner time to come back with usable prints that might help identify the woman in the freezer. Assuming Shepard didn't pull him off after the meeting with the BCA, it would be nonstop from here out.

He'd been neglecting the snow removal around his house so he spent a good part of the afternoon shoveling the deck and the sidewalks and the driveway. In the evening, trying to heed Tim's advice to put himself out there, he drove to the Hopstop under the pretense of needing a beer and something to eat, but really hoping to run into Kyle.

Kyle wasn't working.

Packard ordered his pizza to go and drank a beer and stared at his phone while he waited, then went home feeling sheepish and stupid.

On Monday morning, he sat with Shepard in a conference room that had a screen on the wall and a camera beneath it that recorded the two of them as they videoconferenced with the BCA agent in charge of the investigation. Packard scrolled through a PDF on his laptop as the agent described the 687-page report that started with the written request for an investigation from Shepard. It included statements from Deputy Blanchard and Deputy Baker and transcripts of Packard's interviews with the agent. There were pages and pages of receipts for evidence collected and turned over to the investigators. Measurements. Fingerprints taken from guns. Shell casings. Interviews with witnesses. Copies of internal policies and procedures. Not in the paper report but part of the overall file were photos from the scene and video from Deputy Blanchard's body cam and all the nearby security cameras.

The agent talked about how the investigation was conducted, who was involved, where to find certain information. Autopsy reports for Robert Clark and Mark Quinto, the juror who was killed, had been collected but were redacted from the BCA report as they weren't part of the public record.

Out of the corner of his eye, Packard watched Shepard across the table, fidgeting and looking at his phone. Packard jumped to the end of the report, looking for a summary statement or concluding thoughts. There was nothing.

"Long story short," Shepard said, interrupting the agent. "Do we have to worry about charges or not?"

"The BCA doesn't make recommendations. We lead the investigation and present all the evidence collected to the county attorney to make the charging decision."

"You ever been a cop?" Shepard asked the man on the screen.

"Yes, ten years in Mankato before I joined the BCA."

"Any reasonable doubt in your mind that Packard was justified in his use of force?"

The agent looked down, shook his head. "This call is being recorded. I can't go on the record with any such statement."

Packard felt like he'd been shot full of Novocain. Someone could have pulled all his teeth as he sat there with his mouth slightly open, and he wouldn't have noticed. Six hundred eighty-seven pages about his involvement in the homicide of Robert Clark and still no conclusion. He couldn't help but think of the hundreds of pages of evidence and testimony in Nick's file and how wrong everyone had been all this time about what had actually happened. Until Phil Ayers made his final decision on charges, the matter wasn't closed.

The agent asked Packard if he had any questions. Shepard looked at Packard like he would prefer this call not go on any longer. "I'm sure I'll have questions after I read the report," Packard said. "I'm good for now."

The agent was still letting them know they could reach out anytime when Shepard jabbed a button on the console in the center of the table and ended the call. "Blah blah blah. Thanks for nothing, BCA," he said.

A 687-page report wasn't exactly nothing, but Packard wasn't in the mood to spar with Shepard.

"You really going to read all that?" Shepard asked.

Packard closed his laptop. "I'm sure I'll read most of it eventually."

"Not me. I don't need the report to know there's not going to be any charges. Jim Wolf could go to Ayers and call you a black-eyed murderous sonofabitch and it wouldn't make a damn bit of difference. The circumstances totally met the requirements of the 609 statute."

It wasn't like Shepard to cite chapter and verse. Packard was modestly impressed. It was also nice to feel like he had Shepard's support for once. "We'll have to wait and see if Ayers agrees."

"Have you done your psych eval?" Shepard asked.

"I started it. He wants to do another session," Packard said. He wanted leverage to control his return to work, based on how the next part of the conversation went.

"But you'll be ready to return to work soon," Shepard said.

"What do you mean by return to work?"

"Back to the courthouse," Shepard said.

"Are you sure that's the best place for me considering everything that's happened? How do you think people are going to feel seeing the guy who killed someone right in that spot when they come to court?"

"You didn't do anything wrong. You were a hero."

Packard remembered the last time he was in Shepard's office when Wolf had called him a hero. He hadn't meant it as a compliment. Hearing Shepard use the same word felt almost as insincere. Shepard was trying to win an argument, not bestow praise.

"You know as well as I do that no matter what Ayers decides, there are going to be people who will look sideways at me and at the whole sheriff's office for the death of Robert Clark. That court security position is high visibility, high contact with the public, and it shouldn't be me right after using deadly force."

Shepard didn't say anything. He looked sullen.

"What about the case I'm working? We've got two dead people, an empty bank account, a missing person of interest. I can't follow up on this and work court security full-time."

"You make it sound like I'm asking too much of you," Shepard said. "This 'case' of yours," he said, making air quotes, "has been conjured out of thin air by you while you were supposed to be on administrative leave. Now you want me to make accommodations for something you weren't supposed to be doing in the first place."

"With all due respect, I didn't conjure the body in the freezer out of thin air. I followed the evidence. Finding out what happened to her and Louise is what we do. It's our responsibility."

"Not yours."

Packard didn't know what else to say. "Make it my responsibility. Put me back on investigations. Have you talked to Reynolds? He prefers patrol. Put me where I belong, put Reynolds on patrol where he wants to be, and move someone who's tired of the dog shift to court security. Everyone gets what they want."

"What about what I want?" Shepard asked.

"What do you want?"

"A little respect would be nice."

Packard didn't move. He made his face a stone to prevent even a twitch or the tiniest lift of an eyebrow. He chose his words carefully. "I speak from experience when I say that respect doesn't automatically come with the job title. No one was falling over themselves to show me respect when Stan made me acting sheriff. Were they?"

He waited for a response. Shepard shifted his gaze elsewhere.

"The respect comes when people see you looking out for their best interests. It really is that easy."

Shepard looked like he was hoping for something even easier. He turned in his chair to look out the window. "I need to think about where you're going to land," he said. "You can keep working your case until the official word about charges comes from Ayers's office. We'll talk again then."

There was a knock on the conference room door. Deputy Baker poked his head in. "The coroner's office got Saint Paul PD to submit the prints from the Jane Doe you found in frozen foods."

Fingerprints were sent to the FBI's integrated automated fingerprint identification system where machine learning was used to search millions of records for a match. Results could take as little as twenty minutes.

"And?" Packard asked.

"No match," Baker said.

"Damn it."

CHAPTER TWENTY-TWO

PACKARD SAT IN HIS truck parked on the street in front of the sheriff's office and tried to decide what to do next. Fingerprints would have been nice. They might get a DNA match but that would take weeks. He could start combing through missing person's reports looking for a middle-aged white female, but who knew where she came from? The Twin Cities? Fargo? Wisconsin? Iowa? With most of her face replaced by an exit wound from the bullet she took, it was going to be hard to make a physical match.

Tossed into the passenger seat was the John Sandford library book he had picked up at Louise's house and had been meaning to return for weeks. The library was two blocks up the street. That was something he could do. He grabbed the book, got out of the truck, and walked. The wind was cold on his neck.

Ruth Adams was the head librarian. She was in her seventies with short gray hair that turned in a thousand different directions from cowlicks. She lived on the same lake as Emmett Burr and had no idea of the horrors that had taken place at her neighbor's house.

"Deputy Packard," she said, smiling when she saw him. "Looking for a book to read?"

"Nope, returning this one. Louise Larsen had it checked out. Saw it in her house and thought you might like it back."

"Oh, Louise," Ruth said. "She loved mysteries and thrillers. John Sandford was one of her favorites."

She flipped through the book, removed the business card used as a book mark and slid it toward Packard. "They're tearing down Emmett's house and bulldozing the lot next month," she said.

Packard stared at the card in front of him. The name said DEBORAH SALVO, STATE OF MINNESOTA—FINANCE. Something about it seemed familiar. He'd seen it in the book a couple of times but he'd seen something similar somewhere else. He closed his eyes.

"Hope they're going to let it go back to nature. Seems like the best thing for a place tainted with so much evil. Let the sun and the trees take it over."

The refrigerator.

"One second, Ruth." He pulled out his phone and brought up the photos he'd taken at Tess's house. She had business cards pinched in a clip on the freezer that he'd spread out and photographed. Before laying them out, he'd photographed the freezer. The top card in the clip said DEBORAH SALVO, STATE OF MINNESOTA—FINANCE.

"Ruth, you might have cracked this case for me."

"Crime-solving librarians are not unheard of," she said. "We have several cozy series with characters like that."

"What about your book? I remember you were working on it last time I saw you at the Sweet Pea."

"That's a memoir. In that one I'm committing the crimes, not solving them."

Packard pocketed Deborah's business card. "One of these days you'll have to tell me your secrets, Ruth."

"If it looks like I might get caught, I'll come to you with my confession," she said without smiling.

He couldn't tell if Ruth was joking or not, and he didn't have time to find out. He thanked her, pushed through the doors, and sprinted back to the office.

"Deborah Salvo," Deputy Baker said, handing Packard the first page from a stack of paper he was holding. "Lives in Minneapolis. Works for the State of Minnesota. And"—he handed Packard the rest of the pages—"Minneapolis PD has a missing person's file on her."

Packard was looking at a color photo of a stunned Deborah from her driver's license. This was definitely the dead woman from the freezer. She was fifty-eight years old. From his time on the MPD, he knew her address was near the airport where planes came in so low you could see faces in the windows.

There were more photos of Deborah collected as part of the investigation. Deborah at a restaurant with coworkers, Deborah sitting on a park bench in sunglasses and a wide hat, Deborah accepting an award while awkwardly trying to shake a man's hand across her body.

Packard scanned the first few pages and stopped when he suddenly came to a name he recognized. "I know the officer who wrote this," he said. The name made him feel like his whole time in Sandy Lake had ceased to exist. He was still a Minneapolis cop and this was someone he used to call a friend.

Now a bridge burned, depending on how long hard feelings lasted.

Packard thanked Baker for his help and grabbed his coat from the back of his chair. He stopped at Kelly's desk on his way out. She had daisies painted on her nails like she was trying to manifest spring. Someone had brought in doughnuts and Kelly was dismembering one with pink icing and sprinkles. "Have you seen Thielen today?" he asked.

"She was here while you were in the conference room this morning and then she left with Reynolds. She might have been dropping him off at preschool."

"Nice," Packard said. Teasing Reynolds for his baby face was a game no one got tired of. "How did she look?"

"What do you mean, how did she look?" Kelly bit into her doughnut like a warning.

"She's been sick a lot lately. Has she said anything to you?"

"She did. She said if you asked about her I should tell you to mind your own business."

"Did she really say that or are you messing with me?"

"Doesn't matter. It's good advice regardless." Her phone rang. Kelly put on her headset and turned toward her computer.

Packard reached over her desk and snatched the last bite of her doughnut. "If anyone's looking for me, tell 'em I'm in Minneapolis."

"No one's looking for you," Kelly said. "You're supposed to be on leave."

He drove his county vehicle. This was no longer about him looking into Louise's death as a lark in his free time. He had a real, live dead body on his hands now. This was a murder investigation.

Now that he was headed out of town and wasn't stymied by the identity of the dead woman in the freezer, he had a clearer sense of everything he should have been doing back home. Confirm with Mike Turner the last time he saw Tess Reid. Compare that date with the date Deborah Salvo was reported missing. Go back to Brenda and the rest of the women at the cabin and press them for details about Tess now that she was a murder suspect. Thinking about where he was going, he remembered he wanted to talk to Andrea Hopkins, the state representative who was spending all her time in Saint Paul. Lucky for Packard, Saint Paul was right across the river from Minneapolis. They didn't call them the Twin Cities for nothing.

He asked Siri to find the number for Minnesota Representative Andrea Hopkins and then had her call it. A man answered.

"Representative Hopkins's office. Sean speaking."

Packard introduced himself and where he was from and explained what he wanted.

"I'm going to need some verification that this is all true, if you don't mind."

Packard gave Sean the nonemergency number to the sheriff's office and told him to ask for Kelly. When Sean called back, he said, "Representative Hopkins doesn't have any time on her calendar this whole week. I can schedule you for next week."

"Sean, I'm in town today. Maybe tomorrow. Now I can come by and corner her and we can have a conversation in front of whoever happens to be present, or you can reschedule someone who's not investigating a murder and give me thirty minutes of the representative's time. Either way, we're going to have a chat while I'm here."

Sean was silent while he clicked and typed. "Twelve thirty tomorrow. Twenty-five minutes. She has to be on the other side of the capitol by 1:00 p.m."

"Thank you, Sean. See you then."

———

There was less snow the closer he got to Minneapolis. A few degrees change in the average temperature made a world of difference. The city snow was ugly, trampled and dirty and frozen into treacherous shapes. Traffic hissed on wet streets.

At the precinct building he showed his badge and asked for Detective Easton. "He's out," was the response that came back.

"Can you get him on the phone or the radio and tell him Ben Packard wants to talk to him about his missing person's case. Deborah Salvo."

He waited in the reception area until the woman at the desk said, "He said he's hungry and that you'd know where to meet him."

"I do know. Tell him I'm on my way."

———————

Before settling into a quasi-relationship with Marcus, Packard and Detective Garrett Easton had cruised each other at the gym and eventually hooked up. Thinking about it again, Packard had to laugh at how stereotypically gay he could sometimes be. Hooking up with a guy from the gym? So gay. But come on. Easton had served in the marines before joining law enforcement. At the gym, he wore thin gray shorts and a sleeveless black SECURITY T-shirt from his moonlighting job working events at First Avenue and Target Center. They had fun until the third or fourth time—when Easton confessed to being married. He had a wife.

"That's a deal-breaker," Packard said. "I can't have sex with someone else's spouse behind their back. That's not me."

They transitioned to being friends after that. They saw each other at the gym and played pool at the bowling alley by Easton's house. Over beers Easton would tell him about his other tricks. Packard talked about seeing someone but didn't mention Marcus by name for a long time. Packard felt like he should have encouraged Easton to be honest with his wife about who he was, but who was he to give advice? He and Marcus were no less in the closet.

Packard spotted Easton through the window of the Lunds & Byerlys in Edina loading up a plate at the hot food buffet. This was where they came a lot after working out, to fill up on greens and protein. Easton was wearing a black zippered jacket and black pants. He hadn't slacked off at the gym since the last time they saw each other.

"Look at that hair," Packard said from the other side of the salad bar. It was an inch longer than the buzz cut Easton used to sport. He actually had a part. "Are you undercover as a dirty hippie?"

Easton gave him a less-than-friendly look. "You're an asshole," he said.

"What did I do?"

"You know what you did."

Yeah, Packard knew.

Not many people reached out to Packard after Marcus was killed. They had mutual friends, mostly other cops, almost none of whom knew about their relationship. There were rumors about them in some quarters, but people who gossip aren't the ones who show up when needed.

Packard ignored everyone who tried to reach him. He didn't have the words to express how he was feeling. He didn't want anyone to try to make him feel better, and he sure as hell had nothing to offer someone needing a shoulder to cry on. At the funeral he hid among a sea of matching uniforms. Afterward, all he wanted was to be left alone in the 2000-degree heat of his shame and misery until it burned away all his thoughts and feelings.

Easton had been persistent. Calls, voicemails, texts. *I'm worried about you. I'm here if you need anything. Let me know you're okay.* Packard never responded. He walked away from their friendship, and many others, not even reaching out before he moved for the deputy job in Sandy Lake.

They sat across from each other in a booth, compostable plates piled with chicken and carnitas and sesame kale salad.

"I found Deborah Salvo," Packard said. "She's dead."

Easton put a chicken wing flat in his mouth and pulled it back out clean. "That's where you want to start? I don't give a fuck about Deborah Salvo."

"That's not true."

Easton dropped the bones on his plate. "You're right, it's not true. But I'm more interested in why you fucking ghosted me. I thought we were friends."

"We were friends. We were good friends and then I acted like a shit friend."

"All I wanted was to know that you were all right."

Packard knew that the less he said here, the better. There was no excuse for his selfishness, nothing he wanted to say to Easton to try to make him see things from his perspective.

"I'm sorry. I was fucked up after Marcus died. I couldn't see people. I couldn't talk about it. It felt like being thrown around in a terrible car wreck, and all I wanted to do was crawl away from it. I quit my job and moved three hours north hoping I could leave it all behind."

"Did it work?"

"No."

"Of course not. I could have told you that if you woulda answered the goddamn phone."

"I know."

They ate. They stared at each other across the table, each both present and lost in his own thoughts. It felt like a lifetime since they'd last seen each other. Easton tried to keep scowling but eventually he couldn't help but smile. "It's good to see your face again. Asshole."

"Likewise, Detective."

CHAPTER TWENTY-THREE

AFTER LUNCH THEY SAT in Packard's vehicle and Easton flipped through the pages from the file on Deborah Salvo while Packard told him about Louise Larsen's death, about Tess Reid and the missing money, about the utility bills that had him take a closer look at Janet's Café where he found Deborah in the freezer, and about finding her business cards in Louise's library book and on Tess's fridge.

According to Easton's investigation, Deborah Salvo met several other women at an Airbnb for a knitting retreat that started the Friday of Memorial Day weekend. They said Deborah checked out on Sunday. She never made it home. Never came back to work.

"Deborah was reported missing by her boss," Easton said, reading through the pages he had written himself. "They waited almost ten days to report her missing. Her boss didn't engage directly with her very often, and I got the sense her direct reports were afraid of her and maybe a little glad that she was inexplicably out of the office. As far as family, she's got an older sister in Florida. They're not close. Deborah's not married. No kids. She worked in local government for almost thirty years."

"Cell phone records?"

"Nothing as far as calls out of the ordinary until the Sunday before Memorial Day. She got a call from an untraceable number, which lasted less than one minute. Prepaid phone, bought with cash. No video from the location where it was purchased. We tracked Deborah's phone via cell tower pings to North Dakota, crossing into Manitoba, then eventually we lost it. Canadian border authorities had no record of Deborah Salvo entering the country."

"Her phone did but she didn't," Packard said. "Did you send anyone up north to look for her?" The Airbnb was about sixty miles from Sandy Lake, in the next county over.

"There was nowhere to look. The trail went cold at the Airbnb. Nothing in her personal email, nothing in her phone records to give us a lead. Also, in case the news hasn't reached you guys in Buttfuck, Minnesota, the MPD is a little short-staffed since George Floyd."

Packard was in Sandy Lake when George Floyd was murdered by a Minneapolis police officer kneeling on his neck. The unrest that followed resulted in the burning of Minneapolis's Third Precinct building and scores of businesses across Minneapolis and Saint Paul, many in areas already struggling with crime, poverty, drugs, and homelessness. Cops left the profession in droves in the wake of the unrest, many claiming PTSD. The whole metro area was struggling with a police shortage and still trying to decide what it wanted from its police.

Part of the agony Packard felt over shooting Robert Clark came from contributing to the narrative that had grown louder since George Floyd that police were militarized, thoughtless killers. Yes, there were police like that. They exposed themselves all too frequently. But there were way more good cops who saw the job as one of service and safety and community building. Packard wanted to be part of the solution that addressed the profession's biases, not the guy standing behind the smoking gun.

Packard started the vehicle. "Let's go by her office again and see if we can shake anything else loose. Knowing Deborah was murdered might get someone to talk."

Easton slid out on his side. "The building is on the other side of the river from downtown. Follow me."

He led them across Edina onto I-35 and off again in a semi-industrial area of northeast Minneapolis where they parked in the narrow lot fronting a three-story brick building that stretched an entire block long. A rider on a fat-tire bicycle wearing goggles and a balaclava buzzed by on the bike path. Inside the front door was a lobby with a directory of where to find what businesses, an elevator, and a door to a stairwell. Packard followed Easton through another door that opened into a wide room filled with cubicles. The low din of ringing phones and dozens of conversations mixed with the smell of wet carpet and hundred-degree bodies dressed in winter clothes.

Easton led them through the maze of workstations. They were both dressed in plain clothes and didn't get much attention until they came to a cube near the wall of offices along the back wall. The woman sitting there recognized Detective Easton and looked like she was trying not to swallow her tongue.

"Maryann, remember me?" Easton showed her his badge. Packard did the same. "I wanted to talk to Sam again about Deborah."

"Sam's not in today," Maryann said. She was in her forties with brown hair pulled back in a thick braid and wearing jeans and a yellow sweater. "He's meeting with the governor all day today."

"What do you guys do in this department?" Packard asked.

"Administer the state food and nutrition program on behalf of the USDA."

"And Deborah did what?"

"What do you mean 'did'? Why are you talking about her in the past tense?" Maryann asked.

"What is Deborah's title?" Packard said, ignoring her questions.

"She's the director of finance."

"Who worked most closely with her?"

"That would be me. And a couple of others. Both are on vacation this week."

"Can you tell me what was front of Deborah's mind at work before she went missing?"

Maryann looked like she was being asked to lie under oath. She kept staring at Detective Easton like he was about to produce a pair of handcuffs with her name on it. "We're not supposed to talk about what's going on," Maryann said. "It's supposed to be business as usual."

"Who told you that?" Easton asked.

"The FBI," Maryann whispered.

Packard and Easton exchanged a look. Packard said, "Do you have a card or a name of the agents you talked to?"

"Third floor," Maryann said. "They're in Suite 309. Everything is being run through there. Don't tell 'em I sent you."

They took the stairs.

"I assume you had no idea the FBI was involved in this," Packard said as they went up the echoey stairwell.

"None," Easton said from behind.

On the third floor a sign pointed them left, down a hallway past matching doors with signs for an advertising agency and an architecture firm and a tax preparer. Suite 309 had no sign outside it. The door was locked. A key-card reader beside it was lit with a red light.

Packard knocked hard on the door. Through a narrow window he saw someone look out from what looked like a conference room in the back. He and Easton both pressed their badges against the window.

"Let us in," Packard said, banging again.

The agent came to the door, looked at their badges in the window, and said, "You're not authorized to come in here. Call our office and make an appointment."

"Let us in," Packard said again, "or I'll go downstairs and start asking a lot of loud questions about what the FBI is doing up on the third floor."

The agent looked behind him at a woman standing in the doorway.

Easton said, "You could let me do some of the yelling. This is my jurisdiction, you know."

"Sorry," Packard said.

The agent opened the door. He looked like he was fourteen years old. The other agent was an older woman with deeply dyed maroon hair. Mulder and Scully if they were a May-December romance.

Packard let Easton introduce both of them and tell the agents about the missing person's case involving Deborah Salvo.

Packard said, "It's now a murder investigation. I found Deborah Salvo shot in the back of the head in a walk-in freezer about three hours north of here."

The two agents looked at each other. The woman, who introduced herself as Agent Riley said, "Agent Turner and I are not at liberty to discuss our work with local law enforcement. To be frank, Ms. Salvo's disappearance and murder are your responsibility, not the FBI's."

"I'm not asking you to solve the case. I'm asking whether your investigation might have anything to do with why Ms. Salvo is in the Saint Paul morgue with a hole in her face big enough for me to stick my fist in."

"We're investigating large-scale fraud of the U.S. government involving millions of dollars," Agent Riley said.

"Involving the state's health and nutrition program?" Packard asked. He was thinking of school lunches and kids with change jingling in their pockets for chocolate milk. How did someone suck millions of dollars out of that?

Agent Riley didn't say anything.

"Can you tell me what role Deborah had in your investigation?"

"Deborah was the original whistleblower who noticed a significant increase in reimbursement claims coming through the department. She was already missing by the time the FBI took over the investigation. We've been able to do our work without her involvement. We had to."

"Is any of the fraud originating in Sandy Lake County?" Packard asked.

"I don't know the answer to that, and if I did, I couldn't tell you."

"You're talking about fraud involving millions of dollars," Easton said.

"Deborah Salvo would have to be a very unlucky woman if she managed to stumble onto something completely unrelated that got her murdered."

Agent Riley shrugged. "Again, that's for you to figure out. We're representing the government's interest in the fraud. Now if you'll excuse me."

Packard asked her for a business card and put it in his wallet. Agent Riley followed them to the door and made sure it locked behind them.

"We could get a search warrant for the Sandy Lake records," Packard said as they made their way down the stairwell.

"I got a better idea," Easton said.

They walked the path among the cubes back to where Maryann sat. She had a steaming mug of tea and a half-eaten Luna bar beside her computer monitor.

"Maryann, we talked to the agents upstairs," Easton said conspiratorially. Packard showed Maryann Agent Riley's business card. "We need to see any reimbursement claims originating from Sandy Lake County. Not all of them. Maybe whatever is the latest and going back three months."

"Six months," Packard amended.

Maryann's nervous look disappeared as Easton talked. She folded her arms across her chest. "Cut the bullshit, you two. I know there's no way that Agent Riley said, 'Sure, give those cops whatever they want.' Do you know how on my ass she's been for the last six months? I can't go to the ladies' room without her standing outside the stall and commenting on what I had for dinner the night before."

Packard couldn't help laughing.

"It's not funny," Maryann said. "You don't understand the IT systems they have in place. Every log-in. Every email coming in or out of the department. Documents sent to our networked printers. They're watching it all."

"What if you ran an open search that happened to include the Sandy Lake data?"

"And then what?"

Packard handed her his card. "Call me tonight with the who what where. I'm pretty sure they're not tapping your home phone. Unless you're part of the fraud," Packard said.

Maryann took his card and put it in the purse hanging on her cube wall.

"Can you tell me one thing in return?"

"What is it?" Packard said.

"Is Deborah coming back?"

Packard gave her a grim look and shook his head.

———————

In the parking lot, he and Easton stood between their vehicles. "Do you think she'll call?" Easton asked. The sun was going down, taking the temperature with it.

"We'll see. If she doesn't, I'll start writing the search warrant."

Easton looked at the time on his phone. "Are you heading back tonight?"

"No. I need to get a hotel. I have a meeting in Saint Paul tomorrow."

"You can stay at my place."

"You got a spare room?"

"Nope."

Packard looked away, laughed. He couldn't help but blush under his beard. "What about your wife?"

Easton shook his head, held up his empty ring finger.

"That doesn't mean anything," Packard said. "You weren't wearing a wedding ring the first time we met."

"We got divorced. No wife, no girlfriend, no boyfriend. I'm free and clear." Easton's stare was intense. He didn't blink. Neither did Packard. Seemed like a bad idea to go back across that line with someone he had called a friend. But were they still friends after what he'd done? Maybe things had reset. Standing as close together as they were, he couldn't deny he felt the urge to grab the end of Easton's belt and close the space between them.

"It's been a long time but I remember what you like," Easton said.

"It's been a long time. Maybe I like different things," Packard said, toying with the zipper dangling from the bottom of his coat.

"Maybe you should tell me about it."

"Maybe I'll show you."

Maryann had impeccable timing. She waited until they were done crashing together like train cars coupling before she called. Easton was out of bed, getting them a drink, when the phone rang. He had a wide back, like a giant manta ray, that tapered to a fuzzy peach of an ass.

Packard sat up with a pillow behind him and answered his phone.

"I think I have what you're looking for," Maryann said. "We got reimbursement requests from three different sites in Sandy Lake County over an eighteen-month period. They claimed to be serving a combined total of 3,500 to 5,000 meals a day."

"A day? How many days a week?"

"Five days a week."

"To needy kids in Sandy Lake County? No way," Packard said. "I don't think there's that many kids in the county, let alone needy ones. That's probably thirty percent of the total population."

"And now you know why the FBI is interested. The federal government loosened the rules during the pandemic to allow for-profit businesses to provide meals to the needy and did nothing to fund oversight of the program. Didn't take long for word to get around that the government was cutting checks with no questions asked."

"Is there a signer or contact for the Sandy Lake organization?"

"Yes, Louise Larsen."

Packard was stunned. "Not possible. Total bullshit. Louise Larsen was in her eighties. She owned the buildings but had no idea what was going on in them. She's also been dead since June."

Easton came back in the room with whiskey in a glass for each of them. "Here you go."

"Thanks," Packard mouthed.

"Are you still with that other police officer?" Maryann asked.

"Uh…yes. We had dinner."

"I bet you did. I saw you two talking in the parking lot. You looked like you were one second away from jamming your tongues down each other's throats."

This was the second time in recent memory someone had told Packard she could read his mind when he was standing close to someone he found attractive. What kind of look did he have exactly? They made it sound like he had an erect penis growing out of his forehead.

"How much money are we talking about?" he asked, changing the subject.

"The three sites were reimbursed nearly four and a half million dollars," Maryann said.

"Four and a half million for meals that weren't served? No questions asked? Is it too late for me to submit a reimbursement form?"

"I wouldn't. The jig is up. People just don't know it yet."

"So your department cut checks to distribute these federal funds. Do you have records of where the checks were deposited?"

"In this particular case, it's a Wells Fargo bank in Sandy Lake. The name of the LLC is the account holder."

Packard asked her to text him the names of the businesses being paid in Sandy Lake County and any account numbers she had. She said she had it all written down and would get it to him before she went to bed.

"Have fun with Officer Biceps," she said before hanging up.

"Maryann says hi," Packard said, putting down his phone and tasting the whiskey. "What is this?"

"Weller Antique."

"I like it."

They sat against the headboard, shoulder to shoulder, a sheet pulled to their waists. Easton lived in a one-bedroom condo in Bloomington, near the light-rail station and the Mall of America. Total bachelor pad. His furniture was a big TV and a trail bike hanging from a hook in the ceiling. He had a king-size bed and a giant framed mirror leaning against the wall across from it.

"So you got divorced. Did you tell her or did she catch you?"

"A little of column A, a little of column B," Easton said.

"Was it bad?"

"It wasn't fun. The worst part was having no one to talk to. I never felt so alone in my life," Easton said, staring Packard in the eye. "I know what I did was wrong. Having someone to listen who really knew me would have been nice. I needed a friend and you were gone." His voice caught on the word *gone*. He cleared his throat and drank the whiskey.

Packard blushed. Easton's words were more intimate than the sex they'd just had. Cops weren't supposed to talk like this. "I'm sorry. Deeply sorry."

Easton shrugged. "You had your own shit to deal with. I got through it. Seems like you did, too."

"Some days I wonder. Dealing with shit on our own is not how things are supposed to work. Staying so busy you don't have time to feel anything doesn't help matters either."

"You sound like you've been to therapy."

"More like learning from experience."

Easton held out his drink. "Here's to learning our lessons," he said.

They clinked glasses.

They slept. In the still, dark hours Packard woke to hands moving over his body. He was immediately awake and they went at it again, no light but the moon in the window, aggressive as two animals fighting over a carcass, then slept in the position where they finished. Early in the morning, they showered and Easton made coffee.

"Can you spend another half day on this?" Packard asked. "I want to go back and talk to Maryann and the feds again. I could use your knowledge of Deborah's disappearance to help tie everything together."

"I got time. Let's do it," Easton said.

It was twenty-eight degrees. Easton was parked underground in a heated garage. Packard's vehicle was in visitor parking and needed its windshield scraped. He tried not to be a person who complained about the weather, but the endless string of cold days was starting to wear on him.

He followed Easton back across town to the building where the State of Minnesota had offices. When they got to Maryann's cube, she turned in her chair, a big grin on her face. Gone was the fear of being interrogated by police. "You boys look refreshed."

Packard didn't have time for it. "Grab your laptop and come with us."

The three of them climbed the stairs to the third floor and Packard knocked on the suite door until Agent Riley let them in. Agent Turner was there and so were two other agents.

Packard walked to the conference room and had a seat. He asked Maryann and Easton to have a seat on either side of him.

"What's going on, Detective?" Agent Riley asked.

"I know fraud claims originated in Sandy Lake. I also know Deborah Salvo was killed in one of the buildings claiming to be serving meals in the area. It's no coincidence. You're interested in the fraud aspect. I'm interested in catching a killer. I'm not leaving here until I understand the timeline and have all the information I need to follow the trail back home."

Agent Riley was not happy. "We're building a very methodical case on behalf of the U.S. Attorney's office. Secrecy is still crucial. We haven't executed search warrants yet. This all needs to follow procedure if we hope to bring indictments against those involved."

"Is there a central figure you're looking at in all of this?"

Agent Riley considered her words carefully. "Yes, the head of a nonprofit based in Saint Paul seems connected to a lot but not all of it. He's taken a lot of money in kickbacks. As word of the fraud spread, it popped up more and more independently without his involvement."

"I'm guessing the Sandy Lake fraud might fall into the later."

"It might. We're looking at the centralized cases first and starting with the largest dollar amounts. We'll get to everyone eventually."

"How many murder victims are associated with the central cases?"

"None," Riley admitted.

"Is this everyone working on the case?" Packard asked, pointing at Riley and the three other agents standing with her on the other side of the table.

"No, we're the local team. There are other war rooms and a small army of people back in DC managing all the data that's being collected."

"So give me one hour and access to all the Sandy Lake info you have. If you don't have the bank records yet for Sandy Lake, call right now and get them. I'll go home and catch my killer, and I'll do it without any word of the fraud being mentioned in the press. When the time is appropriate, I'll be happy to thank the FBI for their assistance."

Agent Riley stood with her arms folded, glaring at Maryann, whose unauthorized cooperation had brought them to this moment. Packard knew he had no authority here. Agent Riley could have the three of them arrested for interfering in a federal investigation if she had half a mind.

"I have two dead bodies back home," Packard said. "Deborah Salvo is one. The other is a woman in her eighties whose name and business accounts are being used in the fraud but who I guarantee had nothing to do with it. Someone smashed her skull against a doorframe and then threw her down a flight of basement stairs. She lay there, maybe still alive for hours but definitely dead when they finally found her body a week later."

"Oh my god," Maryann muttered. She put a hand on her forehead. She opened her laptop with her other hand, ready to work.

"Fine," Riley relented. "But I'm in charge here."

It took a couple of hours but when they were done, Packard had a detailed timeline of events cobbled together based on the notes from his investigation in Sandy Lake, Deborah Salvo's missing person's file, and key dates involving the fraud.

Packard worked on one of the FBI's laptops and created an Excel file with events in rows down the left-hand side and months and weeks as column headings. He colored the intersecting cell green for each event. The laptop was connected to a cable coming out of the table that projected his screen on the wall.

"The first record sheets claiming meals were being served from the properties that Louise Larsen owns started in January of last year, meaning the groundwork was likely being laid in advance of that."

"According to the bank records, the business account at the Sandy Lake bank was opened in November," Agent Riley said. The account was in the name of Louise's existing LLC. It wasn't the same account she used to operate her businesses. Packard had a feeling Louise was tricked into creating a second account, or Tess found someone willing to open the account over the phone because she had access to all of Louise's personal information. It would take another search warrant to figure out why this account hadn't turned up as part of Packard's last search warrant for Louise's bank records or as part of Ray Wiley's accounting of Louise's estate. A phony tax ID or a different mailing address might have kept this account isolated from the others.

Packard said, "Deborah's first emails to officials about the fraud begin in early May. As the month goes by, she's sending more and more emails about what she's seeing to her boss, Sam. The last time her key card is used in this building is the Thursday before Memorial Day weekend."

"From there we know she went to the knitting retreat Friday through Sunday," Easton said. "Sam reported her missing ten days later."

"Did you look at Sam?" Packard asked Easton.

"We did. He looked clean. Happily married. Was gone the week leading up to Memorial Day on a trip to Yellowstone with his family."

"Sam is the one who escalated Deborah's concerns about the fraud and got the FBI involved," Agent Riley said.

Packard went on. "Deborah's trail goes cold on Sunday of Memorial Day weekend. I found her business card inside Louise Larsen's library book, which means they had to have made contact before Louise died Sunday evening,"

Packard said. "Louise attended a large barbecue with her neighbors on Sunday. The autopsy showed food from the barbecue still in her stomach, so we know she died Sunday night. By the time her bridge partner reported her missing and a welfare check was performed, she'd been dead at the bottom of her basement stairs for six days. Based on a broken whiskey bottle beside her, my department came to the quick conclusion that she'd been drinking and suffered a tragic fall. Later, I found evidence to suggest otherwise."

Packard told Easton and the agents in the room about also finding Deborah's business card among Tess's personal possessions. "Deborah took advantage of her proximity during her vacation to look up these sites and the person who was claiming to be serving tens of thousands of meals a week in such a rural part of the state. She went to Louise since her name was on all the paperwork. Louise had no idea what she was talking about and told her to talk to Tess Reid, who managed the properties for her."

"You're sure Louise was completely in the dark about all of this?" Agent Riley asked.

"I'm certain that an old woman who read large-print library books and didn't own a cell phone had no idea how to commit fraud on this scale. She died with an estate worth several million dollars. She didn't need more money."

"Deborah meets with Louise. She meets with Tess Reid. The next anyone hears from Deborah is when you find her body in the freezer in Cedar Creek," Easton said. "A lot of roads seem to be leading to Tess Reid. And you have no idea where she is?"

"I don't," Packard said. It looked like sloppy police work on his end. He'd been following leads on this case like a kid with ADHD. The missing $50,000 from Louise's account had led him to Tess. He knew Tess was missing but before he could try to pin her down, he found Deborah in the freezer. Her business cards had brought him to Minneapolis, right to this room with the FBI and their fraud case, which was about to lead him back to Sandy Lake to look for the other players, one of whom was certainly Tess.

"Tess is in the wind. I've got work to do there for sure."

"What does 'in the wind' mean?" Maryann asked.

"Means on the run. She could be anywhere, blown by the wind. Here's the deal, though. I don't like Tess for killing Deborah."

"Why not?" asked Easton.

"Look at the timeline," Packard said, moving the pointer on his screen to highlight the green row of cells indicating the Sandy Lake fraud went from January through October. "The fraud went on for several more months after Deborah and Louise were murdered. If Deborah confronted Tess, Tess must have told someone about it because the other thing I don't like is Tess as the mastermind behind this whole operation. She worked on a landscaping crew and did part-time handy work for Louise. She collected rent, paid bills, and wrote checks as necessary. How do you go from that to setting up the businesses and bank accounts and even having the knowledge that this program existed and was susceptible to fraud? There's no connection there. Someone brought her in on this because of her access to Louise's bank accounts, which allowed them to perpetrate the fraud in someone else's name."

"Smart," admitted Agent Riley. "Most of the people we're pursuing set up LLCs in their own names and started writing checks to other LLCs set up in the names of their friends. They all went out and bought homes and cars and boats in their own names, using funds stolen from the government. It's not going to be hard to nail these people."

"Right. We're dealing with someone with a certain amount of business savvy who knows how to protect their identity. Whoever that person is reassured Tess that they would take care of Deborah's questions. Deborah goes away and Tess keeps working. Does Tess get nervous when Louise suffers a bad accident at the same time? Maybe. But she keeps working June through October. It's not until around November that something happens that freaks her out and she disappears. Maybe she found Deborah in the freezer before I did. I don't know. I know from her landlord that she moved out the same time the fraud stopped. She was scared and she couldn't go to the police because she'd helped perpetrate millions of dollars in fraud."

The room was silent for a minute. Packard didn't know what the others were thinking but he was imagining Tess running through her house, throwing clothes into a suitcase, packing a few boxes, pulling the cords on her computer, and loading everything into the trunk of her car.

Maryann said, "We have invoices that the meal provider was required to submit as proof of money spent on providing the meals. If Tess was the one submitting these claims, she's the one who included the invoices."

Maryann took over the screen sharing and showed a PDF on a letterhead for Lundstrom Food Co-op. Packard had already googled the business and found it was legitimate, located in a small town of the same name in the next county, about thirty miles from Sandy Lake. Maryann scrolled through several invoices as she spoke. "This is some pretty expensive peanut butter, bread, carrot sticks, and fruit cups. This store is invoicing hundreds of thousands of dollars. You can see as I scroll through that it's basically the same invoice every week; only the date is changed. Even the signature at the bottom was scanned and reused."

Easton chimed in. "So the co-op bills Louise for the food that went into the meals and Louise bills the State of Minnesota for providing the meals. If the invoices are phony and no meals were served, where does the money sent to Louise go? Can you track the checks written from her account or any electronic transfers to where they were deposited?"

"Where the money goes from Louise's account and who owns those accounts are two levels deeper than we've gone on our end," Agent Riley said. "What we have going in our favor is that there's no such thing as a totally anonymous bank account anymore. Somewhere along the line, someone is going to have to put down a name, a social security number, an EIN to open a bank account. We'll find out who owns those accounts."

"I'll follow up on the co-op on my way home today," Packard said. "I have a feeling I will get a bunch of blank stares when I show them these invoices. But maybe there's a weak link there."

They wrapped up. Agent Riley was selective in what information she allowed to be released. None of the reimbursement forms, one copy of the food invoices. Packard was allowed to keep his notes and his timeline, which he transferred to a secure server the sheriff's office used. Agent Riley said she'd pass on any info about withdrawals or transfers from Louise's account as soon as she had it.

Outside, Packard and Easton found themselves once again in the tight space between their vehicles. Packard looked at Easton, then looked away. He couldn't stop grinning. The last twenty-four hours had renewed him. It was more than the leads now coming fast and furious on Louise and Deborah. For one day he'd experienced the right combination of work, play, and real connection with another person. Exactly what Tim and, if he was being honest, his mom had been telling him he needed.

"Thanks for letting me crash last night," Packard said.

"Thanks for crashing. That was fun."

"And thank you for being forgiving about my bullshit. I'm sorry for disappearing. I'm glad we're in touch again."

Easton nodded and put on his sunglasses. Mindful that Maryann was probably watching them from a window again, they bumped fists.

"I bet there's some pretty good single-track up where you are. I'll bring my bike and come see you."

"Do it," Packard said. "Anytime. I mean it."

CHAPTER TWENTY-FOUR

PACKARD DROVE EAST ON I-94, took the Kellogg exit. To his right, on a hill overlooking downtown, the Cathedral of Saint Paul's copper dome burned bright in the sun. To his left, the white dome of the state capitol seemed dowdy in comparison.

The appropriately if uncreatively named State Office Building next to the capitol housed the offices of the state representatives. The bland concrete building was dark inside, all the light swallowed by polished marble floors and coved ceilings and ornate wall friezes. Packard checked in with security and was escorted to a set of brass elevators that made him think of the tidal wave of blood from *The Shining*.

He got off on the second floor and went to an office with a brass plaque outside that said Representative Andrea Hopkins. It was after noon—he was fifteen minutes early. There was no sign of the assistant who had made the appointment for him.

Andrea had framed articles about her campaign and photos of her with voters and political bigwigs. *Time* magazine had written about her service in Afghanistan and the IED that killed a fellow soldier. Andrea was featured in a group photo of her unit, all dressed in desert fatigues.

Packard heard the approaching sound of heels on the tile floor. Andrea came around the corner dressed in a blue blazer and a skirt, staring at her phone. She stopped dead when she saw Packard. He hadn't recognized her the day she came to Louise's house when he was there with his mom. In his defense, she had been wearing a hat and a heavy winter coat. In an office with her name on the door she was much more recognizable as the woman on her billboards and TV ads.

"Deputy Packard. You caught me between meetings. What can I do for you?"

She went around him and took a seat behind her desk. She had a mass of springy curls that bounced as she walked.

"How'd you end up in Afghanistan?" Packard asked, pointing to the article on the wall behind him.

Andrea smiled like she was flattered to be asked. She'd told the story a million times on the campaign trail. "The short version is I had an ROTC scholarship in college. Was on the rifle team. Trained to be an MP in the army and got recruited for a new program training women for combat arms. It was the first of its kind."

Packard took a seat across from her in a black chair that had him sitting an inch lower than her. By design, no doubt. "You were in the thick of things. Right alongside Rangers in the field."

Andrea raised her eyebrows and nodded. He was telling her things she already knew.

"I was in town for work," Packard said, changing the subject. "I wanted to ask you a few more questions about Louise."

Andrea looked sympathetic at the mention of her neighbor's name. "I still can't believe her life ended like that. So sad."

"Very sad," Packard agreed. "I talked to Max Scarpetta. He said having Louise over for Sunday night dinner was a pretty regular thing. Did you have anything like that with her?"

"No. Sometimes I got invited to Max and Linda's."

"Did you attend the party they had on Memorial Day weekend?"

"Ah jeez, you want me to remember that far back?" She pulled her blue blazer closed across her chest and leaned back in her chair to think.

Packard sat quietly. He wasn't interested in prompting her memory or leading her to an answer.

"Yes, I was home briefly that weekend. I stopped at the party and said hello to everyone. The next day I walked in the parade in Sandy Lake, then came back to Saint Paul on Monday evening."

"Why the rush to get back? The legislature is required to adjourn by the third Monday in May. Well before Memorial Day."

Andrea looked affronted by the question. There was a hint of her military training in the way she quickly got up, went to the door, and closed it in all but a tactical crouch. She ran both hands through her blond hair, pulled it into a ponytail using an elastic band she had around her wrist, and shook the loose hairs from her fingers as she sat down again. "Between the two of us, Brian and I are in a trial separation. We're rarely in Sandy Lake at the same time anymore. When we are, he stays in the lower level that we converted into a vacation rental."

"I'm sorry to hear that," Packard said. "Was this going on last summer as well?"

"It's been going on for longer than that. He pretty much lives in the rental part of the house. I'm trying to keep up appearances for my political career. Plus we can't really afford a divorce right now."

"What does Brian do for work?"

"He works for an ethanol company whose main customer is in Canada. He goes back and forth a lot."

"Do you have another job besides this one?"

"I don't."

"Any chance of a reconciliation?"

"Unlikely," Andrea said. "His temper has been an issue for a long time. I don't see that changing."

A guy with a bad temper and as many guns as Brian Hopkins had was a bad combination.

"How does he express his temper?" Packard asked.

"Shouts, yelling, furious silence. Smashing things."

"Has he been physical against you?"

Andrea shook her head. "He knows better. I've had combat training. I would drop him."

"But if he had a gun."

"I've got one, too," Andrea said matter-of-factly.

Packard thought back to their first meeting at Louise's house and the heavy object in Andrea's pocket that had made her coat hang funny on her.

"Did Brian have any interest in Louise? Did he spend time with her at all?"

"Not that I ever saw," Andrea said with a shrug. "But like I said, I'm not there as much as I used to be. He did tell me you're looking more closely at Louise's death."

"What else did he say about it?"

"That you think she might have been killed. Do you still think that?"

"I'm more convinced than ever."

"Why is that?"

"Because I found a dead body inside one of Louise's properties who I think was killed around the same time that Louise supposedly fell down the stairs." He was careful not to reveal anything about Deborah's identity or the fraud she had uncovered per his agreement with the FBI. Finding the body had already been made public by the *Sandy Lake Gazette* on their website.

"That's going to upset a lot of people. Stuff like that isn't supposed to happen so far from the Cities," Andrea said. "People move to our part of the state to get away from crime and violence. I blame our governor for kowtowing to special interest groups that want to prevent law enforcement from doing their job. We're just supposed to give criminals a slap on the hand."

"I assure you, when I find out who killed these women, they'll get more than a slap on the hand."

Andrea didn't look convinced. She stood up, indicating their meeting was over. "I'm sorry I couldn't be more helpful. I'm happy to answer more questions some other time, but right now I have to get to a committee meeting on the other side of the capitol."

They walked to the elevator together and waited for the car to come down from the fifth floor.

"Don't you need a coat?" Packard asked.

"There's an underground tunnel that connects this building to the capitol."

"That's convenient. What committee are you on?" Packard asked.

Andrea was staring at her phone. "Children and families finance and policy."

The elevator dinged and the doors opened and they went down.

CHAPTER TWENTY-FIVE

EVERY TRIP BACK TO Minneapolis felt less and less like returning to a place he knew. The city changed so quickly. The parts of it that had burned after George Floyd were already showing new growth. Who would benefit from that growth remained to be seen. In other places, condos and apartment buildings appeared with the sudden alacrity of mushrooms. The quirky Uptown neighborhood he knew as a kid, full of indie coffee shops, bookstores, and panhandling punks, had morphed over the years into a neighborhood of chain restaurants and upscale retail, then changed again into its current incongruous mix of luxury apartment buildings and boarded-up storefronts.

It was a three-and-a-half-hour drive home. On the way he made a detour to Lundstrom, a dried-up small town in the process of transforming itself into an arts community. People came for yoga retreats and pottery classes and writing workshops. It had a vegetarian restaurant and a place that offered sound baths, whatever that was.

The invoices for the food Louise allegedly provided came from a co-op housed inside a low brick building that was once a Rexall drugstore. On the side of the building was a faded PEPSI mural that might have been sixty years old.

Inside, the store smelled strongly of lemon. Being near the end of winter meant local produce was in short supply. Some of the vegetables were beautiful and some of them looked like remnants from someone's root cellar. The products on the shelves came in tiny packages made from recycled paper and were brands he'd never heard of. A bearded young guy in a green apron and a man bun helped Packard find the store manager. They went to her office in the back of the store, and Packard showed her the copy of the invoice he'd gotten from the FBI. She put on her glasses, read, took them off again.

"This is not a legitimate invoice from our business. This is our letterhead. You can get that off our website. Same with this signature of mine, which is used on our monthly letter to members. But these items...JIF peanut butter. Are you kidding me? We don't sell that. Do you know how much sugar is in that stuff? Peanut butter should be peanuts and salt. We have a five-gallon bucket of it that we grind ourselves and members can take home in their own glass jars."

Packard was torn between rolling his eyes at how exhausting it would be to shop at this place and realizing how convenience was ruining the world.

"Who owns this business?" Packard asked.

"We're a co-op. We're owned by our members and governed by our board." She found him a copy of their recent newsletter that had all the board members listed in a column down the left margin. He didn't recognize any of the names.

"Do you own the building?"

"No, that's something we've been working on. We write a rent check and mail it to a law firm. We've expressed interest in buying the building, but whoever the firm represents isn't interested in selling. I don't know who that person is."

"Where's the law firm?"

"It's in Sandy Lake. Wiley something something."

"Wiley, Washington & Prentis," Packard said.

"That's it."

"Interesting," Packard said.

CHAPTER TWENTY-SIX

AT NINE THE NEXT morning, Agent Riley called. "We got the banking data. I've uploaded everything to your secure site."

Packard put his phone on speaker and sat down at his laptop. Frank was at his feet and hadn't let him out of his sight since he'd returned from Minneapolis the day before. Every time Packard went out of town, Frank treated him like a sheep that had wandered and needed to be corralled.

"What did you find?" Packard asked.

"The State of Minnesota deposited money into Louise Larsen's account. Money from Louise's account only goes to one place, another Wells Fargo bank account that was opened in December two years ago in the name of Lundstrom Foods. It was opened online and statements are sent to an address in Sandy Lake."

Packard knew the address Agent Riley repeated. It was Tess's house. Wells Fargo rang a bell as where Max Scarpetta used to work. Didn't necessarily mean anything. A lot of people banked at Wells Fargo.

"The invoices are from Lundstrom Food Co-op. The account name is meant to sound similar but has no relation to the actual store. What's the account holder's name?"

"Robert Clark," Agent Riley said.

Packard was stunned. "Did you say Robert Clark?"

"I did."

Robert Clark was the man Packard had shot at the courthouse. From what he knew about Clark, he was no more likely to be involved in defrauding the government out of millions of dollars than Louise Larsen. What in the hell was going on here?

"You know this man?"

"I killed that man last month after he opened fire outside a courtroom. Can you get me all the personal info associated with the account so I can make sure it's the same person? Date of birth. Social security."

"I can do that. I can also tell you that from Robert Clark's account, the money was moved to a trust account at a bank in the Cook Islands. Confirming the owner of this account is going to be more difficult. The Cook Islands are outside of the jurisdiction of U.S. courts and not subject to U.S. court orders. The trustees named on the account come from an international law firm that will roadblock any efforts to release client information. It's not impossible but it will take time."

Packard sat back from his computer and pinched the bridge of his nose. "Let me see if I understand. The person pretending to be Louise billed the state for meals served and was reimbursed with federal funds. To get those funds, Louise submitted detailed lists of food recipients and invoices from Lundstrom Food Co-op for the food she allegedly served. The manager at the co-op confirmed the invoices are phony. They didn't supply any food to anyone. But if asked, our phony Louise could show payments had been made to an account in the name of Lundstrom Foods where Robert Clark is the account holder. From there the money is transferred to a bank in the Cook Islands and we have no idea who owns that account."

"That's the story we're seeing in the records," Agent Riley said.

"I'm still very confused," Packard admitted. Every revelation seemed to further obscure the truth, which he knew was exactly what the people running this scam wanted.

He said goodbye to Agent Riley and went through the statements from the account set up in Louise's name, tracking the deposits and the outflow to the Lundstrom Foods account in Robert's name. The money that went out added up to almost exactly what remained in the account—nearly two million dollars. A debit card tied to Louise's account was mostly used at Amazon. The largest charge of $1,100 was probably a new laptop. The transfers to Robert Clark's account ended in November of last year, as did the deposits from the State of Minnesota. The final transaction was a debit card charge at a gas station in St. Cloud at the end of January.

The other time St. Cloud had come up in this case was when the owner of the Big Beaver told him Tess's girlfriend, Brenda, lived there when she wasn't at her cabin. Ex-girlfriend, according to Brenda, who said she and Tess had split months ago and were not in touch.

Packard had Brenda's phone number and address from when he last talked to her. He got the gas station address from the billing statement and looked up both online. Nothing was very far from anything else in St. Cloud, but this gas station was literally the closest one to Brenda's house.

Now he knew where to find Tess.

———

There had been a change in the weather overnight. Warm, moist air from the south had pushed all the way into Minnesota, bringing temperatures in the fifties and thoughts of spring. It was weather whose only purpose was to break your heart. It would last two days, maybe three, long enough to make you feel biking and gardening were right around the corner, before the polar temps returned and you realized how far away those activities were.

It was a two-hour drive to St. Cloud. With so many people still working from home since the pandemic, Packard took a chance and showed up on Brenda's front step just before noon. Her house had a huge front yard with a towering multi-trunk cottonwood tree smack in the middle. A long driveway led to a one-car garage set behind the house. Packard rang the bell and heard a dog bark. Brenda's face appeared briefly in the window.

"Uh...just a minute," she said through the door.

He heard her putting the dog in another room and then she came to the door and stood half in, half out of the house.

"Why are you here?" she asked.

"I came to talk to Tess."

"She's not here."

"Cut the bullshit, Brenda. I'll arrest you right now as an accessory, put you in the back of my car, and then I'll go in there and talk to Tess anyway. What's it going to be?"

He expected defiance but Brenda looked exhausted. She came out of the house and shut the door behind her.

"She's scared to death. She thinks you work for him and that you'll kill her when you find her."

"Work for who?"

Brenda was looking over his shoulder at his vehicle parked at the curb. "You should hear it from her. She went to the store to get stuff for dinner. You can come in, but you better move your vehicle so she doesn't see it."

———————

Twenty minutes later, Tess parked in the garage and came in through the back door. "Change in plans. There was a rump roast in the manager's specials section so I'm making a stew," she said.

Brenda stared at Packard from her spot on the couch but didn't say a word. He sat in the chair across from her with Lady Gaga Pinot Grigio MargaretAnn String Cheese Reid in his lap. They heard paper bags rustle and the fridge open and close.

Tess was unzipping her vest as she came through the doorway into the front room. When she saw Packard, she froze, then burst into tears. "No, no, no…" she said as she sank to her haunches and pressed her gloves to her eyes. "I'm not going to tell anyone. Don't hurt us. Don't hurt my dog," she pleaded.

Packard gave Lady Gaga a nudge so she would get down. "I need you to be calm, Tess. I'm not going to hurt you. I'm not going to hurt your dog." What kind of monster did she think he was?

Tess rose to her feet. She was wearing shorts and a T-shirt with the sleeves cut off. It had warmed up but not that much. Packard watched her look behind her, then eye the front door, looking for a way out.

"Don't even think about it," he warned her. "I'm here to talk. If you run, I'll arrest you and then we'll talk back in Sandy Lake with you in a cell and me on the outside."

"How do I know he didn't send you here to kill me?"

"Who?"

"Your boss."

"The sheriff? Howard Shepard?"

"No, the guy who got him elected. Jim Wolf."

The name made Packard go still inside. *Now things were starting to make sense.* Wolf crossed paths with Louise and probably found out about all her properties while helping Max Scarpetta come up with an unsolicited offer for her house. Wolf would have had access to Robert Clark's personal information through the voluminous paperwork involved in a lawsuit. All he needed to open a bank account online was Clark's date of birth and social security number. If Packard had to guess, the Lundstrom Food Co-op building was probably part of Wolf's real estate portfolio. It all made sense when he thought of Wolf as the water surrounding these disconnected islands.

"I can promise you, I don't work for Jim Wolf. Jim did not send me here."

"I told you," Brenda said to Tess.

Tess looked like she still might run. "Sorry that I wasn't willing to take your completely uninformed opinion on matters," Tess shot back.

Packard sensed it had been a long winter for these two. Moving in together under duress—Tess cut off from her friends, from work, and afraid for her life the whole time—couldn't have been easy on their relationship.

"Let's all have a seat," Packard said, nodding at the dining table in the corner of the room. "I have a lot of questions that need answers."

"You guys can talk. I have a conference call in ten minutes," Brenda said. "She's barely told me anything this whole time, so I'm not going to be much help."

Packard looked at Tess, who nodded in agreement.

"I can get you guys some water or coffee if you want," Brenda said.

"Water," Packard said.

"I want a real drink," Tess said.

"No alcohol until we're done talking," Packard said.

Two minutes ago, Tess thought she was about to be murdered. Telling her she couldn't have a drink looked like it was the second-worst news she'd had that day. "Fine," she said.

———————

"Jim came to me with the whole plan," Tess said by way of starting. The way she sat in her chair with her elbows on her knees and her fingers interwoven made Packard think of a football player in detention. "He knew about the federal program, how to submit the forms, what kind of proof we'd have to supply, how to get another bank account set up in Louise's name, every detail. He said we had the perfect cover: legitimate food service sites, an LLC in Louise's name, and access to her accounts. He gave me an old laptop and the printer and said this was going to be easy money."

"What made you agree to do this?"

"The money," she admitted. She still had her vest on. She leaned back and jammed her fists in the pockets. "I mean…fuck. I'm almost fifty years old. You saw my house, I assume. That I rent, don't own. I'm getting too old to keep doing manual labor. The job with Louise was easy work but it didn't pay much.

There's no pension, no 401(k). I've got less than $3,000 in the bank. Jim said I could make more money helping him with this than I'd made in my life. He kept saying there was no way for me to get caught. Absolutely nothing had my name on it. All the forms were in Louise's name."

"What was your cut?"

"He offered ten percent. I insisted on fifteen."

"And Jim got eighty-five? That doesn't sound very equitable."

"He said it was his idea and he was the one taking the most risk since the money eventually had to pass from Louise's account to his."

"The other account wasn't in his name. It was in Robert Clark's name."

"And you killed Robert Clark in broad daylight," Tess said bluntly.

"Jim and Robert were involved in a legal dispute. During the trial, Robert Clark brought a gun to the courthouse and started shooting. I was working security. Yes, I shot and killed Robert."

Saying it out loud never got easier. He would have to own this for the rest of his life.

"I read about the shooting in the *Sandy Lake Gazette* and that Jim Wolf was there when it happened. It felt like an assassination by law enforcement to me. Helping Jim clean up a loose end. And more proof that I couldn't go to the police because you guys were all working for Jim." She looked at him like she was giving him a chance to admit she was right.

This was Packard's fear realized. That no matter the circumstances, people would see him as an assassin in a brown uniform and black boots. *How could he blame them? In his nightmares, he saw the same thing.* "That's not what happened at all," Packard said. "Now tell me about your role in all this."

"I filled out all the forms and submitted them. We started small to test the waters. For the first month we said we'd served two hundred meals three days a week. The next month it was five hundred meals five days a week. By the end it was five thousand meals seven days a week."

"There aren't that many kids in the county, let alone those needing food assistance."

"No shit. I said the same thing but Jim didn't care. And the checks kept coming so there was no incentive to slow down. The worst part was filling out the sign-in sheets. Jim used his connections with the county to get a list of all the families and kids enrolled in Sandy Lake schools. I used that list but it wasn't enough so I had to come up with other names."

"The phone books in your house. I saw them," Packard said.

"Yeah. Found them on eBay. Seemed like a good way to come up with legitimate-sounding names."

"There are sites online that will generate random names."

Tess nodded. "There are. Most of them do one name at a time. I needed thousands."

"So it was as easy as Jim said, except for the names."

Tess rubbed the back of her hand under her chin and shrugged. "Yeah. I mean I filled out the forms, I made the phony invoices from the co-op, I responded to emails when necessary, and the money showed up in the account like magic. At first, I couldn't believe it. It seemed ridiculous that they didn't require any proof of the meals being served, that no one came out here to check on us. They approved everything based on paperwork and deposited the money."

"What did Jim say or do while all this was happening?"

"Almost nothing. He'd check to see if the money was coming in. Every few weeks he'd tell me to up the number of meals. Other than that, there was nothing to talk about. The whole thing was too fucking easy."

"Did it make you nervous?"

"I was never not nervous about this. Especially when we started submitting the huge receipts. We were getting hundreds of thousands of dollars deposited at a time. It started adding up to millions. I thought there's no way this amount of money isn't going to set off an alarm somewhere."

"And then Deborah Salvo showed up."

Tess closed her eyes. Packard wondered if the name conjured the same image in Tess's mind that it did in his: Deborah frozen solid with a huge hole in her face made by an exiting bullet.

"I saw her card on your refrigerator. Tell me what happened the day she showed up," Packard said.

"It was Memorial Day weekend. She rang the doorbell and said she was looking for Tess and wanted to ask her some questions about Larsen LLC and the meals it was serving. I did the only thing I could think of. I said, 'Tess isn't home. I'm her girlfriend.' She asked if she could come in and wait. I said no, we had a mean dog." They both looked down at Lady Gaga, who had her face lying on top of Packard's boot.

"She wanted to know if I was familiar with Tess's work serving meals. I said no. I said we hadn't been dating that long. Just one hundred percent bullshit to try to get rid of her. I asked her if she had a card and told her I'd make sure Tess called when she got home from work. She finally left and I called Jim right away. I was in full panic mode. I said I knew this was too good to be true. I knew someone would eventually come looking for that money."

"What did Jim do?"

"He told me to calm down. He already knew about Deborah. He said he was already dealing with it."

"And then what?"

"And then nothing happened. A few days went by and I finally called Jim again and he said not to worry. Deborah's questions had been answered. We were in the clear."

"I said, 'How are we in the clear? The State of Minnesota is asking questions. We haven't served one fucking meal.' He said, 'Money is the answer to many of life's questions.' He told me to keep submitting the forms. We were good. So I did."

"So Deborah goes away and not long goes by when you get word that Louise has died."

Tess thought for a minute. "Yes, it was in that order."

"How did you find out?"

"I first heard about it at the Beaver. People were talking about Louise like she wasn't a real person, like what happened to her was gossip and not a trag-edy. I pulled up the *Sandy Lake Gazette* website on my phone. They had a small article about it. I called you guys but couldn't get much info out of anyone. It was the worst way to find out."

"What did Jim say after Louise died?"

"He said it was sad and I should take time to mourn but there was no reason to stop what we were doing. We were only using her name and had been doing so behind her back all this time."

"And the timing didn't strike you as odd?"

Tess looked guarded. "What timing?"

"Deborah shows up asking questions about the fraud. A week later Louise is dead. We know from the autopsy Louise actually died the same day Deborah arrived."

"I didn't know about the autopsy," Tess insisted. "What are you saying?"

"Someone killed Louise. She didn't fall down the stairs."

Tess was on the verge of tears. "Why would someone kill Louise? She didn't know a thing about what was going on."

"Think about it. Deborah had to have gotten your name and address from Louise. If Deborah first went to Louise with her questions, Louise would have known enough to start asking her own questions."

Tess dropped her head onto the back of her hand and trembled while tears darkened the thighs of her cargo shorts. Packard got up and got Tess another glass of water from the kitchen, Lady Gaga at his heels. Meltwater from the roof dripped past the window as Packard thought about how wasteful it was to lose your life over money. *Filthy paper. Intangible ones and zeros in the ether. Jim Wolf was already a wealthy man. How much more money did he need? What was he thinking about buying when he smashed Louise's head against the doorjamb and then shoved her down the stairs?*

Packard turned off the faucet. From upstairs came the muted sounds of Brenda talking on a call to a loud man with a South African accent.

Tess's face was red and wet. "I swear to god I didn't know that what I was doing for Jim led to Louise being killed. I swear to god. I honestly thought it was an accident."

"So did a lot of people. And I believe you." He wouldn't tell her it wasn't her fault because it wasn't true. Actions had consequences. What she agreed to do for Jim got Louise killed. "Deborah comes and goes, Louise dies, and you keep submitting reimbursement requests. All the paperwork shows the forms and payments stopped suddenly in November. Tell me what happened then."

Tess wiped her face. "Nancy called me some time before Thanksgiving. She owns Nancy's Hair Hut in Cedar Creek. It's in the building next door to Louise's property there. She said she noticed the condenser for the walk-in freezer was blowing exhaust outside the building. The building was empty and everything was supposed to be turned off so she thought I'd want to know. I told her I'd come take a look."

"You had the keys to the building."

"Yes."

"Did it look like the building had been broken into?"

"No."

"Were the doors locked when you got there?"

Tess stopped to think. "Yes. Nothing was out of place that I noticed until I opened the freezer."

"So someone else must have had keys."

"I guess so. They would need keys to lock up behind themselves."

"Anyone else have keys besides you and Louise?"

"Not that I know of."

"Your landlord let me into your house. I found your keys labeled and hanging on a hook in the kitchen in your house. Could someone have taken them?"

Tess shrugged. "I mean, I was in and out a lot. Never locked the door. I suppose someone could have taken them and then brought them back."

"Or made a copy."

"Maybe."

Jim Wolf lied when he told Tess that he'd paid off Deborah Salvo. Detective

Easton told Packard Deborah's cell phone records showed her getting a call from a burner phone the day she disappeared. Jim could have called her and told her to meet him at the café under the pretense of showing her a site that could have legitimately been serving meals. Packard imagined him telling Deborah that the freezer was full of food, pulling open the door for her to look inside, and then shooting her in the back of the head. He'd already murdered an old woman. What was one more? A freezer in an empty commercial property was a great place to leave a body if you wanted it to not be found for a long time.

Something about the order of events was bothering him.

"Did you say Jim already knew about Deborah when you called him?"

Tess nodded. "Yes, he definitely said that. I asked him if he wanted the number from her card. He said he already had what he needed."

If Deborah showed up at Louise's house unexpectedly and Louise sent Deborah to talk to Tess, how had Jim found out about her in the meantime? Who would Louise have told that would have gotten word back to Jim?

Ray Wiley was the only name Packard could think of. *What if Louise called her friend and lawyer and told him about Deborah's visit?* Packard imagined Deborah drilling Louise with questions about meals and reimbursements and how did she explain the millions of dollars she'd collected? Louise could have called Ray in a panic, given him Deborah's info, and asked him to help her.

And what about the keys? Where did Jim get keys to unlock the café building and lock it again behind him? If Tess called him right away and Deborah was dead later that evening, he couldn't have used Tess's keys. He could have killed Louise, taken her keys on his way out, then arranged to meet Deborah.

"Tell me what you did when you got to the café."

Tess put her face in her hands and shook her head. "I went right to the kitchen, and I pulled the freezer door open as far as I could because the bulb inside was burned out. The light from the room reached in far enough for me to see someone's feet. I thought Nancy was playing a prank and put a Halloween scarecrow or something in there to scare the crap out of me. Then I got close enough to see her face."

"Did you know it was Deborah right away?"

"I ran out and then forced myself to go back in there to get a closer look to try to figure out who it was. It only took a second look. I hadn't forgotten her in the months that had passed. I'd been waiting the whole time for her to show up again on my doorstep."

"So you found a dead body—a clear murder victim—and you didn't call the police."

"By the time I found Deborah, the election was over and I had watched Jim Wolf get Howard Shepard elected."

"That was in November. I was still acting sheriff. You could have come to me."

"And said what? Oh hey, I helped steal millions of dollars from the government, and by the way there's a dead woman in the freezer of the property I manage who came around asking questions about what I was up to."

"So you took $50,000 out of Louise's other account and left town instead."

Tess shook her head. "What $50,000? I didn't take any of Louise's money. I paid myself my regular salary. That was it. Her attorney said I could."

Packard made a note to follow up on the 50K again.

Tess said, "I had to disappear. I didn't know what else to do. If this is what Jim did to someone who asked questions, what was he going to do to me when it was time to shut down the operation? I took the computer, all the paperwork, some of my things and came here."

"Half the money you collected went to Robert Clark's account in payment for invoices. From there it went to an account in the Cook Islands. The other half of the money—almost two million dollars—is still in the account you opened in Louise's name. Why?"

"I don't know. Jim said pay the invoices, transfer the money."

"Did Jim have access to Louise's account?"

"Yes, but I probably fucked him when I changed the password and disappeared."

"Have you heard from Jim since you took off?"

"I'm sure he's tried to get hold of me. I ditched my cell phone and haven't logged into my email or anything else from a computer. I know that's how you guys track people."

"I found you because you used the credit card associated with the account you opened in Louise's name."

"That was…an accident. Brenda's card looks the same. I pumped the gas before I realized I'd swiped the wrong card."

Tess leaned forward and dropped her head. "Do you think I'm going to go to jail?"

"Definitely."

She looked up at him, hopeful that he was making a joke, and when she realized he was not, she went pale. "Even if I didn't spend any of the money? My share is all still in the account. Minus the tank of gas I accidentally charged on the credit card."

"Tess, you stole millions of dollars from the U.S. government. That's going to have consequences. You might have a chance to cut a deal if you come clean about everything and testify against Jim Wolf."

"Are you going to arrest me right now?"

It wasn't his job to arrest Tess and charge her with scamming the government. He was trying to catch a killer. "You should have told someone about Deborah months ago. Lucky for you, failure to report a crime isn't a crime. If I find out you've lied to me about anything, I'm going to arrest you for making false statements and interfering with my investigation."

Tess stood up and put her hands behind her head. The edges of the armholes where she'd removed her sleeves were damp. She talked fast, trying to outrun the tears about to spill over. "I swear, everything I've told you has been the truth. I'll do whatever I have to do to help. What do you want me to do? I'll do it. Anything."

Packard pocketed his notebook. He regarded Tess and her tears without sympathy. "Give me the laptop. Stay here and keep your head down. I've got two dead women on my hands. I don't want it to be three. Do you understand me?"

Tess's face was red and wet and her mouth was open in a funny shape. She looked like a boiling teapot right before it starts shrieking.

"Do you?"

"Yes," she sobbed.

"All right then."

CHAPTER TWENTY-SEVEN

ON THE WAY BACK to Sandy Lake, Packard called Thielen. "I'm hungry and I need to talk."

"What do you want me to do about it?"

"Feed me and listen."

Thielen sighed. "Dinner at six at our place. Bring dessert. Something good."

He spent two hours writing the report from his conversations with Agent Riley and Tess. He saved his work in a file on his computer instead of in the online case file. The FBI info needed to stay secret. He also couldn't be certain Shepard wouldn't tip off his buddy Jim Wolf.

There was time to mix brownies from a box and let them bake while he showered. He put Frank in the front seat and the brownies in the extended cab. The temperature was still two degrees above freezing as the sun went down. Tomorrow was supposed to be almost as warm, then back to the teens after that. The tease of spring would make everyone extra grumpy once it was gone.

Tim was decanting a bottle of red wine when Packard showed up. Dinner was minestrone packed with winter vegetables and pasta and a crusty baguette split lengthwise and rubbed with garlic. When the humans were done eating,

Frank and Thielen's old yellow Lab licked the bowls clean, then collapsed side by side in front of the crackling fireplace, overcome with contentment.

Tim excused himself to do some work while Packard and Thielen moved to the living room. Packard had another glass of wine and Thielen ate a brownie off a napkin while he told her everything that had happened since he went to Minneapolis in search of Deborah Salvo. Where she worked. The FBI. The fraud coming out of Sandy Lake. Round two with the FBI. Everything except for the part where he and Detective Easton got naked and threw each other around like a couple of professional wrestlers.

"Today I found Tess Reid hiding out at her girlfriend's house in St. Cloud."

"Hang on. This is a two-brownie story," Thielen said. When she came back, he told her what he'd put in his report about the fraud Tess and Jim had committed and the timeline for everything, including Deborah Salvo showing up in town, Louise's death, and Tess's discovery of Deborah's body. "She said she watched Jim get Shepard elected and assumed the whole department was now under his control."

"For god's sake," Thielen said, disgusted by the idea. She finished the second brownie and crumpled the napkin. "So...Jim Wolf: double murderer."

She looked at Packard, and Packard looked at her, and they both waited for the other to say something.

"Jim Wolf: double murderer," Thielen said again. She raised a questioning eyebrow.

"We're talking about millions of dollars," Packard said. "And the threat of a nice long stay in a federal prison. Who knows what a guy will do when threatened with the loss of one and the possibility of the other?"

"Hmmm," Thielen said.

"Don't *hmmm* me. That's my line."

"I've always thought he was a dirtbag and I know you hate his guts for a whole list of reasons but...murderer? In all your storytelling that I just listened to, I didn't hear you mention any hard evidence linking Wolf to these murders."

"Wouldn't that be nice?"

"You have none is what you're telling me," Thielen said.

"I mean… I watched the crime-scene team rub a DNA swab over every inch of the freezer and kitchen where we found Deborah. It's going to take weeks or months for results to come back. Same with whatever we collected at Louise's house. Of course, if we find his DNA anywhere in the house, he'll claim the scene was contaminated or that he'd been inside as part of the plan to tear it down. But you're right. I have nothing."

"So, what do you do?"

Packard stared into his wineglass until he realized the reflection was showing him the inside of his nose. "I need to smoke him out. Get him to make a move."

"You can't tell him the FBI is on his trail. You promised to keep their work confidential."

"Right. I'm trying not to burn that bridge in case I need a favor later."

"You said Ray Wiley's firm came up in connection to the food co-op. Why don't you shake his tree?"

Packard pointed at Thielen. "Because anything I ask Ray about will immediately get back to Jim."

"Exactly."

"Great idea."

"I have my moments," Thielen said.

"Do you have time tomorrow to double-team this with me?"

"No."

"Can I have Reynolds?"

Thielen looked too tired to argue. "Fine. On another subject, I've been talking to Northland Search and Rescue. They know we're going to need a cadaver dog when spring hits. They have us on the schedule." She said this matter-of-factly like Packard knew she had been working on this. He had no idea. "And I got buy-in from Shepard that the search for Nick's remains is going to be a priority for me when the time comes. I'll be in charge of coordinating everything leading up to and during the actual search. You will do as I say."

Packard felt warm in the face. It was good to be back in sync with Thielen. That she did all this on her own meant a lot. He would gladly take orders from her.

"Thank you for getting that set up. I appreciate it."

"Any movement on your end?"

Packard shook his head. "I'm at a complete standstill with trying to find Faizah and Faisal Rassin. There's nothing."

"You'll think of something," Thielen said. "Now get your dog and your empty brownie plate and go home. I'm tired."

"Empty plate? There's five brownies left."

"That you are leaving here in exchange for my brilliant advice and the use of Reynolds. You're welcome. Good night."

The next morning Packard had Reynolds come to work early in his regular clothes and put him in an unmarked county vehicle with instructions to locate Jim Wolf and keep an eye on him. "Go by his house. He drives a big black Lincoln Navigator. Lives alone. Make sure he's there and then call me. After that, get yourself in a position where you can see if he leaves home. I want you to follow where he goes."

Forty-five minutes later, Reynolds called. "There were no lights on the first time I went by. If the Navigator is there, it's in the garage. I see lights now, and I think I saw Wolf in the kitchen. I'm in position."

It was still early. Packard waited until 8:00 a.m. to call Ray Wiley's office. Marsha answered the phone. "It's Deputy Packard. I need to see Ray and Lisa this morning. Any chance of them both being there today?"

"They're both here right now," Marsha said. She transferred him to Lisa's extension.

"We have a client meeting at 10:00 a.m.," Lisa said after he told her he wanted to meet. "If you can get here before then, we can chat."

"I'm in the sheriff's office. I'll be right there."

"Want to give me some idea of what this is about?"

"No."

He parked in front of the law office ten minutes later. On the way, he checked in with Reynolds. Jim Wolf hadn't left his home.

Marsha walked him back to a conference room without a word. Ray was sitting at the head of an oval table, Lisa to his left. Packard took a seat on the other side of the table so he could observe them both.

"Ray, I need you to tell me about the deal you made with Jim regarding Louise's house."

"He's getting the listing when it comes time to sell," Ray said. The morning sun coming through the window behind Packard made Ray Wiley look every day of his age. The cuffs of his gray sport coat were grimy, his thick eyeglasses smeared with fingerprints. His white hair was slicked back. Packard tried to imagine who Ray had once been—father to little Lisa, a young lawyer building a law practice in a small town—but all he could see was a man run over by time, like a front porch jack-o'-lantern that had gone soft and sprouted mold.

"He's getting more than that," said Packard. "He told me he'd spent a fortune lining up subs and materials to tear down the house and rebuild it. He's ready to go, but I declared the house a crime scene and put a wrench in those plans."

Ray was silent. He had a twitch in his good eye.

"I'm no lawyer so you tell me... Is it legal for the attorney managing probate for an estate to enrich himself with a plan like this?"

"Minnesota statutes allow the personal representative to improve an estate's assets, including making ordinary or extraordinary repairs, razing existing, or erecting new buildings."

Packard looked to Lisa for confirmation. She nodded almost imperceptibly.

"I'm also entitled to reasonable compensation for my time and expertise," Ray said.

"Did you have the house assessed?"

"Twice," Ray said. "Jim assessed it at $900,000 as is. A second party came in at $995,000 based on condition and comparable sales."

"Was part of this plan for Jim to buy the house outright from the estate?"

"No."

"Why not?"

"He didn't have the funds to buy the house and build a new one."

"Did he ask you to invest in the development of the property?"

Ray hesitated. "At first, no."

"And then?"

"He said he'd run into a liquidity problem and didn't have the money to do the whole job."

"When was this?"

"November or December."

"Did you give him any money?"

"No."

"Did Louise's estate?"

"*Absolutely not*," Ray said, cross-eyed with anger.

"That would be illegal," Lisa said. She had sat mostly silent during the whole exchange. Packard couldn't tell if all this was news to her or not. "It would be a misappropriation of client funds. You'd also have to get a probate judge to approve spending that kind of money from a client's assets."

Packard asked Ray, "Did Jim explain his cash problem? I always thought he was loaded."

"Jim is wealthy on paper. He told me he had the money to cover the job. Later he told me he didn't. I don't know what happened."

Packard wrote in his notebook. November was when Tess took off. She told him their whole fraud operation lived on her laptop. There were millions of dollars in Louise's account that Jim was counting on but lost access to when Tess changed the password and disappeared. If he had spent money assuming the funds from Louise's account would replace it, he would have been fucked when Tess suddenly took off.

"Was the lawsuit against Robert Clark a preamble to liquidating his holdings to cover building costs?"

"You should be asking Jim these questions," Ray said.

"Jim Wolf isn't going to give me the time of day unless he's court-ordered. What about the food co-op building in Lundstrom? Has he thought about selling that?"

Ray tried to remain stone-faced but his overgrown eyebrows revealed he couldn't understand how Packard would know about Jim's connection to that particular property. This was the information he wanted to get back to Jim— the telling clue that Packard was on to him.

"I won't confirm anything about Jim's business dealings without a search warrant and without first notifying my client."

"Never mind then," Packard said. He tapped his pen as he looked through his notes. "So Louise dies the Sunday before Memorial Day. You take over as legal representative of her estate in July. Sometime after that, you and Jim make a deal to tear down Louise's house and build a new one. Things start to progress, but then Jim comes to you in November and asks for money. Something has happened and he's illiquid. He's had a long-standing suit against Robert Clark involving their property line. Before selling, Wolf tries to get a court to side with him and his claim on Clark's land. Clark shoots up the courthouse and I kill Clark. Shortly after that, I find evidence in Louise's house that makes me think her death might have been the result of violence and not an accident. I declare the house a crime scene, which only compounds Jim's problems with the project."

"If you were trying to ruin him, you couldn't have done a better job," Ray accused.

"I wasn't trying to ruin anyone. He was in trouble before I came along. All I want is to find out who killed Louise."

Ray waved a dismissive hand in Packard's direction. "Louise fell down the stairs. You're the only one who refuses to see that."

"Lisa and I found blood evidence in Louise's house that suggests otherwise.

The woman who ran her business is missing," Packard said, counting on his fingers. Ray didn't need to know he'd already found Tess. "I found another woman shot in the head in the freezer of a commercial property Louise owns. And I find out you and Jim have a sweetheart business deal involving her property. You want me to ignore all that and accept the story that the woman at the center of all this accidentally, coincidentally, conveniently fell down the stairs. I can't do it. It's the whiskey bottle for me. It makes no sense that she'd be going up or down those stairs with a bottle in her hand. It's an added detail that's supposed to point our thinking in a certain direction but doesn't make sense at all when you step back and look at the bigger picture. Louise went eighty-plus years not getting drunk and falling down the stairs. I don't buy it at all."

Now it was Ray's turn to count on his fingers. "First, of all, you don't get to make a habit of falling down the stairs and breaking your neck. It only takes once. Second, I've been up and down those stairs personally and I know they're steep and there's no handrail. Third, Louise was not known to never drink alcohol so the fact that she might have had a drink or been about to make a drink is not unlikely at all. Your reasoning would be shredded in a courtroom. Finally, I will counsel you to use your words carefully when you refer to me or my firm or any actions we may or may not have taken," Ray threatened.

"I will sue you six ways from Sunday. I've already told you everything we're doing is perfectly within the law. The plan is for Jim to tear down the house, build a new modern house for a million five, and try to sell the whole thing for three and a half to four million. Louise's estate would get its million for the original property, Jim would recoup his costs and a nice profit, and I will take a legal fee for my assistance. That holds up to any light you want to shine on it."

"You can call it legal all you want," Packard said, "but from the outside looking in, watching the two of you use a murdered woman's estate to enrich yourselves stinks. That's not libel. It's a fact."

Packard flipped his notebook shut and stood up. "I've heard enough. Appreciate the time."

Ray stayed seated but Lisa was on his heels. "Wait a minute, Packard," she said. "Come into my office." He followed her and she closed the door.

"That was a fun fishing expedition," she said, walking around her desk and taking a seat. "I know exactly what you're doing. You expect my dad to call Jim and tell him everything that was said in that room so you can see what kind of reaction you get."

Packard remained standing, arms crossed. Wolf's name in his mouth had dried up his patience. He'd run out of things to say and the desire to say them.

Lisa read the look on his face and sighed like she'd had it with stubborn men. "Fine, you don't want to talk. Don't. I know you know a lot more than you let on in that room. I'm not going to ask what because you aren't going to tell me. I will tell you one thing. You asked me about the $50,000 that was in Louise's business account," she said. "That money was not withdrawn by Tess Reid. My dad had it and the cash in Louise's other accounts swept into an interest-bearing trust account managed by our firm. It's part of marshaling Louise's assets to consolidate cash and sell investments and properties in preparation for distributing the estate. Tess is in the clear."

She opened a folder on her desk and turned a piece of paper in his direction that had a line highlighted in yellow. He didn't need to see it up close.

"I already knew that Tess didn't take it."

Lisa leaned back in her chair. "Meaning you've found Tess. She's not missing."

"I've talked to her. She's scared for her life and she doesn't trust anyone. She won't say why." Lies on top of lies. Telling Lisa something her father didn't know could help track from where information flowed out of this office. At this point in the investigation Packard didn't trust anyone.

"I can help get her counsel if she wants it. Completely independent of our firm, obviously."

"I'll let her know if it comes to that."

"I can also assure you that the deal my father described involving Louise's house is not going to happen. I agree with you that everything about it stinks, and as a partner in this firm, I'm not going to allow its reputation to be tarnished. I will talk to my father. I will get Mark Prentis to vote with me against him if I have to. I know that doesn't help your investigation but maybe it's one less thing that will require your attention."

Packard's phone vibrated in his pocket. The screen said Reynolds.

"I need to take this," he said, leaving Lisa's office door open behind him. He passed Marsha's desk and hit Answer.

"What is it?"

"Wolf is on the move," Reynolds said.

CHAPTER TWENTY-EIGHT

REYNOLDS TAILED JIM WOLF to his office. "I'm sitting in the BP gas station across the street. Want me to stay here?"

"Stay on him," Packard said. "Drive around if you have to. I need to think for a minute about what I want to do."

Packard had moved his truck from in front of the law office and parked by the library. Breakfast behind the wheel was a Clif Bar washed down with a cold cup of coffee.

He took no small amount of pleasure in thinking that Jim Wolf had stolen millions of dollars from the federal government and managed to bankrupt himself in the process. It looked like he was trying to hide half the money in a semi-anonymous offshore account and wash the other half through the project to build a multimillion dollar house on Louise's property.

Sitting back and waiting for the feds to nab Wolf on the fraud wasn't an option. Packard wanted Wolf's head for himself. It wasn't about losing the election, or Wolf's lack of gratitude for having his life saved during the courthouse shooting. Packard wanted justice for Louise Larsen and Deborah Salvo, who did nothing more than have the misfortune to cross paths with a greedy opportunist.

Someone had to show Wolf that the law was the law in Sandy Lake County, no matter who was sheriff. Packard wanted to be the one Wolf saw coming up fast in his rearview mirror, wanted to be there when Wolf realized there wasn't a damn thing Shepard could do to help him.

Packard started the truck and called Reynolds. "He still there?"

"Yeah."

"I'm on my way."

Wolf's office was on the east–west road through town. It had faux log siding and a sign out front that said WOLF REALTY beneath a logo of a howling wolf head in front of a full moon. His neighbor to the east was a car wash, to the west a carpet store. Wolf's black Navigator was parked in the small lot in front.

Printouts of MLS listings for nearby properties were taped to the inside of the front door, a picture of Jim in a suit at the top of each page. He had two office workers and one other agent working for him. An older woman with short, gray hair, a lot of eye shadow, and big rings on nearly every finger came out of her cube and asked if she could help Packard. He got the sense she recognized him a second after asking the question and maybe didn't want to help him after all.

"I'm looking for Jim," Packard said.

"He's not here. He left a little bit ago." She had her head turned so she was looking at him with one distrustful eye. She drummed her fingers against her thighs and her rings clicked together.

There was a closed door at the back of the office. "You sure he isn't back there? That's his truck out front."

The woman looked around him to make sure. "Sure is. He asked to borrow my car to run some errands. I park in the back." She pointed to the door behind her, through which Packard could see piles of gray snow and a blue minivan.

"Any idea what time he'll be back?"

"No. He's a grown man and does what he wants. Not like when he was a boy and wanted to borrow my car. Then I for sure demanded to know where he was going and when he'd be home."

This was Wolf's mom. She had a sign on her cube that said PATRICE. "What do you drive, Patrice?"

"White Mercedes CLS. Custom plate that says WOLFMOM."

Packard handed her his card. "Tell him I stopped by. I'll stop again."

"Can I tell him what this is in reference to?"

Your son defrauded the U.S. government to the tune of several million dollars and killed two women to cover it up.

Packard smiled and shook his head.

Outside on the front step, he paused to locate Reynolds at the gas station across the street, then called him as he got into the truck.

"He's not here. He went out the back. I don't know if he spotted you or assumed we'd be tracking his vehicle."

"Shit. Sorry about that."

"Not your fault. I'm cutting you loose. Check in with Thielen. I'll keep an eye out for what Wolf's driving now and come back later."

After hanging up, Packard sat with the phone in his hand contemplating his next move. Whatever Wolf was doing, Packard wanted him to know it was too late. He scrolled through his contacts and found Wolf's number.

> I found Tess. She told me everything.

He hit Send.

———

Packard hated waiting. It was too much like doing nothing. This point in a case, when he knew who the actors were and what they'd done but couldn't make a move yet, felt like watching clothes tumble and fall around and around in a dryer. All the pieces, all the players, heating up, rubbing against each other, building electricity. Him on the outside, watching.

He drove aimlessly through town, rights and lefts, one eye out for a white Mercedes, then headed further out of town. It still bothered him that he had no evidence to tie Jim Wolf to the murders of Louise Larsen and Deborah Salvo. There was no doubt that everything was connected—Louise's death, Deborah shot in Louise's building, the fraud being conducted in Louise's name. Sandy Lake was too small for all these crimes to occur spontaneously on their own. Jim was behind the fraud. Millions of dollars were at stake. *Who else would have a motive to keep the fraud going and be willing to kill to prevent it from grinding to a halt?*

Packard kept driving. He knew where he was going but still had to shake off what felt like a cold hand on the back of his neck when he stopped the truck and turned off the engine. It had been weeks since he was here with his mother. The site from Stan's map. The place where Dr. Rassin had left his brother's body.

He got out of the truck and started the climb up the trail. It was either a deer path that had been widened by hikers or a little-used snowmobile trail. Warm weather had compacted the snow and the surface gave way like a sugar coating under his boots. How different had this place looked thirty years ago? The hill would have been the same, maybe the trail wider. Trees grew tall seeking the light, fell and collapsed back into the ground, like all of us. How far had Rassin made it up this hill in the dead of winter, carrying the weight of a dead body, the weight of what he'd done? Couldn't have been too far unless fear pushed him to go higher and farther.

Near the top, the ground dropped off steeply on one side. The trees were too thick to roll a body down the hill. It would have hit the first trunk and stayed there in plain sight. Rassin would have had to carry it down from here. Cover it with more snow, hike back out. Packard could see it so clearly, he had to restrain himself from sidestepping his way down the hill, through the snow and the frozen slick leaves underneath, and start digging. It still wasn't time.

Wait.

It was the theme of the day.

He got no response from Wolf to the text he had sent. Packard drove by his office again right at five o'clock and found the black Navigator still there. The reverse lights flared as Packard turned into the lot. He pulled in right behind, honked his horn, and got out.

The windows were tinted almost black. Packard rapped on the rear window and stayed back to allow the driver's door to open. When the window came down, he was surprised to see Patrice behind the wheel.

"Where's Jim?"

"Good question," she said, clearly angry. "I've been calling him all day and he hasn't called me back. He still has my car so now I gotta drive this monster. I can barely reach the pedals."

"I can give you a ride home if you want to leave it here," Packard offered.

Patrice had the wheel clenched tight enough to deform the cheap rings on her fingers. She sighed. "Okay, yes," she said. She put the vehicle in Drive again and moved a few feet forward. Packard waited while she unlocked the office, left Jim's car keys inside, and came out again. He walked around to the passenger side of his truck and helped her up the step into the seat.

They headed south of town. Patrice sat with her purse in her lap and her phone in her hand, like she might need to call for help suddenly. "Is my son in some kind of trouble?"

"I don't know. Is he?"

"I mean from you. You didn't come by twice today for a social call. You two don't like each other enough for that. I know it's not business. If you were looking for a place, you'd go to a hundred other Realtors before you came to Jim."

"We have things to talk about," Packard said.

Patrice stared at him for a long time, then turned away. "You killed that man at the courthouse. He wanted to shoot Jim because of the lawsuit."

Packard nodded.

"Were you scared when he started shooting?"

"There wasn't time to be scared. It all happened in a matter of seconds. It's after the fact that all the emotions catch up with you."

"What did you feel afterward?"

"Everything you can imagine. Sadness. Regret. Anger."

"Does killing someone keep you up at night?"

"It does not sit lightly on the soul," Packard said. "Robert Clark was a member of this community. A lot of people liked him, from what I understand. What happened that day was a tragedy for everyone involved."

"So sad," Patrice said. A minute later, she said, "If Jim is in some kind of trouble, I hope you'll remember the same about him."

"Is this your way of asking me not to shoot your son?"

"I know you don't go around randomly shooting people. I hope you'll remember, whatever your feelings are about Jim, he's a member of this community. A lot of people like him. He's got a mom who loves him."

"I'll remember," Packard said.

Patrice lived alone on some cleared land in a white rambler with a miniature windmill in the yard half-buried in snow. Behind the house, Packard saw a tall deer fence surrounding raised beds in a large garden. He pulled into the driveway.

"Are you subscribed to the satellite program that comes with your Mercedes?"

"You mean satellite radio?"

"I mean the remote start, remote lock. All the things you can do using an app on your phone."

"I use my key fob for all that. Jim bought me the car. He did something on my phone but I don't know what. If it's not Facebook or the weather app I don't use it."

"Can I see?"

Patrice unlocked her phone and handed it to Packard. He searched for Mercedes and found the app. He had to point the phone at her face to unlock it.

"You do have this service. You can use your phone to do everything you do with your key fob. You can also use this app to locate on a map where your car is."

"Well, shoot. I wish I had known. Where is it?"

The cell signal was weak where they were. Packard waited while the map filled. "Looks like your car is...." He zoomed out, zoomed out again to make sure he understood what he was seeing.

"Huh," he said.

CHAPTER TWENTY-NINE

LOUISE LARSEN'S HOUSE WAS on fire.

The early evening light had faded to a plum-colored dusk as Packard drove half an hour from Patrice's to the location he'd seen on her phone. There was no sense of urgency on the way. Mostly he was curious why Jim would go to Louise's after finding out that Tess had spilled her guts.

Packard noticed lights on at Max and Linda's house as he rolled by. Just ahead, Patrice's white Mercedes was parked on the shoulder in front of Louise's. It took Packard a minute to register the smoke that blurred the house and rose up gray against the darkening sky. When he realized what he was seeing, he moved quickly, calling 911 on his cell phone as he got out of his truck. He gave dispatch his location and reported the fire. He kept the call connected and on speakerphone as he ran halfway around the side of the house, calling Jim's name, then came back and kept his head down as he ran up the crooked back stairs.

The back door was open. Smoke coming up from the basement had filled the kitchen. Without thinking, he reached for the drawer his grandmother always kept the kitchen towels in and was relieved to see Louise used it for the same purpose. He pressed a towel over his mouth and looked under the sink for a fire extinguisher. Nothing.

"Jim!"

Dispatch asked him to report his location. "I'm in the house, heading into the basement."

"The burning house?"

Packard didn't respond. He'd idled at low speed all day, his desire to nail Jim rocking him back and forth. Now he found a new gear, now he took the basement stairs two at a time, looking for Jim, not to grab him by the throat, but to make sure he wasn't trapped in this burning house.

Fire crawled between the overhead joists like lava sluicing down a chute. Packard spotted a sputtering road flare jammed in the cross bracing reinforcing the joists. Another flare, pushed up into the first-floor framing, had fallen near the exterior concrete wall. The whole house was lath and horsehair and newspaper insulation, dry as a wasp's nest. Fire scrabbled like rats in the walls above him.

It was a weird time for more childhood memories as he coughed behind the dish towel and felt the heat on his scalp. He remembered a giant oil-fed furnace taking up the center of the basement, pushing air out to a web of asbestos-wrapped ductwork overhead. He used to imagine a spider the size of the furnace living inside that could retract its legs from the ducts and climb out of the burner, huge and hairy, the mother of every other spider found in the house's corners and crawl spaces.

He found Jim sprawled on the floor behind the stairs, a hole in the side of his head. Packard squatted down and put two fingers on Wolf's neck. He shouted into his phone, "There's a male on the floor in the basement, DOA, GSW to the temple. It's Jim Wolf. Confirm no pulse, not breathing. There's a gun partially in his hand. I'm bringing it out because of the fire."

Wolf was wearing jeans and boots and his winter coat. Packard grabbed the gun using the dish towel and hustled back up the basement stairs. The higher he went, the hotter it got. His lungs burned. He coughed. It was too hot to keep his eyes open.

He stumbled blindly through the kitchen, hitting his hip on the edge of the purple peninsula on his way to the back door. He heard a pop, not loud enough to be a gunshot, and at the same time felt a slug punch into the wooden doorframe he was leaning against. A suppressed gunshot. Packard spun to his left and slid to the floor. He didn't see where the shot came from or who was shooting. His eyes stung. Another bullet punched a hole in the partially closed door into the kitchen.

He had dropped his phone in the doorway. He lunged for it, swiped it toward himself just as another shot was fired. The screen lit up, showing the call with dispatch was still connected. He scrambled backward into the bathroom. "There's an active shooter on scene. Someone outside with a gun has me pinned down in the house," Packard shouted. "Three shots fired. I'm trapped inside the back door."

The fire raged louder, pulling cold air from outside to feed itself. The addition where he crouched was a mudroom and a bathroom with laundry inside. Packard sat with his back against the washing machine. The heat wasn't as bad but black smoke was funneling out of the air return. Packard put the dish towel over his mouth again. Every breath hurt his chest.

Another memory—of Nick dressed in his winter clothes…black snowmobile pants and a coat that had three different zippers for all its layers. It was red and light blue and said POLARIS at an angle across the front and again on the back. He had his hand wrapped around the chin guard of his helmet like he was carrying the skull of a black beast.

Another bullet shattered the bathroom window, raining broken glass on top of Packard. He slid lower to the floor. In the mudroom he saw himself at twelve years old, barefoot in flannel pajamas, mouth moving silently as he confronted Nick on the last night anyone would see him. Nick bumped him in the chest with the helmet. *Shut up. Go to bed.*

Nick had seemed like a grown man to him at that age. Not old like their dad but something closer to that than the child Packard was.

Nick grabbed him by the arm and pulled him toward the back door.

He's going to pick me up and throw me in the snow.

Had he ever been as mad or hurt as he was that night, climbing the back stairs as Nick took off in the other direction? Had he ever let his emotions rule him again like he did then? He remembered furious, silent tears. Blood roaring in his head. He hated Nick for treating him like a child. This was the part he had forgotten. How he had gotten half-dressed and stepped into boots without socks. He was hurrying because he could already hear Nick leaving on the bigger snowmobile. He grabbed a coat, no helmet, and was down the stairs and halfway to the garage when he remembered gloves. No, no time to go back. The sound of Nick's snowmobile was already gone.

He took the smaller sled and squinted through the snow pulsing in the single headlight for signs of his brother. It wasn't more than a hundred, maybe two hundred yards before he realized how cold he was. His white-hot fury was no match for a windchill around zero. Nick was long gone. Packard knew he had to go back. On the ditch's steep slope, he felt the sled tip as he tried to turn around, and he launched himself in the opposite direction to keep from getting pinned under the machine.

He left it there, walked home, took off his wet clothes. His feet and fingers were frozen. In bed, he curled into a ball under the blankets, same position he was now in on the bathroom floor, looking for the last breathable air. He coughed. When he tried to inhale, it felt like the shallowest gasp. He heard dispatch calling him by his badge number on his phone, asking him to respond. He tried to make a sound but his throat burned.

He was waiting for the sound of sirens.

Waiting.

The theme of the day, he remembered.

Then he lost consciousness.

CHAPTER THIRTY

PACKARD WOKE IN THE hospital with an automatic blood pressure cuff inflating uncomfortably around his arm. The lights were low and the window beside his bed was dark and streaked with light snow. A clock on the wall said it was 10:15 p.m.

Packard moved his limbs. Nothing hurt terribly, but when he breathed, his lungs felt like he'd inhaled gasoline fumes and swallowed a lit match. A plastic mask over his nose and mouth fed him odorless oxygen. He had electrodes taped to his chest and an IV dripping cool liquid into the back of his hand.

A nurse came when he pushed the call button, sweeping the curtain aside and hitting the hand sanitizer by the door. "Good evening, Deputy."

Her name was Sonja. It was written on the dry-erase board by the door in case he forgot. She brought him a plastic cup of ice water and pointed to the plastic urine bottle hanging from his bed in case he needed to pee. "The hospital kitchen is closed, but I can bring you a fruit cup or some yogurt if you're hungry."

She had him sit up and listened to his breathing with a stethoscope. She asked him a bunch of questions and typed his answers into the computer beside his bed. His voice was hoarse, like he'd been screaming.

"What day is it?" he whispered.

"It's Friday night."

A day since the fire. He had vague memories of an ambulance ride and doctors standing over him. The nurse read through his chart and said they had performed a bronchoscopy to check damage to his lungs. They'd kept him mildly sedated and on oxygen to help his breathing. She didn't know anything about the fire or who found him. "The notes in your chart say the damage was minimal. It could have been a lot worse."

It didn't feel like things could get worse. It felt like someone had scraped out his chest with a fish scaler. He asked if he could check himself out if he wanted.

"I would advise against that," Sonja said. "We're still monitoring you for cyanide poisoning. It can take twenty-four hours for symptoms to develop. Relax, try to sleep. The controller works the TV. The doctor will be back around in the morning."

She was gone with a pull of the curtain. Packard turned his head to one side, then the other, sure he wasn't going to be able to sleep. It was his final thought until it was suddenly 6:30 a.m. and the ICU was buzzing with morning activity. He heard nurses in the next room trying to get an old man to turn on his side so they could clean him. "THESE BED SORES ARE LOOKING BETTER," a nurse said. She was shouting. "IS THE PAIN BETTER?"

The old man moaned low and miserably, causing Packard to shudder.

Things could get worse. A lot worse.

A doctor came to see him around eight thirty but it wasn't his doctor. Packard got more restless as the hours went by. His back hurt from sitting in bed for hours and he smelled and he resented all the things connected to him that kept him tethered in place like a dog staked in a yard. They were taking good care of him but he wanted out.

Thielen stopped by an hour later. She grabbed his foot under the thin hospital blanket and gave it a shake before sitting in the chair beside his bed. "What happened at Louise's house?" he asked.

"The whole thing burned down. It's gone."

"What about the shooter? Was anyone else hurt?"

Thielen shook her head. "No sign of whoever it was."

"No shell casings? No footprints?"

"Nothing. This warm weather has cleared the snow from roads and side-walks. There's pockets of open water on Lake Redwing," Thielen said. "Fire was first on the scene, knew an active shooter had been reported, but didn't wait for a perimeter to be set up. Said they'd deal with a shooter if they saw one. Dispatch said your last known location was inside the house so they went in and got you out."

Packard stared up at the ceiling. "I'm going to have to make fewer jokes about firefighters being second responders."

"I wouldn't worry about it. They'll never stop telling the story about the dumb deputy who ran into a burning building and needed two big, strong fire-men to carry him out. You're the dumb deputy in that story, in case you were wondering."

"I went in looking for Jim Wolf. Found him in the basement. Bullet to the side of the head." Packard drank his water. His voice was still raspy and froggy.

"Suicide?"

Packard could only shrug. It made terrible sense that Packard's text to him that morning was the thing that pushed Jim over the edge. Packard was already asking himself if pushing a man to suicide was any different than shooting him himself. It was a question that needed more thought.

"So Jim started the fire and then shot himself," Thielen suggested.

"I don't know if that's what happened or what I'm supposed to think hap-pened. If I could quit tripping over a dead body every five fucking minutes, I might be able to figure out what's going on."

"You're lucky you're not one of those dead bodies. You never should have gone in that house."

Packard shrugged. Thielen had some papers stapled together in her hand. He saw the words *On this visit.*

"Did you come to see me or were you already here for an appointment?"

"Both," she said.

"What's wrong with you?"

Thielen bent at the waist and dropped her head. "It's nothing. I have a parasite feasting on my insides. They tell me it'll exit through my vagina on its own in a few months."

"Pregnant," Packard said.

"That's another word for it."

"I already suspected but knew for sure after I saw you fake drinking the wine the other night and then snowplowing your way through that plate of brownies."

"You're a real fucking Sherlock Holmes."

"I assume this was intentional and you're happy about it."

Thielen tried to act like she wasn't so sure. "I turned forty and asked myself, did I want to train for another Ironman or did I want to have a baby. Guess I made my choice."

"I bet Tim is excited."

"You mean my fifty-four-year-old husband, known forevermore as Grandpa-daddy? Yes, he's excited."

"Good. I'm excited for you."

"We'll see how excited you are when you get to be full-time Uncle Benjy."

"I already have a lot of nieces and nephews. I know my role."

"Those kids are never around. You're going to babysit, change diapers, and cover for me at work whenever I feel like it. It's your turn to pick up the slack."

"Does Shepard know yet?"

"No. But you're going to owe me double if it's my husband leaving his seed in my lady parts that gets you your detective job back."

"I'll be sure to thank your vagina for its service," Packard said.

There was a knock at the open door then. Kyle from the brewery was standing there, just in time to hear Packard's last comment.

"Am I interrupting?"

Thielen gave Packard a questioning eyebrow, stood up, and said she had to run. Packard said he'd see her at the office when he got out.

She left and Kyle came in wearing a tight-fitting black puffer jacket and a knit hat that said PHISH around the front. "How are you feeling?"

"My voice sounds terrible but I'm fine," Packard said. He wasn't. He was aware how badly he smelled of smoke and sweat. Also how naked he was under the hospital gown draped over the front of him and open in the back. "How are you?"

"Great," Kyle said. He peeled back his hat with a casual indifference to how his hair looked underneath. It looked perfect. "Your mom called the brewery. She didn't know who else to call. She saw on the *Gazette* website or Twitter or something that you'd been injured in a fire and taken to the hospital. She said you weren't answering your phone and the sheriff's department could only tell her that you had been admitted. She asked if I would come see you and report back."

"I'm sorry she bothered you. I'm fine. I'll call her as soon as I find my phone. There's probably a bag of my clothes around here somewhere."

Kyle looked in the cupboards until he found such a bag and set it at the foot of Packard's bed. They talked about the brewery for a bit. Kyle was getting his summer beers ready and trying to hire more employees in anticipation of the warm-weather crowds.

"I'll let your mom know you're okay. You should probably know that she also asked me whether I preferred my sexual partners to have genitals on the inside or outside of their body."

Packard picked up the controller and looked for a button that would raise the foot of the bed until he slid out the top and into a hole in the ground. "Of course, she did. Your mom probably asks people that all the time, too."

Kyle shrugged. "She said if it was the latter, I should call you and find out what else we have in common."

Packard nodded as if this made perfect sense. "So…you need my number?"

"I got your number," Kyle said. "Your mom gave it to me."

It was almost noon by the time Packard got out of the hospital. The doctor told him to expect the raspy voice and burning lungs to last a while. He was supposed to call 911 if he experienced any respiratory distress or lightheadedness.

He'd left his truck with the keys in it at Louise's house. Someone would have driven it back to the sheriff's office for him. It was only a half-mile walk there from the hospital. The cold air felt good in his chest until he tried to breathe too deeply and started coughing hard enough that he had to put his hands on his knees. After he caught his breath, he left a weaving path down the sidewalk through the light snow from the night before as he listened to his mom's voicemails, scrolled through her texts, and sent her a message saying he was out of the hospital and would call later.

At the office he got a lot of handshakes and back pats. People were relieved to see him doing fine. Kelly was the only one who wasn't having it. "You're the only moron I know who almost gets himself killed while on leave," she said. "Do better."

He had a clean change of clothes in his locker at work. He showered and dressed and sat in Shepard's office and told him and Thielen what he'd seen at Louise's. He also told Shepard for the first time in limited detail what he'd found out about Deborah Salvo, the dead woman in the freezer, her job with the state, and its connection to an ongoing investigation by the FBI.

Shepard moved around in his chair like he was sitting on something sharp. He grunted and sighed as Packard told him about Jim Wolf and Tess Reid using Louise's identity and accounts to defraud the government. "It's not going to look great for me when my campaign manager is charged with fraud and possible murder," Shepard complained.

"That is literally the last thing you should be concerned about right now," Packard said. To Thielen: "I dropped my phone in the house but it was with my possessions at the hospital. Did the guys who pulled me out also happen to get the gun?"

"Yes. Dispatch told them to look for it. It's bagged and checked into evidence. I've got Reynolds checking point of origin and whether anyone's reported it stolen."

A gun's serial number could be sent to the manufacturer to find out where it was originally sold. If they were lucky, it wouldn't have changed hands too many times.

"All of this ending in suicide bothers me for a number of reasons," Packard said. "Jim Wolf had to know that money would leave a trail. Someone would come around asking questions about it and he needed to have a good story for it. Half of the money is still in Louise's account, which means it doesn't have Jim's fingerprints on it at all. We don't know who owns the account in the Cook Islands. Might be Jim, might be someone else. I don't think it was my text that pushed him over the edge. He had a plan all this time and it didn't involve a bullet to the head."

Packard stopped to drink some water. His throat felt like he'd been gargling sand. "There's also the matter of the shooter. This morning I was of the mind that Jim was at the top of this pyramid. Now I have to ask: if he was at the top, who tried to shoot me?"

"Tess Reid? Trying to help her partner?" Thielen asked.

Packard shook his head. "Killing me doesn't help Tess at all. Killing me doesn't keep the FBI from knocking on her door eventually. She's had access to all that money all this time and it's still sitting there. She could have disappeared and made herself a lot harder to find a long time ago."

"Maybe it was the same person who took a shot at you last fall," Thielen suggested.

Last September, Packard was investigating the murder of Bill Sandersen when he attended a high-stakes poker game hosted by Leon Chen, a wealthy architect who lived in a huge lake home made mostly of glass. Jim Wolf was there that night, one of the poker game's regulars. Chen and Packard were standing by a wall of windows when someone fired two shots at them from a boat on the water. Both missed. Packard gave chase in Chen's boat but lost the shooter in the dark. They found the abandoned boat the next day and a single .223 shell casing but no clues to the identity of the shooter.

"Jim was at the poker game that night," Thielen said. "He might have told someone you'd be there. Intentionally or not."

"If we think of the timeline, in September Jim was eight months into the fraud scheme. Louise was four months dead, since Memorial Day roughly. The story that it was an accident had been accepted by all involved." Packard avoided looking directly at Shepard. "And Tess had yet to disappear and cock the whole thing up."

Thielen was looking up like she was trying to see something on her forehead. "I can't believe there are that many people running around this county willing to take a shot at you. It's gotta be the same person from Leon Chen's and outside Louise's house. Same person who shot Deborah Salvo and shot Jim Wolf and tried to make it look like a suicide."

"The killings and the fraud all pass through Louise, which means it's someone close to her. Personally or by proximity. Close enough to know she was the perfect front for their plan," Packard said.

Thielen snapped her fingers a bunch of times in a row. "And if they were that close, they might have heard from Louise that the acting sheriff grew up in her house. His grandparents owned it. After Louise is dead, the shooter sees a chance to use the Bill Sandersen murder as cover and make sure you never come around to ask questions about Louise."

"Why would I?"

"Maybe they thought if you were elected sheriff you might take a special interest in something that had escaped your attention."

"I hadn't announced I was running for sheriff at that point."

"Shooting you would make sure you never got the chance."

If the shooter and Jim Wolf were working closely together on the fraud, the shooter likely would have known of Wolf's plan to get Shepard elected. Taking out the acting sheriff—the only other viable candidate—would almost guarantee Shepard the job. A sheriff who never looked too closely at things was invaluable when you were trying to get away with fraud and murder.

Shepard must have picked up on the undertones of the conversation because he looked like the pain in his ass had grown to the size of his whole ass. He couldn't sit still. "Let's stick to facts," he said. "Someone definitely took a shot at you. Might have been the same person as at Leon Chen's. Whether it had anything to do with the election is speculation. We may never know."

We may never know was Shepard's answer to every question he couldn't be bothered to answer during his long career in law enforcement. It should have been his campaign slogan.

"You're right," Packard said. He got up and stood by the window behind Shepard's desk. The view wasn't great—it was of the parking lot—but it used to help him think when he sat where Shepard was sitting.

"I like what you said about the shooter learning something directly from Louise," Packard said to Thielen over the top of Shepard's head. "Louise didn't have a big circle of friends or family. Who were the people closest to her?"

Thielen looked lost. She pointed at Shepard. "Uh...your father-in-law played bridge with her."

Shepard groaned like he was in actual pain. "No, Ray had nothing to do with this. No."

"He's right," Packard said. "Also, Ray is blind in one eye. Give him a gun and he couldn't hit a school bus from ten feet. I'm thinking more literally. Who were the people literally closest to Louise?"

Thielen stared at her hands like she was counting on her fingers. "The neighbors."

"Exactly."

Now his wheels were turning. Max and Linda Scarpetta on one side. Brian and Andrea Hopkins on the other. Max had had his eye on Louise's property for a long time. Had made her multiple offers on it, using Jim Wolf as his go-between. Max used to work in banking before quietly retiring just as fraudulent activities in the area he oversaw became public. Fraud, phony bank accounts, millions of dollars. Sounded familiar. Max was also the first person to tell him about Tess and her job helping Louise with her properties.

On the other side was Brian Hopkins. A man of no obvious means who owned an expensive lake home. Went to Canada for work frequently, which was where Deborah Salvo's cell phone last pinged. Multiple LLCs in his name that had no obvious purpose. A bad marriage. A house full of guns.

"I noticed lights on at Max and Linda Scarpetta's place when I arrived at Louise's the other night. Did they come out or have any involvement that night?"

"Linda is down in the Cities babysitting grandkids, according to Max. He was out getting dinner and got caught outside the perimeter. It was hours before they let him in to go home."

"That's not the tightest alibi in the world. What about Brian?"

"He was home playing video games in his basement. Said he didn't notice the fire until he saw it out of the corner of his eye through the easement window. He actually got burned trying to keep the fire from getting too close to their house. He hooked up a hose in the garage sink and dragged it outside and was spraying his house when the wind changed. He got a little roasted. They took you to the hospital in one ambulance and him in the other."

"Either of those guys could have been the shooter," Packard said. "Brian has more guns than you can imagine. I was in Max's house but didn't get a tour. He could have an arsenal in the basement for all we know."

"What about Robert Clark?" Shepard asked out of nowhere. "Didn't all of this start with him trying to kill Jim at his trial? Maybe whoever shot Jim was seeking revenge for Clark and wanted to take you out, too, for shooting Clark."

"It's plausible," Packard said, coming back to his chair. "We can look into it. I can't be investigating anything to do with Robert Clark since I was involved in the incident. There's a list of Clark's friends and family in the BCA report. If my neighbor theory doesn't pan out, we can send someone around to talk to those people."

"What are you going to do?" Shepard asked Packard.

Packard tented his fingers, thinking. "Wait for Reynolds to report back on the gun. Write a search warrant for Wolf's phone records. Do we have access to his house?"

Thielen opened her mouth, then closed it suddenly. She put a hand on her belly and looked like she was trying to swallow a burp.

"Are you okay?" Packard asked.

"I'm fine," she said, taking a deep breath. "So no, we don't have access to his house. I was waiting for you to get out of the hospital to see what direction you wanted to go. What do we have to put on the warrant?"

"Has anyone notified his mother about his death?"

Shepard said, "We sent a deputy to her house and told her that we had reason to believe Jim was inside the house when it burned down. Outside of that she doesn't know much."

"He drove her car there. Is it impounded?"

Thielen nodded.

"Let me talk to his mom. Maybe she can give permission to search his house. I was with her right before I went to Louise's house looking for Wolf. She asked me about Robert Clark and then asked me not to shoot her son if he'd done something bad."

"That poor woman," Thielen said.

"I need to tell her what happened. She should hear it from me."

"Keep me posted," Shepard said, standing and hitching up his pants.

"Wait," Thielen said, a hand on her belly. "I have one more thing to talk about while you're both here."

CHAPTER THIRTY-ONE

AN HOUR LATER, PACKARD rang the doorbell at Patrice Wolf's house. Jim's black Lincoln Navigator was parked in front of the garage. An ice dam dripped water onto its hood.

Patrice answered the door wrapped in a fuzzy housecoat and Adidas shower shoes over heavy blue socks. He'd called ahead so she was expecting him. Her eyes and nose were red. It was early afternoon but she looked like she had just gotten up or was on her way back to bed.

They sat in the living room where a big picture window looked out over a wide expanse of cleared land that went way back to a heavy tree line. The walls were textured and faintly peach and the furniture was big and floral and pleated along the bottoms. It screamed 1990s mom. She offered him water. He accepted.

"Your voice sounds worse in person than it did on the phone," she said.

"The doctor said to expect it to be like this for a while."

He started off by telling her he was sorry for her loss. "You know Jim and I didn't see eye-to-eye on most things, but I never wanted this for him. I'm not a parent, so I can only imagine how painful it must be to lose a child."

Patrice wiped at her nose with a tissue. "Thank you," she said.

He told her what he'd done since they last saw each other, how he'd gone to Louise's house to find Jim after locating her car there, using the app on her phone. "One of the things Jim and I disagreed about were his plans for tearing down Louise's home. I told him it was a crime scene and nothing was going to happen to it until I released it. Seeing his car parked there and knowing he hadn't responded to your texts all day had me curious."

He told her the house was on fire when he got there. "Jim wasn't in the car. I ran around outside, calling his name. I didn't see flames yet so I ran inside looking for him. He was in the basement. He'd been shot in the head."

Patrice's face contorted. "Shot?" She made a shuddering, keening noise. "Shot?" she said again.

Packard nodded. He moved to sit beside her on the couch and let her cry against him. She cried for a long time. "Oh, Jimmy," she said. "Oh my Jimmy," she said. Packard said, "I'm sorry. I'm very sorry, Patrice."

Packard let her cry for as long as she wanted. When she was done, he set his phone on the glass-topped coffee table in front of them. "I have a recording of my call with dispatch on here. It's unedited. It's not graphic but you can hear me describe for the operator exactly what I found as it happened. I can play it for you or I can tell you what I saw in whatever level of detail you want."

Patrice wrapped her robe around her knees, leaned back, and closed her eyes. "Play it," she said.

It started as he said, with him giving his location and reporting the house on fire and calling out for Jim. The recording captured the dispatch operator talking on the radio, requesting firefighters and deputies to the scene.

Packard: I'm in the house, heading into the basement.

Dispatch: The burning house?

You could hear his footsteps on the wooden stairs, the same ones Louise had fallen down to her death. The phone's microphone picked up a lot of moving air and the crackling sound of fire consuming the dry house.

Packard: There's a male on the floor in the basement, DOA, GSW to the temple. It's Jim Wolf. Confirm no pulse, not breathing.

He explained to Louise the meaning of the abbreviations he was using. Deceased on arrival. Gunshot wound. She nodded, tears leaking from her closed eyes.

On the recording Packard said he was bringing the gun out. A minute later he was reporting gunshots. They weren't audible on the recording. There was a sound of broken glass from the last shot through the bathroom window. The call ended with the dispatch operator calling his badge ID and asking him to confirm his location.

Dispatch: Two one seven. Can you respond? Two one seven? Please report your location. Two one seven, do you copy?

Packard stopped the recording. "You know everything we know right now," he said. "And I'll tell you something I suspect but can't prove yet. Jim's death was supposed to look like a suicide, but I don't believe he killed himself. I think he met someone in that house who shot him. Probably the same person who was shooting at me from outside."

"My son would not have committed suicide. Right or wrong, he would have fought to the ends of the earth. You know that."

"I do know that."

"Did you see the shooter at all?"

Packard shook his head. "It was so smoky. I couldn't breathe. I had my eyes closed running through the kitchen at the end. If I hadn't bumped into the doorway, I might have stumbled down the back stairs and into a bullet."

"So what now?"

"I wanted to ask you if you've seen anything out of the ordinary at the office. Anyone unexpected or unfamiliar come by?"

She said no and shook her head, but he could tell she was thinking of something and was reluctant to say it.

"Patrice, if you know anything, you should tell me. You can't hurt Jim."

She closed her eyes like she was trying to hold back tears. When she opened them, she said, "I can tell you two things. I don't know if they're relevant or not. Number one: he has two cell phones. He has a weird cheap one that I saw him using a couple of times. I asked him about it and he said not to worry about it. The other thing: sometime last year I went to the copier and found a stack of paper in the tray that someone left behind. It was a purchase agreement for a lot and the buyer was Louise Larsen. This was after she had died. The seller was my son. I took him the papers and asked about them because drawing up the papers and putting the little flags for all the signatures and making sure everything gets submitted is my job. I said, 'How come I don't have this sale in my calendar?' He said it was a private matter that he was handling. I said, 'How can Louise buy property? She died.' He said it wasn't Louise, it was her company. Then like the phone, he told me not to worry about it."

A sale of property from Jim to Louise, paid for by money from her fraudulent account would have allowed Jim to wash the funds through his business while being able to claim ignorance about where they originated. He could have backdated documents to before her death if he needed to and had Tess write a check from the account.

"That's very helpful, Patrice. It lets us know to look for a second phone. The purchase agreement is interesting as well." She didn't need to know about the fraud. Not from him. Not now.

"Patrice, it could help us find Jim's killer if we had permission to search his house. I can get a warrant if I have to, but you're his immediate family. We can do it with your permission and save a lot of time, which is our most valuable commodity right now."

Patrice put her hands on either side of her face and shook her head. "I know he would hate the idea of police searching his house," she said. She got up, hugged herself and shuffled to the hall table by the door, then came back slowly, giving herself plenty of time to change her mind. She had keys clenched in her hand. She held them to her forehead, then extended them to Packard.

"It's like you said. Nothing can hurt him now. You have my permission," she said.

Packard tried not to rush out of there once he had the keys. He stayed with Patrice and answered all her questions about what would happen with Jim's body and when he thought she could get her car back and if it was okay to keep driving Jim's Navigator. He asked her if he could search Jim's vehicle and she said yes. He went through every inch of it but turned up nothing useful.

He called Thielen on his way to Jim's house. "I got permission to search and keys from Wolf's mom. Want to meet me there?"

"See you in twenty," she said.

Jim's house was on a spit of land that ran between two lakes. The view from his front yard overlooked one lake and the backyard the other. An acre of concrete driveway led to three large garage bays where a patrol car was idling, driven by a deputy Packard had requested meet him there.

Packard chatted with the deputy on the front step while they waited for Thielen. The deputy had responded to the fire at Louise's and told Packard how lucky he was to have made it to the back bathroom. "If you couldn't get out, that was the best place to be. I drove by again today. All that's left is the chimney stack and the framing for the back addition."

"My grandfather added that on. The house needed a second bathroom."

"He did a good job."

When Thielen arrived, Packard used the keys he got from Patrice to unlock the front door. The three of them stepped inside a large open-concept space: living room, dining room, and kitchen combined. Doors on the far wall looked like they led to bedrooms. Wooden accents were everywhere—shiplap on the walls, faux support beams on the ceiling, heavy trim around the windows. The couches were white linen, the kitchen slightly dated with oak cabinets, a weird square island, and granite countertops with rounded corners.

"What are we looking for?" Thielen asked.

They weren't bound by the terms of a search warrant but Packard didn't necessarily want to pull down the ceiling or open the walls. "Let's look for a computer, any paperwork related to Larsen LLC, a cell phone, possibly a burner."

The deputy stayed by the front door. Packard and Thielen started opening doors, looking for an office. All they found were bedrooms and bathrooms. Packard found it hard to believe Wolf ran a multimillion-dollar fraud scheme out of his work office. There would be too many prying eyes. Too many people with access to his systems. Leaving the contract in the copier that Patrice found probably taught him that lesson.

Packard opened a door off the kitchen and found himself in the heated garage. The floors were lacquered smooth and flecked with color. There were big chairs for seating on an area rug and a long bar with beer taps and a pool table and still enough room to park two vehicles. A set of stairs dropped down to the middle of the room. With all three doors open in the summertime, it would have been an indoor-outdoor paradise.

Thielen was right behind him. "Maybe an office up those stairs," she said.

She was right. The space right above the second garage stall had slanted ceilings, built-in bookcases, and a huge picture window overlooking the lake in the back. A desk faced the window and had two chairs in front of it. On top was a docking station for a laptop and a large monitor. No laptop. The lower drawers in the desk had hangers for file folders that were surprisingly short on papers. Behind cabinet doors in the built-ins were a bar and a coffee station. Their search turned up a frustrating lack of items. In his head, Packard started filling out the search warrant they'd need for Jim's business office.

They did a thorough search of the garage, the kitchen, and Jim's bedroom. They walked through the snow across the backyard to a separate structure that had a kitchenette, a bathroom, and a bedroom. A mother-in-law suite or a short-term rental. It was spotlessly clean. Nothing but basic toiletries and pantry staples in any of the cabinets.

Packard had left the keys in the door. Thielen locked it and handed the heavy bundle back to Packard. "What is that thing on his key ring?" she asked.

Packard looked at the keys in his palm. A magnet wrapped in silicone added weight to the set. "It's a magnet. Probably to stick the keys to the wall."

"That's a monster magnet for sticking to a wall. What about a lock that needs a magnet to release it?" Thielen said. "Ever seen one of those?"

He had.

"It's gotta be in the office somewhere," Packard said.

Back up the stairs in the garage. Packard looked closely at the built-ins again. The lower third of the bookcases all had paneled fronts. He'd tried pulling on them already and knocking against their facades. Nothing budged. He passed the magnet across the framing until it snapped in place. Packard pulled on the corner of the panel. It gave slightly but the other corner still held tightly. When he moved the magnet to the other corner, the first one refused to budge.

"There's two magnets," he said. "We need to find the other magnet."

They retrained their eyes, no longer looking for a cell phone or a computer or stacks of paper. They looked under the desk, deep inside drawers, the light fixture, the toilet tank in the bathroom.

"Found it," Thielen finally said, standing near the coffee bar. "It was under an espresso cup."

With both magnets in place, a drawer slid out. Inside: a laptop, a ledger, a black flip phone, and a digital recorder that plugged into the phone's headphone jack.

Packard used his phone to take a photo of everything in situ. "We'll get the laptop back to Suresh. I'm not even going to try to open it. There's no way there's not a password on it."

He picked up the digital recorder and pressed the Rewind button. Pressed Play.

Jim Wolf said, *"They found a dead woman in the Cedar Creek property. Do you know anything about that?"*

"Who is it?"

"They haven't released a name yet. The news says a body's been found. I asked Shepard. He said she was shot. Didn't know her name."

Packard and Thielen looked at each other. Packard shook his head. Fucking Shepard. He backed up the tape further.

Jim Wolf again: *"She's gone. I mean fucking disappeared. I'm locked out of the account."*

"Why didn't you get the password?"

"I had the password. She changed it before she left. There's no more money coming in without her. There's no getting the money out of that account. I've already written checks against that money. I'm fucked."

Packard hit Rewind again.

Jim Wolf: *"Packard's not letting this go."*

"Did you think you were going to talk him out of it?"

"I thought Shepard would be able to put a collar on him."

"Getting Shepard elected was supposed to help us when we needed a hand or a blind eye from law enforcement. Now we have an imbecile who offers neither. You need to do something about Packard."

"What does that mean?" Wolf asked.

"It means whatever you think it means. Take care of him."

Packard hit Stop. "Aww, they wanted to take care of me. That's nice of them."

"How can you make jokes hearing something like that?" Thielen asked.

Packard shrugged. "Do you recognize the other voice?"

"I don't. Should I?"

"Not necessarily."

"Are you going to tell me?"

"Not yet."

Thielen stood with her hands in the small of her back, lifted her chin to the ceiling, and stretched. "I got evidence bags and a sheet in my car. I'll be back."

Packard listened to more of the recording. No names. The dialogue was purposefully vague. Funny how everything made sense now that he knew who Wolf had been working with this whole time. The hard part was going to be proving any of it.

When Thielen came back, she had her phone in her hand. "It's Reynolds. He tracked down the owner of the gun you found next to Wolf's body."

She put the phone on speaker and they listened to Reynolds tell them about a gun shop in Fargo that received the gun from the manufacturer and made the first sale. "The first buyer lived in Fargo and said he'd sold it to a buddy from

Saint Paul who admired it when he came pheasant hunting. The guy in Saint Paul didn't want to tell me who he sold the gun to. 'There's no national registry for a reason. Gun owners are entitled to their privacy. Blah blah blah.' I told him the gun had been used in a murder, and if he was the last known owner on record, I'd be happy to take his life apart looking for a connection to the murderer or the victim."

Packard gazed fondly at Thielen. "You've trained him so well," he said.

"He learned from the best," she said.

"What did he say after that?" Packard asked Reynolds.

"He didn't like that idea. He told me he traded the gun for another one at a gun show up north."

"Did he remember the guy's name?" Packard asked.

"He did. They exchanged info and emails afterward."

"Who was it?"

Reynolds said the name. Packard wasn't surprised.

"Now do you recognize the voice on the recorder?" he asked Thielen.

"Now I do," she said.

CHAPTER THIRTY-TWO

IT TOOK SEVERAL DAYS to get a plan together. Packard ran it by Thielen first.

"Sounds risky," she said. "Makes sense to move while his wife is out of town. What comes next will be hard to predict."

"All we can do is have a solid plan and execute to the best of our abilities."

Packard called FBI Agent Riley in Minneapolis and told her what he'd uncovered, including the names of everyone involved in the fraud. He told her his plan for arresting the person responsible for the deaths of Louise Larsen, Deborah Salvo, and Jim Wolf. "Sounds risky," Riley said.

"I'm going for murder charges," Packard said. "Minneapolis PD and the BCA are looped in. You're welcome to be there and cuff 'em for the fraud, too."

"We'll sit this one out. What happened to your voice?" she asked.

"Long story," he said.

The sun threw the last of its rays, trying to add precious seconds to the day as four Sandy Lake sheriff's vehicles pulled up next door to the charred remains of

Louise Larsen's house. It was Packard's first time back since the fire. Being able to see straight through to the lake where a house once stood felt like a mirage. Blink and the house would be back. He wouldn't let himself get sentimental about the loss. It hadn't been his family's home for decades. He remembered his walk-through with Lisa Washington and her offer to get him the basement door with all the kids' heights marked on it. It was the only thing he might have wanted. Now it was ash and what he wanted was irrelevant.

Everyone got out of their vehicles. Packard led the way and rang the doorbell. When the door opened, he said, "Brian Hopkins. I have a search warrant for these premises to look for items related to the deaths of Deborah Salvo and Jim Wolf."

Brian had his gaming headphones around his neck and a wireless controller in one hand. He looked disoriented, as if the game he'd been playing had bled over into the real world. "Wait, what? A search warrant for what?" he asked.

"Can we come in?" Packard asked.

Brian stepped aside just far enough to make room for Packard and Thielen. The rest of the deputies gathered outside the door. Packard explained the warrant and what they were looking for. Brian looked bewildered, then angry. Andrea Hopkins had warned Packard about her husband's temper. Packard stood close, crowding him.

"This is… I don't know what's going on. I don't know any Deborah. What does any of this have to do with me?"

"I'm going to answer all your questions, and then I want you to answer some questions for me. We can do it here or you can come down to the sheriff's office."

"Before or after you trash my house?"

"No one is going to trash your house. The search will be orderly and respectful."

Brian looked down the hall. He looked at the controller in his hand like he could push a button and reset the game.

"Am I under arrest? Do I need a lawyer?"

"You are not under arrest," Packard said. "Questioning is voluntary. If you decline, we'll wait to see what turns up during the search. Depending on what we find, I may decide we have probable cause to arrest you. Then things become a lot less voluntary."

Brian looked defeated, exhausted. "Fine. Search. I'll answer your questions."

Reynolds stepped inside and asked Hopkins for his car keys, the key to his gun room, and where to find any tablets, computers, and phones he owned. After a quick initial sweep of the house by the deputies to make sure no one else was there, Packard, Thielen, and Brian had a seat in the sunroom. Clouds stretched away from them over the frozen lake in pinks and purples. Everything that rose above the horizon stood in silhouette. Brian pushed a button on a remote to turn on the gas fireplace.

They sat around a game table. Packard unzipped the portfolio he was carrying and gave Brian a copy of the search warrant. The next thing he handed him was a photograph of the gun used to shoot Deborah and Jim with an L-shaped photomacrographic scale in the corner. At the bottom were the gun's serial number and the contact information for the man who sold Brian the gun. "Do you recognize this gun?" Packard asked.

"Looks familiar. I know this guy you have listed here."

"He said he traded this gun for one you had at a gun show."

Brian looked more closely at the photo. "I don't know if it was this exact one but it looks like this. Could be this one."

"Do you keep a list of all your guns' serial numbers?"

"Yes, I have a spreadsheet online."

"You want to look it up?"

"They took my phone," Brian said.

Packard called for a deputy and asked her to bring Brian's phone. Brian unlocked it and pulled up his spreadsheet. He asked Packard for the last three numbers. Packard saw his answer on Brian's face before he confirmed out loud that it was his gun.

"I found this gun next to Jim Wolf's body in the basement next door."

"You were in the house before it burned down?"

"I was in it while it was burning down," Packard said.

Brian shook his head in disbelief. "I heard there was an injured responder. I thought it was a firefighter. I didn't know it was you." He turned to Thielen. "I told you I didn't notice the fire until the house was engulfed. I was downstairs playing games."

"You did tell me that," Thielen agreed. Her tone made it sound like the information was irrelevant.

"Jim was shot in the head with this gun," Packard said. "We also did a ballistics comparison between a round fired from this gun and a slug we retrieved from a crime scene in Cedar Creek. That slug passed through the head of Deborah Salvo, a worker for the State of Minnesota. They matched."

"I already told you I don't know anyone named Deborah."

"And I'm telling you your gun was used to kill two people."

Brian sat back in his chair. He folded his arms and put an ankle over his knee. His foot bounced like a fish on a dock.

Before Packard could continue, a deputy came in carrying something wrapped in plastic. "We found these in the trunk of the car, under the spare tire." He unfolded two bags and held them up by the seals. Inside one was a cell phone and in the other a wallet.

"Any ID in the wallet?" Packard asked.

"Driver's license and several credit cards for Deborah Salvo."

"That's bullshit. You guys are trying to frame me!" Brian shouted. "I've never met or even heard of Deborah Salvo before."

"The sheriff's office is not trying to frame you. We're here looking for answers," Packard assured him. He dismissed the deputy and handed Brian another piece of paper. "The last anyone saw Deborah Salvo was Sunday before Memorial Day. Those are phone company records showing her phone last in contact with a cell tower near Winnipeg in Canada a couple of days later. Can you account for your whereabouts for that time period?"

Brian still had his phone. He opened his calendar, scrolled back, and shook his head regretfully. "I was in Winnipeg for four days that week," he admitted.

Packard nodded. "Based on the contents of her stomach, we were able to determine your neighbor Louise died on the Sunday before Memorial Day. Only she didn't fall down the stairs like everyone assumed. Someone smashed her head against the doorframe, cracked her skull, then pushed her down the stairs."

Brian stood up and walked around his chair and leaned on the back of it. "I suppose now a deputy is going to walk in here and say she found Louise's bloody fucking housecoat in the trunk of my car."

"Is Louise's bloody housecoat in the trunk of your car?" Packard asked.

"No!" Brian yelled. "That other stuff wasn't put there by me either."

"Answer this for me," Packard said. "Do you have an account at a bank in the Cook Islands?"

"Fuck," Brian said. He put both hands on his head and grabbed handfuls of his hair. "Yes, I have an account like that."

"What's the balance in it?"

"It's zero. I used that account and a blind shell company to hold stocks and investments that we didn't want traced to my wife in any way. Stuff that wouldn't look good for a sitting representative."

"You still own those stocks?"

"No, I got into trading crypto and…got fucked. I chose the wrong exchange to hold my money. It collapsed, all the assets were frozen, and I lost every dime we had."

"Can you check the Cook Islands account balance online?"

"Yes."

"Do it."

Brian on his phone: swipe, swipe, thumbs, scroll. For at least the third time that night he looked like he'd had the surprise of his life. "There's almost two million dollars in this account."

"I can assure you the Sandy Lake Sheriff's Department didn't plant that either," Packard said.

"I don't know where this money came from. We haven't had this kind of money since the exchange collapsed."

"Two more questions. Do you have a rifle that shoots .223 cartridges?"

"Of course I do. I have more than one."

"Last fall someone pulled up to Leon Chen's home in a boat and took two shots at me from the water. It was a couple of days after Labor Day. Was that you?"

"It wasn't me and I'll tell you how you should know. If I ever took a shot at you, I wouldn't miss once, let alone twice. I can hit a five-inch bull's-eye from a thousand yards. I don't miss."

"Were you in town at that time?"

Brian looked at his calendar on his phone again. "No, I was in Winnipeg then, too. My company doesn't give a shit about American holidays. We follow their calendar more than ours."

"Okay, you have an alibi for that. But Louise Larsen and Deborah Salvo were killed on the same day last summer and the next day you left for Canada, where Deborah's phone last pinged before the battery died. We found Deborah's phone and wallet in your car. A gun you admit to owning was used to kill Deborah and was also found next to the body of Jim Wolf. And now you have two million dollars in an account and claim not to know where it came from. What does all this say to you?"

Brian looked like he didn't know if he should sit down or jump out a window. He threw his hands up. "It doesn't say anything to me. I didn't do any of it."

Packard nodded slowly. He swept up his papers and zipped the portfolio. "I know you're not guilty of these crimes. That's why I'm here with a search warrant and not an arrest warrant."

"Then...why? Who?" Brian sputtered.

"I know you didn't kill those people," Packard said. "Your wife did."

CHAPTER THIRTY-THREE

THE SUN HAD SET, turning the solarium's glass windows into black mirrors that reflected the three of them sitting in the room from every angle. The footfalls and quiet conversations of the deputies searching the rest of the house sounded like a haunting.

"Tell me about Andrea," Packard said. The fact that Brian hadn't protested Packard's accusation or insisted his wife couldn't possibly be responsible had already told him a lot.

"We met in college in Kentucky. We were both on the rifle team, won the NCAA championship in 2005 and 2006. Andrea's family was incredibly poor. She was on an ROTC scholarship so she owed the army eight years when she graduated. We kind of broke up at that point because we didn't know where she was going or for how long. While she was serving, she got selected for the civilian engagement team. These were teams of female soldiers deployed alongside special operations forces in combat situations to interact with Afghan women and children. The CETs trained and carried guns and fought when necessary, just like the special forces. Near the end of her time in Afghanistan, the truck in front of hers hit an IED. A woman in her unit was killed and Andrea was wounded in the firefight that followed. She came home after that and switched to the reserves to finish her obligation."

"How did you two reconnect?"

"She tracked me down. I was living in the Cities at the time, working in the financial industry. She called me up, told me she was moving to Minneapolis and wanted to get back together. I told her I had another girlfriend. Andrea asked if it was serious. I said, 'Not real serious, it's only been six months.' Andrea said, 'Get rid of her.'"

Thielen listened with a wary expression. She'd met enough female victims of violence that she was automatically on guard when a man tried to present his wife or girlfriend as an all-powerful witch who used her magic against helpless men. "You must have wanted to get back together if you eventually got married," Thielen said.

"I did want to get back together. We were very compatible. Neither of us wanted kids. We were ambitious in our careers. I wanted to help her realize her dream."

"Which was?"

"To have a career in politics. We moved to Sandy Lake for the express reason that the representative was old and would either be close to retirement or vulnerable to a challenge."

"It takes a lot of money to be a serious player in politics," Packard said.

"At the time, we had it. I was one of the few people who saw the 2008 crash coming. I shorted everything and made a pile. The pile got bigger when the market bounced back. For a long time I thought I could do no wrong when it came to investing. We bought this house. Andrea started making inroads with local players in business and politics. When Representative Campbell announced his retirement, she launched her campaign. Voters loved her immediately. She was young. She was a veteran. She stood for the things people around here care about."

"She's in her second term. How did she go from decorated veteran, popular politician to massive fraud and murder?" Thielen asked.

"She had a hard life growing up. Alcoholic father, a predatory uncle, disbelieving mother. It's given her an eat-or-be-eaten view of the world," Brian said. "She's relentless when it comes to getting what she wants. She was the first in her family to go to college. She joined the army for the scholarship. They must have seen that drive in her when they recruited her for the civilian engagement program. The army trained her for combat. She was a noticeably different person after Afghanistan. I think the year she spent there going on night raids and jumping out of helicopters to sweep mountain villages rewired her brain. She's always in fight-or-flight mode, and when cornered or threatened she will fight."

"When I visited her in her office, she said you were in the process of separating and that your temper was at the root of things."

Brian Hopkins huffed in disbelief. "I'm not the one with the temper. I'm not the one who goes nuclear over the slightest provocation. Being in politics has taught her that she can say or do whatever she wants. It's your fault for not getting it. You're the one who gets belittled for not letting something go and moving with her on to the next manufactured outrage."

"That's a hot take," Thielen said. "What happened to wanting to support her political aspirations?"

"I don't think either one of us knew how corrupting politics can be. Or maybe she did and I'm the naive one. I've become very disillusioned with things while she's gotten adept at swimming in the sewer."

"Is that what broke your marriage?" Packard asked.

"Part of it. The bigger part is that I lost all our money. Crypto kept going up and up. I ignored the warning signs, put more and more of our money into it using a single exchange. The end came in a matter of hours. Insiders started raising concerns about the exchange's stability. The big guys pulled their money and the whole thing collapsed. When the dust settled, we were wiped out. The problem now is we can't afford to separate. She especially can't afford it. Do you know how much a state representative makes?"

Packard shook his head.

"About fifty grand a year. She can't buy a separate house with that. Back when we were flush, we put in a separate entrance here and soundproofed the lower level for guests or short-term renters. Now I live downstairs and she lives upstairs. We can both be here and not know the other is around. We won't be able to stay here much longer. The next tax bill is going to wipe us out. I've been insisting we need to get the house on the market, and she's been saying she'll figure something out."

So Andrea started planning for her financial future without her husband's knowledge. Packard explained to Brian where the two million dollars in the account came from. Andrea would have known about the meal reimbursement program from her work on the children and families committee. She told Jim Wolf about it and he worked with Tess to execute the fraud and split the proceeds among the three of them.

Brian almost looked amused. "She and her cohorts in the legislature see themselves as outside of the government, acting as watchdogs on behalf of the voters. Their message is that the government can't be trusted with our tax dollars or to manage its own bureaucracy. Allowing this kind of fraud to take place is a perfect example of what they're talking about."

"I don't necessarily disagree with her," Packard said. "She's about to find out how proficient the government can be at cleaning up its messes when necessary. The FBI is on to this fraud and getting ready to sweep people up in its net."

"It better be a strong net or she'll wriggle out."

"She's wriggling right now," Packard said. "You realize with Deborah's phone in your car—and your gun used to kill two people and conveniently left behind—that's she framing you for all of this," Packard said. "The FBI has already traced the money to your account in the Cook Islands. Andrea will be able to say it's your account, your fraud. And it'll be easier to do if you're dead and can't deny her version of the story."

Brian paled. Packard could read Brian's thoughts on his face as he considered what Packard was saying and regretfully came to the same conclusion. "I honestly never thought she would kill innocent people to get what she wanted. Does she know you're on to her?"

"She doesn't know about the FBI. She does know that I tracked the fraud to Jim because I told him I knew everything he and Tess had been up to. He would have told her and I'm sure that led to their meeting in Louise's basement where he got shot in the head."

"If she was in town the day of the fire, I didn't know about it. Never saw her," Brian said.

"I'm sure that was intentional. She came up here to kill Jim. She wouldn't want anyone to be able to place her in the area. Burning down the house and shooting at me were last-minute decisions made in the moment."

"She shot at you?"

"Someone shot at me when I tried to leave Louise's house while it was on fire. That's how I got trapped in the back. I didn't know about Andrea when I confronted Jim, but I knew if he was dead and someone was still trying to kill me, there had to be another player. Unfortunately for Andrea, Jim recorded their conversations. She doesn't say much on the recordings, but it's enough for me to know she's the chess master behind everything."

"What are you going to do?"

Packard told him the plan.

"Sounds risky," Brian said.

Packard remembered Stan Shaw's note to him (*Hello, Ben*) on the last page of his brother's file and the risk he took in trading it to Abbas Rassin for the location of Nick's body, everything riding on the chance that Packard would find the file again or figure things out without it.

Sometimes taking a risk was the only option.

CHAPTER THIRTY-FOUR

ANDREA HOPKINS GOT A call from her husband at 9:00 p.m. that night telling her the police had been to their house. They'd asked him about a gun he owned, and when was the last time he saw Jim Wolf, and whether he knew anyone by the name of Deborah Salvo. He sounded panicked. He had to be to call her, considering they'd barely spoken two words to each other in the last several months.

"They won't tell me what's going on or why they're asking. Just question after question," he said. She had connections to the new sheriff. He wanted her to use them to find out what was going on.

"Go to bed," she said. "I'll make some calls in the morning."

She didn't do anything that night. The next night, she and a representative from southwestern Minnesota held a community forum about the agricultural needs of their different parts of the state. After they talked about the current ag bill, most of the audience questions were about voter fraud and COVID conspiracies. She came to talk about the needs of farmers, but if scared people wanted to talk about things that scared them, who was she to stop them? Andrea smiled a lot and made sure not to say anything that would dissuade anyone from their feverish beliefs. Confirming people's convictions bought more political goodwill than any action she might take.

Brian left a message asking if she found out anything from the sheriff. She ignored him.

On the third night, she made her move.

When she was in the army, training with twenty other women for the team that was going to operate alongside Army Rangers in Afghanistan, an instructor told them they'd have one second to find the switch in their minds that turned them from negotiators and communicators into killers. They weren't being sent in as members of an assault team, but they would be right alongside the men who were, and they would live or die by their ability to read a situation and kill without hesitation when necessary. Even when things seemed calm, the instructor said, they were never to forget they were always on a battlefield.

First Lieutenant Andrea Hopkins flipped that switch twice in Afghanistan. Once, standing in a courtyard when insurgents started firing at them from inside a home. The Ranger next to her gave her a quadrant to cover, and she shot a Taliban fighter through a window while a helicopter hovered overhead and dropped brass shell casings from its machine gun into the courtyard like rain. The second time was when their caravan hit the IED and they ended up in a firefight.

Last summer, when she looked out her window and saw the State of Minnesota car parked outside Louise's house, she felt like she was right back on the battlefield. She remembered the smells of Afghanistan: sweat and excrement and diesel and gun oil. She felt the weight of her gear.

It was Sunday afternoon before Memorial Day. Max Scarpetta had invited her and Brian to attend the party they were having. Andrea had no intention of going until she saw the state car. If they invited her, they would have invited Louise. It was the perfect excuse she needed to drop by unexpectedly.

She walked next door, let herself in the back, and found Deborah Salvo asking Louise about the meals she claimed to have served and how she justified the numbers for such a small county. Louise looked like she was being sprayed in the face with a hose. She didn't understand a word the woman was saying.

Andrea put on her biggest smile, introduced herself by her first name, and said to Louise they should head next door for the party.

"I think you should talk to the woman who manages my rentals," Louise said before Andrea could interrupt. "They're all empty. I wish we had people making money and serving meals. My husband thought the rentals would be good investments but my goodness. I think all they've done is cost me money for the last decade." Louise got her purse and read Tess's phone number and address from a little red book she carried.

Deborah gave Louise her card before leaving, said she'd be in touch. Andrea walked Louise over to Max and Linda's, said hi to her neighbors, then used the size of the crowd to sneak away. She called Jim from the burner phone she'd stuck in her pocket before leaving home. "A woman from the State of Minnesota is on her way to see Tess. Tell her to get out of the house or play dumb. I'll catch up with this lady and see if I can deflect her."

Andrea went inside Louise's house, took her keys, and called the number on Deborah's card. "I talked to Louise after you left. She's confused and worried. She asked me to take you around to her businesses if that would help with your questions."

They met in Cedar Creek. Nothing was open in the tiny downtown. On a holiday weekend everyone was on their boat or grilling with friends or drinking somewhere there were other people. There were no people in Cedar Creek.

In front of the café, Andrea introduced herself again, unnecessarily it turned out, as Deborah knew exactly who she was—even knew the committees she served on. Andrea tried to redirect the conversation to how upset Louise was, how concerned Andrea was for her neighbor. Deborah wouldn't be budged from the matter at hand.

"You must be familiar with the meal reimbursement program. There was a lot of debate about it in committee." There was an undertone to her statement. A disbelief that it couldn't be a coincidence that this old woman would be defrauding a program that her next-door neighbor had a hand in green lighting. What were the odds?

When Andrea had first heard of the meal reimbursement program through her committee position and closely read the requirements to participate, she knew it would take only days for fraud to start. Why not take advantage if she could figure out a way to isolate herself? Did she have a problem decrying government waste while picking its pocket? She did not. It was only hypocrisy if you got caught. Voters no longer insisted on virtue from their elected officials. They would overlook anything as long as they hated the other party more than they disliked any particular action of yours.

Andrea unlocked the door to the café. Deborah was still talking about inflated meal counts when they pushed through the swinging door into the kitchen. They looked in the empty freezer. Deborah's last words were "Obviously there's no food prep or distribution going on at this—"

Andrea dragged the body inside the freezer and turned it on. She was wondering what to do with Deborah's car when she spotted the row of garage stalls across the alley. There was a key on Louise's ring that said CC Garage. It would have been used by a renter if the apartment above the café was occupied. Andrea put Deborah's car in the garage space, kept her wallet and phone, and hid them under the spare tire in Brian's trunk when she got home.

That night she stopped at Louise's again under the pretense of seeing how she enjoyed the party. Louise talked about how many little kids were there and the vanilla cake decorated with strawberry slices. When Andrea asked about the woman from that afternoon, Louise looked exasperated. "I still don't understand what she was talking about. She kept saying I was committing fraud." Louise was in her robe and making hot water for tea on the stove. "It's a holiday tomorrow. I'll call Ray on Tuesday and see what he thinks."

She went to the tiny pantry cabinet for the box of tea. When she turned around, Andrea was right there. She palmed Louise's face like a basketball and slammed her head into the doorjamb as hard as she could. The old woman's skull cracked like a rack of billiard balls. It was like a dance, the way Andrea used her other hand to open the basement door and toss Louise down the stairs. She saw the bottle of Evan Williams in the pantry, walked halfway down the steps, and dropped it next to the body. She knew Max had offered Louise a glass of wine. It would look like Louise came home tipsy, decided to have another drink, and tumbled down the stairs. With any luck it would be a week before anyone thought to look for her.

Andrea slept alone in a king bed that night while Brian slept in the basement apartment. She felt no remorse for killing two people that day. Life was a battlefield. You flipped your switch and did what you had to do to stay alive.

Now she was driving a GMC Terrain seventy-five miles an hour, heading north to Sandy Lake. It was after midnight. She'd made this drive so many times, she could do it without thinking. With the cruise control set, her mind could wander as she sailed through the darkness between sleeping small towns, nothing open but gas stations and bars.

A week ago, she'd made this drive after getting a panicked call from Jim Wolf, who had been completely spooked by a text from Packard. They'd driven around half the day in Jim's mom's car that smelled like old-lady perfume.

She'd put up as many walls between her and the fraud as possible. Jim was instructed that Tess should never hear her name. No emails. No texts. She and Jim only communicated via prepaid phones, and even then, she kept her side of the conversation to a minimum. It was too bad the operation didn't run longer than it did. She still didn't know what spooked Tess and caused her to run. Whatever it was had brought the whole thing to a screeching halt. In the months that followed, Jim called to complain so many times about the financial bind he was in that she'd stopped returning his calls. He'd told her repeatedly that he had a rock-solid plan for washing his share of the money through his business. Now he was panicking.

"There was supposed to be so much more money. Enough to make the risk worth it," he whined as they drove around the lake. "Instead, I'm broke and now I've got fucking Packard snooping around, talking about how he knows everything. FUCK!" He pounded the steering wheel while she sat motionless beside him.

"Get it together," she told him. "Stick to the plan. Say nothing. If you've done your job, they won't be able to prove anything. Everything was done in Louise's name. Not yours. Not mine. Even if that dyke told Packard everything, it's her word against yours. Your share of the money is still in Louise's account. How can they pin that on you?"

But what if...? But what about...?

She listened to him for as long as she could. The big, loud businessman who claimed to have Shepard in his pocket, who called Packard a faggot every chance he got, who ran the county board like it existed to serve his whims, was going to crack. She'd seen the same thing in Afghanistan. The loudest, sneakiest insurgents dropped to their knees and pleaded for their lives when the Rangers kicked in the door in the middle of the night and started shouting.

When they got back to the lake, she had Jim stop in front of Louise's.

"Do you have keys?" she asked.

"There's one above the doorjamb that Ray Wiley left while we were working on our plans for the house."

"Come in with me. Louise has some old doors in the basement she said I could have. I'm wondering if you can tell me if they're worth refinishing."

They went up the back steps and Jim brushed the snow from above the door and found the single key left there.

"The doors are behind the furnace," she said as she followed Jim down the basement stairs. He half turned his head when he saw no doors and that's when she shot him.

She left Brian's gun next to Jim, thinking it would be the evidence that connected him to everything. She went to her car, got the road flares, and started the fire in the basement. While she waited outside for it to catch, it occurred to her that now might be a perfect time to eliminate Brian, too.

Make it look like he killed Jim, then committed suicide knowing Packard was closing in.

She hurried to her house and went in through the side door. In the gun room, on a tray in the safe, she found an HK45 Compact Tactical ACP with a suppressor beside it and a loaded ten-round clip. Everything she needed in one place. Because of how they'd split the house for the rental suite downstairs, she had to go in one door to get to Brian's gun room, then go outside and around to the other side of the garage to enter the apartment below. She was standing in the doorway threading the suppressor onto the end of the gun when she saw Packard pull up. She watched him look in Jim's car and run around the house calling Jim's name before running inside.

A few minutes later, when he came to the back door, she shot at him from beside the garage, knowing right away she had missed. The suppressor muffled the sound but fucked her accuracy. She fired two more times. She needed him to die in that house—from fire or smoke, she didn't care. She stayed as long as she could, watching the fire get bigger, watching the flames move behind the windows like people at a party. At the first sound of sirens, she ran to her car and headed the opposite direction.

She kept driving. The night sky was clear and icy cold with stars. Before leaving the Cities, she'd taken two dexies, a drug she'd started using in Afghanistan, where there were no regular hours and lots of night raids and the constant need to be fully energized any time of the day or night. She had more in her bag for the drive home. They had her feeling sharp and pleasantly buzzing. Like being back on the battlefield. It was kill-or-be-killed time again.

When she got home from Afghanistan, she read about the size and the scope of the financial waste the U.S. government had spent under the guise of fighting insurgents. Money for roads that went nowhere, for uniforms and weapons not suited for desert combat, for camps and utilities and equipment that military leaders said weren't needed but were built anyway because the money had already been allocated. Billions lost to fraud and grift and self-dealing.

What did she get? She got a four-year scholarship that required eight years of service to pay back. She got to go to boot camp and patrol a base in Germany, then got nominated for a new program that would put women in combat situations. She got paid $45,000 a year to get shot at, to wear boots that made her feet bleed, to sweat, to hump a forty-pound rucksack, to shoot people, to watch people get shot, to see open sewage pits and dead bodies in the street covered in flies, to see a truck carrying members of her unit leap ten feet in the air after running over an IED, to see those team members come out of the truck in pieces, to take a bullet in the thigh.

Billions wasted.

$45,000 a year for a soldier risking her life.

It was time to take what was hers.

Her husband had become a liability and a disappointment. Good for him that he held the 1,000-yard record at the gun range, and good for him that he was so good at Call of Duty. She had been to war. She had shot an insurgent in the neck. She had seen people blown to pieces. His love of cartoon violence and gun-range swagger embarrassed her. It should have embarrassed him.

Then he lost all their money on fucking cryptocurrency. Fucking cartoon money. Raiding the food program and letting Jim Wolf take all the risk was the perfect opportunity to rebuild her own wealth.

After Brian was dead, she'd move the money to another bank outside of U.S. jurisdiction, in Panama or the Seychelles. When news of her husband's connection to the fraud got out, she could claim ignorance of where the money went, and if that didn't work, she could claim she was protecting her family's property from seizure by government goons. Her constituents would eat it up.

She was still an hour from Sandy Lake. The dexies buzzed through her veins and made her feel like she could take her hands off the wheel and steer with her mind. Everything was under control.

Overhead, too high to make any noise, two simple pulsing lights marked the BCA plane following her every move.

At 2:00 a.m. Andrea killed all but her nav lights and parked in the covered carport beside Louise's garage. When she got out of the vehicle, she could still smell the fire she had started. The back stairs of Louise's house went up to a doorframe that looked like a portal in a horror movie. Through it she could see the drop-off into the basement full of burned timbers and pieces of the roof, and beyond that the lake.

She was dressed in all black with a black nylon backpack and combat boots. The same boots that used to make her feet bleed now fit like nothing else. She wore them hiking and hunting and to any outdoor events with voters. She never passed up an opportunity to mention the boots or remind people of her service.

She still had the HK45 and seven rounds in the magazine. She unscrewed the suppressor and put it in her bag. No one committing suicide would care how loud the shot was.

The entry to the lower level had a keypad so renters wouldn't have to bother with a key. They had four different codes they rotated through. She got it on the second try, was inside the single stall garage with Brian's black Ford Explorer. The interior door's dead bolt wasn't set. Lightly down the stairs, gun at the ready, listening. The bedroom was across the small living area. The door was open. She could hear Brian's white noise machine. Another thing about him that drove her nuts.

The lower level had vinyl floors. A rock in the sole of her boot made a clicking sound as she crossed the main room and peered into the bedroom. Brian's bed was against the wall to her left. He was on his side, his back to her. On her right was the bathroom.

Something had her antenna up. There was something wrong with the feel of the room. Brian didn't move. On his side, he seemed larger than normal. She wanted him on his back for a quick shot under the chin so it would look like he'd made himself comfortable before taking his life now that the cops were closing in.

He was wearing a T-shirt, something he never usually did, even in the wintertime. When she grabbed the shoulder, he rolled to one side like deadweight. It wasn't Brian. The head was plastic. She'd seen dummies like this during her military training. It was a Rescue Randy. Two hundred pounds of deadweight that they had drilled lifting and carrying over their shoulders, simulating a wounded or dead soldier.

A light snapped on to her right. In the doorway of the bathroom she saw Packard in a black jacket. He yelled, "Drop the gun, Andrea!" His voice sounded weird, like it was coming from a blown speaker.

She squeezed off two shots in his direction and watched his image shatter. Another trick. He'd tilted the bathroom mirror so she was seeing his reflection, not him. Now she heard the thump of boots and voices upstairs. She leaped over the dummy in the bed in one move. There was an easement window on the other side with a single latch that allowed it to be pushed outward. She jumped like a cat and crouched for a second in the deep window frame, long enough to shoot again in the direction of the bathroom, then backed into the window well, pushed herself out of the hole, and took off at a dead run.

CHAPTER THIRTY-FIVE

PACKARD LOOKED AROUND THE frame of the bathroom door in time to see Andrea disappear through the window. He ran in that direction, then thought better of it. If she was waiting for him, sticking his head out of the window well like a gopher peeking out of its hole was a good way to get himself killed.

The tactical team was coming down the stairs. "She's running," he said as he went up the stairs opposite the flow of everyone else. He saw Thielen at the top and she followed him out the side door.

They'd had cars parked in Max and Linda's garage that pulled across the road on either side of the house, preventing Andrea from driving away. Their emergency lights were on and Packard saw a spotlight shining across the yard.

"She's headed for the lake," someone yelled.

He and Thielen found her tracks. The warm weather had compressed the snow, but with every step they sank to the top of their boots. Andrea was a black blur, now on the frozen lake. Packard and Thielen crossed the road and stopped long enough to look up at the red and green lights of the department drone as it buzzed overhead. The smart thing to do was let her run and let the drone track her. There would be no hiding from its infrared camera, especially when everything in the background was ice cold.

Packard took off running anyway. His chest still hurt and it was a struggle to take a deep breath. He called after Andrea to stop. His voice cracked like he was going through puberty. It was not the most commanding sound.

The DNR had ordered the lake cleared of icehouses and vehicles two weeks earlier than usual after days of above-average temperatures had created thin ice and open water. He and Thielen splashed through puddles as they chased Andrea down the road that had been plowed across the lake. Where all the snow had melted, they hit patches of black ice, causing them to slip. In some spots it felt like the ice was rocking beneath them, like they were running across a huge waterbed.

Packard kept one eye on the drone overhead, following like a guiding star. He heard a cry and splash. He and Thielen came to a stop. Thielen listened on her radio.

"The drone saw her go in the water. There's a ridge of plowed snow ahead and open water behind it."

They moved closer, as quick as they could, to the spot. Chunks of ice and slush moved up and down on the waves. There was no sign of Andrea.

Packard started stripping off his gear.

"What the fuck are you doing?" Thielen asked.

"I gotta try and save her. It's pitch-black out here. What if she's lost the opening?"

"You'll freeze to death."

"I've been doing cold plunges all winter. I could do three minutes in there if I could hold my breath that long. Give me one minute and then I'm out."

Thielen watched in disbelief as he took off his vest, his belt, and his boots. He shucked his pants and shirt, down to a T-shirt and underwear. It had already been more than a minute since they heard Andrea yell.

"Any excuse to show off that body," Thielen said.

Packard kept his flashlight. "Keep your light right here by the hole so I can find it."

"One minute," she said. "Remember, you still have to be able to pull your-self out. I'm not going to be much help."

Packard pushed a slab of ice away with his heel and dropped into the water, the same way he did at home, letting the shock push all the air from his chest, ignoring the sudden sensation that his skin was on fire. He surfaced long enough to take as deep a breath as his ravaged lungs would allow and then dove down, flashlight in hand, in search of Andrea.

When he was a kid, after Nick disappeared and they pulled his snowmobile from this lake, his family had tried to find joy again in spending summers at his grandparents' house. His worst fear while in the water back then was coming across the missing body of his brother. He imagined a cold hand reaching for his ankle, and behind it, a white face with its eyes open and minnows darting in and out of its mouth.

Now he hoped for a hand or a face to appear in the dark.

His flashlight didn't shine far in the murky water. There was nothing to see, just green-black darkness. He thought he was ten feet down. He dove lower. Andrea went in with all her clothes, including a backpack and boots. The weight would pull her down if she wasn't strong enough to fight it.

Above him, Thielen's flashlight was as far away as the moon. His chest ached. His hands and feet were numb from the blood retreating to his core. He dove lower and the pressure in his ears felt like fists on either side of his head. He had ten more seconds.

He found Andrea near the bottom. Fifteen feet. Maybe deeper. She was floating with her arms out, still holding her gun. When he shined his light in her face, her eyes flew open and the last bubbles came out of her mouth. He tried to grab her under the shoulder. She twisted away, brought up a boot, and kicked him in the stomach. The force pushed her backward, out of his light. In the dark, he saw a muzzle flash, not even a second long but long enough to see it illuminate the inside of her mouth.

All his air was gone now. His lungs were screaming but his body was warm, the water like a bath. How easy it would be to stop fighting and float down here in the dark, to give the lake what it was owed, a Packard for a Packard, now that the lost boy they had imagined living here all this time was about to be found elsewhere. When he touched the soft bottom with his foot, there was a moment of clarity that tasted like lake water in his mouth, enough to make him push off and swim toward Thielen's light, kicking, kicking, reaching up with his arm, trying to grab the moon.

He broke the surface, gasping. He heard people shouting, and then hands, hands, and more hands grabbed him and lifted him straight up, through the slush and the bobbing ice, out of the dark and back into the world.

CHAPTER THIRTY-SIX

DIVERS FOUND ANDREA HOPKINS two days later. The bullet had gone through the top of her mouth and exited above her brain stem. Remembering what Brian said about her always being ready for a fight, Packard had to wonder if she hadn't jumped the snow pile looking for cover to shoot from and found open water instead. He was surprised she didn't fight harder to get out. Maybe she knew it was over. Her blood tested positive for dextroamphetamine. Maybe the drug was what made her so accepting of her fate.

Days later, the final decision from Phil Ayers's office about charges in the death of Robert Clark came out in the form of a letter to the lead BCA agent and Sheriff Howard Shepard. On the county attorney's letterhead, Ayers stated that he had completed his review and found no basis for criminal charges against Deputy Packard. The relief Packard expected at the news didn't come. He couldn't even direct his anger at Jim Wolf anymore. Holding a grudge against a dead man was like trying to punch the wind. It was up to him to figure out how long he would shoulder the weight of events from that day, and when, if ever, he could set them down.

Packard went back to work full-time. Shepard had come around partially and agreed that putting him back on court security wasn't the best look for the department. Shepard gave Deputy Baker the security spot. Packard was on patrol. He worked four ten-hour shifts a week, all day in the car. When he had time, he helped Thielen catalog the evidence against Andrea Hopkins. They found her curly hair in Jim Wolf's mom's car and in the boat that was abandoned after someone shot at Packard at Leon Chen's house. More of her hair was left in the kitchen in Janet's Café, where they found Deborah's body. They had her voice on the recordings Jim made. It was a lot of circumstantial evidence that any good attorney could have torpedoed in front of a jury.

The U.S. Attorney charged the first fifteen people in the fraud case a month after Andrea's death. More charges were coming, he said. He thanked employees working for the State of Minnesota for calling attention to the issue and the FBI for their assistance with the investigation.

When Packard reached out to Agent Riley and asked her if there would be charges in the Sandy Lake area fraud, she said she didn't know. "It's up to the U.S. Attorney. Your two main players, Jim Wolf and Representative Hopkins, are dead. The only one left is Tess Reid, who worked on their behalf but didn't actually spend any of the money. I think she's looking at probation, maybe some workhouse time."

"Now that that's wrapped, I have a favor to ask," Packard said. He shared the information he had and what he was looking for.

"That's not really what the FBI does," Agent Riley said.

"But you know someone in some other agency who could get me what I'm looking for."

"You make it sound like I owe you."

"Don't you? I helped you shut down the whole northern branch of the meal reimbursement cartel."

Riley scoffed. "They shut themselves down. A lot of people ended up shot in the head, as I recall."

"I found Deborah Salvo," Packard offered.

"Shot in the head."

"I helped uncover the representative's role in things."

"Also shot in the head. And currently protected by a gag order from the governor."

There had been a lot of conference calls after Andrea's body was pulled from the water. The first news stories simply reported that she'd died in an accident on the lake. Packard and Thielen and Shepard met online with the FBI and people from the U.S. Attorney's office. Later they had meetings with the governor and heads of the Minnesota House and the Senate, then another meeting with just the governor. Packard explained to him everything he suspected Andrea of, from the murders to the fraud, from planning to kill her husband to the three different times she had tried to kill him (at Leon Chen's, coming out of Louise's burning house, and in the lower level of her house).

"For fuck's sake," the governor said. "And how much of this can you prove?"

"Twenty percent of it. Maybe thirty," Packard said.

"That's not enough. Unless and until there's a public trial, I want zero percent of this discussed beyond this group. I worked with Representative Hopkins. She's a decorated veteran. She's well-liked in the House and among voters. There's nothing to be gained by dragging her name through the mud attached to a bunch of hearsay. Am I understood?"

Packard didn't like it but he agreed in principle. Word would still get out. The greatest threat to the governor's request was Shepard, who couldn't keep a secret with a whole fist in his mouth.

"Agent Riley, I'm not asking because you owe me," Packard said. "I'm asking because I really need the help."

There was a pause. "I'll see what I can do."

CHAPTER THIRTY-SEVEN

LIKE IT DID EVERY year, spring finally returned to northern Minnesota. One day the lakes were solid and chiseled; the next, the ice was out and wind moved across the water. The days got longer. It took less wood in the stove to keep the house warm.

In mid-May, a long row of sheriff's vehicles and pickup trucks were pulled over as far as possible on a dirt road that cut through land that was thick with trees. An old snowmobile trail, which had fallen out of use when ownership of the land changed hands many years back, climbed an incline. People moved along the trail in both directions like ants bringing bits of leaves into their hill.

At the top, Thielen gave orders to anyone who got close or made eye contact. Her primary order to Packard was *stay out of the way.* He was out of uniform, dressed in jeans and work boots and a Carhartt coat.

The other side of the hill was steep. It leveled off at the bottom, then rose again slightly on the other side. Generations of trees grew wild, their bare branches pushing out buds, pushing out new leaves. Ferns as old as time uncoiled like the fingers of a closed fist from soil still heavy with melted snow and recent rain. The air smelled muddy and fetid.

In the low, flat area below, Packard watched a handler dressed in a fluorescent yellow hoodie try to manage a black Labrador retriever on a heavy leash. The handler's voice was muted; her commands to the dog sounded like a made-up language only the two of them knew. Packard had been told that the dog, whose name was Rumor, was one of the best. Rumor could tell the difference between animal and human remains, could locate the scent of decay if it was decades old, if it was ten feet underground, even underwater.

Rumor tugged at the leash and sniffed the ground, following no logical pattern. Where he stopped and sat, a deputy placed a red flag on a metal skewer. Packard felt every dropped flag in his body, like a voodoo pin. After an hour of the dog working the area, almost a dozen red flags dotted the ground. Another man with a metal detector worked not far away and put a yellow flag anywhere his machine gave off a certain tone.

Packard took a break from watching to go back down the hill to the road. News of what was happening had gotten out in advance, drawing lots of volunteers. Deputies and crime-scene techs were there on their day off. The property owner and his family were there. Women from the Legion's Ladies Auxiliary were serving coffee and homemade treats from the tailgate of a pickup. Packard got handshakes and hugs from a lot of people he barely knew. People wanted to help. They wanted to show they cared.

He poured himself and Thielen coffee in paper cups and was trying to figure out how to carry them and two slabs of coffee cake back up the hill when someone called out his name.

"Ben."

He turned around to see Kyle from the brewery coming up the dirt road in sneakers and black Adidas track pants. He had lost the beanie but gained more of a beard since Packard had last seen him in the hospital. The weight of recent events had Packard feeling like he was slowly being corkscrewed into the ground. At the sight of Kyle, he felt his shoulders go up and back. He smiled.

"What are you doing here?"

"Heard about what was going on. Just wanted to see how you were doing."

"I'm all right," Packard said. He offered Kyle the coffee he'd poured for Thielen and they stood by the back of the pickup and ate coffee cake that tasted like butter and brown sugar.

"This day has been a long time coming from what I understand," Kyle said.

Packard nodded, wiped his mouth with the back of his hand. "The accepted story has always been that Nick drowned in Lake Redwing when his snowmobile went through the ice. Another look at the case has led us to this location."

"How's your mom dealing with all of this?"

"She's waiting for a call from me."

It was a lie. If his mom had known this was happening, she would have been on the next plane, probably at the top of the hill trying to get Thielen to join her in a prayer circle. Packard had decided not to tell his family anything until he knew something for certain. He didn't want them watching the calendar, watching the clock, waiting for news he wasn't sure he would have. What if they found nothing?

Thielen came halfway down the hill in their direction. She pushed her jacket back with hands on her hips. Her pregnant belly had started to make itself known. "Are you kidding me right now?" she yelled. "Is he drinking my fucking coffee?"

"There's more coffee," Packard yelled. "I'll be right there." To Kyle, "I gotta go. She didn't want me here in the first place. She'll throw me out if I don't make myself useful."

"I can stick around if there's anything I can do."

"There's no need," Packard said. "Thanks for coming. I'll come see you at the brewery soon."

There was an awkward moment where they didn't know whether to shake hands or hug or rub noses. Kyle stepped close, wrapped an arm around him. "I hope you find the answers you've been looking for," he said close to Packard's ear. Then he turned and was gone.

Packard's face was red. He started across the road, remembered he'd forgotten Thielen's coffee, and spun around again.

By late afternoon, the woods were crawling with people. They moved deep leaves and dirt from around the flags. They were squatting and holding objects, trying to figure out if they were looking at a bone or a rock or a stick. A camera flashed as a photographer shot items where they lay.

"Over here," someone yelled. "I have clothing."

Packard looked at Thielen, who nodded. She was too wobbly to make it down the hill so he went without her, sliding down through the leaves and mud. He stepped over a hollow birch trunk decomposing back into the soil and crouched near a blond woman with her hair back in a ponytail. She was standing over something that looked like a dirty brown towel. Packard had to stare at it for a minute to realize that years of mud and water had washed away the red and blue colors and stained the white parts. The stitching holding everything together had dissolved, leaving layers of fabric on top of each other. Packard knelt down and cleared away more of the leaves and dirt and revealed an unmistakable POLARIS logo.

He turned and looked up the hill and nodded at Thielen. She put a hand over her mouth. He could tell she was crying from there. His eyes burned. He blinked and looked away from her to keep his own tears from starting.

They uncovered more items that day before the sun set.

Pieces of a brown tarp with metal grommets strung with bits of synthetic rope.

A jawbone.

Three vertebrae.

Metatarsals from a foot.

After almost thirty years, they had finally found Nick.

CHAPTER THIRTY-EIGHT

ANOTHER FAMILY ZOOM. HIS brother Joe; his sister, Anne; his mom; and a phone number in a black box representing his father. Some things never changed.

"We found Nick," Packard said.

Everyone started talking at once. Packard watched their faces, how they firmed up or fell apart at the news. He told them about the search and the items recovered and that there was still DNA testing to be done, but he was one hundred percent certain they had found Nicholas David Packard, missing since December 27, 1991.

"I knew this was coming," his mom said, leaning toward the computer. She had tears on her face. "My daily tarot pull has been Page of Cups, Page of Wands, the Hierophant—unexpected news, good news, things about to be revealed." She held her hands up and closed her eyes.

"All right, enough of that, Mom," Joe said.

"Let her talk," Packard said.

"I was going to say you have no idea how long we've waited for this news, but of course you know. You kids have spent your whole lives with this uncertainty. It wounded all of you, but you healed and you grew into the amazing, compassionate, giving adults you are today." She started crying harder, managing to squeak out *I'm so proud of our family* before breaking down completely.

Their dad's line was muted. "Dad, you want to say anything?"

Silence and then the mute came off and his dad's wife said, "Your dad's a bit overcome. He can't speak right now. He's saying thank you, thank you…" She went back on mute.

Joe was in uniform, in his patrol car but not driving. He was a cop in a Saint Paul suburb. Of all of them, he was the one who looked like he wasn't satisfied with the news. "So now we know someone put him there. We still don't know who or how he died or why."

"I'm still working on that," Packard said.

"Is there a chance we'll never know?" Anne asked.

Packard had wanted to postpone this call until he could answer that question for sure.

"I'm confident we'll know everything sooner than later," he said.

"You sound like you know more than you're telling us," Joe said.

"Like I said, I'm still working on things. I don't want to get anyone's hopes up before I'm certain myself. Trust me. I'm telling you everything I know for sure as soon as I know it."

"Well, I'm coming out there immediately," his mom said. "We all need to get up there so we can have a family funeral for your brother and a proper burial next to Grandma and Grandpa."

"That's not going to happen for a while, Mom. Do not come up here. I won't be here. I'm not kidding."

"Where are you going?"

"I'll tell you when I get back."

CHAPTER THIRTY-NINE

PARIS IN THE SUMMERTIME smelled like hot garbage.

A nonstop flight from Minneapolis left at 10:00 p.m. and had Packard in Paris the next afternoon. He'd dressed to be comfortable on the plane and carried on only a small hiking backpack, borrowed from Thielen, with toiletries and a change of clothes.

A train took him from Charles de Gaulle Airport into the city and he got off near a Université Paris Cité campus in the sixth arrondissement. A sanitation workers' strike protesting an increase in the retirement age had mountains of black garbage bags and overflowing bins piled on the streets. Packard checked the address in his phone again, went up the steps of the main campus building, up two more flights of stairs, and came to an office where a young man with round glasses was reading a book at a desk.

"I'm here to see the professor," Packard said.

The young man looked at him quizzically. "*Non*, there is a faculty meeting all day today. There are no appointments."

"I don't have an appointment."

"Of course you do not."

"What time does the meeting end?"

"Late. After six, I would think. I will not be here. The office will be closed."

"The meeting is here in this building?"

"*Oui.*"

"I'll wait."

He wandered through the trees and manicured lawns of the Jardin du Luxembourg, along the rue de Medici and the boulevarde Saint-Michel. He went in and out of a bookstore and a children's clothing store where he bought a baby blanket for Thielen that had zoo animals living in a château. He had an espresso at a café and watched the people walk by. No one looked like they were from Sandy Lake. None of the men had goatees or baseball caps or mirrored sunglasses off the back of their heads. The women looked casually stylish. No bulky sweatshirts. Nary a sports jersey or an American flag T-shirt to be seen.

At five, he circled the university building, noting all the exits. He felt certain the professor would come out the main doors. There was a bus stop across the street. He sat and waited.

At six thirty, a woman in tailored pants and a peach blouse came out the building, followed by a tired, older man in a black blazer carrying a leather satchel. Packard recognized the professor immediately and moved to intercept them at the bottom of the stairs.

"Professor Bodin," he said.

The man and the woman both looked at him, but hers was the face that froze as she suddenly recognized him. Likely the same way he recognized her. From pictures online.

The man and the woman spoke briefly in French. He kissed her on both cheeks, nodded, and said "Bonsoir" to Packard, leaving the two of them standing in the evening shade of the building. She was in her late forties, tall, almost six feet, with rich chestnut hair that had a white streak in front. She carried a purse strung across her chest and a clutch of folders under one arm.

"You are the policeman," she said.

Packard nodded.

"I got your many emails and messages." She had grown up speaking English in America. Now she spoke it with a slight French accent.

The favor Packard had asked of Agent Riley was for help locating Dr. Rassin's two children, last known to be on their way to live with family in Turkey in 1992. He gave Agent Riley their dates of birth and social security numbers from the case file. She responded a couple of weeks later with a name and a university address. Online he'd seen Faizah Bodin's faculty picture and gotten her office number and email from the directory. He'd sent her multiple messages, called and left his name several times. No response. He refused to accept silence as an answer.

"Your messages terrified me. I was paralyzed each time."

"That wasn't my intention, Professor."

"Call me Faizah," she said.

"I didn't mean to scare you, Faizah. All I want is to know what you know. That's it. I'm in law enforcement but I have no authority here, no ability to charge anyone with anything. I just want to talk."

Faizah moved the folders from one hand to the other and scratched the side of her head. "I always told myself if the family reached out to me for answers, I would tell them everything. After all this time, I never expected it to happen. I gave myself permission to forget what happened that night, but you don't get to choose what you remember. The mind decides for itself."

Packard nodded.

"You are hungry," she said. It wasn't a question. "Come, let's eat. I know a place."

He followed her across the campus to a parking ramp. Her car was red and ridiculously small, possibly detached from the swinging arm of a carnival ride. Neither of them fit well inside. She drove with a casual indifference to other vehicles on the road, also to traffic signs and lights. There were so many horns that Packard wondered if French cars honked when you stepped on the gas.

She drove through narrow streets until she found a parking spot, and then they got out and walked around angled street corners and down a cobblestone alley with greenery growing above the doorways of the buildings. She brought them to a restaurant, where they sat outside beside the window, and Faizah lit a cigarette and shook out her hair. Their waiter was a towering bald man with enormous hands who didn't speak, only nodded as Faizah ordered for both of them in French. "You drink wine," she said. Again, not a question.

Packard had never felt so out of his element. He was in Europe for the first time in his life, in a country where he didn't speak the language, surrounded by strangers and the weight of history. He'd spent the day reading plaques and noticing buildings pocked by large-caliber rounds from World War II. Nothing felt familiar.

The waiter came back and poured a white wine. Faizah didn't offer a toast. The mood was not celebratory.

Packard reached into his jacket pocket and took out a photo and pushed it across the table. It was the picture of Faizah with her arm around Nick in the lake, her brother watching from the dock. She gasped. "*Mon Dieu. Nous étions de tels enfants*," she said. Meeting his confused gaze, she said, "We were such children."

She looked at the photo for a long time, and when she blinked, tears streamed down her cheeks. "I've never seen this photo before," she said. She rubbed her fingers across its surface as if she could touch their faces. "The last happy times of my childhood."

"Tell me about that summer," Packard said.

She kept looking at the photo. "I can't even remember how we met your brother. Nick and Faisal liked the same music. Maybe they met at the record store. Or maybe I saw Nick and thought he was so handsome and decided we were going to be friends."

She tapped her cigarette against the ashtray and took a long drag. "My father was very strict. He never would have allowed Nick and me to be alone, but it was okay if the three of us hung out together. My brother would protect my honor."

She tried to give the photo back to Packard. "Keep it. It's a duplicate," he said.

She drank her wine. "I remember your brother had a license and a car and we did not. We listened to tapes and drove all around with the windows down. He and my brother liked such mopey music. The Cure and The Smiths. Ugh." She made a disgusted face. "They never let me play my tapes. I loved Madonna and Janet Jackson. I said, 'We're young and free. We should be dancing. Let's dance.' What do they play? Depeche Mode remixes which were just mopey songs with a heavier drumbeat."

She laughed at the memory. The waiter came with a basket of bread and a pâté and cornichons. He refilled their wineglasses.

Faizah stabbed out her cigarette and reached for a piece of bread. "Sometimes we smoked terrible weed or found another kid who had beer and was selling cans for two dollars. We went to bonfire parties or sat at the diner and ordered french fries and Cokes late at night."

Packard ate bread. He tried the pâté. It tasted of liver and brandy. "Were you in love with my brother?"

Faizah waved her hand. "What does a child know of love? I was infatuated with your brother. I was obsessed with your brother. Look at us in the photo. I wanted to always be touching him, for him to be touching me. I wanted him to take my virginity and do things to me that I only knew about from reading smutty books I hid from my father."

Packard smiled. His was probably the last generation that learned about sex from smutty books. Then it was computers. Now it was phones.

"Did the two of you ever get to be alone?" he asked.

"Not as much as I would have liked," Faizah said. "Sometimes we would sit alone on the dock if Faisal was tired or getting eaten too bad by the mosquitoes. A couple of times we went on a canoe. I treasured those stolen moments with your brother. He talked to me, he listened to me. I would sit as close to him as I dared and find excuses to touch him. One time I got up the nerve to ask him if he thought I was beautiful. He said, 'I think you're very beautiful.'" Faizah put a hand on her chest and closed her eyes. "It might have been the happiest moment of my life to that point. It sustained me through all the times Nick and Faisal didn't want me around. They would go off in the car without me. They thought I was young and annoying."

Packard felt a chill. Those sounded like Nick's last words to him when they were fighting by the back door before he left on the snowmobile.

The sun was nearly set, the restaurant more crowded. Couples and four-somes leaned toward each other, talking and laughing in French, their hands moving like a conductor's. Cars drove by with their headlights on. The waiter came again and took away the bread and left a fried artichoke with sauce in a ramekin beside it. Faizah cut the artichoke in half and put some of the sauce on her plate. Packard mimed her behavior. He'd never eaten a fried artichoke in his life.

"So what happened?" Packard asked. "Did things get more serious? Was Nick coming to see you that night? Did your father catch you together? Or... what?"

Faizah cocked her head and stared at him until her eyes darted away with a sudden realization. She looked down at her plate and delicately separated the choke's lacy fried leaves with the tip of her knife.

"You don't know."

"Know what?"

"About your brother?"

Packard took a deep breath and tried to smile. He felt like a crazy person trying not to be crazy. "I'm asking you...."

Faizah sighed. She reached for her wineglass and leaned back in her chair. "Your brother and I were not intimate. I was infatuated with him, but the feel-ing was not mutual," she said, turning her wineglass by the stem. "It was your brother and my brother who were lovers."

Packard felt the world tilt. It reminded him of running across the ice after Andrea Hopkins, how it lurched beneath his feet. The two glasses of wine he'd had made his head feel like it was full of helium.

"Nick and Faisal were... Nick was gay?"

He felt silly asking a stranger to confirm something so personal about his brother. There had never been any family conversations, never any sibling chatter about Nick being gay. When Packard came out, no one ever said anything about Nick.

"Gay or bisexual or exploring. I don't know. He was only a teenager. He probably didn't know either."

That felt like a modern attitude that Packard didn't remember applying back when he was a kid. Faizah was older than him and should have realized the same. You didn't experiment with your sexuality back then, like trying on hats. You were or you weren't. The fear of being found out and labeled came with too many consequences.

Or maybe that was how Packard felt, and his brother felt differently.

Their entrées came. An airline chicken breast in some kind of sauce with dill and roasted potatoes. Packard put his hand over his glass when the waiter tried to put more wine in it.

"How did you find out?" he asked after the waiter left.

Faizah was still leaning back in her chair, seemingly uninterested in the food she'd ordered. "I didn't find out until the winter when we went back to the lake for the holidays. Your brother came over a couple of times. He and Faisal played the..." She made a motion like she was pushing buttons with her thumbs.

"Nintendo," Packard said.

"Yes. Video games all the time." She looked annoyed, as if this was still a problem with the men in her life. "The first time I caught them together, I came downstairs to see what they were doing. The video game was paused. They were not around. I went upstairs again looking for them. I couldn't see them in the back or in the front. It was winter, it was cold out. Where could they be? I don't know why but I went to my bedroom and looked out the window. Right below my window, they were kissing. Faisal had his back against the side of the house. Your brother had one hand on the side of his face and one hand pressed against his chest, their bodies so tight that nothing could pass between them. It would have been an incredible moment of intimacy to behold if it didn't also destroy me at the same time. I was shocked. I was furious. I felt so stupid and worthless."

Faizah leaned forward with her elbows on the table, rubbing the back of her neck. Packard stared at the top of her head. His heart was beating like he, too, was witnessing something he shouldn't have seen, wasn't supposed to know.

"I can only imagine how heartbreaking that must have been," he said.

Faizah didn't respond. She hung her head. He gave her a moment, then said, "Tell me what happened after that."

"I did nothing the first time. Collapsed on my bed and cried into my pillow," she said, talking to the top of the table. She leaned back. "The next time they were together was when your brother came over very late. I was still awake. I heard the snowmobile stop down by the lake. I heard the lower-level door open. I knew Faisal was still up playing games. Our father was asleep in his room. I waited a while before going down to look. They were in the spare bedroom together with the door closed."

She started cutting her food. Packard realized he'd been eating the whole time and hadn't tasted a thing.

"Please remember I was a child. How hurt I was," she said. Her expression was pleading. Without looking away, she said, "I woke up my father. I said, 'Something is wrong with Faisal. He's downstairs on the bed.' My father went downstairs in his robe and house shoes. Did you ever meet my father? No? He was a huge man. Deep, dark eyes, black hair turning gray, big around. Solid.

"He opened the door and they were in the bed on top of each other, just underwear. It could have been worse for them but not much. My father was enraged. He grabbed Faisal out of the bed and hauled him out of the bedroom and dropped him on the floor. I was on the stairs watching. Somehow, I had failed to imagine how awful this was going to be. My father smacked Faisal across the face. He was yelling in Arabic, yelling in English. *You are no man. You disgrace our family. Disgusting.* He was kicking Faisal when Nick came out of the room, half-dressed. He yelled at my father to stop. I remember his words. 'He's your son!'

"My father turned around, grabbed Nick by the throat. We had a fireplace downstairs surrounded by giant stones. I know my father was furious, but he never meant for what happened to happen. He grabbed Nick by the throat, spun him around, and shoved him toward Faisal, like he was making a pile of the two of them. Nick stumbled, tripped backward over Faisal, and hit his head on the stone hearth. He went limp right away.

"I remember the silence that followed. I could see it snowing outside. I thought I could hear each flake hit the ground."

Packard felt a chill. The memory of the long winter they'd just come through was still fresh. He could imagine the sound of the ragged breathing of everyone still alive in that room. He mimicked it with his own breath.

"Faisal was moaning as quietly as possible. My father was a doctor, remember. An oral surgeon. He went over and lifted Nick's eyelids. He checked the pulse on his wrist. Then he sat on the hearth and sobbed. It was the only time I ever saw my father cry. He put his face in his hands and cried and made a sound like wind through a broken window. It terrified me even more than the violence."

She stopped talking. Packard heard ringing in his ears. He felt a vast emptiness inside him. Faizah's story was a torch raised in a cavern, illuminating the immensity of what had been lost. He saw Nick as never before—not the older brother who towered over him in size and age but a seventeen-year-old boy struggling with the same desires and fears Packard had. He wondered how different his life would have been if Nick hadn't died, if he'd had someone older to show him how to live without shame or secrets. He remembered Detective Easton telling him how lonely he'd been during his divorce. He had no one to talk to who knew the life he'd been keeping secret. Now it made sense how abandoned Easton felt and how empty his own apology had been in the absence of that understanding.

Now he understood. Now he was sorry.

Faizah was saying something under her breath. Again and again. In French. *Je suis désolée... Je suis désolée...*

"I don't know what you're saying," Packard said.

She was crying again. "I'm sorry. I'm sorry for what I did. I'm sorry for what happened to your brother because of my selfishness."

Packard reached across the table with his hand open. He felt how the weight she carried all this time differed from his own. How the grief of not knowing was different than the horror of being there. The fear that one day a stranger would show up to ask questions. He would take this burden from her if she was willing to let it go.

"You don't have to apologize. You don't need my or my family's forgiveness. It was an accident."

"I was selfish in the moment. I was selfish for thirty years to let you go so long and not know about your brother."

"We had our own answer for the last thirty years. To be honest, we didn't talk about Nick for a lot of those years. We had an idea of what we thought happened and where he was and that was enough. It was only recently that things got confusing for us."

It was his turn to talk. He told her in detail about moving to Sandy Lake, his job, looking for the file and not finding it, then getting an empty box from the sheriff's wife after Stan Shaw died. About the letter from him explaining the conversations he'd had over the phone with her father and the photos being the only things left.

"Your father's last actions were to try to continue to protect you and your brother. He asked for the file in exchange for the location of where to find my brother's remains. He didn't want this to come back and haunt you again. Your father had already died by the time I tracked him down in Duluth. I was told his son also lived in Duluth, but it wasn't Faisal. It was a son from his second marriage."

"You cannot meet Faisal," Faizah said. "He is dead. The other tragic part of this story."

CHAPTER FORTY

AFTER THE ACCIDENT, FAISAL was the one who decided they needed to prepare Nick's body. Their father, who moments earlier had been in a rage, was filled with remorse and did as his son instructed. Faizah wasn't allowed to participate because she was a woman. Later, Faisal told her how they removed Nick's clothes and washed his body from head to toe. They dressed him again and wrapped him in a bedsheet and then a tarp. Faisal said they couldn't get his shoes or his gloves on.

"My father drove the snowmobile to the open water and left the glove on the ice. He had Faisal meet him nearby with the truck. They drove the body to the woods somewhere and buried him as best as they could in the snow and the leaves. My father might have gone back in the spring and tried to bury him better. I remember him making a trip to the cabin and us not being allowed to come along."

Packard described the location to her and what the dog found in the search. Some bones, pieces of the tarp, Nick's coat.

"Can I say I am glad you have something of him to properly bury?"

"You can say it. Our family is very happy about it."

Faizah nodded in understanding. "It was impossible for us to act as if nothing had happened after that. My father threw himself into his work. My brother got more and more interested in Islam. I think he was hoping religion would show him a way to not be who he was. I did the opposite. I got wilder and angrier and more defiant. I had nothing to lose. I felt like I had something on my father and my brother that I could hang over their heads to get whatever I wanted. Again, selfish."

The police interviewed their family a couple of times. Her father begged the two of them to stick to the story and say nothing. They didn't see Nick that night. They had no idea where he might have been going. They didn't know anyone else he might have been meeting. Repeat, repeat, repeat.

"My father could have called for help the night of the accident but he was certain there would be no sympathy for the actual facts. He said, 'We are living in George Bush's America. I'm Iraqi and we are at war with Iraq. You are only half-Iraqi but half is too much. You know how it has been. Even your friends see you as a foreigner, as a traitor because of your blood. You were born in this country but they will not call you Americans.' He was terrified of not being able to protect us. My rebelliousness made it clear he had lost control of the situation. His solution was to send us out of the country to Turkey, where we had family."

"I talked to the woman who ran his office for years and years. She told me about the plane tickets and the travel arrangements she made," Packard said.

"I didn't want to go. Faisal did. He convinced me it was better for us to get away from our father after what had happened. I don't know that I ever fully agreed but I went along. We flew to Newark and then Amsterdam, where we had a long layover. Something came over me while we were wandering Schiphol Airport. I decided if I could stay there for twelve hours I could stay there twenty-four hours, then forty-eight hours. I would not go on to Turkey. I was not going to go to a Muslim country and learn to be a proper Muslim woman, my father's dream. I begged Faisal to stay with me. We had a couple hundred dollars between us. Enough to come up with a plan and, if nothing else, a train ticket to France to find our mother."

Faisal refused to stay, Faizah refused to get on the plane. They were both in tears when they parted. He gave her his money. Told her to be careful.

"'You are the one who has to be careful,' I said. He knew what I meant. That was the last time we saw each other."

During the conversation, the waiter had cleared their entrée plates and brought them cheese and olives. Then slices of melon and prosciutto and jam. Then a digestif in a tiny tulip glass. Then dessert, which was a pink macaron and a tiny tart with a single raspberry on top. The courses felt like clowns pouring out of a car. Packard wondered if they would ever end.

Faizah told him she was young and personable and had no trouble quickly making friends in Amsterdam and finding a place to stay. She lied about her age to get her first job as a waitress. She learned French and Dutch and eventually she moved to Paris for college. There was a brief marriage, no children. She had a cold, distant relationship with her mother, who still had little interest in her even as an adult.

"Faisal went to Turkey and finished school. He moved to Iraq after the war ended and did work with displaced refugees and migrants. He traveled a lot between Baghdad and Basra and sometimes stopped in the village where my father's family was from."

She paused, lit a cigarette, and spent a minute watching the smoke. Packard waited.

"Iraq had a culture of fear then," she said. "Everyone was so intent on proving their loyalty to the ruling party. The government sent gay men to prison to be tortured and forced them to report on other men. People spied on their neighbors, on their friends, on their family. Someone was always watching. I don't know what kind of life Faisal was living, but I'm guessing he was not successful in fully denying who he was. I don't know that anyone can be. Not one hundred percent. Not forever."

"I agree. I speak from personal experience."

She regarded him for a moment. "You are homosexual, too. Like your brother."

Packard nodded. The word *homosexual* said with a French accent made him squirm inside.

Faizah sighed and tapped her cigarette. "There must have been rumors, whispers about my brother. Maybe my father told his brother what happened that night. Maybe my uncle told other people in the family. During one of Faisal's visits to the village, a crowd showed up at the house. They dragged Faisal outside into the street. They bound his hands and feet and then stoned him to death. Bricks, rocks, bottles. Whatever they could find. Members of our family participated."

Packard felt every hair on his body stand up. He'd seen terrible things as a police officer. It was a job that presented him with death in all its forms all the time. This was a new one. Stoned to death.

"He was twenty-one years old," Faizah said.

Packard felt watery inside. He blinked. He reached across the table again. "I'm sorry. You've lost so much."

Faizah gave him a half smile and put her hand in his. "We both have," she said. "I'm sorry for you, too. I'm sorry for our brothers and the lives they never got to live."

Faizah finished the last of the wine. There was coffee. She smoked another cigarette. They talked about their own lives. When it seemed there couldn't possibly be anything else left in the restaurant to feed them, she summoned the waiter and took care of the bill in a flurry of French.

"Let me drive you to your hotel," she said as they stood to leave.

"I don't have a hotel."

"Where are your bags?"

"No bags, just the backpack. My flight is first thing in the morning. Let me drive you home. I'll take the Métro to the airport."

"You do not know how to drive in Paris," she protested.

"I'll be fine. You tell me where to go."

Getting her home felt like driving a bumper car around an F1 track. He'd had plenty of defensive driving courses, but the chaos of the streets of Paris was next level. At her home in Belleville, he parked the car and shouldered his backpack.

"I have more wine if you want to come in," she said. She was unsteady on her feet. She looked tired and sad. Packard deeply wanted her not to be.

"I have to go."

They hugged awkwardly with their hands on each other's arms. She kissed him on both cheeks. "I see so much of your brother in you," she said. "The mouth, the eyes. He was very intense, same as you."

Packard held her hand. He blinked his stinging eyes. "I hope in time you will feel unburdened about Nick. There is no debt, no blame. Let it go if you can. If you're missing family, you have a half brother in Duluth, Minnesota. His name is Hamid and he's a tattoo artist. He said if I found you to let you know he'd love to hear from you."

"I have a recent letter from an American lawyer about my father's estate. It mentioned Hamid."

"I'll email you his contact information. Let me know if you ever come to Minnesota."

More cheek kisses. He held her hand as he backed away until just their fingertips touched. It was a summer night in Paris. In another life, they might have been lovers reluctant to part. Packard took another step backward and their hands dropped; then he turned and walked away.

He got on the Métro going the wrong direction, decided it didn't matter, and rode it all the way to the end. He got out at the Nation stop, walked up and down some stairs, and took the train back the other way. He was exhausted, unsure if it had been one night or three nights since he'd slept in a bed. The train rocked and *screeeed*. He dozed, dreamed of a boy being hit with a brick, and jolted awake.

It was after 11:00 p.m. when he arrived at Charles de Gaulle Airport. He made it through the security checkpoint before it closed for the night. The concourses were empty of people. Everything was closed. He wandered for a while until he found an orange couch and decided to camp.

He'd turned his phone off to conserve the battery after finding Faizah's office. He powered it up again, connected to the airport's Wi-Fi. His phone chimed and buzzed with delayed messages.

From Thielen:

> Turns out having your first baby when you're 190 years old isn't as easy as everyone says.

> Doc is putting me on bed rest.

> Told Shepard.

> You're getting your job back thanks to my geriatric love child.

> You didn't hear it from me.

> Act surprised when he tells you.

> And grateful if you have it in you.

From his mom:

> Where are you?

> Are you still traveling?

> Any news?

> I called what's-his-name at the brewery again.
> He didn't know where you were either.

> Have you smashed that yet?

> Will you share your phone location with me? Anne and
> I share. We can always see where the other is. It's fun.

> Call me.

From Kyle:

> Just checking in.

> Hope you're good.

> Your mom wants you to call her.

Packard lay down on the couch and held the phone to his chest. He closed his eyes. He thought about Nick and Faisal. He didn't know if it was right to imagine them as star-crossed lovers. They might have just been two horny teen boys who recognized in each other the secret they shared. Either way, he was glad Nick had found someone like himself.

Once upon a time he had an older brother who had been happy, who drove around with friends, listening to music and laughing, drinking and dancing, who kissed another boy and felt the heat of his body.

Once upon a time he had an older brother who had lived.

Packard thought of Kyle as he tried to sleep, one foot on the floor through the straps of his backpack. The last time they saw each other was at the search site for his brother. Kyle's mouth close to his ear.

I hope you find the answers you've been looking for.

He had.

He had all the answers now. He thought of Nick, who had been his oldest brother, then a ghost, then a collection of small bones and muddy clothes sniffed out from a hillside. Faizah's story had put the flesh back on him. Packard would carry her words back to his family, answer their questions as best he could, and they would all recover in their own ways and in their own time, and he would make sure that from here on they talked about Nick and the seventeen years he'd lived so that none of the details were forgotten.

Packard's eyes grew heavy. A towering glass wall beside him looked over an empty runway, a line of lights in the dark. His last thoughts before falling asleep were of all he had waiting for him back in Sandy Lake. Friends and family. His old job. He saw the view from his back deck of the lake that had reemerged from the ice, where he'd been swimming in the cold water for a month already, watched by owls and a three-legged corgi. What a life he had made in this place that had been the source of so many good memories for his family, and would be again now that they knew Nick was there, had always been there, waiting for his little brother to come home and find him.

READING GROUP GUIDE

1. Describe the culture of Sandy Lake, Minnesota. Would you say it's a good place to live?

2. After the courthouse shooting, Packard must finally contend with his long-buried emotional baggage. How does he do this? What does he have to process?

3. What is Packard's last memory of his brother? Is it accurate?

4. Why do you think Packard can't let Louise's death go? What are his motives for investigating?

5. In *Where the Dead Sleep*, an anonymous figure takes a shot at Packard. Who was it, and why did they attempt to take his life?

6. Grief affects everyone differently. How did the loss of Packard's brother change him? By contrast, how did it change his mother and father?

7. Consider what it must have been like for the Rassins in Sandy Lake. What prejudices would they have run up against?

8. What role does Jim Wolf play in the plot? Who is really pulling the strings?

9. Now that Packard has closure on what happened to his brother, what do you think is up next for him?

A CONVERSATION WITH
THE AUTHOR

This is now your third book set in Sandy Lake. What's it like returning to such a familiar landscape?

I'm having a lot of fun writing about this small town and this North Central Minnesota setting. It's fun to come back and shine a light on parts of the community we haven't seen yet and ask what's new in the lives of the people closest to Packard. The fact that each book builds on the last in relatively short order means I get to play with the changing seasons and use the Minnesota weather like another character in the story.

The dynamic between Packard and his mother is completely delightful. What inspired it?

I envisioned someone the complete opposite of Packard who had dealt with the grief in her life in ways he would never consider. I also thought it would be fun if she had no filter and could make Packard cringe.

Chris and I spent some time hiking in Sedona a couple of years ago, and at the top of this steep climb, we encountered two older women wrapped in scarfs and shawls with ribbons and beads in their hair. The had this whole tableau laid out on a blanket with tambourines and smudge sticks and photographs and crystals. It looked like they were doing a ceremony for a friend who had died. I saw them and knew immediately that I was looking at Packard's mom.

A Long Time Gone finally closes the chapter on the mystery of Packard's missing brother. Was it daunting to tackle such a long-standing thread? Was it a relief?

It was both. I had no idea what happened to Nick Packard when I sketched out the bones of his disappearance in _And There He Kept Her_. One thing I felt from the beginning was that it had been thirty years since Nick disappeared, and I didn't see Nick's story being resolved with a steeplechase or Packard in a shoot-out with a bad guy. Michael Connelly did an excellent job handling the cold case of the murder of Harry Bosch's mother this way, but I wanted something more intimate, more heartbreaking than that.

After college, I had a roommate who had a very strict immigrant father. I was never allowed to answer the phone in case he called. She said, "He'll show up and kill both of us if he finds out I'm living with a man." I said, "Even a gay one who's not trying to have sex with you?" She said, "That's not the rationale you think it is."

I kept thinking about young lovers and a strict father and a night that ended in tragedy for everyone involved. It was daunting knowing I had left everyone hanging at the end of _Where the Dead Sleep_ and owed them a resolution. I hope readers will be satisfied with what I imagined.

Packard wonders what it would be like to have had a queer role model growing up. How important do you think that is for folks who are still discovering their own identities?

There's a fine line between embracing what makes you unique and feeling like you're the only one of something. Everyone wants to seem themselves reflected back to them. When Packard was a kid, he would have had few gay role models. He's a decade younger than I am, but things weren't a whole lot better in the '90s than they were in the '80s. Growing up queer at a time when religion and politics and popular culture was telling you there was something wrong with you made the coming-of-age experience so much harder. Life can be a bit easier when someone who's gone before you helps illuminate the path.

We have to ask: Kelly, the sheriff's department administrator, is obsessed with Barry Manilow. Of all musicians, why did you pick him? Were any other artists in the running?

I love writing Kelly and all the ways she keeps Packard in check. Kelly the Admin was inspired by Kelly my coworker. When I started at my day job, she taught me everything I needed to know. Kelly is the kindest, funniest person you'll ever meet. We worked side by side for many years until COVID and a corporate reorg separated us. There was no question about Kelly the Admin's love for Barry Manilow. Real-life Kelly has seen him in concert more than two hundred times. I told her in advance that I had a character in *Where the Dead Sleep* named Kelly who loved Barry to make sure she was okay with it. I had no backup plan if she said no. Maybe I could have made her a Dead Head. Luckily, Kelly and her husband both have gotten a kick out of it.

You humanize Jim Wolf by having Packard interact with his mother. Why did you choose to do make the reader feel empathy for such a cruel individual?

Jim Wolf is selfish and arrogant and greedy. He and Packard have been enemies since the first book. I wanted another scene where Packard had to deal with the public perception of him following the shooting that opens the book. In the moment he was most angry at Jim Wolf, I also wanted him to be reminded that there were other sides to this man. We all contain multitudes. Even villains have mothers who love them.

In this story, Packard juggles two cases: his brother's disappearance and Louise's death. How did you go about finding balance between those two subplots?

The short answer is I have two very good editors who made sure of it.

I knew Nick's story wasn't enough to drive an entire book. The connection to the family home helped link Nick's story and Louise's death and created the opportunity for Packard to struggle by himself to resolve both. It was a matter of looking for small ways to keep Nick's story from dropping completely from the reader's mind while Packard was deep into the investigation surrounding Louise, then tying everything together using help from the FBI involved in catching Louise's killer to locate the missing person Packard needed to find to finally get all the answers about Nick.

Over the course of the series, Packard has gone through the wringer. Now that he's finally put his family's greatest tragedy to rest, can you hint at what's next for him?

In the next book, a strong wind blows a new darkness into town. That's all I can say for now.

ACKNOWLEDGMENTS

It's hard to believe how quickly I've gone from zero books in the world to now having three. Everything happens so quickly. I feel like Lucy on the line trying to shove all the chocolates into her mouth. It's chaotic, but I'm having the time of my life. Thanks to my agent, Barbara Poelle, for putting me here.

I've never had a baby, but I've heard you get amnesia about how horrible the experience of childbirth is and that's what allows you to do it again. Writing a book might be similar. I've forgotten the pain of this one because I'm suffering through the next one already. I do know my editors, Anna Michels and Jenna Jankowski, took a horrifying first draft and helped shape it into the book in your hands. I'm incredibly grateful for their patience and wisdom.

The only reason anyone knows about my books is because of the work of Mandy Chahal. She's in these streets shouting about Ben Packard like no one else. When she told me she sobbed at the end of this book, I knew I had done my job. Mandy, I value our working relationship and friendship more than you know. Thank you for everything.

I want to thank everyone on Instagram, TikTok, and Facebook (shout-out to all the Psychological Thriller Readers) who has taken the time to read and spread the word about my books. I don't dare make a list for fear of leaving someone off. You know who you are. Every single post, comment, review, DM, tag, and email feels like a gift, and I take none of it for granted.

Thank you to all the authors who lent their time, names, and creativity to the praise offered on the back and in the first pages of this book. I'm such an admirer of every one of you. Thank you for your generosity.

Gretchen Anthony is the best writing partner a guy could ask for. Thank you for the Saturday morning accountability, brainstorming and cheerleading.

Thank you to Dr. Roger Waage for the story about the woman with the fishing lures stuck to her hand.

Thank you to all my coworkers, past and present. My bio says I work in medical devices, and it's been especially gratifying to hear from people I don't know who found my books and then found me in Outlook or on LinkedIn and let me know how much they enjoyed them. Thank you to everyone I work with now who picks up the slack when I'm off doing this job.

This book is for Lisa. We've been friends for thirty-five years. Thankfully, all our worst behavior predated digital cameras and the internet. So many adventures, laughs, fights, trips, side-eye, inside jokes—all the things that make a long friendship. Thank you for answering all my lawyering questions. Any legal errors in this book are 100 percent your fault for not knowing everything about every single type of law ever practiced in any state or the entire world.

Chris—you were my partner for the sixteen years and two books that preceded this one. We're married now. Whose idea was that? Probably yours 'cause it was a good one. I love you.

ABOUT THE AUTHOR

 Joshua Moehling is the critically acclaimed author of the Ben Packard series and a two-time Lammy Award nominee for Best LGBTQ+ Mystery Thriller. He lives in Minneapolis with his husband.